A HOUSE DIVIDED

Also by Genevieve Lyons

SLIEVELEA
THE GREEN YEARS
DARK ROSALEEN

GENEVIEVE LYONS

A HOUSE DIVIDED

Macdonald

A Macdonald Book

Copyright © Genevieve Lyons 1989

First published in Great Britain in 1989 by
Macdonald & Co (Publishers) Ltd
London & Sydney

British Library Cataloguing in Publication Data
Lyons, Genevieve
A house divided.
I. Title
823.914 [F]
ISBN 0-356-17908-7

Typeset by Leaper & Gard Ltd, Bristol, England
Printed and bound in Great Britain by
Mackays of Chatham PLC, Chatham, Kent

Macdonald & Co (Publishers) Ltd
Headway House
66-73 Shoe Lane
London EC4P 4AP
A member of Maxwell Pergamon Publishing Corporation Ltd

To three great ladies;
My mother,
Annette,
and Finn, with my love. And Michele.

Acknowledgement

I would like to thank Alan Williams, Master Brewer at The Orange Brewery, Pimlico, for his invaluable help.

PART ONE

Chapter

1

THE house was full of the smell of cooking fruit. Jam-making time had arrived again and the air was heavy with the sharp, seductive, aroma of oranges and apples, damsons and plums, blackberries and loganberries. The scent of cinnamon and spices, cloves and bubbling brown sugar drifted from the kitchen below-stairs clear up to the attic at the top of the house.

The Connollys' fat dumpling of a housekeeper, Mamie by name, directed the delicate operation like a Sergeant-major in charge of recalcitrant troops. Mamie's admonitory tones penetrated at least to the second floor as she issued instructions and tried to control the youngest lady of the house, Celestine Connolly, and her helper, the maid-of-all-work, Miffy Mulligan.

'Yiz are an unholy hindrance, the pair of ye,' she cried, exasperated.

'Then what are we doing here in this heat?' Celestine Connolly asked, her big brown eyes snapping in her pretty heart-shaped face, which was puce with the heat and effort.

Mamie picked up a large copper spoon. 'The point of this exercise is te teach ye the housewifely art of jam-makin' an' chutney-makin',' she said firmly, jabbing the ladle in the air to punctuate her speech. 'So ye can do it by yerself and not need me behind ye every blessed minute in case ye banjax the whole undertaking.'

Celestine sighed and cast her eyes up to heaven, and Mamie wagged the spoon at her.

'I saw that, Miss, an' don't think I won't tell yer Ma. An' if ye think yer here because I want ye to be, yer makin' the mistake of yer life,' she said succinctly. 'It takes all my patience and forbearance to put up wi' ye at all in my kitchen, Miss Celestine. But yer Mam is anxious that ye learn, an' learn ye will.' She sighed. 'If it kills me!' she added.

Celestine and Miffy were encased in huge starched white aprons so that they would not stain their clothes. They had both managed, nevertheless, to spatter their skirts with bright red spots, which made Mamie purse her lips and tut, for she doubted if the stains could be removed.

'*Keep* stirring,' she ordered, for the umpteenth time, and wiped a straggle of grey hair out of her eyes with her arm. They were all perspiring in the steam and the heat of the kitchen.

'Drippin' with sweat,' Mamie said, as Celestine paused for a moment to push a stray curl back from her forehead. Her cheeks throbbed, bright red, and her soft brown mahogany-coloured hair was damp at her brow and the nape of her neck.

'Oh I'm so hot, Mamie dear,' she sighed. 'I'm sweating like a pig.'

'Miss Celestine! Don't talk like that. Yer a disgrace.'

'But you just said . . .'

'I'm different,' Mamie sniffed. 'Ladies don't sweat and they certainly don't *say* they do.'

'Well, perspire then.' Celestine wiped her poppy-red cheeks on the edge of her apron and, pursing her lips, blew upward to somehow cool her face.

'Not perspire either,' Mamie said firmly. 'Ladies don't sweat, or perspire, or even get hot. So there.'

Celestine stirred the thickening bubbling fruit with an effort, pushing the spoon against its will round the huge copper pot. She sighed again and slackened her pace. Mamie looked at her flaming face and nodded. She knew, even before the girl spoke, what was coming next. Celestine had her 'determined to escape' face on, and Mamie knew she had lost. Miss Celestine had had enough of jam-making, so willy-nilly she would go now to her mother, who was drying flowers and herbs in the conservatory.

But Mamie could not find it in her heart to be angry with the youngest, prettiest Connolly, for Celestine, a joyful, happy little body, was rarely wilful and was blessed with the sunniest of dispositions. 'However,' Mamie thought, 'when that girl makes up her mind about anything there's no shifting her.'

'Where's Mother?'

4

'Your mother is in the conservatory, sorting the herbs and rose-petals for her *pot-pourri*,' Mamie said tartly. 'An' I know just what yer goin' to say next. Well, Miss Celestine, she does not need yer help. You just stick to the jam.'

'I wasn't going to . . .' Celestine protested.

'Oh yes ye were. Every year it's the same. The work gets to the difficult bit an' off you go to help someone else. I know you, me fine young lady.' She wagged her finger under the girl's nose, then clapped her hands together. 'Stir now! Put yer back into it. Stir now. Stir,' she urged.

'Oh, can't I rest for five minutes? Please, Mamie. Maa..mieeee. Pleeease.'

'No staying power.' Mamie shook her head. 'Why can't ye be more like yer sister?' It was a rhetorical question, often asked, for Mamie constantly bickered with Celestine whom she adored. Clothilde, the elder Connolly girl, was another kettle of fish entirely in Mamie's view, and while she rarely scolded Celestine's sister, she did not pet her either.

'Well, I notice Clo isn't here, is she? *She's* not trying to stir this goo that's as thick and unmanageable as tar, so it is. *And* it does not *want* to be stirred, so it doesn't.' Celestine said, biting her lip in vexation.

'Miss Clothilde is in her room finishing a letter to her Auntie Nellie. You were asked which you would like to do; help me with the jam or write to your auntie. You chose this so now you'll stick with it. Stir.'

'I don't think Clothilde is writing to Auntie Nellie at all. I expect she's on her knees suffering for Jesus.' Celestine glanced at Miffy Mulligan whose lowly position as maid-of-all-work forbade her from taking part in this dialogue. Miffy, catching Celestine's merry look, dissolved in guilty giggles.

'Miffy, get on wi' yer work,' Mamie said sharply. 'And, Miss Celestine, don't you be disrespectful.'

'Well, can't I go and write to Auntie Nellie now?' Celestine asked hopefully. She put out her tongue and caught a salty drop of moisture that had trickled down from her temple. Miffy saw her and giggled again. Mamie gave the maid a gentle cuff.

'Get on wi' yer stirrin'. Honest yiz are awful, Miss Celestine. Every year it's the same. Ye *want* to stir the jam. Beggin' me, ye are, to help. Then after ten minutes . . .'

Celestine let out a protesting shout. 'Aw, Mamie. That's not *fair.* We've been stirring since *lunch*, and it's nearly five now.'

She had glanced at the grandfather clock in the corner of the big rambling kitchen and Mamie, without looking, corrected her.

'Four, Miss. Four o' the clock, unless I'm going blind.'

'Aw, I've worked so *hard*,' Celestine wailed.

'For the first half-hour ye did nothin' but *eat*. I saw ye, an' yer mouth is all stained bright red.' Celestine started to rub her lips guiltily with the back of her hand, and Mamie continued, 'An' after the corned beef I cooked for lunch an' all those custard tarts you gobbled up, I don't know how you managed it. Yer a terror, so ye are.'

Celestine heard the affection in the old voice and she quickly took advantage.

'Well, an' since then I've worked so *hard*. My best. And now my back is breaking and my arms are just about to fall off.'

Mamie sighed and wiped her hands on her apron. 'Exaggeration, exaggeration. Ye always exaggerate, Miss Celestine. Oh well. All right. Just five minutes, mind. Miffy, take over from Miss Celestine.'

Celestine lifted the starched apron to her face and blotted it dry. Miffy shrieked.

'She's let the spoon drown! Oh Janey Mac, Mamie, the spoon's, gone to the bottom. Sunk. It's sunk in the jam, Mamie.'

'Hush up, ye little fool,' Mamie cried sharply.

'But I din do nuthin'. Twasn't me. Twas Miss Celestine.'

'I said hush up, Miffy, and I meant it. Here, stir with this.' She handed the agitated girl the ladle she had in her hand, and gave her a little shove towards the pot.

Celestine sat at the table fanning herself with the bottom of her apron. It was boiling hot in the kitchen. Flies buzzed about and eventually got stuck to the long yellow sticky papers that hung from the ceiling. The kitchen was large and ran the full length of the house in the basement. It had a larder and an all-purpose room off it. The all-purpose room was used mainly for washing and ironing. It had a door to the yard and the back where Mamie hung the washing on a fine day. There was a flight of uneven stone steps that led from the yard up into the garden, but you could not see it from the kitchen window. The garden was on a level with the ground floor, and when you were

6

in it you could not see the kitchen or the yard and certainly not Mamie's washing.

The garden was oblong: a lawn bordered by roses with a rockery about three-quarters of the way down. A white-painted trellis separated it from the fruit and vegetable area which took up the remaining quarter. The plums and apples and logan-berries they were using for the jams and chutneys came from this little garden. Auntie Nellie O'Dwyer had brought the blackberries up from the country and the oranges came from far-away Seville on a clipper-ship that docked at Dublin Harbour. But that was becoming very infrequent now, with the war on.

Celestine was fed up with the jam-making. At first, each year, the prospect had enchanted her. She loved the pungent smell of the berries and licking the ladle. Then, as was her wont, her initial enthusiasm faded. Her arm ached from stirring and she felt queasy from all the sticky fruit she had eaten. She stood up and untied the apron.

'I'm tired, Mamie,' she said with sudden determination. 'I'm going up to Mother.'

'I said ye wouldn't last. I told yer mother. I said "Don't let Miss Celestine into my kitchen for she'll start like the hare and grind to a halt like the tortoise".'

'It was the tortoise that won,' Celestine sang out trium-phantly.

'Well, an' Missy, who's talkin' about winnin'? Winning's no great feat. *Finishing* is. There's a difference.'

But Celestine was not listening. She had gone upstairs.

It was cool and dark in the hall. The wine-coloured carpet covering the floor was worn at the edges. A border of polished wood surrounded it. The small square hall led to a study and the dining-room on one side and the parlour on the other. A hat-and-coat-stand stood behind the front door which was draped in a deep red velvet curtain to keep out the draughts. The coat-stand had an oval mirror at eye-level and here Celestine stood, humming under her breath, and tidied her wayward curls and with her handkerchief cleaned her stained mouth. Her mother was very particular about tidiness.

She smoothed back the soft brown tendrils at her temples and tucked the escaping ringlets behind the large floppy blue satin bow that held the mass of tresses neat at the nape of her neck. Her large eyes, shiny and chestnut-coloured, stared back at her in a small heart-shaped face. She sighed. She did not approve of what she saw. She felt her face lacked the dignity she craved, and that her older sister Clothilde possessed in abundance. Normally her skin was smooth as cream and the same colour, but now she saw to her disgust it throbbed, scarlet and damp. She blew down the front of her dress of soft Liberty-print wool to cool herself, then shook her head and retraced her steps past the study and the dining-room towards the little door that led to the conservatory.

Her mother had the doors open, the one Celestine had entered by and the one that led to the garden, for it was very hot and the openings created a pleasing current of air.

The conservatory, green and white, contained a lot of growing plants that Ellen Connolly loved to tend and nurture. There were rubber plants, ferns and ivies purchased from the Botanical Gardens near Phoenix Park and given to her by her sister, Lady Gorman. May sent them up to her older sister from her beautiful estate, Avoca House in Wicklow.

Ellen was sitting at a bockity old wooden table sorting piles of sweet-smelling herbs and flower-petals into baskets — the baskets were made by blind girls in a Home for the Blind in Clondalkin. She looked up as her daughter entered, a smile lighting her face as she thought how pretty and fresh Celestine looked, her face flushed so rosy a pink, her eyes dancing with vitality.

'Ah, Celestine. Finished with the jam?'

'Not really, Mother. I'm afraid Mamie was right. I got tired.'

Her mother smiled again at Celestine fondly. Ellen was a faded, pretty, plump woman with a sweet-tempered resigned expression. Her pale blue eyes had lost their intensity and her soft fairish hair had strands of grey liberally sprinkled through it.

'Well, it doesn't matter. It's getting late and I'm dying for a cup of tea. Tell Miffy to make the tea now. And tell her we'll have it under the chestnut.'

'Miffy's taken over from me, Mother. I'm afraid she's elbow-deep in blackberry jam.' Celestine said, dimpling at the thought of Miffy on tiptoe trying to stir the jam.

'Oh dear. Well, never mind. Tell Mamie, then. We'll have it in a quarter of an hour. It's lovely to be able to have it in the garden at this time of the year.' She sighed. 'September. Long may the weather last.' She stared into the garden, seeing the plants and shrubbery still green under the golden radiance of the sun, and feeling grateful that it was so.

Celestine went out into the garden. She stood for a moment in the shadow of a tall lime and relaxed, letting the soft breeze cool her down. The sunlight was dappled and the shadows shifted, casting shimmering patches of light on the jade-green lawn. Then she ran down the steps to the kitchen back-door, opened it and said quickly 'Mother wants tea outside in fifteen minutes, Mamie, please,' withdrew and ran lightly back up the steps to the conservatory.

Her mother was still sorting the herbs and petals. Her hands moved swiftly and efficiently.

'Smell these, Celestine. Aren't they beautiful?' Her voice was wistful. She held a bunch of pale dried rose-petals in her palm. Celestine took her mother's wrist, raised the open hand to her nose and sniffed at the sad sweet scent of tea-roses.

'Ummmm. They are lovely, Mother.'

Her mother nodded and brought her hand back and lifted it to her own nose.

'That particular perfume always reminds me of my mother,' she said.

Celestine thought of Grandma O'Meara, that little dried-up woman alone in the house in Ely Place, and thought, 'Yes. Yes, the smell of old tea-roses is exactly right for Grandma O'Meara.'

'And the lavender, darling.' Ellen ran the small mauve seeds through her fingers. She looked lovingly at the piles in front of her, murmuring appreciatively. 'Camomile. Lemon-mint. So many mints. And this is rue, so sweet.' She sighed. Her skin was baby-soft and creased with wrinkles about her mouth and eyes and Celestine felt her heart overbrim with a sudden surge of love for the little, soft, plump woman. She put her arms around her mother and hugged her.

Ellen smiled, kissed her daughter lightly and said, 'Oh, Celestine, go and remind Mamie about tea, do. I asked you.'

'I *went*, Mother. But then you made me smell the rose-petals . . .'

'I didn't *make* you, Celestine. Oh, do go down and hurry her, I'm dying for my tea.'

Ellen stood and brushed the skirts of her pale-grey silk

tea-dress free of the lavender stalks and the bits and pieces of leaf and seeds. She went into the garden, thinking that if Mamie saw her there she might hurry up the tea, forgetting that Mamie could not see her.

She loved her garden. She felt the cool September breeze on her face with gratitude. It was soothing and pleasant after the humid heat of the conservatory. The sun shone low, a primrose yellow in a pearl-grey sky. The smell of the cooking fruit drifted from the kitchen. She walked slowly down the gravel path looking at the late roses and the ground-plants — mauve aubretia, night-scented stock, alyssum, cotoneaster and potentilla — plucking off deadheads and snipping faded roses with her secateurs, taking her time. It was the hour she liked best: tea -time. The chores of the day were over and her husband's return would not be until later. She could relax, bask in the peace of the garden with her daughters and her sons — for a wee while, anyway.

Normally she had done her best, organising the running of the house and putting her greatest efforts into caring for the well-being of her family. She had nothing to reproach herself with. She could sit under the chestnut and sip her tea and take her ease before Neill and Breffni came home. They would be followed by Garreth, her husband. She felt the usual tension in her neck at the thought of her husband's return, but she put it firmly out of her mind. She did not need to think about that yet. His return would inevitably have to be faced, as she had faced up to it with fortitude every day of her married life. She had learned over the years to put off anticipating the moment. Best not to think about it until she heard his key in the lock.

She told herself that she loved her husband, looked up to him in all things, but she found him 'difficult'. She expected that. A wife had a duty to her husband, to anticipate his every need and want, to ease his burden. After all, he had provided the house in Rathgar, the comfortable life they had. He was a good provider. She and her children were totally dependent on him and the weight of responsibility for them all must lie heavy on his shoulders. Naturally he was entitled to have erratic moods, moods that affected the whole family. He controlled the atmosphere in the home, as surely as a captain controlled his ship. If he were happy, they were happy; if he were out of sorts, so were they. He was not often happy. She felt it was natural that he was authoritative, and expected his slightest command to be obeyed. How on earth could he have run his business successfully if he were not so constituted?

She had tried to accept her marriage and Garreth, reasoning in this manner because that was how she had been taught. Grandma O'Meara was quite adamant. A man was king in his own home, she maintained. But deep down Ellen chafed against the role she had to play. There was a fiery resentment that she concealed beneath gentle smiles. No one knew about these feelings, except Fr Grogan, to whom she remorsefully confessed her irritation at having to bow her head before her husband's unreasonable demands.

'Ah, child, it's a cross you have to bear. A cross you have to bear,' Fr Grogan told her firmly, and she accepted her cross because Fr Grogan told her to, but deep in her heart she thought God was as unreasonable as her husband to ask such self-sacrifice of her. So she found her marriage difficult and a strain.

Yet marriage was not so for everyone. Nellie and May, her sisters, were shockingly familiar with their husbands. She thought of her sisters now, with fondness. Everyone had admired the O'Meara girls: May and Nellie and Ellen. They had been beauties in their hey-day and all of them had done well. May was the baby of the family, fussed over — spoiled, some said — and much younger than her sisters. She was the most beautiful and to her mother's delight had married one of the Wicklow Gormans, a title, no less. She had met him at a ball in the Vice-regal Lodge, and he had fallen for her beauty in an instant. They now lived in luxury in Avoca House, and if Ellen looked at her sister with a slight sigh of envy it was more because of the obvious camaraderie that existed between Lord Gorman and his wife than over the prosperity of their circumstances. Nellie, the eldest, had been smitten by Gerald O'Dwyer, a gentleman farmer from Kerry whom she had met at the Dublin Horse Show. They lived together in harmony and with a sense of humour and fun that Ellen was quite jealous of. She, the middle sister, had married Garreth Connolly of Rathgar. He owned the brewery. Connolly's Brewery was famous. He had built it up from a tiny beginning, and he had acquired the land and property that surrounded it — quite a little gold-mine, acquaintances said. For he had no friends.

Garreth Connolly did not believe in friendship. He believed in Family, with him at the head. He had started the brewery from scratch and had bought the property around it, and upon this land were the crumbling ruins of three streets and a square of ruined but beautiful Georgian houses. They were occupied by his workers. He was both their employer and their landlord.

Often Ellen thought she had simply married him because she had not had the will-power to refuse. When Garreth came courting she had been overwhelmed by his masterful ways, and he had rail-roaded her into marriage. She had said yes without really thinking about it. She was good-natured and hated to upset anyone. He had hustled and hurried her and she had been overawed by him and had weakly surrendered to his pressure and agreed to marry him. In one moment she had consented and in the next they were married. Or so it seemed to her.

Shortly thereafter he had proudly shown her over the brewery. It was the first and last time. She had enjoyed her visit, but on leaving, their carriage had made its way through a street of horribly run-down houses and on inquiring about the terrible place and its pathetic inmates, her husband, surprised that she showed such interest, explained to her that this terrible place was his, the homes of his tenants. She had been appalled and had told him so in all innocence, not expecting the scene that followed. He had been terribly angry with her and she had discovered then how violent her husband's temper was. On that day she had felt the first stirring of fear. She had the trusting disposition of someone who had known only gentleness and love in her life. But now a worm had entered and begun to eat at her soul. However, her sensitive mind shied away from her husband's guilt. Brought up to be intensely loyal, she found excuses for him.

They never discussed his beginnings, his childhood. It was another subject she had learned never to mention if she desired peace in the house, and she desired peace above all else. Perhaps, something in his childhood had shocked and hardened him to the suffering of others.

But deep down she knew there were no excuses. There was no excuse for the awful conditions her husband's workers lived in. Someone, in a more prosperous time, had optimistically called the place Paradise Row, Paradise Square, and Paradise Street. Ellen had thought about what she could do. Her husband implacably refused to discuss the subject with her and became quite violent with her if she brought it up. But she belonged to various charitable institutions in the city, such as St Vincent de Paul and the Catholic Mothers's Institution for Help for the Deserving Poor, and she briskly set about making the Paradise area the major focus of her charitable work and energies. She never told her husband that she had made sure that her area of concern would be the territory he owned, was landlord of. He never asked where she went, or even what she did in her work for charity. She had always done charity work. She had been taught that it was her duty. Now she found herself calling on her husband's tenants, which deeply shamed her and them. But at the same time she felt she was doing what she could to mitigate the injustice meted out to those workers by her family.

Garreth never knew. He was not interested in what she did. She was a good and virtuous woman. Charitable works were part of her life, a woman's trivial pursuit, something she did to pass the time until he came home. He was fond of saying that it was thanks to his generosity that she had time to be philan-thropic. And it was also his generosity that enabled her to have two servants and thus have time free to lead the life of a lady of leisure.

Ellen sighed. Sometimes she thought how ungrateful she was and she made sure to apologize to God when they said the family rosary each evening. She was so lucky. She had a comfortable home and a family she adored. Yet she allowed worry to plague her and tiny resentments to flourish deep in her mind. Not at all the way a good Christian should behave. There dwelt within her — side by side with her efforts to keep the peace, her resignation, her fear, her obedience to and accept-ance of her husband as lord and master, as dictated to her by Fr Grogan and the Church — an iron-hard resistance to Garreth's unfairness, and an evergrowing determination to preserve both herself and her principles. It was when her children were in trouble that this came most to the fore, for though she rarely contested his rulings openly, she often circumvented his punish-ments, deflected his wrath, and cheated by assuring him she had seen punishment meted out, when in fact she had done nothing whatsoever to see to any such thing.

She was a peacemaker. The world saw her as weak, a pawn

13

her husband moved about at will. She was in fact enormously strong, for singlehandedly she held together a family, a family, who, because of its head, was horribly split, put upon, manipulated and bullied. Ellen held it together by her tact, loving-kindness and bravery, and at enormous cost to her nerves. But for how long would this strength, eroded from years of stress, hold out? she often wondered. 'One day I'll snap,' she thought, and snipped another deadhead from the Princess Alice rose bush, putting all distressing thoughts aside.

Mamie was waddling across the lawn to the round wrought-iron table under the chestnut tree. Miffy trotted after her, looking flustered. Miffy was illegitimate, a shameful fact that consigned her at birth to a very servile and lowly position in the scheme of things. She was a tiny slip of a thing, a twig, Neill called her, and she had been taken from the laundry-room of the convent in Whitehall where she worked like a navvy from 5 a.m. until 10.30 p.m. by Mrs Connolly, who needed a maid-of-all-work.

The illegitimate girls lined up, once a month, and the ladies of Dublin City came and looked them over with a view to suitability, docility and sturdiness. Miffy had been passed over so many times her heart had near given up on her. She had stood meekly the first Wednesday of every month, trying her very best to look strong and reliable, biddable and nice, but her lip trembled in anticipation of her return, rejected to the dormitory, and the toil and the loneliness of her life in the institution. She was desperately anxious to be chosen, but she never was until Mrs Connolly picked her out. Of all the girls there, this beautiful kind lady had chosen her! Miffy's heart leapt within her, and Ellen Connolly had acquired a devoted slave.

Now, in the Connolly family circle, she worked from 5 a.m. to 10.30 p.m. and sometimes later, but she thanked God daily for his goodness to her and her luck in landing up with such a wonderful situation. Except for Mr Connolly. Her soul, starved for a crumb of affection, blossomed under the casual acceptance into this family, the only one she had ever known. She would cheerfully have died for any one of its members. But she was mortally afraid of the master of the house. However, she reckoned it a fair price to pay for the gentleness and kindness she received from Mrs Connolly, Miss Celestine, Miss Clothilde, Master Neill and Master Breffni, and most of all from

Mamie, who scolded her and bullied her gently and ordered her about, but who loved her wholeheartedly and was the closest thing to a mother that Miffy would ever have.

As they crossed the lawn, Mamie heard Ellen cry, 'His senna . . . my goodness, his senna pods . . . I forgot!' Dropping the secateurs, she put her hands to her cheeks in anxiety.

'Ah, never fear, Missus woman, I did them. They'll be cool for after breakfast and then tomorrow he'll have a good movement. Don't you fret,' Mamie soothed her.

'Oh, Mamie, what would I do without you?' Ellen sighed with relief and picked up the secateurs, then helped Mamie set out the tea things. 'Will the jam be ready to bottle soon?' she asked.

'Yes, Mam. Yes. Don't worry. I'll see to it.'

The garden was full of the chatter of starlings, and a swallow glided from lawn to tree and back again. The sun filtered through the leaves, freckling everything in silvery-gold. The old tree had gnarled grey sinews and Ellen touched it briefly and affectionately with the flat of her hand.

There was a yell from the house. Both women turned and looked up at the third storey window from where the loud voices of Clothilde and Celestine were raised in argument.

'. . . told you not to barge in here without a by your leave . . .' Clothilde's voice floated down to Mamie and Ellen below. They stood, action suspended, still as statues, each holding one end of the table-cloth which fluttered like a banner between them.

Simultaneously, Celestine's voice over-rode her sister's, '. . . shutting yourself up and doing nothing, nothing to help and today I made all the jam . . . all the jam for the next year.'

'Girls! Girls!' Ellen cried, and the faces of her two daughters appeared at the third-floor window. Her voice was clear and thin and they had heard it instantly and responded at once.

'Oh, Mother, Celestine came barging into my room without knocking . . .'

'And I found her kneeling in her chemise, not writing to Auntie Nellie.'

'Mother, Mother, don't listen to her . . . don't. I . . .'

Ellen's calm voice was raised just a fraction as she shaded her eyes with her hand against the sun's pale glare and called up to her daughters.

15

'Little birds in their nests . . . little birds in their nests . . . you *know* I hate to hear you quarrel. At any rate, it's tea-time.'

The heads instantly disappeared and in moments the girls came running across the lawn and joined their mother and Mamie in the pleasant ritual of laying out tea. Both girls were dressed in white, the finest white cambric edged in bands of Limerick lace. Celestine had changed. There was a bunch of blue silk flowers on a blue satin ribbon sash about her small waist, and a blue ribbon in her hair. Clothilde's identical adornment was pink.

Clothilde was taller by a head than her sister. Her face was dominated by fiercely brooding eyes and she had an intensity that was sometimes uncomfortable.

'All Clo wants is to be a martyr. A saint, no less,' Celestine chided her.

'Oh shut up, Celestine. Leave me alone.'

'Well, you can't be a saint. You're not good enough, so there. And you've a terrible temper,' Celestine taunted her, face still flushed.

'Mother, make her stop. She's awful.'

'Leave your sister alone, Celestine, and help me with this.'

Ellen handed her daughters the pile of saucers and spoons, waiting until they set them down before she put a cup on each shallow and delicate vessel.

When they had set the table, gently bickering all the time, their mother's voice light-heartedly admonishing them and Mamie tutting at both, Miffy made her appearance, staggering across the lawn with Grandma O'Meara's silver teapot.

'Oh lord, Miffy . . . is everything too heavy for you?'

'Missus . . . missus. The jam's reached its peak. It's needin' ye.'

'All right, Miffy. Calm down. Mamie'll see to it. Just leave the teapot there like a good girl and go and help Mamie.'

Miffy set it on the table with a bang, apologized, gave a bob and turned and trotted after Mamie, who was waddling purposefully towards the back entrance to the kitchen.

Ellen sighed. 'Poor Miffy. She's so tiny. Almost everything she tries to carry is too heavy for her. But we mustn't say that. She worries so. I cannot bear her to be hurt. She's had quite enough pain in her short life already.' She sat back in her chair. 'Ah. Peace at last. How good it is. Now, girls, I'll tolerate no more arguments. And I don't want to hear the whys and where-fores of anything, anything at all. I simply want a little peace.'

The girls knew their mother well enough to know she meant what she said. This time was sacrosanct. It was not that she was angry if they broke the peace of the early evening, the peace she craved so much. On the contrary. She simply seemed to dwindle into herself, losing her starch, sadly exhausted and drained. The girls hated it when this happened. It frightened them. It made them uneasy, as if the balance had shifted and they had assumed the role of mother, responsible and in command, and she had become the child in need of care and attention. It only happened if they were stroppy at tea-time, their mother's sacred time. So they were quiet.

There was peace in the garden and Ellen sighed again in satisfaction. This time regenerated her energy and gave her the courage for the evening and Garreth. The clink of the china blended with the evening chorus of the birds. It was soothing, and Ellen sipped her tea, savouring its fragrance as the thirst-quenching liquid slid down her throat. She smiled at the girls, put down her cup and patted their hands, one on either side of her.

'You're good girls. Very good. I feel better now. Top up my cup, please, Celestine.'

She watched as Celestine stood and refilled the cup, her movements graceful. Her youngest child, Garreth's favourite, was seventeen. In his eyes she could do no wrong. If the others, Clothilde and Neill, the twins, twenty, and Breffni, eighteen, wanted anything from their father — permission to stay out late, or buy something, or go to somewhere special — they always asked Celestine to intervene. Garreth liked to keep his family under his own roof, and under his thumb, and it was sometimes difficult to go anywhere, but Celestine could coax him into giving permission.

She was a happy, good-natured girl, looking forward to life with an expectant optimism, her mother thought, admiring her daughter's smooth white brow, her thick hair and velvet-brown eyes flecked with amber. Clothilde looked calm enough, but underneath the surface a coil of intensity lurked, an ardent seeking, a yearning, a passion that worried Ellen. She was aware of the tight rein her eldest daughter held on her feelings, and she was often alarmed at the girl's control. Clothilde had

17

confided in her mother her burning desire to become a nun.

The sun lingered, unwilling to set, and the birds agitated the leaves and sang their hearts out, and as the three Connollys sipped their tea, a hush held everything still for a breathless moment.

Clothilde leaned her dark head on her mother's shoulder and yawned. Ellen looked at her fondly, thinking about the possibility of her daughter really having a vocation, then realizing what that news would do to Garreth, and deciding, as always, that at this sacred time it might be better to dwell on more trivial things. So much of her time was spent shelving unpleasant thoughts, training her mind to dart away protectively from what might be reality, cloaking it in its best light, trying never to have to face up to the facts of life. She had never once admitted to herself that she was terrified of her husband, that he was difficult and unkind and that her whole life was spent smoothing things over between him and her children, avoiding trouble, confrontations and arguments and trying to keep the peace in the house. This 'peace' was a fragile edifice she built up with care and tact and the dexterity of a brilliant politician or diplomat. It was as precarious as a castle built with cards and the maintaining of it was exhausting and sometimes she could feel her heart fluttering under the little bunch of medals and scapulars she wore on a chain about her neck and tucked into the top of her chemise where they snuggled warmly between her breasts. She often thought her heart would jump right out of her chest. A sparrow had once been trapped in the conservatory and had kept slinging itself against the glass, not understanding why it couldn't fly through the transparent panes. It was panicked and when Ellen caught it, holding it firmly between her hands, taking it outside and setting it free, its heart, thudding against its breast, had felt like her's did sometimes, and she knew exactly how the small creature felt.

And yet her life was good. She had a lovely home and her children were healthy. She reminded herself of this often and rebuked herself for her ingratitude. But it was not enough. Under the lightness, the meals, the everyday commerce of greetings and squabbles, chats and heart-to-hearts and laughter, there simmered the passionate wishes of her children in opposition to their father, and her own iron determination to prevent a fatal clash. But that clash was coming.

18

Up to now she had been able to control things, to stage-manage their lives, going to any lengths to avoid confrontations. It had been easier when the children were young. But they had grown. Soon, wanting to go their own way, the children would stand in opposition to their father. It was bound to happen and she could foresee only division and disaster. She had no doubt at all where she would stand then: firmly and squarely behind her darlings, completely partisan, even though Garreth had all the power. She wished Ireland was not so behind the times. She had heard that in London and Paris things were much more advanced and girls and boys were much freer to lead their own lives. Well, in Dublin, thanks to Holy Mother Church, it simply was not so.

Reminded of the Church, she prayed to God that the eventuality she envisaged would not happen, but she knew her prayer would not be answered. Although she would do all in her power to prevent the conflict from taking place, it must happen eventually. Neill and Clothilde, twin souls as well as twins in actuality, both wanted to take religious orders. Garreth, however, had decreed that Neill would take over the brewery and Clothilde would marry. Neill was his heir and he, therefore, must perpetuate the respected name in a business that his father had created. He should also, in Garreth's opinion, be eternally and verbally grateful for the honour his father bestowed upon him. Breffni, the child closest to his mother's heart, was a tousle-headed dreamer and idealist. He was a poet and an artist, impulsive and emotional, even unstable, she feared, and his father was as incapable of understanding him as he would be if one of Monsieur Jules Verne's characters from another world came to call. She shuddered when she thought of what would happen, must happen, soon. Breffni, for all his dreamy ways, was curiously obstinate. When he decided upon his chosen artistic pursuit he would come up against a father who thought all art a waste of time, a folly, a daft and useless appendage to real life. Religion too, in Garreth's opinion, was an added, quite trivial extra. He was only too pleased to have the females in his house devout, but for a man it was the height of folly and positively interfered with his freedom to act, as Garreth put it, in 'an uncompromising way as one must at times in business'. What must happen when Neill told his father of his desire to become a priest caused Ellen to shiver and cross herself.

19

Once more she pushed all such unbidden speculation away. She was constantly doing this during the day and it was not too difficult then. Such thoughts would come and they had to be nipped in the bud, so that she was constantly censoring herself. But it was at night, listening to her husband snoring beside her, his presence unavoidably there, that the worries came in their hundredfold to plague her and she could *not* make them go away. Conversations, and permutations of conversations, went round and round in her brain, and ideas of such terror pressed upon her that she lay in bed paralysed by fear, while her husband grunted and snorted and rolled over in his sleep.

Sometimes he could not sleep. She hated him then, for she was terrified that he would hear what was going on in her mind, as if her thoughts were being shouted aloud. She would pretend to be fast asleep, and she lay, her body tense as a violin-string, waiting for him to stop tossing and turning and slip into the arms of Morpheus. She resented then her helplessness, her dependence upon him, the fact that her wishes were of no importance as far as he was concerned.

Sometimes she was filled with an almost irresistible impulse to hit him, beat at him with her clenched fists, rain blows upon him. Terrified by the impulse she would cross herself and say Hail Mary's and often that was not enough . . .

She looked now from the shade of the tree to where the fruit and vegetables grew behind the white trellis. She thought about gathering the last of the loganberries and some Granny Smiths for a pie for dessert tonight. Perhaps there were still some black-berries left. There was nothing Garreth Connolly enjoyed more than one of Mamie's apple and blackberry tarts with thick cream. The leaves would be falling soon. The winter wouldn't be far behind. Autumn did not last long in Dublin. This meant that Paradise Row, Paradise Square and Paradise Street would need her desperately. The inhabitants would get sick and die without her ministrations. Their bodies had no resistance. It made her feel so useful to help them, but her feelings were contradictory, for if it were not for her husband's abominable insensitivity and greed there would not be a Paradise Street and its environs. She had at times pleaded with Garreth to repair the slum houses, to make them even partially safer and a little less dangerous, but it was a sure way of sending him into a thunderous black mood, of the kind that nearly frightened her to death.

Ach! There she was again. It seemed all avenues of thought led back to Garreth and his moods and wishes. She looked at the sweet faces of her daughters and wondered what their thoughts were, wondered if they thought about their father.

Celestine thought of him tenderly. Her darling Papa. She loved the strength of his arms encircling her, the smell of his clothes, the tobacco he used. She thought of how tonight she would fill his pipe with the new tobacco that had arrived from Argentina. Then she would sit on his knee, as he liked her to do while he talked to the family. His voice, deep and firm, reassured her and sometimes she did not listen to what he said, but rested content, her cheek against his chest with the deep rumble of his words in her ear. Tonight she would curl his beard around her little finger and coax him to allow her to order material for a dress in Cleary's. She wanted something new and pretty for the Military Ball at the Curragh on the 30th September. Yellow-striped silk, she thought. That was her best colour. Papa would say yes, to her. He always did. She wondered briefly why he was such a cross-patch with the others. But she did not give it serious consideration. She could not bear distressing thoughts or angry words. She was like her mother in that, but unlike her mother she had a way out. Her father was besotted with her, so he was always gentle and kind to her. And she would do what she could to help the others, trying to influence him. No, she could not bear to be upset. Even an altercation with her sister distressed her. Clothilde wanted to be a nun. She'd have to curb her temper if she wanted to live in a convent. Tempers were not allowed in convents, Celestine knew. Poor Clothilde. Wanting to give up the world and become a Bride of Christ. Heavens! Celestine could not understand her sister. She loved the world. She loved the parties they went to. Auntie May was giving one for her in September. It would be her official coming-out party. Then she could go to the Military Ball and waltz with all the officers. She loved life. Each day for her was exciting and new. She loved shopping with her mother and visiting the sick and needy. It made her feel good and sad, both at the same time. She loved helping Mamie, except at jam-making, and she especially loved the evenings after dinner when she could sit on her father's knee and give him his pipe. She would play the piano and sing to him and the others. She thought that tonight she would play 'Kathleen

21

Mavourneen' for him. It was one of his favourites, for he loved sad, sentimental ballads. They made him weep real tears.

On her mother's other side Clothilde's thin beautiful face quivered in anticipation at the inevitable row that would follow her announcement that she wanted to take the veil. Her face was not in the fashion of the day and lacked her sister's round softness. But it grew upon you. It was beautifully fine-boned. Her eyebrows were heavy and straight and her lashes thick and dark over her malachite eyes. They were slate coloured, their expression fierce, not because of her personality but because of the intensity of her thoughts. She was an ardent, passionate girl, and ever since she could remember rosaries came easier to her than conversation. She felt more at home at devotions than she did at the parties at Auntie May's that Celestine loved so much. She desired nothing more than to lose herself in a spiritual ardour that satisfied her in a way that nothing else could. She did not know why. She had never queried her spiritual aspirations.

She wanted, most of all, to be a martyr. Celestine was right. (She hated her sister for being so knowledgeable about her.) She wanted desperately to die for Jesus. She wanted to give up her life in some noble tremendous gesture. She wanted to be burned at the stake, be pierced by a thousand arrows, to be shot in front of a firing squad of weeping soldiers. Sometimes she stood in her nightgown at her open window at night in the winter: it had to be winter; when it was raining was best; and cold; preferably icy. She would chant the Hail Holy Queen and get soaked. She would want desperately to close the window and snuggle down in bed the way Celestine did, hardly finishing her sign of the Cross before she jumped under the covers. But Sr Imelda had told her that suffering for Jesus was a most salutary and sanctifying act, a purge of sin and a gift of great love, and so she stood there, allowing the freezing wind to chill her and the driving rain to drench her. Then, shivering, teeth chattering, she would eventually close the window and go to bed exhausted, but, she felt, cleansed.

She had spoken to the Reverend Mother in the convent in Rathfarnham. The Reverend Mother had put a hasty hand to her mouth and said, when she had recovered, that pain was not something to be actively sought. That misguided actions such as getting drenched for God were more likely to lead to pneumonia than to sainthood. The Reverend Mother was anxious to point out to her that religious life was not, could never be, an escape from life. 'We seek rather to embrace life, my dear, but from a different angle, a more selfless, less self-preoccupied one. We try to be more concerned with the well-being of others than perhaps an unwholesome desire to suffer would give us the energy for.'

Clothilde was not too sure about that. She felt the Reverend Mother was perhaps not the stuff saints were made of. She laughed a lot, which Clothilde felt was inappropriate, and had been seen skipping in the playground. Sister Imelda, on the other hand, was pale, with dark circles under her eyes. She coughed a lot, never smiled and was constantly to be found in the chapel murmuring Ave Marias. Clothilde adored her.

Mamie had told Ellen that there were damp patches in Clothilde's room. 'Just under the window, Mum. The wallpaper is ruined. I don't know where it's coming from.' Clothilde was alarmed, but as Ellen did not want to broach the matter to Garreth nothing further was said and the matter dropped.

Clothilde thought Celestine was excessively silly to want to marry and have babies.

'That's all right for the *hoi polloi*,' she said loftily to her sister. 'If you are *ordinary*. But God has called me, so it's different.'

She knew that her brother Neill shared her religious fervour. They often went to church together and although they did not talk about it too much they understood each other. However, Neill had reservations about his sister. She was so volatile and emotional. He was fond of telling her, much to her fury, that she would have to pray for balance if she intended to take a vow of unquestioning obedience.

'You're too emotional, Clo.' He would shake his head, then smile his warm reassuring smile. 'But I'm reckoning without the good Lord. He'll sort you out, if you ask Him, never fear.'

Brother and sister had decided that they could not put off the evil day any longer. Their father would have to be told. Clothilde hoped that because she was a female it might not be as bad for her as she anticipated, but Neill's task was almost impossible. Everyone in the family was aware that their father had brought his sons into the business so that they could, would, take it over in a year or two, under his direction of course. Neill and Breffni were already going to the brewery for a

23

full day's work, in order, their father asserted, that they learn the business from the top of the tower to the cellars. Breffni, who hated and feared his father, had told Clothilde about it.

'He drags us around and shows off, talking all the time in a loud voice. Then he lords it over the workers. They hate him, Clo. They really do. All except that little rat O'Brien. Then he just leaves us to hang about. I never know *where* to put myself. I feel so useless. I'm no good at judging the hops, or seeing whether the malt is split or riddled with thins and cracked grains. I'm just no good at it. And I'm not interested. I cannot for the life of me work up any enthusiasm for the business and I can't help it. I'm sorry.'

'I know, Breffni, I know. Don't worry about it, dear,' she soothed him. He was so vulnerable and so young, she thought. She could not bear to see his distress, but what could any of them do in the face of their father's implacable authority?

Breffni said brightly, 'I wrote a poem about it though:
"All the fires of Hell are there
All the faces too,
Made fearsome in the flickering light . . ."
Oh, it's not tidied up yet, but I'll work at it.' He gave her a little deprecating smile and she kissed him.

Breffni was always scribbling. Their father didn't know. He would have a fit if he ever found out, Clothilde thought. Sometimes she hated their father with a fierceness that frightened her. She remembered the Reverend Mother's words: 'You are too passionate, Clothilde. Sometimes I think you are afraid of the passion within you. You must not be.'

For a moment Clothilde wondered if perhaps she was wrong, if perhaps she did not have a vocation after all. Then she shrugged the thought away.

'What are you thinking, dear?' Ellen asked.

'Nothing, Mother. I'm just content to be here. With you.'

She kissed her mother's hand and Ellen smiled. It was at moments like this that she forgave Garreth for all his faults and was glad she had married him, for she would not change a hair on the heads of any one of her children and their affection for her was worth everything.

'Mr Goldblat told me today that he has Father's jacket ready for him,' Celestine said, sipping her tea. 'I'll mention it to Papa tonight.'

'When did you see him, dearest?' Ellen asked.

'When I went to get the sugar with Miffy. We needed extra sugar for that horrid jam.' She wrinkled her nose. 'I was in the Waltons and Mr Goldblat came in and told me.' Mr Goldblat was the bespoke tailor who had a shop on Rathgar Road.

At that moment, through the conservatory door, Neill and Breffni came to greet their mother. Neill was tall and thin and serious, very like Clothilde in looks. High cheekbones, and steady slate-grey eyes whose gaze was straight-forward, unafraid and direct. Breffni had his younger sister's velvet eyes and thick curly hair. The boys kissed Ellen's cheek and sat while she poured them tea. Her children were all about her now and her moment of complete content had come, the pinnacle of her day. Her heart was full of the warmth of their love for her and her's for them. It was a blessed time. She had felt this sensation of joy every evening of her life since they had been born, and it was the main reason she found excuses for Garreth, for he had given this to her. These were the moments she savoured most, sending up a silent prayer of thanksgiving and gratitude. Everything was worth this. It negated any suffering she had had to endure, any pain she had felt. It made her feel strong as a lioness. She could not know, as she sat, the sun slipping away, the shadows lengthening, her loved ones around her, that it would be one of the last times they all sat thus, as a family.

Mrs Danagher, their next-door neighbour, popped her head over the garden wall.

'Evenin', Mrs Connolly,' she called.

Ellen waved. 'Lovely evening,' she replied.

'Long may it last. Sure it'll soon be winter. Mr Danagher says it'll be any day now. Then we'll be up to our neck in leaves, an' then the frost an' snow, God help us.'

Celestine tried to control her giggles and Ellen gave her daughter's hand a gentle tap. Mrs Danagher's head had disappeared down the other side of the wall, then it popped up again like a jack-in-the-box. Celestine's giggles became out of control and her mother gave her a reproving glance.

'Oh, Mrs Connolly, d'ye mind if I prune the crab-apple tree? Only it's just that the branches are dipping over into the flowerbed. I wouldn't ask if I thought ye'd mind. But I don't see why ye should, an' what harm can it do?' She peered at Ellen, her chin resting on the wall, her round, red, wrinkled little face cocked slightly askew as she asked her convoluted question.

'Sure, why not indeed Mrs Danagher? Twill do it good, no doubt,' Ellen replied tranquilly.

Mamie came hurrying down the garden path with more hot water to top up the teapot. The family, as if by secret signal, raised their faces to catch the last of the sun. Breffni fanned himself with his Panama hat and teased Celestine.

Clothilde said softly to Neill, 'Tonight's the night.'

He nodded. His skin was taut on the sensitive bones of his face, and Clothilde could see the ripple of the muscles just above his jawline, a sure sign of inner tension.

'Yes. It cannot wait any longer,' he murmured firmly.

Although occupied with pouring the tea, and although they had spoken quietly, Ellen heard them.

'Please, dears, don't upset your father tonight. I don't think I could bear it.' She pressed her handkerchief to her forehead and passed the boys their refill of tea. 'Have some of Miffy's marble-cake. She has become adept at making it. It's really quite delicious.'

Neill noticed that the plate in her hand trembled and she looked at him with pleading eyes.

Breffni was munching the cake and nodding.

'It's top-hole, Mother. Really first-rate,' he said enthusiastically, and continued without a pause, 'I was looking at the advertisement today. Old Kitchener. Your Country Wants You. Might go. Get me out of the boring old brewery and from under Father's feet.'

Ellen had gone white and Clothilde, glancing at her mother, cried, 'For pity's sake, Breffni, think what you are saying.'

The boy's eyes under their spiky lashes glowed with excitement. 'But it would be thrilling. To go off to war to . . .'

'Shut up, Breffni. You really are the most tactless little . . . Shut up and think what you are saying.'

Breffni looked injured. 'But I believe in the cause of freedom,' he said heatedly. 'I believe in peace in the world. I must fight on the side of right. I have a duty.' His eyes snapped and he pushed the curls back off his face as he protested hotly, 'We have to save democracy. We have to do what we can. I *want* to go, Mother, and you can't stop me.'

'Shut up,' Neill cried. 'Don't fret, Mother. He doesn't mean it.'

26

Breffni opened his mouth to protest but caught his brother's stern gaze and noticed for the first time how pale his mother had gone.

'I want you to promise me Breffni . . .' she began, then stopped, and bird-like, tilted her head, listening.

The others heard nothing but she had caught the sound of the key; through the length and breadth of the hall, two rooms and a kitchen, she had heard it.

She stood up and brushed her skirts and sighed.

'Come along, children,' she said, knowing her short moments of peace were at an end. 'Come along. Your father's home.'

Chapter

2

ELLEN Connolly went to greet her husband as she had for the past twenty-five years, and, as usual, Garreth, still edgy from his day at work, treated her brusquely.

He was a large man. His face gave an impression of joviality, but the cold eyes held no comfort in them and the mouth held no humour. He was square-shaped, his shoulders heavy, a florid, superficially good-looking man whose manner, outside his home, aimed to charm but did not succeed. He was a man who liked to show his power. He had the same brown eyes as his younger son and daughter, but they were, unlike his children's, curiously responsive to a direct gaze. He had a fine straight nose and was bearded and moustached. He laughed a lot, but his laughter held no joy, no spontaneity, rather it was a cover-up, a noise he hid behind.

Everything in his house, the furniture, the accoutrements, the servants, his children, and most of all his wife, irritated and pleased him in equal proportions. They pleased him, for they were a constant reminder of his achievement in rising from nothing to the peacock-preening position he was in: a well-to-do businessman, a prosperous householder, father and husband. It irritated, because however long he lived in this prosperity he could never become at ease in it, never take it for granted. He always felt that initial stab of inferiority to his wife and his children, especially Ellen and Breffni. Ellen with her breeding, her titled sister, her knowledge of what was right and wrong in society, what was 'done' and what was 'not done'. And Breffni; carelessly charming, unconsciously graceful, poetic, eloquent. Quite unconsciously Breffni made Garreth feel fat, ungainly, uncouth, ineloquent, a clumsy peasant, a yokel.

When Garreth was irritated he was bad-tempered.

Ellen said, 'Good evening, Garreth,' and tried to kiss his pendulous cheek, but he brushed her aside. Her nose had touched his sideburns and the wiry hairs itched her.

'Ellen, I'm very tired. I've had an appalling day. I must bathe and change.'

She took his coat, hat and scarf from him and hung them carefully on the coat-stand in the hall. He went quickly up to their bedroom above the parlour and she followed meekly as usual. He sat down on the bed and stuck out his leg. Ellen bent down with a little grunt and unfastened his ankle-high boots, unhooking them, removing them.

While he was in the bathroom she laid out his clothes for the evening, a clean starched shirt, a smoking jacket and his socks and slippers. He liked her there as he changed, an audience for his monologue. Long ago he had enjoyed watching as she got ready for dinner, but those days were long gone. She had never liked that time when he had held her pinned under an avid gaze as she tried to get dressed.

Now while he was in the bathroom Mamie came up, and she took off Ellen's tea-gown. Ellen splashed herself with water from the ewer, then dried herself, dabbing some lavender-water on her neck and shoulders. The scapulars around her neck smelled strongly of lavender, for she never took them off and they had a daily douse in the scented water. She let Mamie, who kept a weather-eye on the bathroom, slip her dinner-gown over her head and tidy her hair. Then she left to attend to her duties downstairs.

Ellen's jewellery was modest, although Garreth could easily have afforded to deck her out in the best. May, her sister, badgered her to nag him about his meanness, but Ellen did not have the nerve. Besides which, she was not a greedy woman and was quite content with what she had. Tonight she wore a lavender silk and with it her garnet necklet and earrings.

All the time her husband's voice came to her from the bathroom. Tonight he was talking about the workers at the brewery, a favourite subject and one she knew by heart.

'Those men don't seem to understand how lucky they are. All they have to do is put in a little overtime. That's all I ask. A few hours here and there out of their petty little lives. Why on

29

earth should I pay them for that? I ask you. Where would they be if the brewery went out of business? I'll tell you. In the gutter. That's where they would be. I'm their bread and butter. And if Neill says another word on the subject, then he's put out of this house for ever. Needn't darken this door again. He's *your* son, Ellen. I don't know where he gets some of his ideas. Crack-pot. Lunacy, I can tell you.'

She never listened to what he said. She let him ramble on. It was easier so. It was always better if she did not react antagonistically to anything he talked about.

He sometimes tried to provoke her. Prodded and goaded her like a matador a bull. But she bravely resisted his attempts. Sometimes, to her cost, he succeeded. Sometimes he did not. She never knew which was better, for when he made her angry it seemed to placate him and his tirade usually ceased. When she did not take the bait he could simmer all evening and into the night and only Celestine had the power to soothe him.

Whenever he had a complaint about the children they were her's, and so tonight Neill had become 'your son' as he listed Neill's misdemeanours to her. He continued in this vein until he was ready to go, and then, without asking whether she too had completed her toilet, he turned and left the room.

She followed him downstairs into the parlour. Mamie had poured his sherry and was putting it carefully on the table beside his deep leather armchair. She spilled a little, then sighed and mopped the drops up with a cloth she held over her arm against such a contingency.

She shuffled out and when she had closed the door behind her he said, 'That woman will have to go, Ellen.' He sipped his Amontillado, smacking his lips. 'She's getting too old for us.'

Ellen seated herself opposite him. The children were in their respective rooms where they would remain until the dinner gong sounded. Ellen's crocheting lay on her chair and she picked it up and fiddled with the wool. She made little shawls and rugs for the poor women in Paradise Street, but she was not thinking of her needlework now. She was praying for the right words to steer her through the mine-field of this evening's conversation.

She knew she could not bear to live without Mamie, and Garreth, knowing it too, often used her need as a weapon against her. Mamie had been in the service of her family since she was a young girl. She had come with Ellen when the latter had married Garreth Connolly. They never discussed Mr Connolly. There was no need to. Without words Ellen knew that Mamie saw everything, noted everything and was squarely on her side. Garreth Connolly knew it too, and it irked him. He could not fault Mamie's behaviour. There was nothing you could put your finger on, but her loyalty to and her love for her mistress was inherent in everything she did and Garreth could not bear that. After all, he was master in his own home, was he not?

Ellen worried about his remark. Not its essence: he had been threatening to expel Mamie for twenty years now. But Mamie worked for nothing and a replacement, essential in his position, would have cost him a hundred pounds a year, money that he would not willingly be prepared to lose. She worried now, not about Mamie leaving, for that she knew was nonsense, but rather how to field the question without provoking a quarrel. How to deal with it? To argue with him could set him off, to keep silent might do the same. On the other hand, if she simply said nothing, his mind might drift to other matters. She never knew what to expect. Uncertainty was the worst part; her evenings were fraught with danger.

She made up her mind and held her peace, saying nothing. It did not work.

'Lost your tongue, Ellen?' he said sarcastically. 'Or gone deaf? Talking to myself, am I?'

'No, Garreth. I was thinking . . .'

'He gave a loud guffaw. 'Thinking?' he said. 'Women? Thinking? Ellen, spare me. Serious thought would addle you. Women don't think. Men think.'

'No, dear. Of course.'

'No, dear. Of course.' He mimicked her. 'No, dear. Of course. Think by agreeing with me I'll forget Mamie, do we?' His eyes glittered and Ellen flinched. He was right of course. That had been precisely her line of thought. 'Well, I'm not. One day, quite soon, I'll fire her. We need a young girl here. Not old bones. Someone young and energetic. I'm surrounded by ageing women at home and fools and hotheads at work. Look at you, Ellen. And that old crone of a servant your father foisted on us.'

This was so unfair that Ellen lost her judgement and was stung to a sharp retort.

31

'Oh, Garreth, that's not true,' she cried, distressed. 'Father gave us Mamie as a present. He paid her salary for all the years he was alive and when he died Mamie ceased to earn. She works for nothing, and you know it.'

Ellen instantly regretted her outburst. Horrified, she snapped her mouth shut and stole an anxious glance at him. To her surprise he seemed quite calm, all anger gone. As long as she lived, she thought, she would never understand him. For the first time since he had arrived home he had relaxed. He had achieved his aim and his tension had been channelled into another. Ellen's distress worked a miracle in her husband. Garreth became all benignity.

'Oh, my dear Ellen, don't take on so. I was rambling on . . . you know me. You must not pay any attention.'

And if I did not, she thought, you would goad me into it as you've just done. But she suppressed such unworthy ideas and accepted his change of mood with relief. Her heart resumed its normal pace.

At that moment Celestine came into the room. She ran over and plonked herself on her father's knee.

'Papa! Welcome home, Papa.'

Garreth pinched her cheek, hugged and kissed her smooth forehead.

'My pet. At last I feel at home. This is what Papa works hard for. How is my little girl? Tell Papa what you have been up to?'

'I went shopping, Papa. At least, I did not buy anything, but I saw the most, most beautiful yellow silk brocade, and dearest Papa, it's quite perfect for the dress Madame McGinty will make for me for the ball Aunt May is to give for me at the end of the week. Oh do say I may buy it, Papa, do!'

Her father smiled indulgently at her. 'Of course you may. Forgive me, poppet. I don't understand these things, but should you not wear white at that ball?'

Celestine shrugged. 'Well, maybe. Mother?'

'Perhaps you could wear yellow. In any event you have the white lace upstairs that you've never worn. Ask Papa if you can buy the yellow material, then you could wear the yellow to the military ball and the white to May's.'

Garreth kissed her cheek. 'Capital,' he said. 'Capital. I'll give you some golden guineas tomorrow, see if I don't.'

'And I'll sing "Kathleen Mavourneen" for you after dinner.'

32

They were both delighted: he by being able to bestow upon her, this child of his heart, something she wanted; Celestine because she could see that she had created a peaceful atmosphere and got something she really desired.

Garreth felt that great familiar surge of love within him that always overwhelmed him when his Celestine smiled at him like that: her eyes bright as stars, the love she felt for him glowing in their depths. Tears pricked his eyes. He knew he would give her anything her heart desired. It was the only way he could show his love for her. He would not, could not, ever let her go, the light of his life. He smiled at her and she smiled back.

Ellen relaxed in her chair opposite her husband. She let her crochet rest in her lap and a momentary peace steal over her. All was well for a moment at least. Garreth was holding his daughter lightly on his lap and Celestine had her head on his shoulder as he sipped his sherry.

The parlour was large and full of furniture. It ran the length of the house. There was a piano draped in thick Irish lace near the back window that looked out over the now darkening garden. Framed photographs stood on it and a vase of late roses. There was a large gilt-framed painting of Garreth Connolly over the fireplace, seated, his elbow on a table lightly resting on a book he had not read, looking stiff, formidable and hirsute. Opposite it on the other wall was a matching portrait, obviously done by the same artist, of Ellen in her presentation ball-gown of cream satin and pearls. She looked very much as Celestine did now, innocently wide-eyed, trustful and sweet-natured.

Ellen was glad her husband was soothed and did not know why she suddenly felt so ill-at-ease, like an interloper who should not be there. The room was peaceful, the grandfather clock ticked, tranquillity in measure. She could hear the clatter of dishes from the kitchen where Mamie was preparing the dinner and the smell of apple and blackberry tart with a residue of the scent of jam-making floated up through the floorboards. The fire crackled in the grate and the clink of cutlery sounded from the dining-room across the hall where Miffy was setting the places for dinner. The deep voice of Ben-the-Boots could be heard faintly somewhere at the back of the house. He had driven Garreth home in the motor car. Ben-the-Boots was one of Ellen's 'lame ducks'. She had found him starving to death in Paradise Row and had brought him to Rathgar, fed him, nursed

33

him, much to her husband's fury. Then she suggested that as Garreth was determined to buy a motor vehicle and as he could not possibly drive himself, Ben would be a wonderful chauffeur. He would work for his board and keep and a few coppers. Against his will, Garreth saw the sense of the idea. Driving a motor car presented problems, and as he hated to admit ineptitude or ignorance about anything and it was a sure thing that he would have to if he tried to drive the vehicle, Ben-the-Boots was a perfect scapegoat to harangue when anything went wrong. So at the ripe old age of thirteen Ben became chauffeur and boot-polisher and jack-of-all-trades in the Connolly household.

That had been five years ago. He did not remember or know or want to divulge his surname. He had become Ben-the-Boots by accident. He had given Mamie a shocking fright when unbeknownst to her he had got out of bed at five o'clock in the morning, frightening them all with the noise he made, for they thought he was an intruder. When Mamie had gone to see, creeping down the kitchen stairs, Ben was discovered blackening the boots and polishing them in the kitchen. He then and there acquired the name Ben-the-Boots, and had been so called ever since.

Ellen heard him laugh now. He was a cheerful boy, although Garreth Connolly berated him constantly and sometimes beat him. Perhaps he was used to it and did not mind, but for a lad in his position he was curiously content. Now she could hear Neill's voice talking to him. She glanced at her husband. He hated his chauffeur talking to any of the family barring himself. He owned him, after all. But Garreth did not seem to notice tonight.

The boys would not come to the parlour. They never willingly went where their father was. Neither would Clothilde. They would stay away until the gong sounded for dinner. She hoped tonight the meal would be peaceful. She hoped in vain.

Miffy sounded the gong with all her strength. She hated the noise it made. She closed her eyes tightly before she banged it and would have put her hands over her ears if she could. However, she needed both hands and when she struck the gong it left her shuddering from head to foot.

Garreth stood at the head of the table with his back to the window. He would wait until all the children had taken their

34

places. He had taken his fob-watch out of his waistcoat pocket and was looking at it. He would not take his eyes off it until everyone was in their correct place. Ellen sat opposite him at the foot of the table and Celestine sat on his right. The other three seats remained vacant.

Ellen stood up. 'I'll tell them . . . ' she began, and started for the door.

'Sit down, Ellen.' His voice halted her in her tracks.

'Perhaps they did not hear,' she said uncertainly.

'The gong, Ellen, was loud enough to wake the dead. Sit down.'

Ellen obediently sat. They waited. The seconds ticked by. Three minutes seemed a long time, waiting in silence. The door opened and Clothilde came in, followed by Neill. She stopped short when she saw her father at the table already. Most days he was not this prompt. It depended on how long it had taken him to drink his sherry. Tonight he had gulped it and had finished it before the gong sounded and consequently he had arrived almost immediately as the last reverberation had died away.

'Sorry, Papa.' Clothilde muttered and took her place beside her mother.

Neill shuffled in, a sober hang-dog expression on his face. He had been crossing swords with his father all day in the brewery and was weary of it. And he knew he had to speak tonight about his vocation; he had promised Clothilde. He said nothing, silently taking his seat at his father's left side and opposite Celestine.

Garreth Connolly never lifted his eyes from the watch which he held in the palm of his hand. There was another pause while everyone waited uncomfortably and another two minutes ticked by. Then the door burst open and Breffni rushed in.

'Oh crumbs! Sorry, sorry, sorry, Papa, everyone.' He hurried to his place beside his mother, touching her hand as he passed.

'Well, it's about time. Five minutes and four seconds. How nice of you children to condescend to grace this table at all! I'm not accustomed to be kept waiting and you are all aware of my ruling on the matter. All of you, except for Celestine, were late.'

Miffy arrived at the doorway, a large silver soup tureen in her hands. As she moved forward, Garreth's voice stopped her.

'No, Miffy. Stay there. I would like an explanation before we begin. Clothilde?'

35

Clothilde turned up her eyes. Her thin intelligent face revealed an impatience that verged on contempt. She was not good at dissimulation.

'I didn't hear the gong. I'm sorry,' she said in a monotone.

Ellen was watching Miffy in an agony of anxiety. The soup tureen was heavy and hot; Miffy could barely manage it. Now she was stuck in the doorway, desperately trying not to drop it.

'Garreth, Miffy is . . .'

But he interrupted her. 'Are you deaf, Clothilde? Miffy struck the gong quite hard, I thought.' He glanced at the servant but did not notice her predicament.

'Garreth, Miffy is . . .'

'Ellen, will you kindly let me straighten out this time problem with my children without interruption? I will not tolerate unpunctuality.'

But Miffy could hold the tureen no longer. It fell to the floor; soup spraying everywhere. Breffni gave a snort of laughter which he tried to stifle; and it ended in an agonizing whinny. Miffy, overcome with terror, uttered a strangled scream and stood shaking from head to toe like a leaf in the wind. She whined like a whipped puppy and jumped when Mr Connolly turned to her.

'What the devil do you think you are doing, idiot girl?'

'I was trying to tell you, Garreth. The tureen was hot and too heavy for her to hold and . . .'

'I do not care what she was trying to do,' he shouted. 'I only care about what she has done. This carpet, Miffy, is Indian. It took many people months to weave and it has lasted a hundred years. It has taken you two minutes to destroy it. You are a stupid, silly girl and if you are not very careful I will send you back where you came from.'

'Do not speak to her like that, Father.' Neill's voice was calm and cold.

Ellen found her heart give a great leap within her. It pained her as if someone had squeezed it; then it started thumping as if it were trying to escape the confines of her chest. Breffni covered her hand with his.

Garreth's face had turned plum-coloured. He looked at Neill in disbelief. No one had ever spoken to him like that in his own home before, or anywhere else, for that matter. As soon as his attention shifted from her, Miffy disappeared.

36

'You forget yourself, boy. How dare you address your father in that fashion? Apologize immediately.'

Neill, seeing Miffy had escaped, smiled his severe little smile. 'I'm so sorry, Father. I apologize most humbly,' he said graciously. There was a breathless silence in the room. Everyone wondered what would happen now. They were not left long in doubt.

Mamie came wheezing up the stairs with a basin and cloth, the sniffling Miffy hiding behind her bulk. When she entered the room, hostility oozed from her every pore, was inherent in her every move.

'Thank you, Mamie,' Ellen said as calmly as she could.

They sat in silence at the table while the two servants, the old and the young, laboured to clean up the mess the soup had made. Ellen desperately wanted to rise and help them but Breffni's firm hand restrained her. Only Mamie seemed to exude an 'I dare you' attitude as if she hoped Garreth would utter one word of condemnation so that she could give him a piece of her mind. But he said nothing. He simply sat in stony silence at the head of the table, waiting.

At last it was over. Mamie gave Miffy the bucket and threw soupy cloths into it with a defiant gesture. She turned and looked directly at Garreth Connolly.

'Shall we serve the meat now, Sir?' she said with heavy sarcasm.

If she thought to disconcert Garreth, she was wrong. He stared back at her and said icily, 'If that would not be too much trouble, Mamie.'

It was an uncomfortable meal. Garreth ceased attacking and now sat in brooding silence. Every clink of knife on fork, every sound of swallowing or the click of tooth on tooth seemed unnaturally loud and was a thin scraping across Ellen's nerves.

Mamie served the meal. Ellen knew that she would not allow Miffy into the dining-room again this evening. She bullied the girl, kept her hard at work, but she loved her and was fiercely protective of her. The result was that they had to wait while Mamie, taking her time, wheezing and panting up the stairs, brought everything from the kitchen in separate journeys. First came the roast pork, a pause, then the apple-sauce, carrots and peas, then another pause, and then the roast and mashed potatoes. While this was happening, they waited at the table in silence, and Ellen had to squeeze Breffni's hand as the desire to giggle shook his body. She knew that Mamie was doing it deliberately and she wished heartily that the servant would not behave so. It was misplaced loyalty, as the family would be the ones to suffer from the backlash of Garreth's annoyance. Mamie kept darting malicious looks at Garreth under her creased eyelids, her little blackcurrant eyes snapping aggressively.Her movements verged on the cheeky but never became audacious enough to warrant rebuke. Ellen knew that Mamie would love Garreth Connolly to admonish her, would welcome a chance to look at him with mock-innocence and swear loudly and long that he had completely misjudged her. He was well aware of this, he had played this game with her before and lost, so he did not give her the opportunity. In fact he turned the tables on her. It was his most confusing characteristic, a trait that disturbed and bewildered his family.

When Mamie brought in the apple and blackberry pie, Garreth clapped his hands together like a child and beamed up at her.

'My favourite. Oh Mamie, what a wonderful surprise. You make the best apple pie in Ireland.'

Mamie nearly dropped the pie. She plonked it down in front of Ellen and left to get the cream. Breffni had snorted again and although his father gave him a brief glance, he had obviously decided to ignore any partly-concealed defiance that could be denied, thereby making him look foolish. Garreth Connolly hated to look foolish.

The tide had turned, but for how long no one knew. At last the meal was over and the family repaired to the parlour for coffee. Clothilde sat on a footstool at her mother's feet, her little kid boots sticking out from beneath her dress, and Breffni stood behind them. Neill isolated himself by the front window: tall, tense, brooding and withdrawn. He stood with his back to them all, watching the carriages as they clopped by in the street and the lamp lighter as he lit the lamps and they glowed yellow in the blue night.

Celestine lit her father's cigar, smiling up at him; then, without being asked, went to the piano and opened it. Her fingers slipped over the keys and she settled herself, flicking some pages of music.

' "Kathleen Mavourneen, the grey dawn is breaking,
The horn of the hunter is heard on the hill,
The lark from her light wing the bright dew is shaking,
Kathleen Mavourneen, what, slumbering still?' "

She sang in a high pure voice, clear and sweet. Her father closed his eyes and puffed on his cigar.

Ellen visibly relaxed. She poured her husband a brandy from a decanter on the side-board and set it on the table beside him. He nodded without looking up and relief flooded her. His face was at rest, his eyes closed, listening. She sat down and Breffni put his arm over her shoulder, leaning against her slightly. She loved his nearness to her and she drew comfort from the careless embrace.

Clothilde rested her head against her mother's knee and Ellen gently stroked the soft, dark hair. The girl's thin face became smooth as glass, her eyes vacant as tension left her. Peace had come into the room. Only the tall eldest son stood apart, quivering, tightly-strung, looking out on the street.

Celestine finished her song. The last sweet note hung on the air and she smiled across at her father. She rose slowly from the piano as Neill spoke from the shadows.

'Father, I want to talk to you.'

Ellen's heart leapt into her throat. She touched the scapulars at her breast. Breffni's arm tightened about her and Celestine sat down again abruptly on the piano stool and bent her head. Clothilde raised her's and rubbed her eyes and murmured, 'I was nearly asleep . . . Mother?'

'Well? Well, what about, Neill?' Garreth asked.

'Could I speak to you in private, Papa?' Neill's voice was calm and steady.

'Private? Private? Good heavens, no. If you think I'm going to leave the comfort of my fireside and the bosom of my family to listen to some more of your twaddle . . .! Piffle it all is. Do you know, Mother, what he was ranting about today?' He always called her 'Mother' when he wanted her on his side. 'In front of the men? When I was trying to make sure the beers were roused? A crucial moment, and not one when I like to be interrupted?' Ellen realized dismally that her husband was becoming furious. Angrier than he had been for a long time. This was the second time in an evening that his eldest son had crossed him, and she imagined that they had had words already that day at the brewery.

Garreth's voice shook, his face became mottled. She sometimes thought when he was like this he might fall in an apoplectic fit and die. She tried to quell the little snake of hope that thrilled through her at the idea. Saying a quick prayer under her breath she tried to concentrate on what he said. She never listened when he spoke to her alone, but when her children were involved she tried to grasp the content of what he was saying in order to come to their defence if it proved necessary, even though she was terrified and she rarely achieved a fair response.

'Strikes! Overtime! Threatening me if I did not increase their wages. And he talkin' to me in front of them! Me own son! God help you when you take over. D'ye want to bankrupt us? Send your mother and the girls te the workhouse? Have us all thrown into the gutter?'

He struggled to control himself. He always lost his accent when he lost his temper. The gutter-language of the slums returned from their burial-ground deep in his memory to haunt him and trap his tongue. He could hear it and they could hear it and he knew they must despise him.

'Don't exaggerate, Father.' Neill interrupted, his voice cool. Everyone looked at him. It was as if Neill was a stranger with a stranger's detachment. Garreth whipped around in his chair to face his son.

'Now listen to me, you young whipper-snapper . . .' he began. That was better, but Neill interrupted.

'No. You listen to me, for once. You drive those men at the brewery mercilessly and you know it. Twenty-four hour production! My God! All they are looking for are their basic human rights.'

'Don't you dare speak to me like that! Are you finished?'

'No, I'm not. That is not what I want to talk to you about. I wanted to tell you — privately — what everyone here already knows: that I don't want to work in the brewery any more. I want to become a priest.'

There was a stunned pause. Ellen gripped her scapulars which were working their way out of her bodice as her agitation mounted. Clothilde had lifted her head and sat bolt-upright on her stool staring at Neill and her father. Celestine bent over the piano, hunching her shoulders, her hair almost covering her

40

face, as if to disappear behind it, to vanish from the room. Breffni held his mother's shoulder like a vice. He did not realize how strong his grip was.

After a moment Garreth sat down again and puffed on his cigar. The silence lengthened.

'Well, Father? What have you got to say?' Neill asked finally.

'Nothing.'

'But, Father . . .'

'I tell you I've got nothing to say to you.' Garreth's voice was cold and even. He had his pronunciation under control. They all looked at him, and he could not resist continuing. 'The idea is preposterous. You are my heir. The business goes to you, though God help us, you make a sorry businessman. What will happen to your poor mother and the girls after I've gone does not bear thinking about . . .'

Ellen, on cue, tutted, 'Oh no, Garreth, don't talk like that. Please God, you'll be spared to us for many a year yet.'

Garreth nodded comfortably. This was more like it. The conversation was running in familiar grooves; predictable.

But Neill said again, 'I don't want to be your heir. I want to be a priest.'

'I have just told you. You can not,' Garreth said and smiled.

'Then I shall have to go ahead without your consent, Father.'

Garreth Connolly rose from his chair again. It was a very agile movement for a man his size. He stood in front of the fire, cutting off the heat suddenly from Ellen and Clothilde on the other side. He gave a short snort of laughter.

'I don't think you understand, boy,' he said calmly. 'It takes money to be a priest. It takes parental consent and co-operation. You have to study. How do you think you will live while you do that, eh? The Holy Roman Catholic Church is not a charitable institution, eh, Mother?' They'll not want you without your settlement from us. Certainly your fees must be paid. No matter what your mother thinks. Oh no. And when I make it plain that it is completely against my wishes, your father's wishes (remember the fourth commandment?) then they'll no more want you than they'd want the leader of the Orange Lodge.'

Neill looked shattered. Garreth had the satisfaction of seeing him crumble, his bold stance wilting under information he had

41

not taken into account. He realized that his father's logic sounded irrefutable.

'But, Father, I'm sure I have a vocation and . . .' Neill stammered, loathing the pleading tone that had entered his voice.

'Well, you'll have to forget it, then, won't you?'

'But it's my whole life, Father.'

'I'll not give my permission, and that's final. I need you in the brewery.'

'But you don't, Father. Not really. Breffni and I are no good. You say so yourself. Oh, we could do the mashing and the rousing with the other workers, but you won't let us do that. And I'm no good at management.'

'Well now, that is really beside the point. When I go, you can leave most of the paper work to O'Brien. But as your saint of a mother points out, I'll be here a few years yet . . .'

'God willing . . .' Ellen murmured.

Garreth stared at her a moment, then continued, 'It's *my* firm, *our* name, and I intend it goes to my sons and grandsons. You'll obey me. Without me you are nothing, boy.'

'Don't say that, Father.' Clothilde stood up, standing beside her father in front of the fireplace.

'Oh, missy? Are you daring to question your father's commands? Remember "And He went down to Jerusalem and was subject to them". The blueprint for Catholic family life, Eh? You'll all do as I say. That is what your precious Church commands. And the state too, come to that.'

'Father, you must listen. If Neill is called by God, it is like a command from heaven itself.' Clothilde felt her face flush.

'Oh? God is speaking personally to my son? What have we done to merit this honour? Really, Clothilde, be your age.'

'Father, Neill is not the only one. I too want to enter religious life. I know how he feels. It's a burning desire . . .'

'The whole family's got religious mania,' Garreth said in astonishment and he looked at his wife who sat stiff in her chair, fingers interlaced, her knuckles white. 'This is your fault, woman. Don't I know it. Force-feeding them like geese with all that Latin hocus-pocus.' Then as he glanced at her horrified face he continued, 'Not that I'm against it, don't get me wrong. It is fine and proper in its place. Women need it, the Church. But the brewery needs Neill, and there he must make his future or like as not we'll all starve. There is no Santa Claus you know.

You ought to know it by now, though you all behave like gullible infants.' He shook his head disbelievingly. 'I work for all this. The house, the food you put in your mouths, the clothes you wear. I bought everything you see around you.'

'You did not.' Ellen cried silently. She would not, could not, say it aloud. It would make matters worse. She looked at the piano, a present from her mother, and the fireside chairs and the portraits, her father's wedding gifts to them. Her sister May's china cabinet a present to her, stood in the corner full of knick-knacks collected by Ellen over the years of her marriage.

'I employ Miffy.' He was going to add Mamie, and would have if Ellen had not been present, but he thought better of it. 'I pay for everything you do, eat and wear. And . . . ' he glowered at Neill '. . . that shiftless bunch at the brewery . . . I *support* them. My money keeps them and their families. They're lucky to be in work. Half Dublin is unemployed. Did I say half? More like three-quarters and my lot get paid regularly. I put the bread in their mouths.' His face was mottled a curious liverish colour as he waxed righteous. He was in full stride now, well into a familiar monologue. He droned on and on, his chest expanding as he reassured himself of his generosity, his justness, his open-handed and genial nature.

Neill and Clothilde stood looking at him, baffled. Breffni batted his eyelashes nervously and Celestine drooped lower and lower over the piano, her face curtained by her hair.

Ellen was not listening to her husband's words, but she gave a start when Clothilde interrupted him.

'That's as maybe, Father, but I'm going to become a nun whatever you say. I can enter a poor order without a dowry. I don't care how menial the work is, how humble I have to be. I want to work among the poor and needy anyhow. Can't you understand? I long to help . . . to help . . . ' Her eyes were full of tears and they burned with a fervour her mother had not noticed before. She looked at her daughter amazed. So did Garreth. He stared at Clothilde, his mouth slightly open as if he were looking at an odd specimen in a museum. He shook his head.

'I do not pretend to understand you,' he said. 'But you can both forget about these insane ideas.'

Ellen took a deep breath and her courage in both hands.

'Garreth, if God has called the children, don't you think it's . . .'

43

Her husband interrupted. 'If God has called them, then God can pay for them. There is no such thing, my dear Clothilde, as a convent that takes you in without a dowry. You can ask Miffy about it. I don't know what kind of nonsense your mother has been filling your heads with, for I've no doubt it is all her doing. She and Canon Geraghty have a lot to answer for.'

He stretched his arms and yawned, then patted himself on the stomach. He was in charge. His word was law. He knew it and they knew it.

'Now I'm tired and I'm going to bed.'

Ellen started. 'But the rosary . . . ' she began.

He turned a disbelieving stare upon her. 'I cannot think where you get the nerve, Ellen, after your two eldest children have defied their father, broken the fourth commandment, to suggest the rosary to me. We have quite enough religion in this house already, don't you think?'

He glanced about the room, making sure he had everyone's attention. Celestine looked up from the piano.

'Before I go, I would like to say this. Your futures are quite decided upon. Neill and Breffni will take over the Connolly Brewery. Celestine — ' he held out an arm and his daughter rose from the piano and moved to her father's side. He put his arm around her. 'Celestine will stay at home with her mother and me. Our little girl, eh?' He patted her cheek fondly.

'And Clothilde. Clothilde will marry Owen Mulcahy. As soon as it can be arranged.' He caught his eldest daughter's expression of horror and smiled. 'But you knew this, Clothilde. Why are you so surprised? You know I keep my word.' He did not wait for her reply, and, turning to his wife, added, 'Ellen, you know how I feel about this alliance. The Mulcahys are a good family. Brendan Mulcahy owns Mulcahy & Son, the wine merchants just up the river from us. We are both interested in a merger. His firm needs new blood, and new money,' he laughed. 'And his business and our brewery can compliment each other, provide for both our families comfortably, which is what we men are supposed to do instead of spending our days on our knees muttering mumbo-jumbo suitable only for women and fools.'

He paused and looked around the room at each one of them in turn.

'Well, I think that is all. Ellen, say goodnight to the children.' He was not going to leave the family in the parlour to mull over what he had said. 'Neill, Breffni, kiss your mother goodnight.'

Breffni leaned over and laid his cheek on his mother's touching her shoulder with a reassuring pat. Neill bent stiffly to kiss her and his lips were cold. It was her hand that pressed his, trying to impart something, anything to lessen the blow he had been dealt. They left together, the brothers, silent, sullen.

Clothilde looked at her mother with wild despairing eyes, then kissed her and rushed from the room.

'You must not be upset by your sister and brothers, Celestine. They are an unruly lot. Your mother was never strict enough with them.'

'Please, Papa,' Celestine murmured. He knew she hated any criticism of her mother. Or the family. To her credit, she never abused her position as her father's favourite, the one member of the household who in his eyes could do no wrong. Rather she used her privileged position when she could, to smooth the paths of the other members of the family.

'Dear child. Why cannot they be more like you?' he asked smiling, his face full of the love he felt for her. He took her chin in his fingers, his thumb underneath, feeling the delicate bone and soft tissue. He kissed her gently on the lips then released her. She embraced her mother, then followed the others to bed.

'Well, Ellen? I hope you are proud of yourself?' he said, then added, 'Come to bed, woman.'

And she dutifully trotted up the stairs behind him.

45

Chapter

3

SOMETIMES Garreth watched her as she undressed. He realized that even when it had pleased him two decades ago, she had hated his scrutiny. Now he did it for the pleasure of humiliating her. If he was in a bad mood he made vulgar derogatory remarks about her body. Tonight was not one of those nights. He was flushed with success. He had routed the children, defeated them completely in a display of his authority and power over them. He could feel he was the big man again. The boss. He wondered why he always felt so small, so inadequate inside. Why he always felt inferior. Especially in front of his family. He shouted at them to force them to feel his power but it did not make them tremble as it should, as he had done before his own father. Neill's ascetic face and Clothilde's burning honesty unmanned him, and Breffni's careless charm and elegant manner destroyed his confidence. It was not much better in the brewery. Except with O'Brien. He was always secure with O'Brien, for the man worshipped him.

Ellen sat on the side of the double bed and wished wistfully for the millionth time that she had a room of her own, or, failing that, at least a bed. Then she would not have to undress in front of him. Exposed to his eyes she felt diminished as a woman. She wanted to apologize and did not know for what.

She unlaced her corsets and watched him in the mirror, scratching his belly as he removed his longjohns. He put on a night-shirt and got into bed with a grunt. His side of the bed sagged, his heavy weight bearing it downwards. It meant that she often rolled over towards him against her will. And sometimes, though rarely now, he would take her in the marriage act

46

without preamble, without love.

She knew that women had to endure a husband's lusts. She accepted that. It was her duty. But she was not stupid and she realized dimly that there was a completely different perspective to that beastly peformance Garreth inflicted upon her in the darkness of the night. She could not imagine what it could be, but her sister May, when Ellen had complained at an earlier time of Garreth's sexual appetite, had said, 'Oh Ellen darling, it can be such fun.'

She had never asked her sister what she had meant. She could not in her wildest dreams imagine Garreth's physical release as being 'fun'. Yet she knew too that it must be exciting for some people. She had read 'Romeo and Juliet' and 'Heloise and Abelard' in the old editions in her father's library in Wicklow where she had grown up. She knew that the Shakespeare had beeen edited and was available now only in a censored version. All Shakespeare's plays had been censored.

'The best bits taken out,' May had said.

'Best bits?' Ellen asked.

'They don't like you to enjoy sex,' May said. Then when Ellen looked blank. 'The priests, silly, though I can't think why not. They want us to breed so badly, don't they? I'm tired of listening to the clergy insisting that sex is "solely for the procreation of children". If they told us it was extremely enjoyable, just think how many children there would be.' She threw back her head and laughed, her lovely face alive with merriment.

People in Shakespeare had enjoyed sex. Heloise and Abelard had not been able to keep away from each other and they a nun and a monk respectively. Other writers she had read, poets too, like Shelley and Keats and wicked men like Lord Byron, prized the union between man and woman as something wonderful, or exciting, or obsessive, and she did not understand it. She felt sad that she had obviously missed something good that life had to offer.

Meantime the bed sagged and Garreth bounded about in his sleep, muttering and grunting as she lay wide-eyed awake beside him. Then, as usual she drifted into a deep peaceful state of unconsciousness, impervious to her husband's struggles with the bedclothes and pillow.

For Garreth, in the night, were the demons. He did not

understand why he was an insomniac, which is what he called himself. He resented Ellen's tranquil sleep when he was awake. His heavy build made constant movement uncomfortable yet he often tried, unsuccessfully to keep his wife awake. He hated tossing and turning and hearing her breathing peacefully beside him. How dare she rest when he was far from sleep?

Then he would drift off into a doze, a half-unconsciousness peopled with monsters, fearful shadows and menacing intangible images that filled him with alarm though he did not know why. He tried to keep them at bay but they kept advancing; and he was helpless, a feeling so foreign to him that it frightened him very much. He lay at the mercy of vague terrifying shades that held some terrible threat and over which he had no power at all.

Then he was outside his mother's little house in the muddy lane. Big boys, faces like gargoyles, huge and ugly, were beating him, tearing at him with dirty broken jagged fingernails and kneading his face with their hands. He tried to escape. He ran into the house, but there was no safety there. He screamed as he saw the brutal, drunken face of his father turned to him in hatred. He knew that if he ran outside the bully-boys were waiting, but if he stayed his father would beat him to a pulp. His father's rage was a terrible thing. He stood petrified between the twin terrors and thought he would die of fright. Then the edges began to dissolve and curl into shapes again, eerie and lurid. His father's face melted and the gargoyle heads of the bully-boys slewed about, cheeks dragged out of shape, eyes popping slowly and bloodily out of their heads, a crimson cloud drenching the curtain of his mind as demons and monsters rode past like nightmare wraiths.

Then beyond these formless terrifying visions there appeared suggestions of obscenity. He dreaded this moment, the knowledge that he was semi-conscious and there was no way to stop what was about to happen. There he lay, inert, incapable of moving, at the mercy of the filth that was about to engulf him. He cried out to God, to no avail, and the gross images boldy encroached on his dreams, engulfing him: fat women's legs spread-eagled, the soft hairy centre revealed, throbbing, pulsating: heavy breasts suckled by goats; a satyr obscenely coupling with a howling woman; a dwarf with a penis the size of an elephant's trunk cavorting with a lewd and toothless hag. The

48

colours were repulsive too. The faces when they appeared (for mostly the visions were of grotesque parts of bodies floating in limbo) were of such lewd expression that he found them unbearable. And yet . . . and yet . . . part of him responded to the devilish nightmares and that was worst of all.

He would suffer from these haunted nights once or twice a month. Then their frequency would increase to once or twice a week. Eventually he would not have a peaceful night at all and then he knew the time had come when he must go to London. He struggled against this inevitable journey, but when he knew he had reached the end of his tether, he gave in completely and a fever of excitement seized him and he could think of nothing else but the red-lit, rather grimy house in Paddington where he could indulge his wildest impulses, give in to a week of total debauchery, taking no heed of normal disciplines, allowing his unbridled lust to run its course, until, exhausted and sated, the demons put to rest, he returned home to the peaceful house in Rathgar, to his wife, children, servants, to sleep tranquilly once more. Until the next time.

He could not be said to enjoy his visits to the house in Paddington. He was afraid of the desires that took charge of him and he was only content when he was in control.

Now the dreams had been escalating once more. Tonight, he told himself, they had been aggravated by the trouble with his children. He always had heated debates with himself, trying to justify his impulses and actions. It was Neill's fault, Clothilde's fault. He thought of Ellen now in this marriage bed but he found the idea distasteful. Her body was old, her breasts sagged, middle age and childbearing had spread her hips and caused her stomach to lose its elasticity. He longed for . . . what was her name? Maggie. Yes, that was it, Maggie. Plump as a chicken, round and sweet as jam roly-poly, but firm as ivory and full of tricks to make a man feel young and virile. Her mouth was full and generous and she ate him like a rich desert. Her hips engulfed him, wide and amorous. He tossed and turned, his small wife beside him, lying peacefully asleep. What could she know of his needs, his desires? All these years, lying back and suffering his embrace? She was, in his considered opinion, a religious maniac. In his mind there were only two kinds of women: the bad were exciting; the good were a bore. She, he thought, had filled the children's heads with a load of sanctimonious rubbish. Priests and nuns! Neill didn't know what he was talking about. Let him try celibacy. Just let him. When the sap rose and the blood got hot and there was iron between your legs? Ha! But he should know that by now. He was, after all, twenty. Perhaps Neill was like his father in that one area. Garreth had started slowly. He had been a virgin when he had married Ellen. Fumbling about her that first night had been a nightmare. He shuddered when he remembered the humiliation of it. But he had soon got the hang of it. Ellen, however, had been hopeless; a dry, tight, unresponding apology of a woman, in his opinion. She behaved as if her body were china and would fly apart at any moment. Her cries were cries of pain and never the animal cries of satisfaction Maggie uttered so frequently in their sessions together, sounds that drove him to ecstacy. No. He would have to go to London. It was time. He would go immediately. Then this fire within him could be quenched, the fever calmed. Then he could forget his rebellious children and his boring wife. His mind made up, he fell asleep.

Chapter

4

THE household awakened the next morning to the news that their lord and master was making one of his periodical business trips to London. Relief flooded into every heart, steps became lighter, voices were joyous, eyes danced and sparkled and a holiday atmosphere invaded the house in Rathgar.

'And my dearest Celestine, you may go into Cleary's today and buy that . . . what . . . er . . . stuff for your dress. And a bolt too for your sister. Although I'm not sure she deserves it.'

Garreth smiled expansively at the assembled family around the breakfast table and placed a little pile of coins beside his youngest daughter's plate.

Celestine jumped up and hugged him. 'Papa! You are the best, best father there is,' she cried and meant it.

He smiled at her tenderly and pulled her on his knee. 'Ah! If the others were only like you,' he said, looking around the table again. 'This is my house. What I say is law here. You must all be guided by me. I have your best interests at heart. I am, after all, your father.' He smiled at them benevolently. He shifted in his chair and Celestine rose and reseated herself, holding the coins in the palm of her hand.

'Ellen, where are my senna-pods?'

His wife sped to the side-board. 'Here they are. Oh dear. I hope it's not too late for you to take them?'

Garreth was disposed this morning, due to his impending jaunt to London, to be magnanimous.

'No, my dear,' he said. 'Not at all.' He looked at the yellow liquid in the cup his wife held out to him. The pods floated in the bottom like transparent fish with black eyes.

51

'If I drink it now I'll have a movement about ten o'clock,' he said. 'That will be quite satisfactory. I'll have finished with the boys and O'Brien by then and can spend a quarter-of-an-hour reading the paper in the lavatory.'

He tossed off the drink, pulled his lips back over his teeth and uttered a deep grunt. Then he looked around the table for the third time, sighed and said, 'I don't know what I did to deserve such headstrong children. Headstrong and stubborn. Except for Celestine, sweet child.' He patted her cheek. 'You'll never leave your Papa, will you, dear child?'

Celestine shook her head. 'You know I never will, Papa.'

He wiped his moustache with his napkin and gave a sigh of contentment. 'Now to work for me. Hard work keeping the wolf from the door and the ladies in fripperies.' He turned to Ellen. 'See my cases are packed. I'll have O'Brien purchase my boat-train tickets today and find out the precise times of sailing from Kingstown. He knows them well. I'll be off tonight with luck.' Ellen sent up a silent prayer that it would happen exactly as he planned.

'Come now Breffni, Neill. It's time for work.'

He liked leaving the house with his sons. He liked to carry on a monologue and have them turn to him attentively, respect-fully, for all the world to see.

Garreth puffed up like a pouter pigeon on the way to the brewery. He swelled with pride and self-importance. And also with enjoyment. He was so proud of the elevated position he had worked himself up to. No-one knew, he thought, no-one could guess on this prosperous street at his humble begin-nings, and thinking this he walked taller, his chest and belly extending.

He bowed graciously to everyone he met. Sometimes he took the car, always driven slowly, and sometimes he walked, particularly if the weather was fine, and had Ben-the-Boots drive beside him. He enjoyed his royal progress down the road.

'G'morning', Mr Connolly.'

'Good morning, Mr Goldblat.'

'Good morning, Mrs Danagher.'

'Good mornin', Mr Connolly. Nice day.'

'Mr Blessed. Mr Callaghan. Nice weather we're having.'

'Thanks be to the good God, Mr Connolly.'

He raised his hat, bending courteously from the waist. He

liked the fact that Ireland was half a century behind the rest of Europe, a fact, he reflected in amusement, due not entirely to its position on the globe but also to Holy Mother Church. A decorous Victorian pace and formal manners prevailed here. Women were still biddable and modest, subservient to men, which Garreth thought was exactly as it should be. They were totally dependent on their fathers and husbands, and could not lift a finger without their permission or their money, a very satisfactory state of affairs, in Garreth's estimation. In England he had heard they were becoming much more advanced. Well, please God it would never happen here, not in his time. Ellen and Celestine, he thought, were happy with the situation. He would have to see that Clothilde got rid of this stupid streak of independent thinking. He was her father, he knew what was best for her. For them all.

He suddenly felt very good. Proud and happy. The terrible memories of his childhood were buried once more, the demons were at bay. He was going to London. His family would have to do as he said and there was an end to it. His workers would obey him. Flanked by his sons, he strode taller than they, his head held higher.

After the men had left, Ellen, Clothilde and Celestine dawdled at the breakfast table, discussing plans and fabrics and dressmakers.

'It's the perfect material, Mother, and it will look wonderful at the party at Auntie May's.'

'Who'll make it, Cel?' Clothilde asked.

'Madame McGinty is the best,' Celestine said eagerly.

Her sister snorted. '*Madame* McGinty, is it indeed? And why does she call herself Madame, I ask you?'

Celestine blushed furiously. 'She's from Paris, that's why.'

'You're such a snob. You think that just because she's Madame, that makes her a better dressmaker? Paris? Is it Paris? Rosheen McGinty has never set foot in France. She's from Ballybunion, so she is. Paris, morra-ya!'

'Well, she has a sheaf of new patterns from Paris,' Celestine said, mortified.

'Lord, she's certainly a terrible liar. Doesn't she knew there's a war on? How did she get the patterns from Paris, I ask you?'

Ellen put her hands up. 'Now, now, girls. Pax? All right. Rosheen McGinty may not be from Paris, Clothilde, but I fail to see how that matters if she makes a good job of the dresses.'

'Oh she will, Mother. She will.' Celestine cried breathlessly. 'She made my white one and it's gorgeous.'

'And Clothilde,' Ellen said severely, 'don't be be so quick to criticize people's little vanities.'

Clothilde buried her head in her hands and groaned. 'There I go again! Oh Lord, I'm sorry. Mother, forgive me? Celestine? Oh, oh, oh, I'm the most awful sinner.'

'Don't be silly, Clothilde,' her mother said with some asperity. 'Poor Clo. You don't really care about any of this, do you?'

Clothilde smiled ruefully. 'I don't know,' she said. 'I like to be well-dressed. I shall probably care about the cut of my habit, for I *will* be a nun, no matter what *he* says.'

'Now, Clothilde, you must not speak disrespectfully about your father.' Ellen said severely.

'Oh, you know what I mean, Mother . . . he's so . . . ' She paused and bit her lip. 'No you are right. If I'm to join the *religieuses* I cannot back-bite or criticize like that. I must have forgiveness. I must curb my tongue and show patience in adversity, like The Little Flower. I must learn to pluck out resentment.' She sighed. 'But oh, it is so hard.'

Celestine looked at her sister, the intense eyes, the fervent mouth.

'What is it that makes you want to be a nun?' she asked. 'What makes you want to give up everything?'

Ellen smiled fondly at her daughter. 'God has chosen her,' she said softly.

'Yes, but how does Clo feel?' Celestine persisted.

'I feel . . . I feel as if I have no option. All that I am, all that I do belongs to God. I yearn to give him . . . everything. It's hard to explain.'

At that moment there was a knock at the dining-room door. 'Come in, Mamie.'

Ellen knew it would be Mamie to clear the table. But Mamie stood just inside the door shifting her weight from one flat foot to the other.

'If ye please, Missus, Miffy's in a state. Throwing up half the night, she was. It was fierce awful. Sick as a drunken sailor she was.'

'What's the matter with her?' Ellen asked, concerned, immediately sympathetic.

'She's got it in her head she's goin' to be sent back to the Institution. After last night.'

Ellen looked blank.

'After the calamity with the soup,' Mamie said in exasperation. 'After'n' she dropped it. An' what Mr Connolly said. She's like a wild thing, sobbin' an' throwin' up an' carryin' on. Will ye talk to her, Missus? For if she goes, I go with her.'

'What nonsense, Mamie. There's no question of anyone going anywhere. Send Miffy up here to me.'

'Right ye are.' Mamie bobbed.

Celestine ran around to the fat servant and hugged her. 'Oh Mamie, Mamie, don't ever go. What would we do without you?'

Mamie blushed. 'An' where would I go, I ask you, Miss Celestine? Not that ye thought so yesterday, an' it jam time! Let me loose now till I get Miffy, the creature, an' put her outa her misery.'

She left the room and a moment later reappeared with Miffy in tow. She had not exaggerated. The girl was a shaking, shivering mass of barely-controlled hysteria. Her eyes were the size of saucers, ringed with dark circles in her small pinched face, and her mouth had all but vanished in a puckered line. She stood in front of Ellen like a prisoner waiting to be executed.

Ellen called the girl to her, her voice soft and kindly.

'Come here, Miffy. Don't worry.'

Tears sprang into the maid's eyes at the sympathetic words. 'Yes, Missus.'

Ellen put her arm around the girl and gently stroked her hair in soothing rhythmic movements.

'Now listen, Miffy. Last night was not your fault. Do you hear me?'

Miffy sniffed. 'But it was, Missus. 'Twas me that dropped the tureen.'

'It was not your fault, Miffy. You had to stand with it in your hands for too long, and it was hot. I know.'

Miffy nodded, her nose beginning to leak. Ellen took out her handkerchief.

'Forget all about it. No-one is going to send you anywhere, do you hear me?'

Miffy hiccupped and nodded again. 'Yes, Missus.'

'You are part of this family, Miffy; do you understand? As

long as I'm alive you are going to live with us. Now dry your tears and get on with your work.'

She patted the girl's face with her handkerchief and pressed it against the maid's nose. Miffy blew into it obediently. Her face had lit up. Doubt vanished and an expression of great relief flooded the tear-stained and swollen countenance.

'Oh Mam, Mam, how can I thank you? A saint you are. Oh Missus, I was so worried. God help us, I couldn't go back there, I couldn't, now that I know what it's like outa it.'

Ellen hugged her again and the maid tried to kiss her mistress' hands.

'No, no, Miffy. That's enough. Now off with you. Tidy up and get on with your work.'

When Miffy had gone, Ellen rose from the table.

'Time for Mass. And we must plan our shopping trip tomorrow,' she said, and, although no one remarked on it, they all knew that tomorrow had been chosen since by then Mr Garreth Connolly would be in London.

Chapter

5

THE brewery was a sweat shop. It bent or broke all the laws of the land, and the laws of humanity. Garreth Connolly had convinced himself that it was only right and fitting that the poor laboured and the rich lived off the fat of the land, even at the expense of others. Neill often looked at his father on a Sunday morning at Mass when the Gospels were read. So many of them pertained to the giving away of excessive wealth and to the responsibilities of the rich to the poor, and stated that the beloved of Christ were the meek and the poor. Yet his father did not seem to think that the messages had anything to do with him.

He strutted, Neill thought, over the bodies of his less fortunate fellow men. And women. And children. Neill's heart broke in two as he watched them, haggard-eyed women with cheerless faces, and gaunt children, sallow from their twilight existence down below ground level in the bottling room. They worked early and late to scrape together a few pennies. Neill was filled with a terrible rage at their plight. Their lives were lived mainly within the walls of Connolly's Brewery. What little remained was spent in the slums called Paradise Street, Paradise Square and Paradise Row.

'Money is the stuff of life,' Garreth used to say.

'He does not know what it is like, to be so helpless, so poor,' Neill thought. He did not realize that his father despised his workforce because he knew *exactly* what it was like, and his workers frightened him. He could so easily be one of them. His hold on power was based on fluke, on bluff; very precariously. He was aware of how tenuous was his good fortune, of how ignorant he was, unlike Brendan Mulcahy, who had had a grand education with the Jesuits behind him. Garreth Connolly despised his workers because they stood for it. He could not understand why, if he could do it, they could not. He did not see that they lacked his greed, his driving ambition, his ruthlessness. He had only contempt for them, and for Neill and Breffni an exasperated impatience: at their lack of gratitude; that they could not see things as he saw them. He often thought of his brutal, loutish, drunken father and wondered how his sons would have coped with such a man. He had had to, to survive. To survive you have to stop at nothing. O'Brien now, O'Brien was a different kettle of fish, a man who respected him, who admired him for his unscrupulous practices and who listened to everything he said and obeyed his slightest command.

The three of them stood facing him, dark-suited with high starched collars and respectful expressions: Neill, Breffni and Mr O'Brien. Mr O'Brien was hanging on Garreth's every word. Or appearing to. Neill remembered when he too had been interested in all this. Two years ago he had been eighteen and his father had 'set him to work in earnest'. He had listened eagerly then, anxious to understand, to join the world of men, the initiated. Above all, he had hoped he could win his father's approval and somehow overcome his terrible fear and dislike of Mr Connolly.

The brewery shocked him. He simply could not bring himself to accept the fact that anyone at all in the fair green land of Ireland should be doomed to labour morning, noon and night in a twilight world, for a pittance. He had practised hardening his heart, but had not been able to build a defence against the children's docile exhaustion, the women's desperation or the men's helpless despair and loss of pride. They were paid less here than anywhere else, but jobs were scarce and there was massive unemployment. Eighteen shillings a week was better than nothing, it took the sharp edge off starvation. And if your wife and a couple of children worked, why, life was not totally hopeless, though most of the money went right back into Mr Connolly's pocket as rent.

The hours were what offended Neill most. They were working a fifteen-hour day, most of them, and now Garreth had proposed an eighteen-hour stint for some of the men in order that he could produce more beer and fulfil more orders without having to hire more men.

The brewery sat on the banks of the Liffey at Islandbridge, its back to Phoenix Park. To the right, a stone's throw from its tall chimneys, lay Paradise Row, Paradise Street and Paradise Square. The hard, crystal-clear brewing water was drawn from a well near the river. Garreth Connolly owned the whole shebang, and the tenement houses were mainly inhabited by the brewery workers.

The front of the building was almost like the residence of a prosperous man — six windowed, with decorative wrought-iron balustrades encircling the sills and a glass globe lamp hanging over the elegant doorway. CONNOLLY & SONS, BREWERS it said across the front of the building in tall gold letters and higher up, under the roof, ESTABLISHED 1884.

At the side was the cask-yard and the loading exit. The noble teams of shire-horses stood there, docile and patient, harnessed to the drays which were ready to be, or were in the process of being, loaded with the wooden casks for local delivery.

The rest of the building sprawled out behind, huge, barnlike, red brick, its few tiny windows blocked up, its sheer face descending vertically into the river.

This morning, all memories of Miffy's misdemeanour forgotten, his coming visit to London and all it entailed filling him with an unholy excitement, Garreth lectured his lieutenants on how the brewery was to be run in his absence.

'I've bought another tied house, Neill,' he was saying. 'That makes seven we can boast of. Not up to the Guinness standard, m'lad, but more modest, more realistic. Those fellows are getting too big for their boots. Heading for a fall, I'll bet. No. Can't gamble. Risk!' He clicked his tongue behind his teeth. 'Not something I could every approve of. Always cover your tail. Have enough put by to know whatever happens you are secure. Solid.'

Neill knew that his father had no capital, that everything was in the brewery and the Paradise property. His father did not worry. He loved the feel of money. He was mean. A self-made man, nervous of returning to the poverty from whence he came, he scrimped and cut corners. The result was that although cash was in ready supply, the brewery and the Paradise property were in a shocking state of repair.

Garreth deplored his rival firm Guinness, although they produced different brews, for what he called their 'wanton extravagance'. He was convinced that Connolly's would be standing, thanks to his prudence, long after Guinness had fallen apart.

It was lucky that they were in the business of beer, Neill thought, for had it been any other, the employees might or, indeed, would, have been killed by the old and faulty equipment. But the process of brewing needed no modern inventions to be successful, and Connolly's beers were of superior quality.

'The brew has been in the fermenters for five days now, Neill. See to it, lad. See to it.'

The Manager, O'Brien, had taken Neill and Breffni through the works each Christmas holiday from school and they had learned the whole process of brewing when they were still young. Neill found it as boring now as he had then, and he believed Breffni did too.

Connolly's was built on a tower principle. The sacks of malt were winched to the top of the building; dark malt for stout, crystal and pale ale. There the grain was crushed and the grist was put through the mashing machine mixed with hot water into the Mash Tun. The liquor was 166°C. and the room small. The men who worked there lost weight in the heat. It was vital to get and maintain the correct temperatures. Malt sugar solution, wort, was run off from the 'Mash Tun' through the 'Underback' to the 'Copper'. It was tested for gravity-sugar content. Hops were added and the mixture was boiled fiercely. Spent hops were then filtered from the 'Hop Back'. The liquid then passed through the cooler into the fermenting vessels where yeast was added and fermentation took place. Then dry hops were added to cask-conditioned beer, while next door to that the beers were kegged and bottled by the women and children.

Neill and Breffni were as familiar with the workings of the brewery as they were with the alphabet. The problem was that their father never allowed them to become part of the process. Neither of them had ever mashed or roused the beers. They had never participated in the making of the brew, but rather stood about and watched. They watched their father issue commands from his Olympian height as owner and supreme boss, wielding, as he did, the power of life and death over his workers. The workers were as much his slaves as the black men had been in America, Neill often thought. His father owned their homes and they had little choice but to obey him. The alternative was unemployment, the inability to pay rent, then eviction and the workhouse if they were lucky. Or starvation. Death.

Yes, the boys understood the beer-making process from the top of the tower to the bottling room — understood, but did not relish it. Neither of Garreth's sons was interested in their father's business. Neill saw only its injustices; Breffni was bored by the place and ached to be set free, to escape, to go where there was excitement and romance, where the smells and the sounds were of God's natural world rather than those made by man's devilish creation.

Breffni blinked his eyes and tried to look interested as he stood with Neill and Mr O'Brien before his father. Mr Connolly had seated himself behind his large mahogany desk in his padded leather chair. He had chosen a pipe from the rack and was pressing the golden tobacco into its bowl. The room was painted pale green and it was large and light; the only bright room in the building. There was another portrait of Garreth on the wall behind the desk, similar to the one in the parlour at Rathgar, but showing Garreth at a slightly more mature age. On the other wall was a price list. It had 'CONNOLLY & SONS, BREWERS. EST. 1884' printed in large green letters on a beige background, the drawing of an Irish wolfhound with *Trade Mark* written across it and below, a list of prices:

ALES	PER GAL.
*ALE	-/10
**MILD BRECKNY	1/-
***BRECKNY	1/4
***OLD MELLOW	1/6
Invalid Stout	1/6
PRIZE OLD ALE. Made from the choicest	
Malt & Hops	1/-
PALE ALE	1/4

All kinds of wines and spirits in stock. Delivered free in casks of 5 gallons and upwards.

Breffni read it as he had done a thousand times before, not taking in a word but trying in vain to blot out his father's monotonous voice. Men came in and out, servile, desperate to please, tipping caps or forelocks with constant dipping motions of deference.

'We mashed in, sir. At 5 a.m., sir.'

'Malachy and Tom are digging out the spent grain, sir.'

The grain merchant came in and Garreth attacked him.

'I paid good money for Premium Malt but what you sent is split and raddled with thins and cracked grains. You'll deliver a new consignment in its stead, replace every sack, do you hear me? And at no further cost to myself.'

'But sir, some of the sacks must have been all right. Surely you can't . . .'

'Oh but I can. And do. See that it is attended to at once or you'll see no more of my trade.'

An unfortunate was given a roasting because he had been responsible, or so it was alleged, for allowing the beer to fall below temperature and as a result the liquor was cloudy. The man shook in his shoes while Garreth yelled at him and eventually he scuttled out of the room, breathing Ave Marias of gratitude that he had been let off so lightly. Why don't any of them tell him to shut-up? Neill asked himself, despising their servility yet realizing full well that they had no choice. The knuckles of his hand stood out white against his skin and he pressed his lips close together.

Outside the lace-curtained window he could see Ben-the-Boots polish the Ford with his rag. His lips were pursed in a whistle but Neill could not hear him, for the windows were closed. All he could hear was his father's voice. Garreth now turned to O'Brien. O'Brien was manager in so far as anyone could claim to have any authority at all in the brewery apart from Connolly himself.

'What's all this nonsense about John Joe Reilly?' he asked.

Bill O'Brien was a smarmy little man, in Neill's opinion, but he was a good manager. He kowtowed to his betters, a regular fawner. Thin, with carefully parted hair drawn tastefully over his bald pate, protruding teeth that were brown-edged from the foul cigarettes he smoked and a pair of bright eyes that darted about like goldfish in a pond, he missed nothing, saw everything. His clothes looked faintly as if the cat had been at them.

'Oh, it's this Union business, Mr Connolly, sir. Terrible it is, sir. Terrible. But . . .' He shrugged cheerfully. 'Nuthin' that need worry us. Not if it's nipped in the bud at onst. If ye get my meanin'.' He winked at Garreth Connolly.

'Well, and what is it all about, Bill? I still don't fully understand.'

'Well, it's John Joe's idea that the brewery workers here should join the Union. He says they are not paid enough. He's a fierce awful troublemaker, sir. A troublemaker.' He gave a little snort and drew Mr Connolly into his confidence. 'You an' I know, sir, that they'll take advantage of you, sir . . . if you let them. A firm hand, sir. A firm hand. He tried to have a meetin' here last night, only I broke it up. Me an' Dorsel.'

Dorsel was O'Brien's son. The same age as Breffni, he worked as a jack-of-all trades about the place. He was a chip off the old block and a veritable copy of his father in thought, deed and action.

Connolly nodded his head. He glared at Neill. 'You see what all this . . . agitation can do? Tell him, Bill. Tell him.'

'Oh, they'd close us, Master Neill. Shut, we'd be. An' then what?' He looked around mournfully. 'Penury. That's what.'

'Why can't we pay them the going rate? Why can't we do that?' Neill asked.

'O'Brien and his father gazed at him aghast. Neill thought he was going to faint. The room was hot and stuffy and filled with Garreth's pipe smoke.

'You see, Bill?' Garreth looked at the manager, a despairing, helpless expression on his face. 'My own son. It's obvious, m'boy, you know nothing of profit margins or you could not suggest such a thing. Bill, Bill, have you ever heard such nonsense?'

Bill O'Brien shook his head. His secret hope was that Neill and Breffni, who had made their feelings clear, would follow the inclinations that they talked of and refuse to work in the brewery. Then Mr Connolly's only recourse would be to let Mr O'Brien and his son Dorsel run it for the family. The thought caused a surge of excitement in O'Brien.

Garreth stood up now in the stuffy office. They knew he was going to make a speech. O'Brien put on an attentive look and stuck his hands in his pockets.

'No member of my staff, no worker, bottler, cooper, masher, delivery boy or *anyone*, is to join anything so evil as a trade union,' Garreth said. His voice was soft, hardly raised, and it was cold and brooked no argument. 'The Church is against them. I am against them. Look what happened only a year and a half ago.'

He began to strut again, up and down, up and down, his footsteps making no sound on the thick green carpet. He hooked his thumbs in the little pockets of his waistcoat.

'Look at the Irish Transport Union. That confrontation ended in a *strike*.' He paused to let the terrible word sink in. 'Strike. Lockout. No one can tell me that was good for the workers. It means no pay, and no pay means no food. They had to eat humble pie in the end and give in.' He looked into Neill's face. 'They got nothing, do you hear? Nothing.' He turned to O'Brien. 'Remind them of that. All of them. And sack John Joe Reilly. You may all go.'

'But, Father, you can't sack . . .' Neill started to protest.

His father looked at him coldly. 'Don't tell me what I can or cannot do, boy. Away with you now. O'Brien, have you been in touch with the Booking Office? First Class on the boat-train . . .' He likes saying 'First Class' to O'Brien like that, Neill thought. It pin-points their difference. He loves to show-off, to wield his authority and power like a bludgeon.

As he and Breffni turned to go he heard his father say, 'Keep an eye on those two, O'Brien, while I'm gone. They disappoint me, that they do. Younger generation's got no guts, no get-up-and-go. Now in my day . . .'

Neill sighed and closed the door behind them. As they walked down the corridor they saw John Joe Reilly approaching. The loader wore a collarless shirt with armbands. His trousers were dusty from his work and he wore a big apron. He was a hugely-built, good-looking chap. But he had, Neill knew, a deep sense of grievance within him. He did not meekly accept his lot as the others did. He railed against a fate that gave some so much and him so little through no fault of his own, for he was a good worker, a man who gave value for money. It was because he placed this value upon himself that he got into trouble. All he wanted was a fair wage. And because of this pride, this individuality, the high value he placed on himself as a worker, Garreth Connolly hated him.

'I wouldn't go in there now, John Joe,' Neill said.

The man's brown eyes opened in surprise. 'Why not, Master Neill? Why?'

Neill decided it was best to tell the truth. There was nothing to be gained by dissimulation.

'Father is sacking you, John Joe. I'm truly sorry.'

The man's face went a horrible putty colour. His eyes flashed in anger.

'You're sorry? God's sake, man, you're *sorry*? An' what would you know about Mary an' her chest an' the young wan an' her dysentery? An' it's all yer Pa's fault. What would you know about livin' in one of his pig-sties?'

The man was working himself up into a righteous rage. Neill knew he was entitled to. He had been with Connolly's for nearly ten years. He had a genuine grievance but he was not going to do himself any good by shouting a couple of yards away from Mr Connolly's office.

'Hush man . . . hush . . .'

'I will not hush. That's the trouble here. People have been hushed for too long. A disgrace it is.' He was beginning to look and sound wild and desperate. 'If I lose me job here, we'll starve, I'm tellin' ye. An' for why? I'm a good loader . . . the best. There's no one can deny that. It's not for that. It's because of the Union. Isn't that so? Well, isn't it?'

'O'Brien's face, quivering with curiosity, popped out of the door to the office, his body remaining safely inside the room.

'What's the noise, the boss wants to know? Shut up or you'd wake the dead.'

'It's me, John Joe Reilly. I hear ye've got a complaint against me? Are ye man enough to tell me?'

'O'Brien looked up as the huge loader loped down the hall, although Neill and Breffni both tried to stop him. He simply brushed them off as if they were flies. O'Brien licked his lips nervously and pushed the door closer so that he looked as if he were being decapitated sideways.

'Yes I am, Mr John Joe Reilly. Yiz are fired,' he cried, his voice shrill and triumphant. 'Do ye hear? Orders of Mr Garreth Connolly, proprietor of this establishment. Fired and finished.' He swiftly pulled his head in and it disappeared from view as he slammed the door firmly shut.

John Joe began to thump on the door with his fists. 'I'll get ye for this. I'll call on the Union. They'll fix things for me. See if I don't.'

John Joe was shouting and thumping when the door suddenly opened again and he nearly fell inside. Garreth Connolly stood

65

in the entrance, his bulk filling the gap.

John Joe drew himself up to his full height. 'I appeal to you, Mr Connolly . . .'

Garreth held up his hand. 'Do not speak to me, Mr Reilly. Just get off my premises. You are trespassing. And any other member of your precious Union will be asked to do the same. Now leave before I get the police.'

He closed the door and Neill and Breffni watched in horrified silence as the big man seemed to dwindle before their very eyes. All the fight went out of him, the bravura and confidence, and he faltered as the anger left him and realization dawned.

'I'm done for,' he said softly and Neill and Breffni watched in amazement as tears filled his eyes and he sank slowly, his back sliding down the wall, into a sitting position. He started then to blubber, like a snotty-nosed boy who'd been bullied. Great sobs tore his chest and he wiped his eyes with the back of his hand, then covered his head with his arms.

Neill motioned to Breffni. They went to him and each of them took one of his arms.

'Come along, man. Let us buy you a drink.'

His painful sobs turned to hysterical laughter as he looked up at them. 'Buy us a drink, is it? Jasus Master Connolly, 'n this a Brewery an' you're ownin' it, an' ye want te buy us a drink? Christ, that's rich.' And he laughed again and sniffed and tried to stem his tears. But he choked on them.

'It's Mary, see? She's worn out. An' the child. Delia's got the runs. She's wastin' away. Aw God, what am I goin' to do?'

'Come and have a drink with us, man. Come on.'

They dragged him to his feet and got him somehow out the front door. Neill put his finger to his lips as Ben-the-Boots saw them and stopped whistling 'Good-bye Dolly I must leave you'. He made as if to speak to them, but changed his mind and went back to his polishing. 'Though it breaks my heart to go'.

Garreth Connolly and Bill O'Brien watched them through the window as the three of them turned the corner at the bottom of the street. How dare Neill and Breffni go off with a traitor like that? How dare they leave the premises with the enemy? And be seen to? Ben-the-Boots watched them, and the men who were nearby looked on as Mr Connolly's sons went arm-in-arm down the street with the man their father had just sacked. He could feel the anger simmer within him and he rapped sharply on the glass of the window.

'Get on with yer work out there.' They could not hear him but they got the message.

'See that man never sets foot in this place again,' he said and turned from the window.

Mr O'Brien nodded and smiled, pleased as punch at the sight of the three men going down the road together.

'I'll see to it, sir. I'll see to it, never fear.' O'Brien licked his lips. 'An' sir, the insurance. It's due, Mister Connolly. I hate to remind you again but . . .'

'Don't bother me now,' Garreth said as he moodily watched the three men disappear around the corner. It was something, something he could not put his finger on. He, watching from behind a window while others went arm-in-arm . . . somewhere. What was it that made him feel so defeated when he had just won a battle?

Then he saw what irritated him. Neill and Breffni were arm-in-arm with John Joe Reilly and he could not remember, ever, in the whole of his life, being arm-in-arm with anyone. No-one, ever. How strange, he thought, and a deep melancholy laid a heavy hand on his heart.

O'Brien was watching him. He turned from the window.

'What are you standing about for, man? Get on with it. Get on.'

O'Brien left the office and Garreth looked around it, feeling suddenly like an intruder. Then he shook his head. Silly. It was foolish to be so downcast, to allow 'them', those clever, educated ones, to make him feel bad. Why, he was off to London. First class. Arm-in-arm? Who the hell wanted to be arm-in-arm? He laughed mirthlessly to himself. He could think of better positions to be in. Maggie would know a few. He sat down at his desk and pushed the evil mood away firmly.

Chapter

6

NEILL and Breffni frog-marched John Joe down the road and propelled him into a public house called 'The Golden Harp'. It was not a Connolly house. Connolly's had tied houses, but 'The Golden Harp' was not one of them. The Quinns did not do business with Connolly Senior, though they were great friends of the Connolly brothers.

It was a pleasant pub. The slum-dwellers in Paradise Row, Paradise Street and Paradise Square on the other side of the brewery did not come here. They frequented a dingy tavern called 'The Paradise Arms', a title that made you laugh the other side of your face, Philomena Quinn was fond of saying.

The proprietor of 'The Golden Harp' was a happy-go-lucky gingery, hirsute, gentle, kindly fellow called Kipper Quinn. His wife, Philomena, was a buxom, motherly woman who adored Kipper and their two children, Darragh and Kerry. They all had Kipper's hair; a smoky golden amber, the colour of the treated fish. People had remarked on the similarity when he was but a wee lad and the name stuck.

Philomena had a heart overflowing with the milk of human kindness. Cruelty was the only quality that appalled her and she doted on Neill and Breffni, and tried, like the good Catholic woman she was, to pluck out of her heart the rage and loathing she felt for their father.

'A shit of a man,' she often said to Kipper, she who never used bad language. 'Keepin' those poor sods in Paradise in a state my Kerry uncle wouldn't keep his pigs in. Hoity-toity, an' I know where he comes from! Sure, an' some people's memory is short. Think he's foolin' me? Not on yer life. Ha! He's a handsome man, I grant you, but look in his eyes. There's a snake-pit in there.'

Philomena came from Kerry and had named her daughter after the pretty county she loved and missed. She was a large full-bosomed woman with flaming red hair piled softly on the top of her head and fixed precariously with combs. Strands were constantly descending, escaping from their confinement onto forehead, neck-nape, cheeks and ears. She had dimples everywhere — cheeks, chin, elbows and at the corners of her bright green eyes. The latter were quite small and often almost concealed by the contortions of her laughter or her tears, for she was an emotional woman.

When she saw the three lads arrive in the pub, she hustled over to see what was up. Breffni and Neill did not usually come into the pub of a morning and John Joe Reilly looked near to collapse.

'Good mornin', boys. What's up wi' him?' she asked, jerking her head at John Joe.

'He's had a shock, Mrs Quinn,' Neill said. 'Da's sacked him.'

Philomena looked horrified. 'Oh God help us, no! Never. For what?'

'He wanted some of the fellas and girls above in the brewery to join the Union. Or start one of their own. Can you imagine my Da findin' out about that? I dunno. All John Joe was looking for was fair play, God help him.'

Neill tended to pick up the vernacular when he spoke to the Quinns. His eyes darted wild in his head now as he wrestled with overwhelming feelings of rage and impotence. He looked nearly as fervent as John Joe himself usually did. But the latter now sat, mute and shocked at the small table in the snug.

'Get him a brandy, Mrs Quinn. He needs it awful bad.'

John Joe looked up. 'Where de ye think I'd get the money for a brandy?' he asked. 'An' I'll take no charity.'

'Hold yer whist, man. It's on the house. Effen I can't do ye a kindness on such a mournful day, then how can I count meself a neighbour?'

And with that Philomena hustled over to the bar. Breffni followed her, leaving John Joe to his brother's care. In Philomena's presence he always had an urge, which horrified and frightened him, to push his face into her cleavage. She liked to wear low-cut bodices, and the round half-moons of flesh thus revealed had a peculiar effect upon him, giving him an almost uncontrollable desire to nuzzle her, smell and feel her soft flesh against his lips and face. Philomena was well aware of her effect upon him and far from being shocked was quite flattered at the young man's lusty desire.

She patted his cheek now, laughing in a kindly way. 'Keep those thoughts locked up tight, Breffni me lad, or you'll have to go to Confession on Saturday or miss Communion on Sunday, an' then what would yer Ma, God bless her, say?'

Breffni blushed crimson and took the brandy she had poured back to the snug. Neill held it to John Joe's lips but the big man pushed it away.

'Now calm down, man, do,' Neill said in as soothing a voice as he could muster, wishing he could take his own advice.

'John Joe looked at him haggard-eyed. 'How can I calm down when I've just received a death sentence?'

'Drink this, John Joe. Whatever is wrong it'll help. For a wee while at any rate. I *do* understand. My mother has talked to your Mary and the young one. I know . . .'

'You may *know*. Indeedn' you may. But *living* it is somethin' else. You'll go home tonight to a large meal an' a soft bed in a warm dry house. How can you really *know*? Oh I know you are sympathetic to the likes of us. Ye have a kind heart, Neill Connolly. But it is not enough. In the end it is not enough.'

Neill said nothing, but silently held the glass to the man's lips. He realized that what John Joe said was true. As John Joe drank Neill felt some measure of relief. If he could get him to talk, perhaps some of the heat of his rage would evaporate and he would not do something hot-headed and silly that might land him in even more trouble.

'Ye see, I know ye'll tell yer mother an' she'll come to Paradise Row tomorrow or the next day laden with stuff, food an' clothes an' so on, from the goodness of her heart,' John Joe said. 'Grateful we are for the help but it shouldn't be necessary.' He turned to Neill and grabbed his coat-collar, looking at him with pleading eyes. 'I'm a man. Husband and father. I don't want to have to accept charity. I'm strong. I'm a good worker. All I'm askin' is to do a job an' get a fair wage. That's not unreasonable, Master Neill, now is it?'

'No, John Joe. No. I'm bound to admit it's not.'

'Then can't ye speak to yer Da? Can't ye get him to see?'

John Joe knew it was a hopeless question. Neill did not reply and the two men gazed at each other, mutual understanding in their eyes. All the energy left John Joe Reilly and he slumped on the wooden seat, letting go of Neill's jacket.

Breffni said, 'It's no use, John Joe. Our father is a bastard. A real bastard.'

But Neill shook his head. 'No. He's stupid. He's afraid. He has no compassion. He just doesn't see things the way we do.'

'Then what will I do, Master Neill? Answer me that. What will I tell Mary? What about little Delia? We'll starve. If I don't work, I can't pay the rent. He'll put us out on the street, so he will. He's done it to many another. What will we do?'

There was silence in the place. It lasted on and on, for no one had an answer to his question.

Chapter

7

ELLEN and the girls went to ten o'clock Mass in St Hilda's around the corner from where they lived. There were a dozen churches in Rathmines and Rathgar but Ellen liked St Hilda's best. She liked Fr Denis Grogan, the parish priest, and she was fond of Fr Gerald Devoy, a cheerful young cleric, active in good works in the community and of great assistance to her in her charitable activities. He was also guaranteed to give an inspired sermon at the Women's Sodality, first Wednesday of every month.

St Hilda's was small, and Ellen loved its cosy intimacy. The other church near them, the large one on the Rathmines Road, was a huge echoing building and made Ellen feel far away from God, as did the priest there, a remote austere man, no doubt a saint, but impossible to communicate with. The general consensus was that he lacked the 'common touch' and certainly Fr Denis and Fr Gerald had that attribute in abundance.

Ellen knelt in St Hilda's in the light of a hundred candles, swathed in clouds of incense, murmuring the Latin responses and praying for fortitude and courage in the coming battles with Garreth over Clothilde's and Neill's sacred vocations.

'For you can help them, my dear Lord, and only you. Do I do wrong to go against my husband? Oh, I wish I knew for sure the right thing to do. Ah why can't you see your way to sending me a sign?' Then she added hastily. 'No, I didn't mean that. Why should you, and you with so much on your mind? Important things like the war. My problems are not all that big for me to worry you about.'

She sniffed into her handkerchief and Clothilde put an arm

protectively around her. She loved holding, touching her mother. She loved Ellen's scent, the incredible softness of her skin when she touched her hand or her cheek. She loved the clouds of incense, the heady smell. She loved the stained-glass windows, the martyrs: St Agnes with her lamb; St Mathilda; St Clare with lilies in her hair. Above all St Philomena. Virgin and Martyr. Tall in her mediaeval gown, rich crimson velvet edged with gold braid. Golden braid around her waist with tassels falling in the folds of her dress. Bare feet in golden sandals, a palm clasped between her long white fingers, her eyes cast downwards. She had died for her religion, pure and undefiled. Clothilde was not one hundred percent sure what it meant, to be undefiled, but she knew that she desperately wanted to be like St Philomena. For God. She loved the odour of sanctity, the robes of the priest, the reassuring sexlessness of him. Her soul was full of love. A huge surge of giving that had no other outlet, winged its way ardently upwards with the words, the scents, the devotion.

They stayed for Benediction, much to Celestine's chagrin. She was dying to get to the shops and her mind was preoccupied with whether in fact she was right about the striped yellow silk brocade or whether a heavy wine brocade would be more dramatic and if her mother would allow it. She began to get restless, pulling her gloves off and on until her mother gave her hand a gentle tap. Clothilde, however, found the ceremony soothing.

The priest, it was Fr Denis, had a fondness for the Litany of the Blessed Virgin and Clothilde shared his delight in the voluptuous language. She let the beautiful words flow over her, resting her head on her palms.

Mirror of justice,
Cause of our joy,
Spiritual vessel,
Vessel of Honour,
Singular vessel of devotion,
Mystical rose,
Tower of David,
Tower of ivory,
House of gold,
Ark of the covenant,
Gate of Heaven,
Morning star . . .

73

How could anything in life go wrong with those words, that comfort in her ears? Yet she knew it could. It all depended upon her father. Dear God, that she could escape his tyranny. Hastily she crossed herself, decided to be grateful for the coming respite, wondered if that was a terrible sin, and gave the whole thing up and herself over to the pleasure of the last words of the Litany,

Queen of the most holy Rosary,
Queen of Peace,
and Amen.

They ended up with a rousing chorus of 'Star of the Sea'.
'Virgin most pure,
Star of the Sea,
Pray for the sinner,
Pray for me.'

'You have my heart and my soul, dearest Lord,' Clothilde murmured fervently as the service ended. Thoroughly refreshed, she smiled brilliantly at her mother and Celestine, who made a face at her. Then they genuflected, made the Sign of the Cross, and left the church.

They hailed a hansom cab which took them to Cleary's and they told the jarvey to wait. There, after Ellen had persuaded her that the wine brocade was too old for her, they purchased the striped yellow silk for Celestine's ball-gown. That satisfactorily accomplished, Celestine decided for Clothilde that the old rose georgette was perfect for her sister, for Clothilde could not seem to drum up an interest in materials today, vacillating as she was between the salutary effects of Benediction, which made her absentminded, and intense anger at her father, which made her sullen. She tagged along behind her mother and Celestine, who was in her element.

Mrs Connolly decided they needed tiny pearl buttons, some white petersham and cambric for underskirts. Celestine told her mother that underskirts were out of fashion. Ellen said she did not care what the fashion was, her girls would have underskirts. The boxes were carried to the cab which then took them to the 'Irish Lace Industries Depot' in Grafton Street where they bought quantities of lace for trimming from the neatly uniformed girls whose assumed English accents kept slipping into Dublinese.

'We can cut the bodices quite low, Mother. It's the fashion

74

. . .' Celestine began and Ellen sighed.

'I only hope your father . . .'

Celestine wrinkled her nose. 'Oh, I'll coax Papa. You know I can. It will be all right. Madame McGinty has impeccable taste,' she said with confidence, glancing at Clothilde from under her eyelashes.

They had lunch at the Shelbourne Hotel. Sitting under the crystal chandelier and taking in the *ensembles* of the other fashionable women present, they enjoyed game soup, a plump partridge and jam roly-poly to follow. Clothilde remained locked in her thoughts and Celestine became impatient.

'Clo, I wish you would show *some* interest in absolutely *anything*. You sit there, staring into space like a goop. Oh Mother, tell her to wake up.'

But Ellen smiled and told Celestine to pay her sister no heed. 'Clothilde has loftier things to think about,' she said to Celestine's fury and Clothilde's shame, for at that moment she had been planning how she could defy her father.

It was at times like this that Ellen felt that all her difficulties with Garreth were worthwhile. She looked at the faces of her daughters: Celestine's bright and happy, excited by her purchases, full of an eager expectancy; and Clothilde's ardent beauty, the thin nostrils, the wide eyes. They were dear sweet girls and her heart swelled with love and pride. She wished, she just wished that they could both be happy. Garreth had put his foot down about what Clothilde thought was her vocation in life. She wondered if it was really God the girl yearned for, or if a good man might satisfy her passionate nature. The practical Reverend Mother thought so. And Celestine: the child was ripe for love and romance. What would happen when she realized that Garreth meant exactly what he said, and that his intention was to keep her at home with him? She thought of Neill. A born priest. His spirituality was as much a part of him as his breathing. God grant him a way to reach his goal. And Breffni. She visualized his charming smile, the idealistic eyes, and her heart melted within her. Breffni, her sweetest, her best. She would never tell him or let the others guess that he was her favourite, but deep in her heart she knew he was the pearl of great price. And he was not at all ready for life. She thought of his suggestion last evening. A soldier? She felt suddenly cold. 'Thank you, Lord, for all of them,' she prayed to herself, then looked at her daughters again and smiled in sheer delight at the mere sight of them. She looked around the crowded room and knew she would not change places with anyone.

They were having coffee in the lounge when Clothilde suddenly came to life.

'I wish you'd persuade Father to let me take the veil, Cel,' she said. 'He always listens to you.'

Celestine looked acutely uncomfortable. 'I can't, Clo. You know I can't. I never cross Papa. That's why we get on so well.'

'Oh that's a fine thing. What kind of love is that? You can't disagree? You can't have your own opinions?'

'It's like your God, isn't it?' Celestine countered gently. 'Your God asks complete obedience. Blind faith in His word. You have to trust He knows best.'

'Oh Celestine, don't be disrespectful.' Ellen was shocked. So, in another way, was Clothilde. She had not thought of the situation with her father from this viewpoint before. She looked into her sister's gold-flecked eyes.

Celestine continued, 'Papa is the head of our family, the way that Christ is the head of the Church, and we owe him obedience and love, however we disagree with his dictates. Isn't that the teaching?'

Clothilde was confused. 'Yes,' she said doubtfully. 'But not if our father here on earth asks us to do something wrong.'

'But he is not asking you to do anything wrong. He is simply telling you that you are mistaken about your vocation, that he will not give you permission to become a nun and he wants you to marry Owen Mulcahy, who —' she flashed her sister an amused and knowing glance, '— you like. I know.'

Clothilde blushed, but whether from shame or anger Ellen did not know.

'Anyone would like him,' Celestine continued. 'No sensible girl could actually object to marrying Owen. We are supposed to obey our parents. It's our duty. If you ask me, Neill would also be much better off trying to right some of the wrongs he says Father is responsible for at the brewery, instead of wanting to be a priest and doing good from a lofty position.'

'Now Celestine. You must not upset your sister,' Ellen rebuked her daughter gently. 'And I don't think you have a right to criticize either of your elders.'

Clothilde looked at her sister open-mouthed. She had never

76

heard Celestine speak so before, and was quite unaware that her sister harboured any opinions on such serious subjects at all.

Celestine rose from the table. 'I'm sorry if I have offended anyone,' she said with fragile dignity. 'It's just my opinion and I can't help it. I am going to the "Ladies", Mother. Please excuse me.' She left the lounge watched in amazement by the others.

Ellen sighed. 'My little bird has grown up,' she said. 'She's right, you know, Clothilde. I believe she's right.'

Clothilde saw she was fighting back her tears. Whether they were there because her daughter was growing up, or because Celestine was right and all that that implied, Clothilde did not know.

'Oh Mother, Mother. I'm so confused,' she cried. 'Everything is so muddled.'

Her mother patted her hand. 'I know, dearest. I know.' she said. 'But it will all right itself, you'll see.'

Clothilde sighed. Then she too rose and holding her head high followed her sister, leaving their mother to settle the bill.

Left alone, Ellen thought of all the problems duty brought with it and wondered briefly why Clothilde and Neill couldn't do as they wished and take Holy Orders. Would it be such a tragedy if they were allowed their own way? And did parents always know what was best? She wondered, too, how Celestine was going to react when the realization dawned that her father's plan for her was that she remain in the house at Rathgar with them for the rest of her life. What price obedience then? To be condemned to spinsterhood? The girl would not find out until she fell in love. Then there would be the devil to pay, for Garreth would never allow her to marry, that Ellen knew was a certainty. At the moment, Celestine saw her father's will as good and right. What would happen when she realized that she was fated to spend her whole life being at home for Garreth Connolly?

Perhaps that would content her? Perhaps she had no desire to leave the security and protection of the family for a husband's arms and the demands of children? Perhaps the thought of such responsibility alarmed her and she would choose to remain under the roof where she was adored and cossetted by a doting father?

Ellen shrugged. It was no matter now. All that was in the future. She was going to have a whole week of freedom.

Garreth was off to London. Her heart sang as she gave the waiter an extraordinarily large tip and with a dazzling smile left the room.

Chapter

8

JOHN Joe Reilly had inevitably to return home to his wife and child. Mary had borne him three babies, only one of which had survived. It was in the nature of things in Paradise Row, the survival rate there being very low.

Neill and Breffni Connolly had been very sympathetic and kind in the 'Golden Harp', but, John Joe wondered, how could they possibly comprehend the seriousness of his predicament? Without his job he was doomed. Mary and Delia, his beloved family, were doomed with him.

Their room was on the third floor of the third house up Paradise Row. They had hoped it would be a good omen for them, as Mary said that three was her lucky number. But that had been when they were laughing youngsters not yet acquainted with the harsh facts of life in a Dublin slum.

Mary adored her strong husband and was by nature an optimistic little person, energetic and prepared to make the best of things. More accurately, she had been so ten years ago, John Joe mused, and he wondered when the change had taken place in her, when exactly the joy had been knocked out of her as the strain of daily living took its inexorable toll.

He trudged up the street from 'The Golden Harp' to the ramshackle row of houses leading to Paradise Street. He remembered her bonny smiling face and plump breasts, her warm and willing body, her easy laugh. They had had such hope then, such dreams. He shook his head as he walked. There were tears on his cheeks for her bravery, her gallantry in the face of increasing hardship. It touched and disarmed his stoic manhood and left him weak as a woman, a prey to the sobs that had wracked his body in the hall outside Mr Connolly's office and threatened now to engulf him once more.

Without her he was strong, angry, unafraid. She was his weakness, his Achilles' heel, his tenderness. Thinking of her, her pain, her dependence on him, her trust in him, undid him, so that he felt like a baby crying in the night.

Mary had given birth to Delia that first year and things had seemed good. But they became trapped on Mr Connolly's little roundabout. John Joe found that if you lived in Paradise Row or Street you had to work for Connolly's Brewery, and so perforce had to work for your landlord. When he was laid off he fell behind in the rent; then, when they needed him again, the relevant amount was deducted from his wages and sometimes there was no take-home pay at all. He was laid off, a few days here, a few days there, when there was no loading or delivery at Connolly's. True, it did not often happen, there were usually malt or hops arriving in sacks or being returned as faulty, or barrels or crates of bottles to be piled on the drays for the tied houses and the other customers. But at least once a month the five-day fermenting period overlapped with the non-arrival of sacks of grain or the advent of a full store, and there was no work. These days were deducted from his wages along with his rent arrears and, but for Mrs Connolly's charity and kindness, there would be no food in the house in those times.

John Joe resented this. He bitterly objected to his being under an obligation to Mrs Connolly. He did not accept the circumstances that made her help essential. He knew it to be unfair and he wanted to fight for fairer working conditions and realistic terms for the underprivileged and put-upon.

He had joined the Irish Transport and General Workers' Union but had stayed out of the strike two years ago in 1913 when 24,000 Dublin men and women had come out against the dismissal of members of the tramway workers who were also Transport Union members. But the lock-out failed and the following January, in the cold and fiercely inclement weather, the workers had totally capitulated.

Garreth Connolly had issued an ultimatum: any member of his staff who attempted to join a union would be summarily dismissed. John Joe thought ruefully that Mr Connolly had simply kept his word. Where was the evil in that?

He mounted the stairs and when he entered the room Mary

knew at once that something was wrong.

'Yer home at this time smellin' of brandy, ye who rarely let the booze cross yer lips, an' a face on you like an undertaker's mourner,' she said.

Her eyes had always been big. Now they dominated her face, dark-circled, shadowed by fatigue and malnutrition. She and Delia were martyrs to coughs and colds and John Joe nervously crossed himself as the dreaded thought of tuberculosis skirted the periphery of his mind only to be firmly pushed aside and buried alongside the other unbearable, unacknowledgeable facts of their lives.

He sat at the table while she brewed some tea. Delia lay sleeping on a pallet in the corner of the room. She had spent most of her short life in that place. She had no vitality and she lay there consumed with fever, and listless, semi-comatose.

'Mrs Connolly'll be here today, thanks be to God, wi' a drop of soup for her,' Mary said.

John Joe banged his fist on the table in anger.

'God, I'm sick to death of the Connollys,' he said angrily. 'Why should we have to depend on their kindness when I work like a slave down there all the hours God gives?' He jerked his head in the general direction of the brewery.

Mary kept the room tidy. She worked hard to keep it nice. A lot of women around Paradise Row gave up, for the fight proved too much for them. But Mary tried, even though there were damp spots on the ceiling and walls and the tap leaked. She had a nice white cloth, carefully and neatly darned, on the table and some chipped china cups. She had purchased those china cups when they were first married, from a stall in the market at St Patrick's Close, and had treasured them ever since, washing them, polishing them with her petticoat. She had, too, a picture of The Sacred Heart over the fireplace and a small glass bowl of holy water under it.

John Joe glanced at it now with contempt. 'Ye better say yer prayers, Mary, for I've been sacked this day.'

She turned even paler than her naturally pale complexion and sat down abruptly on a butter-box that substituted as a chair. She hid her shocked expression from him as best she could and tried to control the emotions of despair and panic that threatened to overcome her. John Joe relied, she knew, on her hopeful spirit; often he had fed off it and it had given him the courage to go on. She never let him know at what cost to herself.

'Well, John Joe, something'll turn up, you'll see,' she said bravely.

'Ach what? What, woman? Don't be so daft. You sound like those damned Connolly sons now, so ye do.'

Quick tears sprang to Mary's eyes. He had never, until now, said a rough word to her. Things must be very bad indeed to make him break the habit of a lifetime. But he was instantly at her side, apologizing.

'Oh I'm sorry, love.' He embraced her, feeling the sharpness of her bones through the thin material of her dress. 'Oh God, I didn't mean to be sharp wi' you. It's just that I'm worried outa my mind. Forgive me, love.'

He wiped the tears from the corners of her eyes with his thumbs. His gesture was infinitely tender. She summoned a smile from somewhere and put her palms to his cheeks, looking at him with love in her eyes.

'It's all right, me darlin', all right. We'll survive somehow. We will. You've got to believe it.'

There was a tap on the door and Mrs Connolly came in. She found them gently wrapped in each other's arms, Mary's head resting near her husband's heart. There was such an atmosphere of love between them that Ellen felt for a moment overcome by shyness and an acute sense that she had intruded on some precious privacy. Mary, however, put her at her ease. She broke away from her husband and dusted the seat of the only chair in the room. She and Delia used the butter-boxes.

'Sit down, Mrs Connolly, Mam, do,' she said and John Joe was once more overcome with rage that his wife should have to be so obsequious to his boss's wife. Ex-boss, he thought ruefully, and knew his rage misplaced. Mrs Connolly neither asked for nor expected servility.

'How is Delia?' Ellen asked briskly.

Away from her husband and in her capacity as social worker she acquired an admirable authority, both kindly and direct. Without waiting for a reply, she went over to where the pale little nine-year-old slept, fitfully coughing and spitting, even in her sleep, into a pink-flecked cloth. Ellen felt her forehead then shook her head. Mary watched her apprehensively.

'John Joe. Mary. I've been making enquiries. I hope you

won't mind. It's for the child's sake. There is a chance, well more than a chance, that I can get Delia into the Peamount Sanatorium.'

Mary let out a sharp cry and Ellen instantly put her arm about the panic-filled woman.

'I know this comes as a shock to you . . .'

'For God's sake, Mrs Connolly, yer suggestin' ye take her child from her,' John Joe said in shocked tones. Mary moaned.

'To save Delia's life, John Joe. She'll die otherwise.' Ellen felt Mary shudder in her arms and strengthened her clasp about the woman. 'You know that, deep down, just as well as I do. But you hide the truth from yourselves and you keep pretending that things will mend. That one day you'll wake up and Delia will be better. Well, she won't.'

'Oh I know that, Mrs Connolly.' John Joe could not keep the anger out of his voice. 'Deed'n' I know that. Hasn't your husband sacked me this day?'

Ellen was dumbfounded. 'You're not serious?' she asked.

'Ye don't think I'd invent a story like that?' John Joe asked sarcastically.

'Oh my God. Oh, I'm sorry, John Joe. I really am.'

'A fat lotta good that'll do us, any more'n yer sons' sweet sympathy,' John Joe said.

'Well at least let me help you with Delia. The Peamount Sanatorium is a wonderful institution.'

'Ay. Institution,' John Joe cried contemptuously.

'As you know, I'm a member of the Women's Health Association,' Mrs Connolly continued, ignoring the interruption. She was interrupted again as she tried to continue, 'And . . .'

'Well, ye don't seem to be able to do much about the health-trap this place is an' us rentin' it from yer husband . . .'

To John Joe's surprise Mary turned on him her enormous eyes, pools of misery. 'Ah stop it, John Joe. Please. Yer not doin' us a blind bit o' good talkin' that way. Forgive us, Mrs Connolly. It's just that we're so anxious . . . so anxious.'

Ellen noticed how great and touching her loyalty to her husband was, for she included herself in the apology, yet she had done nothing wrong, said nothing amiss.

'I'm sorry.' Ellen faltered for a moment. 'I appreciate . . . Well at least let me . . .' Everything she had been going to say seemed somehow crass. To offer food. To offer financial help. It deprived that tall strong man of his dignity and pride and chipped away at his gentle wife's self-esteem.

Mary glared at John Joe, but there was no malice in her admonitory look, only an expression of loving rebuke.

'Please go on, Mrs Connolly. We interrupted you.' 'We' again.

'The Peamount Sanatorium, is there to care for victims of tuberculosis.'

John Joe looked at the floor and shuffled his feet.

'We could not pay,' he muttered through his teeth.

'You would not be expected to. Delia would have the best of care. They have special milk there and . . .'

'We can't refuse, John Joe,' Mary said tiredly, her body sagging as she tried not to think of the loneliness and heartache she would feel at the loss of her beloved child, the only one of her bairns she had managed to keep alive. 'An' it'll give me a chance to work.'

'No. No. I'll not have ye . . .'

Mary pushed her hair behind her ears. There was infinite weariness in her gesture.

'Not now, John Joe. We'll talk of that later.'

The man bowed his head in defeat.

'Do I take it I have your consent?' Ellen asked.

Mary nodded. 'Yes, Mam. It'll break my heart to part wi' her. But if it'll make her better, then right grateful we are an' you thinkin' of us.'

'That's not necessary, Mary. Now I have here some nourishing soup for Delia.' For a moment Ellen thought guiltily of the fine filling luncheon she had partaken of that day at the Shelbourne. Mary turned to her, a victim, trying to thank her benefactor. 'No. No. Mary, don't say any more. It's the very least my family can do for you. The very least.'

She emptied the basket she had brought. Soup in a flask. A packet of tea. Some jam. A loaf of Mamie's best bread. Sugar. John Joe sat in his chair at the table. Each item she put there seemed to diminish him and he shrank into himself. When she had finished, he did not raise his head but sat motionless, his chin sunk on his chest, his shoulders hunched.

Mary opened her mouth to thank her again but Ellen forestalled her. She felt deeply ashamed.

'Hush, Mary,' she said as she left. 'I'll arrange it all for you

84

. . . Delia and a place in the Peamount.'

She stood for a moment outside the closed door to regain her equilibrium. There was no sound from within except the monotonous coughing of the child. Then, just as she was about to descend the stairs, she heard the sound of a woman's heartbroken weeping.

Chapter
9

WHEN Neill left 'The Golden Harp' he started walking back to the brewery, then changed his mind. He could not be responsible for his behaviour if he met his father, so it was best to stay away. He was boiling with anger and resentment so he turned around and started walking in the other direction. His father was always in a lenient mood when he was going away and there would likely be no comment about Neill's absence.

One of the difficulties he and Breffni had was knowing when to be around and when to disappear. Their father hated them to stand about getting in the workers' way, yet he gave them little to do and was furious if they did not appear to be busy, although ready to do his bidding. It was an impossible situation. They did some of the paperwork for him, checking invoices and filing them, replying to letters. O'Brien made trouble for them if they made a mistake. He was jealous of them, though Neill was certain he had no need to be. He and Breffni were simply glorified office boys.

Neill walked along the road, his thoughts falling over each other, moiling and roiling in his mind so that his temples throbbed and he thought his brain would burst.

He knew the Reillys, had known them since they had come, a happy healthy couple from the country, to live in Paradise Row and work in the brewery. Neill had been a little boy of ten and John Joe had seemed to him a giant then. He had tickled Neill and made him giggle and gave him piggy-backs hoisting him up on his enormous shoulders. Mary kissed him on the cheek when she met him in the street and called him 'young Master'. They had been grateful for the work, delighted with their cheap accommodation. They had not seen the trap yet. They had been hopeful, expectant of a good life ahead, if they worked hard, and they were both more than willing to do their share.

Neill had been aware of the change in them over the years; the gradual loss of vitality, the disappearance of the ready smiles, and the jovial greetings that were suddenly hollow. They both became thin and tense, and worried expressions replaced the open spontaneous happy looks he had been used to from them.

Well, his mother would say that that was normal. Life did that to you. That was what growing up meant. Maturity wore a serious mien and meant a natural preoccupation with the important things of life. But Neill knew that John Joe's and Mary's worry was lethal. It was *too* serious. The stakes were too high. The consequences could be death. It consumed, this worry, and it destroyed; a cancer of the spirit. Life was not supposed to be like that. And it could all be put right by one word from his father. No man should have such power!

There was nothing that he, Neill, could do. If he or his mother spoke to Garreth Connolly on the Reillys' behalf he would be certain to exert his power and show them who was boss by extending the punishment. John Joe and Mary could find themselves evicted on the morrow. They had made that mistake before, he and his mother. It had never worked and they had ending up by doing the families a disservice. No, there was nothing they could do except dole out charity. And charity erodes. It feeds upon a man's spirit and takes away his self-respect. Good God, he felt so helpless.

He walked down the banks of the Liffey, passed the Phoenix Iron Works, down Victoria Quay and Usher's Quay, Merchant's Wood and Essex Quays and found himself in Dublin City. The river, molten in a golden autumn day, blinded him with the glow it bounced back from the great orange sun. But he did not notice, so engrossed was he in his thoughts. The trees were shedding their leaves of amber, bronze and yellow, but he was unaware of the separation of leaf from tree.

He got on a tram going to Rathmines. People jostled him, sitting close to him in a companionable way, talking and laughing in their soft Irish voices, but he neither saw nor heard. When he arrived at the Rathmines Road, he got off the tram and walked to Rathgar, scuffing the few leaves that had drifted down, sending them scurrying in little golden cascades before him. But his eyes were blind and he did not see them. Finally he came, as if by accident, to the church of St Hilda's.

It had seemed to him that he had not known where he was going, yet, when he found himself in front of the presbytery door, he realized he had known all along that this was his destination. His father was wrong. There must be some way that he could take Holy Orders and fulfil his heart's desire. Then, perhaps, he could do something about the poor, the oppressed. He could shake off the mantle of his father's name, his father's reputation. They listened to priests in Ireland. They respected a cleric's word. It was the condemnation of the Church that had worked against the Transport and General Workers' Union and took the fight out of them.

He rang the bell. Sister Angela answered. She came from the convent down the road and looked after the priests with the help of Sister Clare from the same order. She was a plain-looking woman, indeed, downright ugly would be a better description but her face was so full of loving-kindness and good-humour that you forgot the bulbous nose, the porridge-coloured lumpy cheeks and the heavy eyebrows almost at once. She remembered everyone's name if she had heard it only once, and she greeted Neill now with a broad smile that lit up her face.

'Ah Master, or should I say Mister, Connolly. My dear Lord, you've grown, you've grown that ye have. Come in, come in. Don't just stand there gawping. What a fine young fella you've turned into. Yer Mammy must be burstin' wi' pride. An' isn't it a gorgeous day, God bless us, that the good Lord has given us?'

'Yes, Sister. Sister, is it possible to see one of the priests?'

'Sure, of course it is. I'll get Fr Grogan for you now. He's on duty, so he is. Come into the parlour. Would ye like a pot o' tay to wet yer whistle?'

Sister Angela and Sister Clare had developed a reassuring patter over the years. Visitors were often in a blue funk coming to see the priest and it put them at their ease.

'I would, Sister. I'd appreciate that, I really would.' Neill could still taste the brandy in his mouth and he did not like the flavour in the daytime; it reminded him of being sick.

He sat in the silence of the parlour, and the peaceful cluttered room restored his equilibrium somewhat. Religious pictures adorned the walls. There was St Christopher ploughing across the stream with an incredibly ugly baby Jesus on his back, a copy of Raphael's 'Holy Family' which Neill thought beautiful, and his favourite, Giotto's 'St Francis with the birds', which he had loved as a little boy and marvelled at as a man. Then there was St Sebastian, which Neill found embarrassing. The saint was like a bloodstained pin-cushion, riddled with arrows, his eyes cast up to heaven so that you could only see the whites, and he was tied to a pillar, naked except for a loin-cloth. He had a beautiful body, and Neill felt the whole thing was in terrible taste though he would never have admitted it, and felt the fault was in himself.

The room was obviously well used; the armchairs sagged and the cushions had lost their body and were shedding bits of stuffing. On the occasional table were copies of religious publications, 'The Messenger' and such like.

Neill found sitting still too difficult to manage and although he had calmed down considerably he was still very much on edge. Fr Grogan, a relaxed, kindly man, came into the parlour followed by Sister Angela carrying a tray. He was a small man with a mane of grey hair, shrewd eyes buried in a concertina of wrinkles and a high forehead. He held out his hand and shook Neill's firmly.

'Ah it's grand to see you, Neill. Sister, you're an angel. Just put the pot there and we'll manage, we'll manage.'

The nun left the room and Fr Grogan pointed to a chair.

'Sit you there, Neill. It's less tough on the bum.' He winked. 'The springs are all astray in this lot.' He indicated the other chairs. 'That one's not too bad.'

Neill hesitated. 'But what about you?' he asked. The priest laughed and plonked himself down in the chair facing the one he expected Neill to occupy.

'Ah, I'm used to it, Neill. I'm used to it. Put me down in a decent chair and I don't know what to do with myself. I tend to drop off, that's what I do, and we can't have that now, can we?' He turned his attention to the pot of tea, removing the knitted cosy and pouring the strong brew into the pottery cups on the tray. The cosy seemed familiar to Neill and he had a strong feeling that his mother had made it.

The priest did not speak while he performed his tasks. His movements were slow and deliberate. He handed Neill a cup and nodded his head at the tray.

89

'Help yourself to milk and sugar and take a slice of Mrs Mahony's fruit cake. It's so good it's a mortal sin. She tells me the secret is a measure of whiskey.'

He seemed in no hurry, eating Mrs Mahony's cake with relish. Neill added sugar and milk to his tea and ate the fruit cake which lived up to the build-up, all in companionable silence.

At last Fr Grogan asked, 'Family all well? Nothing amiss there?' Neill shook his head. 'It's me, Father. I think . . . I know I have a vocation. I want to become a priest.'

'Isn't that grand? That's a wonderful thing; to be chosen by God for his ministry.' He looked at Neill who sat on the best chair clenching and unclenching his long fingers, his face rigid with tension. 'But why the long face? What's up with you? Surely it's a matter for rejoicing?'

'It's my father. He's dead set against it. But you can tell him, can't you, Father, what a grand thing it is?'

The priest looked cautious. 'Hold your horses, Neill, now, there's a good chap, and tell me the whole of it.'

'It's my father. He says you need money to become a priest.'

'Well, that is true. Undoubtedly.'

'And he says he'll never give it to me. Never allow me. Not in a million years.'

'If it's simply a question of money . . . if your parents are short . . . though I wouldn't have thought so . . . A case could be made out . . .'

'No. No. My father is rich.'

'That is what I understood. So I don't see . . .'

'He does not want me to be a priest. He wants me to take over the brewery. He says he will never give his consent. But I'm twenty years old. I'm a grown man. You'll see him, won't you, Father? Get him to change his mind?'

Even as he asked this, deep in his heart Neill knew it would not happen.

The priest folded his hands and thought. 'That puts an entirely different complexion on the whole thing I'm afraid, my son,' he said after a moment. 'You see, if your parents were poor some way could, perhaps, be found to accommodate your circumstances, But your father refusing to give you his blessing is quite another matter. The Church encourages the young to take the advice of their guardians, and assumes that the guardian knows best. It preaches filial obedience.'

He looked into Neill's face and rose. The boy's expression was despairing.

'There, there, Neill. We'll see what we can do. Tell your father I'd like to see him.'

Neill could not imagine his father agreeing to this. For Garreth Connolly, the hour he spent in Church on a Sunday was more than enough time in the company, however tenuous, of the clergy.

'Perhaps you could call in for tea, Father, in a week's time? My father is going to London and won't be back until tomorrow week.'

'Fine, my lad, fine.' As Neill rose, Fr Grogan slapped him gently on the shoulder. 'You're a good lad, so don't worry. All will turn out for the best. You'll see. Your mother, a saint if ever there was one, and I will arrange it all between us.'

With that Neill had to be content. He had walked miles to-day and he was tired. It was late afternoon. He was hungry, for he had missed lunch. He decided to go home and wheedle some wheat-cakes out of Mamie and try to talk to his mother before tea-time. She would not discuss problems at tea; he knew he would be wasting his time if he tried. He felt more optimistic, more cheerful on leaving the presbytery, but in his heart of hearts he still felt it was a lost cause. Once Garreth Connolly had decided against something, there was little or no chance of changing his mind.

Chapter

10

BREFFNI had remained in 'The Golden Harp' after John Joe Reilly and his brother had left. The snug was dimly lit and quiet and he felt curiously elated. He wanted to write, so he took out a notebook and pencil and wrote: 'Sorrow's sad face', then scratched it out.

'The cold hand of poverty . . .' he wrote, then nodded in the grip of an idea. All his anger and resentment, his rebellion and irritation, his search for truths and wisdom were, unlike his brother, translated into words on paper. Neill had to act. Action was the medium he worked best in, Breffni thought, whereas for himself, his pen was his sword.

It was quiet in the pub. He could hear the ticking of the clock and the voices of children chanting outside:

'Ring-a-ring-a-rosies
A pocket full of posies,
A-tishoo. A-tishoo,
We all fall down, followed by shrieks of laughter.

A shaft of sunlight blazed through the top of the window above him. The glass was engraved with bunches of grapes and the word, 'Guinness', in a tasteful scroll. A lace curtain covered the bottom half of the pane and the light that filtered through fell on his table in dappled patterns of gold. The beer in his glass was gold too, clear as crystal, and he sipped it occasionally as he wrote and frowned and thought.

He was conscious of Philomena Quinn's presence behind the bar and she soothed and comforted him. All his life he had been aware of the gentle presence of women in the background and for him it completed his content. It was necessary for his equilibrium, that fractional awareness of some soft creature hovering about.

'The heavy hand of death . . .' he wrote, then crossed that out too.

He was chewing the tip of the pencil when he became aware of someone standing over him. He did not look up but said, 'Another beer then, Mrs Quinn.'

'So ye take me for Mam now, do ye?'

He looked up into the twinkling blue eyes of Kerry Quinn, eyes which sparkled and danced. A blade of brilliant light from the window made the freckles across the bridge of her small nose and her cheeks shimmer like stardust.

'Ach, Kerry! Yes I did. I did. I thought it was your Mam.'

She stood, hands on hips, looking at him with an amused smile on her face. She wore her red curls tied back in a ribbon like his sisters, but her curls seemed finer, less biddable, and escaped to frame her heart-shaped face. She was a pretty, lively girl and she looked at him saucily under her lashes.

'There must be something wrong with yer eyesight, man. There's a difference in our shapes, or can't ye see?'

Philomena, behind the bar, shrieked. 'I like that now. Me own daughter! I'll tell ye there's many a man as 'ud prefer my shape to your's, Miss Skinny-ma-link, so now.'

Breffni laughed and Philomena winked at him and disappeared into the rooms behind.

'Oh, Kerry, I know,' he said. 'You're a sight for sore eyes, that pretty you look standing there in the sun. A sun-drenched maiden. Oh I'll write that down.' He frowned, 'No. On second thoughts, I won't. It's all the rage now to be very realistic. In London that is. A Mr Eliot. And it's the only place that has the discernment to understand poetry. This is too romantic. I have to write about gutters and exhaust fumes and factories, and stuff like that.'

'What are ye writing?' she asked.

'A poem.'

'Oh. What is it about?'

'Poverty. How it kills. No, decays. Not kills. Killing is quick. Decisive. Poverty takes men slowly.'

He glanced up at her, fearful she might laugh, but she stared at him in sympathy.

'I'm sorry, Kerry,' he said. 'It's rude to talk like that to you.

93

Sure, what would a pretty young girl like you know about it?'
He realized at once how foolish the remark was.

'I'd want to be blind and deaf and dumb not to,' she
answered tartly. 'Gawney Mac, Breffni, where do you think I
live? Walled-up here? In a convent? Everyone in Dublin knows
about the poor. They pretend, some of them, not to. The
English, now, call us too stupid to better ourselves. The Anglos
exploit us. And so do some of our own people. The new Irish
rich don't want to know about their oppressed brethren. They
want to join Society. They want to climb up in the world. They
betray their heritage by pretending to be more English than the
English themselves. They don't want to be bothered with the
sick and the poor and the starving of Dublin. Like your father,
Breffni! Like bloody Mr Connolly!'

'Oh god help us, Kerry, don't talk like that, me darlin',' Mrs
Quinn's voice came to them as she reappeared behind the bar.

'An' why not, Mam? It's the way I feel.' Two red spots had
appeared on Kerry's cheeks and her eyes flashed.

'My mother . . .' Breffni began.

Kerry shook her head and a few more curls escaped the green
ribbon. 'Oh, yer mother's a saint, Breffni Connolly. God bless
her. But that's not what we're talkin' about.'

She sat down beside him on the narrow wall-seat. He could
smell the sweet scent of roses from her and it reminded him of
his mother's pot-pourri.

'Do you remember the day, Breffni, when you, me, Neill and
Darragh went to Killiney Strand? How lovely it was there, how
quiet. Just us and a few families. We played about at the water's
edge and you splashed me. We gathered the shells we found
there and wondered where they came from. We could hear the
seagulls calling.' She paused, her eyes closed as if she could
visualize the scene, as if it were indelibly painted there behind
her lids. She opened them. 'And then the soldiers came.
English soldiers. They were handsome in their smart uniforms.
They were with their wives and families and I'm sure they
meant no harm. But they just . . . took over. We retreated. We
backed away. All of us did. We pretended not to mind. They
did not ask us to move. Nothing was said. It was attitudes. We
were the occupied countryfolk. They were the bosses, the over-
lords, the conquering heroes. Authority.'

She lowered her voice. 'An Army of Occupation. That's

what they are. The people here forget it, they've been here so long. An' I'll never rest until every man Jack o' them has left this land!'

He looked at her in astonishment. 'That's a silly thing to say. We're still Irish. We can go about freely.' He felt suddenly very cross, as if something inside him had been disturbed. 'Oh you're being silly, Kerry. The soldiers are wonderful. Half of them are Irish themselves. I've been thinking I'll join up myself. To get away from Papa. He couldn't get at me over there in France. Anyhow, we were talking about poverty, not English soldiers.'

'It's the same thing, Breffni Connolly. An' if you can't see it, you must be blind.'

She had succeeded in making him feel stupid, so he got angry. 'Oh leave off, Kerry, do. You're only a girl, so shut up. England's at war now and she needs every man she can get to help her.'

'And why should the Irish help? Tell me that? What do we owe the bloody British?'

'The British protect us.'

She laughed derisively. 'From what? I ask you? Ourselves?'

'Kerry, if they left, this land would have such poverty as has never been known.'

She looked at him with withering contempt. 'More than "The Great Famine"? More than that? It is possible, Breffni?'

'Yerra, for God's sake, Kerry, that's ancient history.'

'Old sins come home to roost. Countries have to pay for what they did in the past. Quite a lot of the time it destroys them. One day England will have to pay for her great Empire. The score will have to be settled. She is leaving a legacy of hate. Yer blind if ye can't see that.'

'All I know, Kerry, is that England is at war to ensure freedom . . .'

Kerry hooted with derisive laughter. 'Freedom! Ye think we're free? God, man, ye're an eejit. We give our young men to a foreign power so they can die for a freedom they have not got . . .' She shook her head, then sighed and looked at him fondly. 'Let's not quarrel, Breffni, love. I've no quarrel with you. That's our trouble, Breffni. The Irish trouble. The way we fight amongst ourselves. We never have gone out to war against other nations like the English and the Germans, the Spanish or the Italians. We simply stay home and fight among ourselves. Come on, let's be friends.'

She put out her hand and he raised it to his lips and kissed it. She smiled at him and lifting the hand he had kissed, touched his hair with it. Not knowing why he did it, Breffni leaned forward and kissed her parted lips. They were warm and soft beneath his own. She drew in a sharp breath as he pulled back. He did not apoligize and she looked at him, the expression in her eyes unfathomable. They sat for a moment, the veil of their childhood falling from their eyes as they discovered the adult in each other.

Then Mrs Quinn called from behind the bar, 'Kerry, can ye come an' help me? The tap here is stuck. I been cleaning it an' a bit o' rag musta got jammed in the join.'

Kerry kissed her index finger and touched it gently to his lips. She stood up and went to her mother, leaving Breffni sipping his drink in the shadowed amber light of the snug, his feelings in total confusion.

A little later the door swung open and Darragh Quinn came in from the street. He, like his sister, was good-looking and had a vitality and a purpose in his manner. He exuded a strong masculine authority and was as unlike the tentative Breffni as chalk is from cheese.

'Mam. Mam,' he called as he entered, and as the heads of his mother and sister appeared from beneath the counter he continued, 'The meeting's tonight. Liberty Hall. Ah God, after the foul-up we've had . . .' He caught the expressions on their faces and the direction of their glances and he looked around swiftly, saw Breffni and crossed to him, arms outstretched.

'Breffni, me ould friend.' He embraced him energetically then dropped him back on his seat. Darragh was very tall and Breffni only came up to his shoulder. 'Maybe you'd like to come? To the meeting? Although it'ud be ironical, to say the least to have the boss's son there. One of the most hated employers in the city of Dublin.'

'Leave him be, Darragh. It's not his fault, you know that.' Kerry's face was soft.

''Course. 'Course I know it, and Breffni knows I know it.'

Breffni leapt to his feet. 'I don't want anything to do with Irish causes or Transport or General Workers' Unions or anything like that,' he said, near to tears. 'Nothing, do you hear? At the moment. . . .' He paused and looked around. 'At the moment, England is doing us no harm at all. Without her protection, things would be a lot worse.'

Darragh sucked in his breath, his eyes blazing, as full of fire as his sister's had been earlier.

'You're talking rubbish, old son . . .'

'You're the same age as Neill, Darragh Quinn, and who are you to talk to me as if you were my father?'

'God forbid,' Philomena Quinn muttered beneath her breath.

'An' don't tell me I talk rubbish as if it were a fact. It's rubbish in *your* opinion. Half the people in Dublin agree with me.'

Darragh sighed. 'Yer right. They do. More fools they.' He looked at the distressed boy who, in fact, did look years younger than himself. 'Don't you see it can't be right to have another country's army marching all over your land and seeing that the natives don't get too uppity? To be servants in your own houses is not right. We'll forget how to be anything else. Don't you see that, Breffni?'

Breffni shook his head sadly. 'No, I don't. I don't see it that way at all. I see the poverty. Here. And in England. A lot of places. I see our freedom threatened by the Bosch. I see us fighting to end all war. That's what I see and write about.'

'Yes, you write because you're Irish,' Darragh cried. 'So many of the great writers are Irish.'

'Goldsmith, Swift, Wilde, Sheridan, Shaw, Yeats and Farquhar, Le Fanu,' Kerry added with enthusiasm. 'Think of the Book of Kells, Breffni, written before any Englishman put pen to paper.'

But Breffni was not listening. 'The rest is . . .' He waved his arm aimlessly about. 'Trivial,' he said.

Darragh felt a great rage rise up in him but he controlled himself, reminding himself that Breffni Connolly would, of course, see things differently. They lived in different worlds. Breffni's world collaborated with the British occupation and Darragh's never would, never could. Reminding himself, too, that they had been friends these many long years and that friendship counted for a lot he said in placating tones, echoing his sister, 'Look, old fellow. Let's agree to disagree.' Then he smiled his charming smile. 'We've been blood brothers, remember? And I'm the same age as Neill,' he said with a grin, 'And you are the same age as Kerry, and we four sat under that tree in Portmarnock and cut our thumbs and swapped blood.'

They all burst out laughing and the tension was gone.

'Have a drink on the house,' Philomena said and began to pull a pint, but Breffni shook his head.

'I've had enough. Besides, I'll get into trouble if I don't get back. I really must go.'

He left them there in the cosy interior of the pub and he felt he had left something very important behind, though he didn't know what. He rarely talked politics with the Quinns. By tacit agreement, the explosive subject was avoided. What Darragh and Kerry had said in the pub had unsettled Breffni. He had never been told in so many words that the English were better, that to be English was more desirable, that the Irish were some-how inferior, but underneath all conversations, from the moment you opened your mouth and your accent was heard the underlying assumption was that to be English, to sound English, was infinitely preferable to being Irish. School had taught him to sing each morning:

'I thank the goodness and the grace
Which on my birth have smiled,
And made me in these Christian days
A happy English child.'

Teachers preached of the great Empire of which Ireland was a part. They were told in school that the correct way to speak was in a clipped Oxford accent as foreign to most of the students and as difficult to manage as Chinese. The manners from across the sea were *de rigeur* for any self-respecting Irishman or woman who hoped to be considered a gentleman or lady or to rise in the world, even though the manners and mores of their own civilization were charming and warm and much more politely hospitable than any English form. Firms, employers, mothers seeking nannies and governesses, desired above all at least a pretence of an English accent. You 'did well' if you married into an English family or worked for an English company, and to go to London was the pinnacle of people's ambition. To be and sound Irish was, in the eyes of society, to be uneducated, unsophisticated, uncouth. The native cultural heritage and manners of the Gaelic people were to be despised, and served only to prove their inferiority and the superiority of Britain's civilization.

Breffni had never looked proudly on his heritage before. What Kerry and Darragh had said about Irish writers had thrown him into confusion. It was all too complicated to explore now, but it was a novel if blasphemous conception.

His whole mind now was occupied by his own ambition and to deviate from his hardening decision was to complicate matters. So, he firmly put all thoughts of Irish writers and their importance out of his mind.

He wanted to get away, out from under the shadow of his father. All his life he had felt oppressed, his personality squashed, by Garreth Connolly. At least when he had been at school he had only seen his father morning and evening. Then the glorious escape. He could feel in those days his heart and his mind joyously running free as well as his body. But now, for twenty-four hours a day he was under his powerful father's thumb. All day, every day. Never free of the overwhelming presence. Might as well be in prison.

He liked to be quiet. He liked to watch people. He liked to sit close to his mother. He liked to write down what he felt. Yet his father made him feel that all these things were, as he put it, namby-pamby, and he jeered at his son if he caught him 'at it', as he said. He had seen his father last night noting Breffni's hand on his mother's arm or shoulder. Well, he would not stop doing these things. His father couldn't make him! Even as he thought this he knew it was not true. He often stopped himself to avoid Garreth's constant heckling. He had sworn that Garreth could not make him work in the brewery. Well, that was a laugh. Where was he now, if not in the brewery? He was an eejit to think he could ever get his father to understand. It would be wonderful if he could. He would have liked more than anything to have his father's approval. He wanted the big bully's approbation. Why, he did not understand. But it was impossible. So too was fighting his father. Neill and Clothilde thought they could cross swords with him and win, but Breffni knew that any mutiny was doomed to failure. In any fight Garreth must win.

So Breffni was escaping. He would get out from under the terrible shadow, and perhaps one day his father would look upon him with respect, with understanding. He was not going back to the brewery. He had lied to the Quinns. He knew exactly where he was going. He was going to join the British

Army. He felt it should be a moment of rejoicing in his life. He was going to be a soldier. He could not understand why he felt like crying.

He walked down the Quays an hour behind his brother but when he got to Sackville Street he did not take the tram. He walked up the busy main street until he reached the doors of the Recruiting Office. Straightening his shoulders and lifting his chin he went in.

Chapter

11

ELLEN finished her work in the conservatory and peeled off her gloves. She removed her apron and sighed. Yes, she had done her best that day and she felt at peace. It had been a good day. She wished only that she could do something more for the Reillys. She was very fond of Mary, admired the girl's bravery and was slightly envious of the obvious physical love she felt for her husband. It was a love that lacked any fear; she did not do things for John Joe because she was afraid of him but because she wanted to. Ellen sighed again.

She went into the hall. Garreth's cases sat there. Garreth would be taking the night train and boat to Holyhead, then London. She felt again that flood of relief she always felt when he was going away. It was as if she was carrying a great load on her back, and as soon as Garreth left or even intimated he was going, the weight fell away and she felt free. She suffered, then, pangs of guilt that she was capable of being so disloyal to her husband.

She decided now not to worry too much about her feelings. Pangs of guilt could overcome her, but later, on another day. Looking at herself in the mirror in the hallstand as she tidied her hair, she noticed that her lips were smiling and there was a dimple in the corner of her mouth she had thought had gone forever. Her smile grew broader and she giggled. She felt like a girl again. She suddenly wanted her daughters to come home so that she could ask them about their dresses. The girls had gone to Madame McGinty to look at designs, discuss styles and be measured in case they had become a little thinner of gained a little weight.

She felt full of energy. She went down the steps to the kitchen and called to Mamie for tea.

'De yiz want it under the tree?' Mamie called back to her.

'Yes, I think so, Mamie. It's a lovely evening, and the weather will break any day now.'

'It can't last much longer. Right you are. I'll get it now, Mam.'

Ellen stood for a moment listening to the clatter of dishes, then went back up into the hall and out into the garden. Golden shadows dappled the green lawn. The sun was a huge orange ball in the sky, yet it was cool in the garden. The fierce light blinded Ellen and she could not see the flowers. She shaded her face with her hand, holding it slanted to her forehead as if she were saluting. She walked in a leisurely fashion, light-stepped, to the tree and with a happy little sigh, seated herself and fell to daydreaming.

The girls found her like that when they returned a few minutes later. Celestine's excited voice broke her reverie.

'Mother. Mother, they're going to be beautiful. Very modern. A bit short.' Then, when she saw her mother's face, she added hastily, 'Tincy, wincy bit. Very modest, I promise you. Madame McGinty said it was *haute mode* in Paris.'

Ellen smiled at their flushed faces. Clothilde kissed her cheek and sat on a stool at her feet and laid her cheek on her mother's knee. She always did that when she was worried or upset. Ellen thought her daughter was probably anxious about this vocation business, but could not bring herself, just now, to get upset on her daughter's behalf. Today she felt that nothing could disturb her content.

Celestine sat beside her mother, holding her hands and keeping up a steady stream of chatter that was echoed by the birds.

'The styles are wonderful, Mother. So free. Madame McGinty says she'll put a bunch of silk roses at my waist. Huge golden ones, like cabbage roses to match the yellow. And Clothilde will have lily-of-the-valley. And yards and yards of ribbon. Lace inset. That lace we bought, the narrow bands from Connemara, are going to look sweet across the bodice. Oh Mother, Mother, we are going to look divine.'

Mamie lumbered up from the kitchen with the tea, Miffy close behind. Neither of them could see where they were going with the radiance of the sun blinding them and no hands free to shade their eyes.

'Help them, Celestine. They can't see a foot in front of them,' Ellen said laughing.

Mamie and Miffy looked like blind people in an unfamiliar place, and the expression of terror on Miffy's face would have been comical had it not been so patently real and agonizing.

'Oh, Mother, poor Miffy. She think's she's going to drop the tea things now. Oh I must help her,' Celestine cried as she rose to her feet and ran to Miffy and steered her to the table beneath the tree. The look of relief on Miffy's face was wonderful to see and Celestine gave the maid a quick hug. Miffy had wound her way into Celestine's warm heart and she harboured a great fondness for the little orphan girl.

Ellen poured the tea and was handing around the cups when she saw Neill emerge from the kitchen. He mooched over to them and plonked himself down on the grass.

'Were you in the kitchen, Neill? Aren't you going to greet me? Don't lie on the grass. It's autumn. You'll get rheumatism. What were you doing in the kitchen?'

Neill lowered at them all, then reluctantly got to his feet and kissed his mother. His gloom cast a damper on Ellen's content.

'Yes, I've been in the kitchen. Why? Can't I go there if I please?'

'Oh, Neill, you're just like Papa. Don't be bad-tempered, please. It's not fair to Mother.' Clothilde looked beseechingly at her brother.

'I'm sorry. Sorry, Mother.' He sat down. 'I'm upset, that's all. It's been a beastly day.' He caught his mother's warning glance. 'But we won't talk about it now. It's simply that I missed lunch and was stealing some of Mamie's wheat-cakes to keep me going.'

Ellen was instantly anxious. 'Oh Neill, you must eat. Why didn't you say so? Celestine, run and tell Miffy to bring Neill a ham sandwich.'

Neill's face cleared and he laughed. How handsome he is when he smiles, Ellen thought.

'No. No, Cel. I've had two large slices of Mamie's side of ham, and mustard and pickles so I'm fit to burst. So don't fuss over me. It's not necessary.'

Neill, Ellen, Celestine and Clothilde were all laughing when

Breffni erupted into the garden, running across the lawn, whooping. They were to remember that moment, to hold it close for evermore: the golden sun dazzling them, the tea things scattered about, the slight September chill in the air, the raucous birdsong and the scent of the late roses; and their laughter, their joyous laughter.

The moment held, and was broken. Breffni hugged his mother and for a moment she could not understand what he was saying. She caught the words 'joined up' but still she did not understand. Then she heard 'soldier', and her breath left her and she turned pale. The others laughed on, their laughter contagious so that Breffni was laughing too.

Ellen held her hands up. 'Hush. Hush a minute. All of you, stop.'

They looked at her in surprise, their laughter petering out. She was usually so grateful for a morsel of gaiety.

'What did you say, Breffni? Tell me I've heard you incorrectly? Tell me I'm wrong.'

'I've joined the Army, Mother. I'm off to Colchester next week. I'll be in France soon, they told me.'

The excitement suddenly left him. The buoyancy that had lightened his footsteps from Sackville Street to Rathgar deserted him at the sight of her face. She looked as if someone had stripped her brutally of her remaining youth, all in a moment. She looked devastated.

'Ah God, no. No, Breffni. You can't. Ah God, you can't,' she whimpered.

Celestine said, 'I think it's dashing and romantic, I really do.' Then she, too, was shocked into silence by the look on her mother's face.

'The British Army?' Neill asked in disbelief. 'You're joining the British Army?'

His brother's question rescued Breffni from the discomfort of his mother's distress.

'What else?' he asked. 'It's the best army in the world.'

'That's true enough,' Neill said. 'How much'll they pay you?'

'When I start, as a private, one shilling a day. But they say I'll soon get to be a lance-corporal and then I'll get one and threepence.'

'My God, I can't believe it,' Neill said in disgust.

'But it's more than I get now. Papa gives us nothing.'

'Oh, I didn't mean that. I simply meant that I cannot imagine my little brother in the army and I think it's terrible and disloyal that you should fight for the bloody British. Maybe die for them . . .'

'Oh stop it, please stop it.' Ellen's cry was wild and full of pain.

Neill looked at her, aghast.

'Oh, Mother, I'm sorry. I'm sorry. I didn't . . .'

'Shut up, all of you,' Celestine said firmly. 'You are upsetting Mother and it's spoiling tea. We won't talk about it.'

'No. No. This is much too serious,' Ellen said. 'Besides, I couldn't think of anything else now. Breffni, we will not allow you, do you hear? I forbid you to go. Your father will forbid you.'

'It's no use, Mother. I'll go anyway. No one can stop me. Don't you see, I *want* to go, I *have* to go. I have to get out from under Father's thumb. He's stifling me.'

'But I cannot bear it if you go.' Ellen found to her horror that she was weeping and wringing her hands like a peasant woman. 'I cannot stand the pain if you go to war . . . to fight.' She broke down completely and Breffni put his arm about her. The others were surprised at his calm, his determination.

'Mother, you'll get over it. Really you will. You'll have to lose us all some time and I'll return, I promise you.'

Ellen thought, 'He's right. He's right. I have to lose them all. Then what will I do? Then I'll be left alone with my husband.'

She looked at him, her face swollen from her tears. 'Breffni, you don't know what you are doing. Listen to me. You are a poet. A sensitive boy. You've always been tender and soft . . .'

'Ah, Mother . . .' Breffni looked acutely embarrassed and rolled his eyes to heaven.

'No. No. Listen. I know you. I'm your mother, after all.' She hiccupped, but no one smiled now. 'War is terrible. You don't know. People will be killed before your eyes. You'll be shocked, stunned by the horror of it all.'

'Mother, you're a woman. I would expect you to feel that way. But I'm a man. Poets write about war. Think of all the wonderful battle hymns. Now, Mother, quit this weeping and wailing. I'm off to war, so you must wish me luck and make the best of it.'

Ellen looked stubborn. 'Your father won't let you, and in this instance I'll back him to the hilt.'

Neill shook his head. 'Oh no, Mother. Not this time. He may be able to stop me and Clothilde from doing what we want, but he can't stop Breffni. You don't need money to get into the army.'

'Well, your father will think of some way to stop him,' Ellen said with conviction. She was appalled at how sure she was that Garreth would stoop to any mean strategem to get his own way. 'He needs you in the brewery. He's always saying so.'

It was her one hope, that Garreth would wield his enormous power and prevent her dearly beloved son from going to war.

Chapter

12

BUT to Ellen's dismay, for the first time in his life Garreth was full of admiration for his son. She should have known better than to rely on any predictable reaction from her husband.

Ellen had rushed into the hall at the sound of his key in the door. If he was surprised at his reception he gave no sign.

'Garreth, you have to stop Breffni,' she cried, removing his scarf and twisting it between her fingers.

He looked at her with distaste. 'What is the matter with your face, Ellen? You look as if you have spent the day in a tavern.'

She did not react to his insult but plucked his coat sleeve and repeated. 'You'll have to stop Breffni. He's joined the army and is off to Colchester next week. Tell him he cannot go. You need him in the brewery, don't you? You are always saying you do. Forbid him to go, Garreth, please.'

Garreth turned to his son and clapped him on the shoulders. 'Breffni, me boy. That's a gallant thing you've done. Joined up eh? Off to war? Show you're a man? Dammit if I'm not surprised. Didn't think you had it in you. The brewery'll wait. We'll keep your place open for you, never fear.' Neill wondered what place he meant exactly.

Garreth Connolly saw himself strutting about the town, the brewery and his club, nonchalantly dropping the news that his son was at the Front. How proud he would be. How impressed all those envious little people would be of him this day.

'Beat the Hun.' he said, expanding. 'That's the thing to do. Stop snivelling, Ellen. Damned women. What are you doing with my scarf? Don't understand a man's place in the world.' He turned to Neill. 'One up on your brother, eh, Breffni?

107

Namby-pamby wanting to be a priest. Never heard such rubbish! Well, you can look after the store while we're away, Neill. Take the opportunity to see how you can run a brewery while the men are out . . .' He waved his arm but could not find the word he was looking for. The words he wanted were 'drinking and wenching', but he did not think them suitable for Ellen's ears. 'Breffni, get your things now, m'lad and come with me. We'll leave together tonight. I want to take my soldier son to London. We'll have a fine time there, and I can show you the . . . er . . . sights. You can travel to Colchester from there.'

Ellen held onto her son's arm, moaning, feebly protesting. Her tongue felt too big for her mouth and she could not get the right words out. Breffni tried to push her away gently but she held on to him like grim death. She was reeling with the shock, terrified like a child in the dark and she only had him to cling to. As long as she held him, he could not go anywhere.

'Ah no, no, no. Not yet. Ah, don't do that, Garreth. A week. Give me that last week with my son,' she pleaded.

'Hush, woman, hush. Stop behaving like a harridan. Garreth looked at her holding onto Breffni's arm. 'Get off him. Leave him alone,' he said coldly. 'Your son has behaved like a man and you want to spoil it. You're a disgrace.'

'Papa, please.' Celestine spoke gently but he turned to her instantly. 'Let's all go into the parlour,' she said. 'I'll get Mamie to bring some coffee and biscuits. Papa, I expect you would like a sherry. Are you having dinner tonight in the Grand Hotel in Kingstown?' It was his custom when he travelled to London.

'Yes, my darling, I am. We are. Breffni will come with me. The boats are never crowded at this time of year. And with the war . . . In any event, they jump at my word. They'll make room or I'll know the reason.' He winked. 'Money is everything, m'boy. The pound in your pocket carries more clout than half-a-dozen friends. Remember that.'

Breffni was elated. At last he was important in his father's eyes. Garreth had joined in his excitement, helped him to feel that he had done a great thing. His mother's reception of the news had upset him and confused him for he was, in his secret heart, not at all sure he was doing the right thing. His mother's words had shocked him in spite of himself. But his father had arrived and was giving him the feeling that he was behaving like a hero.

108

They went into the parlour. Garreth was in commanding mood.

'We'll have a good time in London, Breffni m'lad. We'll have a fine time. Mamie, pack his trunk.'

'Now, Sir? Janey Mac, there'll never be time.'

'Get Miffy to help you,' Garreth ordered.

'I don't need anything much, Papa.'

'Course you don't, m'boy. Anyhow, if there is anything, we can get it in London. Eh? That's how you can behave when you have money.'

'Your missal,' Ellen said. 'Don't you forget your missal.'

Garreth gave her a withering look. She felt its impact. It froze her. She could not feel her fingers. She kept blinking her eyes and shivering and she did not seem able to breathe. In a state of shock such as she had never felt before, she mindlessly repeated the Hail Mary under her breath: 'Hail Mary, Full of Grace, The Lord is with Thee, Blessed art thou amongst women and Blessed is the fruit of Thy womb Jesus . . .'

Clothilde was the only one who realized how close to toal collapse her mother was. She knew there was nothing she could do just at that moment; that any plea for tact or delay would be the cue for another spate of verbal abuse. She kept silent, but held her mother closely and firmly, her arm about her shoulders.

Miffy and Mamie worked like lightning. The spur was the imminent departure of Garreth Connolly from their midst. Far too soon all was ready and Ben-the-Boots sat in the motor car outside. The luggage was safely stowed; goodbyes were being said.

Ellen held Breffni as if she would never let him go. Dazed and confused, she was mumbling platitudes because the power of rational thought seemed to have deserted her. All she was aware of was the bustle and fuss of a departure she had not been prepared for. Her beloved son, the child of her heart, was leaving without preamble. One moment she was holding his warm body in her arms, breathing in the special smell of his skin and hair, and the next her arms were empty and the wind blew in her face. There was a cacophony of voices, arms were waving, people were rushing about in the silver twilight. The car door banged and then there was silence. An appalling, awful silence.

She stood behind the shut front door, numb, her head bowed, feeling empty and betrayed. Cheated, too. Why had it happened? What had she done? Why had God taken away her best-beloved? Her day had been good. She had been happy, looking forward to being alone. Ah! There was the sin. She had wished for her husband's departure and so she was being punished. She sighed and turned. The dark hall was full of shadows. Ghosts from the past flitted for an instant down the stairs, in this house where she had lived all her married life: Breffni as a toddler holding Mamie's thumb. Breffni sitting half-way down, sobbing because he had lost his favourite toy — she had held him in her generous arms, murmuring endearments until he was soothed; Breffni descending in his school uniform, looking suddenly grown up and very vulnerable at the same time; Breffni leaping down the stairs two at a time in his cricket whites, waving a nonchalant hand as he rushed out of the house to his game. Now Breffni was gone. Gone. That awful word. He would be a soldier. He would fight and kill and perhaps be killed. He might never walk down those stairs again. He would never be her baby, the child of her heart, again. She had lost him this night, and the pain was overwhelming. She felt the world blur before her eyes, a haze come over her mind and she fainted.

Chapter

13

CELESTINE, Clothilde, Mamie and Miffy took care of Ellen. Neill went to the public house to telephone Auntie May, Ellen's sister, Lady Gorman. It was felt that as she was nearly next door, in Wicklow, she should come. It seemed a bit unrealistic to send for Auntie Nellie in Kerry. It would take her a long time to get to Dublin and she did not have a motor vehicle, while Auntie May did. Besides, Aunt May was a bright, brittle, no-nonsense woman. Beautiful and selfish, a charmer who always got what she wanted, she would surely, Neill felt, bully and cajole his mother out of the pool of despair she seemed about to drown in.

She arrived the next day, dressed in the height of fashion, as slim as a willow-wand, beautiful as a saint (Mamie's words) trailing a very seductive scent behind her. Mother had always said that except for lavender or eau-de-cologne, perfume was vulgar and only used by 'females of the night'. But Celestine had discovered that exciting scents were also worn by her aunt's rich friends.

She looked breathtakingly stylish this morning, like a portrait from a glossy magazine, come to life. She wore a pale-blue silk shantung suit. The skirt was pencil-slim. It wrapped over, revealing slim legs and dainty ankles and little blue shoes with soft suede bows on them. Her fitted jacket had a peplum and beneath it she wore a frou-frou of lace. The colour of the suit exactly matched her eyes and on her head was a tiny blue hat trimmed with ostrich feathers and a gossamer veil which covered the delicate little face. Her skin was white and fine as porcelain, the tints pastel. Delicate brows like swallows' wings

111

slanted over long lids, pale mauve. The eyelashes were dark gold and the cheeks were barely tinted pink, the fine curves of her lips coral. The face was perfectly proportioned. Celestine always thought she was like a Dresden shepherdess. She adored her aunt, who was also her godmother.

'Oh Auntie May, you look beautiful,' she cried, admiring May's clothes and noting the shorter skirt.

'Oh nonsense, Celestine,' her aunt cried good-humouredly. 'Now what is the matter with poor Ellen? Take me to her at once.'

Celestine and Clothilde took May upstairs, chattering all the time. Clothilde did not warm to her aunt, although it was impossible to resist her beauty and her devastating charm. Clothilde could see through that charm and knew her aunt, though amiable about most things, was quite ruthlessly selfish about anything she wanted. Whatever it was she would have it, and God help anyone who stood in her way. Being a very beautiful woman with an indulgent husband she rarely had to battle for anything, but Clothilde wondered what her glamourous and lovely aunt would think if she knew that her niece realized that behind her exquisite facade she was just as relentless as Garreth Connolly.

However, Clothilde was very relieved to see her. She was worried about her mother.

Ellen sat up in bed, sipping tea, her hand trembling. Mamie stood to one side near her, holding the saucer and looking fierce as a lioness defending her young. On the other side Miffy looked anxiously at her adored mistress, hopping nervously from foot to foot, a damp cloth in one hand and a phial of spirits of ammonia in the other. The girls sat on the bed, one on either side, while Neill hovered in the doorway.

'Heavens, Ellen, look at you. My poor, poor darling. Has that awful man been barbaric again?'

In spite of herself, Ellen giggled. 'Oh May, don't. Oh it's awful, you don't know.'

May knew very well, but she allowed her sister to talk, well aware it would do her good. She raised her veil, turning it back gently over the hat and feathers while Miffy watched, fascinated. She embraced her sister swiftly, then sat in the chair Neill held for her and prepared herself to listen. Ellen blurted out her story with hiccups and moans and a deal of sobs.

112

'Thank you, Neill. How handsome you are.' May touched his arm with pearl-tipped fingers. 'I hope *you're* not thinking of joining up.' Neill blushed and shook his head and May said triumphantly, 'There, you see, Ellen. At least you have one of them left. Poor Milly Parkinson has lost six to Kitchener. Dashed hard on her.'

'See, Mother? Auntie May is right. You've still got Neill.' Celestine grasped at the straw gratefully. 'And me. And Clo.'

'But Breffni is only a baby.'

'Stop this at once, Ellen.' May shook her golden head. 'Breffni is a grown man. I cannot have you drowning in self-pity. Oh, I know I'm being harsh but it's what you need at the moment. Now . . .' She looked around the room at the circle of faces watching her, gave her bewitching smile and continued, 'I've booked a box at the theatre for tonight. A very tolerable 'La Bohème' is being sung.'

'Oh no, no, no, May,' Ellen protested weakly. 'I couldn't. I'm prostrated.'

But May continued, 'And I think you and the girls and Neill should dine with me at the Shelbourne. Then tomorrow we'll all go to Avoca House and leave Mamie and . . . er . . .'

'Miffy, m'Lady.' Miffy was trying to impress the beautiful visitor. Her face was appalling to look at in its exposure of large teeth bared to the gums in an anxious grimace, and, in her excitement, she kept waving the ammonia under Ellen's nose.'

'Yes . . . Miffy. Miffy and Mamie will do the tidying up and sorting out while you rest in Avoca House and get your wits back together, Ellen.' May, in spite of her selfishness was very kind and intuitive. She realized what was happening to the small servant. She leaned over and patted Miffy's hand. 'Can you manage to help the girls pack, Miffy, while Mamie and I see to Mrs Connolly? You look very competent to me.'

In a transport of ecstacy and importance Miffy cried, 'Oh yes, Mum. Yes.'

'Good girl. I knew I could rely on you.' Miffy squeezed her eyes tight shut in bliss.

'You, Neill, will have to manage on your own.'

'Ben will help me,' Neill said.

May laughed. 'Heavens, you would think I was the eldest sister, and not years younger than your mother. Are you the sensible one in this house, Celestine?' she asked gaily while

Ellen spluttered on about the impossibility of going to the theatre now that darling Breffni was going to have his head blown off.

Ellen knew she would be contradicted, which was why she said it. She wanted desperately to be contradicted, to be reassured. She watched her sister. May twisted people around her elegant little finger. She cast her spell over everyone. She could not resist wooing all and sundry that she came in contact with and her charm was as gossamer as the spider's web and just as lethal. Ellen knew that May privately thought that she, Ellen, gushed, was too fulsome in her dealings with people.

'You must be a little more subtle, dear,' she would remark to her puppy-dog sister.

'But I can't, May. I love people so. I get such joy from the presence of friends. I know I'm too exuberant but I just cannot help it.'

May was not charmed by others, Ellen realized, but she gave the impression that she was. She could not bear to be rejected, everyone must love her.

But, after all they were sisters and they loved each other, and May's charm hurt no one, Ellen thought; it only made people happy.

'Have his head blown off? Phoo. What nonsense,' May cried lightly. 'And you lying here in bed on a fine sunny morning will prevent it? I suggest a light lunch, Mamie,' she added briskly.

'Yes, Lady Gorman.' Mamie, a tiny bit jealous, glanced at Miffy as she said this. Miffy put her hand to her mouth, aghast that she had called m'lady 'Mum'. But May saw, smiled and patted the servant's rough hands. She gave her a conspiratorial smile and as the others left the room she whispered to Miffy, 'Remember, I rely on you.' Miffy blushed in delight and scuttled out in seventh heaven.

'Now we're alone, Ellen, I want to hear all about it. But no hysterics, please.' Ellen looked crestfallen and May, seeing her look, amended, 'At least, not unless you cannot help it. Listen, Ellen, I know it's easy for me to talk. Barth is such a pet. You don't know how . . . ' She looked disconcerted for a moment, almost embarrassed, Ellen thought, but she hurried on. 'You have to cope with Garreth and that cannot be easy. It leaves you without any reserves for the shocks that life brings.'

Ellen did not know what to say. To agree with her sister

114

seemed disloyal to her husband, to disagree seemed foolhardy and hypocritical.

May said gently, 'Tell me what happened.'

Ellen was only too delighted to comply. It all came out: Neill and Clothilde's vocations, Garreth's 'difficult' nature, as Ellen phrased it; and Breffni joining up.

Mamie brought in cold cuts on a tray, salad and chutney, hot rolls and butter and a cut-glass jug of wine. Ellen, in the telling of her woes, began to recover. She perked up no end when she had eaten some of Mamie's delicious pork pie and had drunk a glass of fine French wine.

When she had finished she cried a little, but it was a very mild weep, and a touch resigned. She wiped her eyes and blew her nose and looked at her sister beseechingly. 'What am I to do, May? Tell me what?'

Her sister patted her hand. 'Well, Ellen, I must admit you have quite a lot to worry about.' She shook her head, frowning. 'Oh my dear, we live in another age in Ireland, we really do. To be in such a predicament in the twentieth century is quite ludicrous. We are very backward. Any self-respecting modern young thing in London would laugh their heads off if they knew about the little dramas here. They would tell you, too, that there were no problems at all.'

Ellen looked confused, her soft cheeks flushed from the wine, and May smiled at her fondly.

'Well, now. That's not much use to you, is it? First things first. Why don't you talk to Barth about Neill? Oh my dear, you know how he is about family. He loves to help. I know you're the soul of loyalty.' She had caught a glimpse of Ellen's face. 'It's one of your great virtues, my dear, but my husband is a powerful man and you need not directly refer to Garreth. Everyone, after all, needs help with their children at the stage yours are. Barth is the obvious man to go to.'

'But Garreth . . .'

'Garreth doesn't have to know. Better still, get Neill to go to his uncle. Barth will give him good advice.'

'But Garreth would be furious,' Ellen said.

May saw her sister's worried face and patted her hand. 'Oh Ellen, you're so much stronger than you know. You've put up with more all these years than most of the rest of us could bear to without going mad. You've done it for the children, I know.

115

It took a lot of courage, dear. Sometimes I've wondered where you got the strength from.' She looked thoughtful. 'I think it's because you bend. I don't. I snap.' She sighed. 'Oh Ellen, I envy you that ability, to be able to bend and not to break.'

Ellen looked dazed. So much was happening to her that was out of the ordinary, and now May, her beautiful self-sufficient sister who gave the appearance of being invulnerable, was complimenting her and envying her. She blinked.

'Now a little more courage is needed,' May continued, smiling. She saw her sister's face had cleared somewhat. 'As for Clothilde . . . Well, we'll come back to that. What's worrying you most, I know, is Breffni. Well, there is nothing in the world you can do, pet. Nothing at all. Breffni has gone, and all we can do is pray for him.'

She knew how serious it was, the terrible war that all the young men were travelling to so hopefully and that their mothers, sweethearts and wives were so reluctant to send them to.

'But being depressed is not going to help Breffni in the least. Or you. Or the girls. Or Neill. From what you tell me they need you now. Are you sure Garreth is not of a mind to let Celestine marry?'

Ellen nodded vigorously. 'He says to her often 'You'll stay at home with us,' but she doesn't *hear*. She is excited about the ball next week. I tremble to think . . .' Ellen faltered to a halt.

'Well, Garreth will just have to be made to change his mind.'

Ellen's eyes widened. 'You don't know him, May,' she said in a shocked voice.

'Oh don't I? Just leave it to me, Ellen. You are not firm enough with him. He does not frighten me. I'll take Celestine under my wing.' Hit by a bright idea, her face lit up and she looked at her sister in excitement.

'I've got it. Why doesn't Celestine stay on at Avoca House after you've come home? She can stay with us for a few months. Garreth can hardly come and drag her away. You know how he hates to look a fool in public, and I would make sure it was. In public, I mean.' She clapped her hands, delighted at her idea. 'We'll take her to all the Wicklow parties. The Vestries are having a party at Mount Rivers and there is a Hunt Ball at Usher. She'll meet *everyone*.

Ellen looked crestfallen. 'I'll be losing another of my babies,' she said and sighed, but smiled at her sister. 'However, in this case it will be for Celestine's happiness.'

'She'll be a great success,' May said, 'For she's a beauty, that one. Clothilde is perhaps more beautiful in a classical way, but there is a remoteness about her that is off-putting for the young men. She gives one the feeling that she is thinking of something else, and her mind is on other, more important things, and young men cannot bear that. But she has passion. Such passion. That's frightening too.' She paused and smiled. 'You must thank Garreth for their noses if for nothing else, Ellen. He gave them their perfectly delightful noses. But Celestine is like an excited and friendly puppy. Playful and affectionate. And she has a latent sexuality . . .'

'Oh May . . .' Ellen was shocked but May continued serenely.

'Society will love her.'

'And what will I do about Neill and Clothilde? Tell me that?'

'I think Neill, as I have said, must talk to Barth. Sadly I think he would make a first-class priest.' She giggled. 'And he would look so handsome in black skirts. *Everyone* would want to go to confession to him . . . the women, I mean.' She sighed. 'But what a waste it would be of such a beautiful man.' She held up her hand as her sister started to protest in shocked tones. 'You know how irreverent I am, so it's no use scolding me. But after all, celibacy is a man-made prerequisite for a priest. It's not in the Bible to my knowledge. You know what spoil-sports they were in the Middle Ages. They so loved to suffer, and chastity is such a ridiculously overprized virtue.'

'Oh May, you must not speak so.'

'I know I mustn't, pet and I'll stop right now to please you. But I think, much as I hate to say so and I know you'll be displeased, that Garreth is right about Clothilde. Owen Mulcahy would be a perfect match for her and I feel that if she took the veil she would be sadly out of countenance about it all very soon.' Realizing what she had said, May burst into a peal of laughter. Then, seeing her sister's blank face, she remarked, 'No pun meant. Veil, countenance . . . oh, never mind, Ellen. You are too worried, my poor dear.'

She looked around the bedroom. Its heavy furniture, the large dressing-table, the ornate wardrobe, the knick-knacks and large bed made it seem a small room. There were lace curtains on the windows and the velvet drapes were half-drawn.

'This house stifles you, my dear. Not like Holly Lodge. Home. Our rooms there were so light, so airy. Oh Ellen, how do you bear it?'

The moment the words were out she regretted having uttered them. Ellen never complained about Garreth or their life together. To complain about her husband or to indulge in conversation about his weaknesses seemed to Ellen in the worst possible taste. After all, no-one had forced her to marry him and the marriage vow stated clearly that it was 'for better or for worse'.

Ellen took a deep breath and pushed the pillow up behind her back. 'I've been so selfish, May,' she said. 'I haven't asked about your family. I apologize.'

May knew precisely what her sister was doing and she swiftly latched on to the new turn of conversation.

'My dear, there's no need. You've had a really nasty shock and well, yes, the family are well, thank God. Barth is in fine form and getting plumper all the time. He must take more exercise, I tell him, but he pays no heed. Of course he spends a lot of his waking hours in the saddle, but that hardly counts. I think he sometimes sleeps quite peacefully on Harriet, his mare. Lelia is lovely, a fair and happy child, if a little naughty at times, but then, aren't most children? She is looking forward to seeing her cousins. Being only twelve, she is envious of them. She thinks she'll never grow up. And little Barth is the apple of his father's eye. As you know, we call them Big Barth and Little Barth, and he is beginning to mind. "I am eight years old," he says. "I am big now".'

She was rattling on in a bright, brittle voice and for the first time Ellen realized there was something not quite right about her sister. She had made a few uncharacteristic remarks and she spoke now quite feverishly as if to drown out her own thoughts. Ellen took a closer look at her. May's blue eyes were bright as stars, her cheeks flushed pink as a Princess Alice rose. Added to that, the cupid-bow mouth, so admired, was pursed and red as if the blood flowed near the surface. There was a deep frown on the smooth porcelain forehead.

'May, what is it?' Ellen asked softly.

'May raised her eyebrows. 'What, Ellen?'

'You. There's something. I didn't really *look* at you before. I was being selfish. But there is a difference. You look as if you have a fever.'

May blushed and giggled. It irritated her sister. There was something secretive and complacent about the laugh. Something unpleasantly girlish, not at all dignified. That laugh was not appropriate for a married middle-aged woman. Ellen wondered how May had managed to keep her figure. Of course, she was much younger than Ellen; added to that, her husband adored and pampered her and she had only borne two children, but it was nevertheless uncanny how young she looked.

'Well, I was going to tell you anyway, though I'm quite sure you'll be shocked. But you must not scold me. Really you musn't. I'm not like you, dear Ellen. I'm not . . . *good*. You are, truly good, but I'm simply not, so don't expect me to be. Well, Ellen pet . . .' She paused, hesitating. 'I'm . . . I've got a lover.'

Ellen looked at her sister as if she were stark staring mad. She tried to speak but all that emerged from her stiff lips was a strangled squawk.

'Oh don't lecture me, Ellen dear, please.' Ellen saw that tears had sprung into the wide blue eyes. 'It's not as frivolous as you may think.'

Ellen at last found her voice. 'That's the last thing I would think,' she said with some asperity. Then seeing the stricken look on her sister's face, she hurried on. 'Darling May. It's not up to me to judge you. I'm not going to lecture. It's just that I'm puzzled.' Ellen hesitated, trying to form and utter her thoughts without being too tactless, whilst inwardly she fought her incredulity. A lover! At her age! To do 'that' with a man not one's husband! It was unbelievable.

Ellen pulled herself together. 'Oh I do hope you know what you are doing,' she cried feebly. 'Barth is such a kind husband.'

A tear spilled down the soft pink curve of May's cheek. 'Kind? Oh yes. He's kind. And dear. And loving. Good. And dull, dull, dull.'

Restlessly, she got up and walked to the door, but there was no room to pace, so she sat down again. She looked fragile and delicate.

'You should have married Barth, Ellen. You two would have suited perfectly.'

Ellen looked aghast. 'What are you saying, May? For God's sake . . .'

'But you would. Everything you need so badly that Garreth lacks, Barth has, and you would have been content with what he has to give. But it is not enough for me. He is so predictable. He would be so good for you. He is gentle and kind and tolerant. Come to think of it, I might have fared better with Garreth. Rough-hewn. Untamed. God, I would have given him a run for his money. He would have had a time with me, I can tell you. Oh, don't look so bewildered, Ellen. I'm just running on.'

'But . . . but . . . the . . . er . . . lover?'

'Captain Charles Cavendish.'

Ellen creased her brows. She was quite taken out of herself now. She had forgotten her own problems in her fascination with this totally unexpected drama in her sister's life. She sat up perkily in bed, eyes alive with curiosity.

'I remember that name,' she said.

'Yes of course you do. Remember, Ellen, a young lieutenant of eighteen calling at Holly Lodge? I was seventeen. Mama horrified. Nipping it in the bud. I was half out of my mind with love. You were of course married already. Do you remember?'

Ellen nodded, caught up in the memory of them as girls. The past flooded over her, enveloping her suddenly in a nostalgic dream of starched petticoats and the scent of apple-blossom, of constant mindless chatter in high voices when the sunshine and a happy heart were constant things. No, that was before her marriage. When May had fallen for the lieutenant, she was already a serious young wife and mother. Where then had that other time gone? Those far-off days when Mama and Papa were the sole arbiters of power in their lives? Life then was full of dreams and prayers, a curious mixture of innocence and desire. And May had fallen for the handsome soldier in the smart uniform. She and Nellie had been let in on the secret of May's passion. They had played a game of deception, deflecting their parents' attention from the lovers, for they had spent many hours at Holly Lodge in their young married lives. Their presence allowed May and Charles to romp in the summer meadows, steal kisses in the rose-arbour, pledge vows in the apple orchard.

Ellen remembered that summer vividly, and she recalled the excitement of being drawn into the conspiracy. There was in Ellen then, in the first flush of her disappointment in marriage,

120

a deep hope that her little sister would find real romance, true love. Garreth had been working that summer to improve his business. She had wished the relief and the gratitude she felt had been for his diligence, and not for his absence. Nellie had been there, too, expecting her first child, little Donald, who had died six weeks after his birth. Both of them had felt dull and staid in the face of May's butterfly beauty and her dashing young officer's romantic devotion. They wished that May should savour the sublime feelings so lauded in poetry and song. And as the summer days had drifted past in sunny tranquillity, they had conspired to conceal their young sister's sweet love affair and protect her from the rude awakening they both knew was in store for her.

It inevitably came. Their mother was horrified that her youngest had been cavorting around the countryside with a young lieutenant, a nobody, with no money or social position. Lord Gorman's son and heir had been presenting himself as a contender, among many, for the hand of the fairest of the beautiful O'Meara sisters. The offer was too good to resist. The O'Mearas had always felt that Ellen had married beneath her, although Garreth showed signs of making a lot of money. Nellie, too, had done well, but when all was said and done Joe was only a gentleman farmer. They felt that if the youngest O'Meara sister became Lady Gorman, all that would be tolerable. What a triumph it would be. And now here was this young upstart of a lieutenant paying indiscreet court to their daughter without their permission.

May suddenly found herself whisked over to London that September. She was surprised to find Barth Gorman almost constantly in their party and he proved to be a sympathetic friend, a considerate and faithful attendant; and, when May had realized that her parents were inplacable and that she would never see Charles Cavendish again, she sensibly recovered from her broken heart. She was a realist. She had no money of her own. There was, for her, no avenue of escape from parental control. She was not sure in any event that she wanted a complete breach with her parents. She was quite sure that she did not want to be poor. She was used to comfort and privilege. It was a cold and hostile world outside their social circle. She and Charles were too weak, too powerless, her parents too strong for them to fight.

121

She gave in gracefully and, giving in, fell into Barth Gorman's open arms. Their wedding was the event of the year. He had been a very satisfactory husband. Ellen thought again of the 'fun' May had told her Barth was in bed.

She sighed now, thinking of the past. So much had happened since then. She had grown old; she was plump and forty-six now, her hair greying, her waistline non-existent.

But May sat opposite her, a mature thirty-eight years of age, mother of two, yet she looked no more than twenty. The hair that peeped out from under her hat was wheat-golden in the sunlight that filtered through the lace-curtained windows. There were no lines beneath the bright blue eyes and her skin was like a baby's. She was as slim and supple as when she had run light-footed through the woods with Charles Cavendish. Ellen thought of Holly Lodge, gone now, sold, lived in by strangers. Their father had died. Granny O'Meara, as she had come to be known, lived now alone and doddery, drowsing before the fire in Ely Place, Ellen and Nellie had matured and settled down. Only May had not changed. And now she was saying that the young Lothario she had loved in the springtime of her life was once more there, her lover.

Ellen didn't know what to say, how to react, what to think. It was not the sort of thing that happened to anyone she knew. But then she realized sadly that she knew hardly anyone at all. Garreth had seen to that. Only the Sodality ladies, the people she helped in her charitable work; those were the only intimates she had outside the family.

When they had first married, she and Garreth, she had tried to keep up with her friends. She had given little dinner parties. Musical *soirées* had always been a favourite pastime in Holly Lodge and in a modest way she had organized an evening or two in Rathgar. They had been successful and she had been delighted, but her husband had not.

Garreth had put a stop to all such 'frivolity and waste', as he called it. This was where the Church came in handy for him. He used it as a whip to encourage Ellen to believe that such evenings were a waste of the good God's time and, incidentally, an excess that consumed his money unnecessarily.

The truth was that Garreth was uncomfortable with his equals or superiors. He was only happy in the company of those he considered inferior, those he could manipulate, those in his power. He was not a social man. He had no polish and he was bad at concealing his feelings. He had little or no sophistication and could not make or take a joke. His wife's popularity made him jealous, and he hated to have to join in the general laughter when he had not the faintest notion what was amusing the company. Haunted by his poverty-stricken past he was out of his depth, and it was a feeling he loathed. So he made it obvious he wanted no more such social occasions held in his house in Rathgar, nor did he wish Ellen to accept such invitations as they received.

Ellen, of course, bowed to his will. She always did, feeling it her duty. But it was the beginning of Ellen's disillusionment.

Her sister held her hand. 'Don't be shocked, Ellen. Please don't be angry with me,' she pleaded.

Ellen realized that her face had probably revealed her feelings. She squeezed her sister's hand.

'Oh, May, I'm not. In fact, if you want to know the truth, I was just realizing that you are still as young and beautiful and full of life as you were long ago that summer when Charles was in Wicklow. I was thinking how old and ugly I have become.'

A sob caught in her throat and May put her arms about the woman who looked old enough to be her mother.

'Darling, Ellen. Your looks don't matter one whit. You are eight years older than I am and you have had two more babies and the miscarriage, *and* you are married to that dreadful man . . . no, don't protest. He is, you know he is. So it's a wonder you don't look older than you do. But you have always been the sweetest person, the dearest, most loved girl in the world. I am not nearly so nice. Everyone who knows you adores you. You cannot say that about me.'

Ellen smiled at her sister. 'Then it's more fool they who cannot,' she replied. 'Please tell me what happened.'

May shrugged. 'Charles came back into my life. Oh darling, when these things happen, well . . . it was like a bolt from the blue. My whole world was changed. There I was, quietly leading an exemplary life, deep in the country, content with my dear husband and children, and then one night . . . one night I go to a party at the Countess of Athy and who is sitting across the table but Charles. Oh Ellen, you don't know! Have you ever felt that lurch? When your stomach falls and your heart races? I have never been drunk, but I imagine it must be like that. A madness.'

Ellen tried to comprehend. She listened carefully, hoping to hear something — a sentence, a simile — that would give her some recognition of what her sister was talking about. There must be some area of identification somewhere in her life, before or after she married and had children, when she had felt the same feelings as May, had the same sensations. But no. There seemed a whole arsenal of emotions she had never explored. She knew what love was. She loved her children to distraction, would cheerfully give her life for them. She had loved Mama and Papa. But it was not that kind of love May was speaking of. It was the love she had missed, the romantic love Shelley, Byron and Keats wrote of, that Shakespeare spoke of as madness. May talked of not being able to help herself, of being *madly* in love, of dying without him.

She was crying now, her pretty face blotched as she tried to explain. 'I dote on him, Ellen. All caution has fled and I am consumed. It is hopeless, hopeless. I am terrified. Half the time I'm so happy I feel I can fly, and the other half I'm in despair, wanting more and even more of him, his time, his love. And having to pretend, play elaborate games. What am I to do? Barth would let me go, I know. He is a fair man. And he loves me. But he would never let me take Lelia and little Barth. And I do not know whether Charles would want me, how long he would remain in love with me on those terms. It is one thing to have an *affaire* with a married woman who is protected by her husband, who lives in comfort provided by him, in surroundings and fashionable clothes supplied by him, and quite another to have to provide for that woman yourself.'

Ellen began to see that the complications were enormous. She felt briefly relieved that the problems were May's and not her's. It was all very well to want the love written of by the poets. It was quite another matter to watch someone totally gripped by an obsession, a destructive vice, and to witness the storm of emotion it caused.

May, she could see, was at the mercy of a fervid passion that she seemed to have no control over. Ellen shivered.

'I don't understand, May,' she said. 'You said he loved you, that you were passionately in love. How can you even think that he might not want you?'

'Oh Ellen! Life is not like the fairy tales we read as children. This sort of passion spends itself. I am not so besotted as to forget that salient fact. I could never be secure. I wish I could escape it, run back to the safety of my husband's arms. But I am trapped by my passion. I'm driven, Ellen, driven. Oh you don't know how lucky you are.'

Ellen looked at her sister, amazed. 'Me? Lucky?'

'Yes. You are free of such overwhelming emotions. I feel I'm drowning. I've become appallingly possessive and I know Charles finds it irksome. I hear myself, sometimes, quizzing him. I hear my own voice and I know that he finds it irritating. I cannot help myself. If I go on this way, I'll lose him.'

'Oh dear. We are both in the most awful trouble,' Ellen said. 'We'll simply have to help each other.'

There was a knock at the door and Mamie's voice called, 'I've some tea for you, m'lady, Mum. Miss Celestine thought you might like it.'

May dabbed her face with a minute piece of lace and took a deep breath.

'Life goes on,' she said, took another deep breath then sang out, 'Come in Mamie, come in.' Then she looked at Ellen, a changed person, all emotion eradicated from her face.

'What a pretty creature Celestine is,' she said brightly. 'I only hope Lelia turns out as well. Oh dear! What a pair we are. Ellen, you must get up when we have our tea. We have been disgraceful, sitting here here half the day gossipping. We most put on our finery. Mine is in the Shelbourne with Brindsley.'

Ellen recalled the stern face of May's maid. She had always envied May her personal maid, yet at the same time knew that if Brindsley were her's she would be too terrified to give her any instructions at all.

'Tell your daughters to look their prettiest. We'll go to the theatre tonight. Out of pure bravado. And to thumb our noses at Fate and show we are not afraid.'

Chapter

14

THE crowds around the theatre entrance were so dense that the Connolly car came to a stop at the top of Grafton Street. People jostled each other and hawkers tried to sell the latest edition of the 'Evening News'. The flower sellers pressed their fragrant posies on gentlemen and ladies who were hurrying to the theatre. Groups of young people following Mamas and Papas were noisy as parakeets, twitting each other, teasing, talking together, their voices shrill and full of laughter in the mindless way of youth.

Ellen found the crowds alarming, and wondered for the hundredth time since May had left Rathgar for her hotel, whether her sister was a witch that she had persuaded her to come to the opera on tonight of all nights.

'And what would you do if you were at home?' Celestine, who desperately wanted to hear 'La Bohème', asked her mother. 'Stay in and mourn Breffni's departure and make yourself ill.'

Neill was leaning out of the car window to see what the hold-up was, when he gave a yell of pleasure that startled his mother and sisters.

'Kerry. Darragh. What are you doing here?'

'Going to the gods. To hear the opera. Think only the toffs appreciate good music, eh Neill?'

The voice, male, was deep, the accent heavily Irish, and Ellen knew at once its owner was not a gentleman. Two faces appeared at the window. The man was obviously a contemporary of Neill's and he was nearer the window than the girl. She stood behind him and Ellen could see her face over his shoulder.

They were a handsome couple, vaguely disturbing in their vitality. There was something strong and electric about them both that made Clothilde shrink back and both Celestine and Ellen scrutinize them with wide eyes as if they came from a foreign place.

'Havin' a motor car makes no difference to the speed yer gettin' to the show, eh Neill?' the big man taunted, and then laughed and Neill laughed with him, much to Ellen's discomfiture. He was not in evening dress, she saw, and neither was the girl. He wore a rough tweed jacket and a high collar and tie. The girl had a lace blouse under her velvet jacket and her fine red hair framed her face, ungroomed and wild. Their appearance made Ellen suspicious that they were not suitable people to introduce her daughters to. Clothilde wished they would go, and looked purposefully out of the other window, averting her face.

'The traffic is awful,' Neill said, and as he said it Ellen realized who they were. The Quinns. Darragh and Kerry Quinn. But how odd that they were here, going to hear the opera, even if it was from the gods. Of course, they were Neill's and Breffni's friends whose father owned a public house near the brewery and Paradise Row. Garreth deplored his sons' friendship with them and had, on more than one occasion, forbidden the Connolly boys to have anything more to do with them. But the friendship prevailed.

Ellen glanced at Clothilde and Celestine who sat behind her in the car, at a loss for the moment. These were certainly not calling-card people, nor were they Paradise Row charity cases. They dwelt in the no-man's-land of ambiguity where the rules were not clear and Ellen did not know how to behave towards them.

'Why don't ye get out here and walk down South King Street? It'll be quicker than sittin' there stuck.' Darragh looked at Ellen as he spoke and she had an uneasy feeling that he had divined her thoughts.

He looked further into the car and Neill said, 'Oh Darragh, Kerry, my mother and sisters, Celestine, the baby, and my twin, Clothilde.'

The girls bowed stiffly. Clothilde blushed under Darragh Quinn's bold stare. She could see the freckled texture of his skin and the sandy-gold of his lashes and brows. It was the most open scrutiny she had ever been subjected to, and the man's obvious admiration filled her with furious resentment.

'Come on, Darragh. We won't get a seat. Mam is standin' in the queue,' Kerry explained to Ellen as if it was the most natural thing in the world. 'She's keepin' a place for us.' She sounded excited and she plucked at her brother's sleeve. 'Come on,' she said again.

'You mean your mother is alone down there?' Celestine asked, leaning out of the car and looking down the crowded narrow street where the lights of the theatre winked and blinked in the darkness.

'Oh no. Me Mam is around the corner down the alley. There's a long queue that goes right the way around, but the commissionaire says we'll get in all right.'

It was obvious the girl wanted to leave and saw nothing wrong in her mother being alone in a queue down an alleyway in the night. She was unaware of the impact her little speech had on the women in the car. The two girls stared at her, and Ellen gazed in disbelief. Clothilde glanced from Kerry to her brother. She was startled to see the comprehension in Darragh's eyes and the amusement there. He knew what they were thinking and he was laughing at them.

'They are people out there. Not wild animals,' he said lightly. 'They won't hurt us. They are all going to the opera.'

'Auntie May will be waiting for us, Mama. We really must go,' Clothilde said, trying to evade those eyes, to hurry their departure and finish this conversation.

'Well, you may be right, Clo. Although if she is there already it beats me how she managed it.' Neill frowned and Clothilde had an almost irresistible urge to hit him. She controlled herself as best she could although her foot tapped the floor of the car impatiently.

'Can we go, Neill?' she said, her voice tight and expressionless.

'I don't see how we can, Clo. Ben can't budge the car either way.'

Clothilde was angry. How dare he call her Clo in front of this stranger, who still stared at her in the most objectionable way. The more she squirmed beneath his gaze the more broadly he smiled.

'Why don't you leave the car to him,' he said and thumbed

128

in the direction of Ben-the-Boots, 'and I will escort you to the entrance? We will see that you are all right.'

'No. No. Under no circumstances.'

Clothilde had snapped the refusal with more vehemence than she had intended. Ellen had been just about to comply with Darragh's suggestion, as it seemed the most practical thing to do in the circumstances and she looked at her daughter in surprise.

'Why ever not?' she asked. 'I don't see what else we can do, unless we wish to remain here all night. Ben, you take the car and find out what time the performance ends and be outside for us, as near as you can get.' Ellen was suddenly decisive, and she turned to Darragh and smiled at him. 'We will be glad of your protection, sir, as far as the theatre.'

So saying, she opened the door and alighted. Neill and then Celestine followed and Neill took his mother's and sister's arms so Clothilde was perforce left to the care of the impudent Darragh. He bowed, smiling a broad mocking smile and held out his arm, crooked, to her. His sister fell into step on his other side, peering around her brother, waiting for Clothilde to take Darragh's arm. Clothilde stared for a full moment at the man, fearful of touching the rough tweed jacket, furious at her fear and his amusement while Kerry tried to conceal her impatience.

At last Clothilde laid her gloved hand on his arm and in an instant he drew her protectively close to him and set off towards the short crowded walk to the theatre. He made his proximity seem natural but Clothilde knew he was doing it deliberately. She could smell the disturbing maleness of him and she prayed they would soon reach their destination. Contrarywise she wished the walk would go on forever. She was overcome by a desire to lean nearer to him and was petrified by this strange inclination.

At the entrance Neill turned around. 'Thank you, Darragh. I'll see you and Kerry next week,' he said.

'It was awfully nice of you to come to our rescue,' Ellen said uncertainly, and nodding, turned and entered the theatre on her son's arm. Celestine, raising her skirt a little above her ankles the better to negotiate the steps, followed.

Darragh put his other hand over Clothilde's arm. He gave her a look, intent, personal, that made the blood rush to her face, rising from her neck right up to her hairline where her

129

soft dark hair clustered on her milky forehead. He pressed her arm while she gazed at him speechlessly. Then he let her go abruptly, so suddenly that she nearly fell. His sister moved forward. She glanced over her shoulder to where they stood looking at each other.

'Come on, Darragh,' she called.

'Goodbye,' he said softly, and raising her gloved hand, he kissed it.

'Goodbye,' he repeated, and then he was gone and Clothilde followed her family into the theatre. For a few moments in the foyer she felt disoriented. She could not imagine what had come over her. But she was a sensible girl and she decided, quite ruthlessly, to put the whole incident out of her mind, and, being a woman of considerable character, she succeeded, intermittently, in doing just that.

Chapter

15

THERE was a buzz of anticipation in the theatre. People in evening dress, decked in jewellery, crowned by tiaras and swathed in furs, arrived in carriages and motor-vehicles, chatting, laughing and excited at the prospect of Melba's 'Mimi'. The murmur of voices in the auditorium was like the sound of rolling thunder and the noise increased as more people arrived and the audience raised their voices to be heard above each other. People greeted acquaintances, exclaimed in delight, both real and feigned, as they welcomed their friends, and exchanged casual gossip.

May wore egret feathers in her blonde hair. They were pinned with diamonds and she dazzled like one of the brightest jewels nestling in her golden curls. Ellen was soon to realise that she had not come to the theatre, as she had said, to thumb her nose at Fate. She had come to meet Charles Cavendish. The audacity of her sister's behaviour stunned Ellen, and left her bewildered. She felt gauche and unsophisticated in the light of May's *sang-froid*. May had procured herself the most impeccable chaperonage and Ellen felt that she had been taken advantage of, but she could think of no way to extricate herself with civility. Besides, she loved music, and so she determined to follow her sister's advice and enjoy the evening. Outings like this were few and far between for the Connolly family, so in spite of a heavy heart she decided to put Breffni and Garreth to the back of her mind for the time being and bask in the excitement of the theatre, surrounded by the love and attention of her children.

She was so proud of Neill, tall and serious in his evening

131

clothes. He looked after her every need, removing her wrap, procuring programmes for them all and ordering champagne for the interval.

Celestine and Clothilde were like two blossoms, sweetly scented, fresh and beautiful, she thought, with their soft dark hair piled high and studded with tiny flowers, white lace and satin. Virginal. She was very proud of them, too, and felt herself blessed, encircled as she was by her happy, healthy family. At least they were happy tonight. The girls giggled and whispered together, excited to be in a box, peering into the house to see who was there and reading their programmes.

May seemed restless, Ellen thought, glancing about her as if she were looking for someone.

He was in the box before Ellen realized he had arrived. She could smell that indefinable masculine smell: soap, tobacco, brandy, and the leather of his boots; and something more, something exciting and unsettling and unfamiliar to her.

'Dear Colonel. You remember my sister, Ellen?' May was saying.

For a moment Ellen was confused. She realized then that Charles had been expected and the thought made her sad. The man was certainly handsome, Ellen could see that. But, she thought, slightly prejudiced, his were superficial good looks. 'Handsome cad'. The phrase came to her mind. He was very charming and he could not help flirting, even with her. She found herself responding to him, almost against her will, but his ways were winning and it was impossible not to like him.

'Dear lady. How could I ever forget? You were always so kind to me.'

His eyes were twinkling, and she smiled. His face was full of oddities that served only to make him seem more handsome: a cleft chin; wide dents in his cheeks; a mole on his cheekbone; even teeth that he revealed in flashing smiles; and a lopsided grin. He had a supple build, was tall and graceful, and it all gave him an attraction and a dash that labelled him, in Ellen's mind, a 'ladies' man'. She would not trust him an inch.

Still, it took her mind off Breffni and her own troubles. In that, at least, May had been right. She watched her sister, fascinated, as she sweetly asked Celestine to move down one chair and patted the red plush of the seat she had vacated. Charles sat there beside her as May peeled off her long gloves in

132

the most provocative manner. Charles whispered something to her which made her laugh and look absurdly pleased with herself. Ellen looked away from them, embarrassed, and her glance alighted on her daughters, heads together, cheeks flushed with excitement, elbows on the edge of the box. They had paid little attention to the new arrival, being too interested in the orchestra's entrance to the pit.

'Mother, the harp is beautiful,' Clothilde breathed. 'Beautiful.'

The overture began and Verdi's lush romantic music filled the theatre. As the lights dimmed Celestine's programme fell to the floor. Captain Charles Cavendish bent down to pick it up, and so did she. Only Clothilde saw the look that passed between her sister and the soldier as they bent to retrieve the fallen programme, for all eyes were on the stage. Clothilde shivered, for like her mother she was not won over by Captain Charles Cavendish's charm.

Celestine and Charles stared into each other's eyes in a look that excluded all others. The man's face lost its animated social mask. His expression was suddenly naked and vulnerable and he caught his breath as he returned the programme. Clothilde saw the colour leave her sister's face and an expression of astonishment cross it, followed by a blush and a lowering of her lashes in confusion. Then they both straightened up and sat stiffly, staring at the stage.

It was a wonderful production of 'La Bohème'. Never had Mimi seemed more pathetic or Rodolfo more romantic. Celestine thought her heart would break. She watched the stage transfixed, but was constantly aware of the man on her right. Charles Cavendish watched her, not the stage, the enchanting curve of her cheek, the tears as Mimi died, that lay on it momentarily before she wiped them away with her handkerchief. He could see the flutter of her eyelashes as she blinked rapidly in emotion and the delicate ear, a pendant pearl, moving with her movements, hanging from its pink lobe. She was very moved by the opera, he could see, and he could not believe what was happening to him.

He fought it, this tide of emotion that threatened to engulf him, but it refused to be stopped. May had told him how she felt about him, explained to him, insofar as she could, the tangled disruptive emotions that he had caused her to feel, and he had not understood her at all until now. And, now, he felt like crying, 'Eureka, May, I understand.' All his life, previously, he had thought that perhaps it was the fair sex that were liable to these tumultuous feelings, men being spared such excesses in order to attend to the more serious things in life.

When he was eighteen, he had been in love with May, but not to the extent that she now was with him, not like Rodolfo on stage, singing out his passion for Mimi. Not even enough to interfere with his career. He was a soldier first and last. He loved the army, it was his life. He had missed May when she had gone to London, whisked away from him by her anxious, ambitious parents, but not enough to follow her, thereby jeopardizing his advancement. Shortly afer her departure, he had been sent to Africa, and the war there had preoccupied him and prevented him from pining. He had risen quickly, doing well, and when it was over he had returned to London and a series of mistresses, mainly ballet dancers, and a jolly life of drinking and gambling and generally hell-raising. He had been told that May was married and he had accepted the fact without too much discomfort. He was sad, but had soon allowed himself to be consoled.

When war had broken out again he had been in France from the start. A shell had taken off part of his knee and he had been sent home. He had been lucky, but then he had always had the luck of the devil. He could have been killed; many of his friends were dead. He could have lost his leg; medical help at the front was not always one hundred percent successful or efficient. But he had survived. He had been sent to Surrey to recuperate and all he had now was a limp, a minor irritation that women found attractive.

He had been sent to Ireland pending his return to France, for, 'We need someone there to keep an eye on the natives. They do get restless,' they told him. He was only at the Curragh until he was perfectly fit for active service again, which he hoped all things being equal, would be quite soon.

And now this had to happen. He had, at a glance, fallen in love for the first time in his life, with this young niece of May's.

It had been lovely to meet May again after all these years and find her more beautiful than ever. His childhood sweetheart (as he insisted on describing her) had matured into a passionate experienced woman and he enjoyed their liaison immensely. He loved intrigue, it added spice to an amorous adventure, and May was a sophisticated lady, emotionally mature and in charge. At least, so he had thought. The situation had suited him perfectly, or had done until now.

But recently May's attitude had become a trifle possessive. She had become a little intense and emotional. She had begun, almost imperceptibly, to irritate. He had decided he would return to the front via London, as soon as he could persuade the big brass that he was fitter than the doctors declared him to be. Which would not be difficult, he knew, for they were desperately short of men and needed everyone they could get. Now he realized he had fallen hopelessly in love like any green schoolboy. In one moment. In a second. In the blink of an eyelash. He had glanced at the girl beside him and felt the world stop still.

It had not been his plan at all to have this happen. Ever. He was very annoyed with himself. He felt like an idiot. But there it was; that lurching stomach when he looked at her, that suffocating heartbeat, that almost ungovernable desire to touch, to please, to stay beside the person who had aroused the tumult within him. All these things May had told him, in those very words, that she felt for him. He now felt for the first time the same feelings, for this chit of a girl beside him.

He did not know how Celestine felt. He wanted desperately to ask her. He thought ruefully that one of the things about May that irritated him most had been her constant inquiries about how he felt. Now he understood that, too.

She smiled at him, provocatively, he thought, a young inexperienced girl's flirtation. Did she look at all men, or rather, boys, that way? he wondered. Or did she feel something too? For once in his life he did not know and was afraid to find out.

In the intervals they drank champagne and Celestine looked into his eyes in a way that gave him a glimmer of hope, for she appeared breathlessly confused and shy. Oh surely she felt something too? He touched her twice: once when he picked up the programme and once when he offered her a chocolate. Her skin scorched his fingers, but she did not look up either time so he could not fathom her reaction. He was angry too at his helplessness, his loss of confidence. At this stage in his life, the last thing he needed was this unexpected emotion, these sharpened feelings, this uncertainty.

The opera moved to its end. He could see Celestine's shoulders shaking as the curtain fell and knew she was in tears. She must have a soft heart, he decided, and watched her clap, wildly applauding as the singers took their bows, Nellie Melba receiving a bouquet.

May looked faintly surprised when he helped Celestine on with her cloak before he helped her, but she obviously thought nothing of it and laughed up at him when they stepped out into South King Street.

'Let's walk to the Shelbourne,' she said, gazing into the dark-blue star-strewn sky. 'It's cold and it's a beautiful night: two good reasons for walking.'

The hotel was directly ahead of them down Merrion Square and Charles wished it was miles away, somewhere in the direction of wherever Celestine lived. He looked at her now and was as awkward in this moment of leave-taking as any beginner in love, afraid to see her go, unable to think of something to make her stay. She shivered in the fresh chilly night and he longed to put his arms around her to warm her. She should not be cold, he thought tenderly. Her mother was waiting for their motor car which appeared around the corner in a queue of carriages and cars. Charles felt a moment's complete desperation as they piled into the car, Ellen, Neill, Clothilde and the focus of his interest, Celestine. Panic seized him as he thought she might be disappearing from his life, that he might never see her again. He certainly could not ask May for her address.

But it was all right. As Ellen said farewell, kissing May, she pledged an early start for Wicklow on the morrow and in the fragmented remarks that followed he realized then, in the cold star-filled night, that the girl he had fallen in love with was coming to stay at Avoca House the next day. His heart sang with joy. He felt an elation he had never felt before — at least, only when they were pinning medals on him. He hummed as he tucked May's arm in his and walked with light-hearted steps back to the hotel.

Chapter

16

'HE'S beautiful. I want him.'

Clothilde pondered Celestine's words whispered to her sister in the motor car before Ben-the-Boots had started the engine and they drove back to Rathgar. Celestine had watched the tall figure of the soldier as he started down Merrion Square, Auntie May leaning on his arm. Once, Celestine saw Auntie May look up at him and laugh and she felt a pang of — something? She did not know what as she watched May's perfect profile turned to Charles.

The emotion Celestine had felt for the man was overwhelming and she was shocked at herself. She was not sure that such a powerful feeling was either permissible or desirable, but there seemed nothing she could do about it. Even to think of his name, Charles Cavendish, caused such a churning within her that she went hot and cold and her knees trembled. All she knew was that she would see him tomorrow and that was a blissful and exciting thought.

'He's beautiful. I want him.'

Clothilde was worried. She alone had sensed the true nature of things, and her worry caused her to forget her meeting with Darragh Quinn, so preoccupied was she with her sister. She had noted her aunt's proprietorial air over the soldier and their instinctual behaviour with each other. They were used to intimacy, she could see. They were cognisant of each other's small needs and had performed such services for each other often. It showed. He knew how to place the cushion at May's back where she needed it most: Clothilde had noticed that when her aunt had sat on the small gilt chair after the interval.

137

She had paused expectantly and, without words, Charles had put the cushion directly at the base of her spine. She had leaned against it silently, content. He had chosen a chocolate he obviously knew she liked and popped it in her mouth; a very intimate gesture, to Clothilde's mind, even if it was accompanied by laughter. He had been physically comfortable with her, too. Clothilde had noticed that men and women who had lived together intimately were usually so familiar with each other's bodies that they were careless. They touched, often grabbed an arm or the lapel of the other's jacket, bumped into or against each other's body, all without remark or comment. Or even notice, Strangers or friends would apologize for the contact. They would avoid unnecessary contact as if by being careless of the other they were invading a privacy, a space that was entailed. May and Charles touched each other a lot without remark and Clothilde had an unerring impression that they were physically very familiar.

It was obvious to her that Celestine had fallen for the dashing Captain and she was curious about his reaction, for, to her, it seemed as if he too had become enamoured. Yet he was certainly already involved with May. What a tangle it all was. Ellen had noticed nothing, Clothilde was relieved to see. Her mother needed no more strains to worry her, no more tensions to stretch her almost breaking nerves.

Ellen had dozed in the car going home, worn out by the events of the last two days. She had relaxed in part because of the music and also because she was looking forward to a break and the pleasures of Avoca House, and Clothilde felt it best to keep her in innocence. Neill seemed lost in a world of his own and there was no contacting him. He often drifted off into a meditative dream and Clothilde doubted if he had heard a note that was sung. He had sat through the whole opera, his arms folded across his chest, his eyes glazed.

When they arrived home, she followed Neill into the parlour whilst the others drifted up to bed. She found him kicking at the dead embers of the fire.

'You'll spoil your shoes,' she remarked casually.

'Do you think that matters very much?' he parried lightly.

'What is it, Neill?' she asked gently. 'You haven't been with us tonight.'

'I could not get John Joe Reilly's face out of my mind all

138

evening,' he said. Clothilde remembered what Celestine had said in the Shelbourne the day before. 'Perhaps you could do more good if you, in fact, did as Father wished and took over the brewery. Perhaps then you could help the workers and . . .' She broke off and he thought a moment, his eyebrows creased in concentration.

'I know, Clo. What you say makes sense. And I expect I'll have to do it in the end. But it breaks my heart. I want so much to do it another way. God's way.'

'How do you know that Father's way is not God's?' she asked.

He shook his head. 'I'm quite certain he has called me. Deep down I know.' He looked at her. 'Don't you?'

She thought, seeking for the truth deep within herself. Then she sighed.

'I believe,' she said, 'I don't *know*.'

'Even if I did it Father's way it would take a long time and I'm in a hurry. Everywhere around me I see misery and poverty and injustice. I cannot see Father giving up the reins for many a year yet. I'm afraid I cannot wait. Yet I must. Then there is the other thing . . . I need . . . I need . . .' he mumbled uncertainly.

'You need God,' she said quietly. 'I understand. It's not something easy to explain. It's a great yearning.' She thought of Celestine and Charles. 'Like falling in love must be, only more temperate.'

He looked at her and smiled. 'I wonder,' he said. 'I should have thought they were quite different. Yet it cannot be. Papa will never allow it. And he's delighted with Breffni. Off to be killed like a lamb to the slaughter. How quickly they grabbed him. England at war means automatically that Ireland is at war. On the same side. Not that it's difficult getting Irish recruits. Look at Breffni. They are queuing to become the King's soldiers, happily volunteering to join the British bloody Army and get blown to pieces in France.'

'Hush, Neill, hush. It's supposed to be a war to end all wars. There'll never be another, they say.'

Neill snorted. 'There'll never *not* be another war as long as there is injustice, as long as nations plunder nations, as long as some men are treated as inferior to others and as long as there are banks and the greatest power we know is Finance.'

'Oh Neill, you sound so cynical. Don't let it all upset you so. You'll never survive otherwise.'

139

'Oh Clo, don't you see? There'll never be peace and love in the world until men listen to the word of Christ. Exactly His word. Not our interpretation of it. Just Christ's. The Sermon on the Mount. The parables. What He said. It's the only thing that makes sense. Love each other. How often He said that. Love your neighbour as you do yourself. Not shoot him in the back.' He put his hands on his sister's shoulders. 'Dear Clo, I'm sorry. I must not upset you. You have enough troubles of your own. But do you know what I was thinking tonight? Looking at that crowd of empty-headed people all of whom had paid a fortune to hear Melba sing? I was thinking that each ticket would have kept the Reillys for a week or a month, I'm not sure. Sive Jeffries' diamonds would have kept them for life. It is so grossly unfair. And the only thing that makes any sense to me at all was something Darragh Quinn once told me Parnell had said.'

At the mention of that name, Darragh Quinn, Clothilde found to her horror that she had blushed deeply and her cheeks had become scorching hot. She could see her face in the mirror over the mantelpiece and she turned away before her brother noticed.

'What was that?' she asked, keeping her voice as neutral as possible.

'"We must," Parnell said, "pave the way for Ireland to take her place among the nations of the world." That's what he said. If we had Home Rule, then we could make up our own minds whether we wanted to go to war or not. We could decide for ourselves. But the fools in Redmond's Volunteers believe that by fighting for Britain in this war they are earning Ireland's right to Home Rule. They are wrong. They are fools. Idiots.'

'Neill, I don't know what you are talking about, I really don't. And I'm not sure I approve of your friend Darragh Quinn. I think he is very impertinent.'

Neill threw his head back and guffawed. 'Impertinent? That's rich. He is a free man, Clo. How should he be, for heaven's sake? Did you want him to touch his forelock and say "Yes, Mum. No Mum"?'

Clothilde shook her head angrily. 'I'm sure I did not,' she replied hurriedly. 'It was his manner. Oh, I don't know, Neill. I'm tired. Let us go to bed, please, and be cheerful for Mother's sake tomorrow. Promise? She depends on us now.'

He nodded, the abstract expression returning to his face. She

140

kissed his cheek and left the room, and went upstairs to say goodnight to Celestine.

She found her sister in bed, her rosary clasped loosely between her fingers, her hair spread out over the pillows, the satin ribbons of her white cambric nightgown tied beneath her chin.

'He's beautiful,' she whispered. 'I want him, Clo. And I'll have him.'

Clothilde said nothing. Celestine stretched out her arms sleepily and her sister, bending to kiss her, found herself clasped in a fierce embrace.

'I love him. Oh, I love him,' she murmured as Clothilde disentangled herself. She gently pushed her sister's hair from her face and kissed her forehead.

'Be careful, Cel,' she said at last.

Celestine smiled like a cat. 'Why? I love him,' she repeated and turned over and fell instantly asleep.

Chapter

17

THE journey next day was lighthearted. The Connollys decided that Ben would drive them in the motor vehicle to Amiens Street and there they would catch the train. They would be met at the station and driven to Avoca House by the Gormans' chauffeur. May (and Charles) had left the Shelbourne early for the country.

It was nice to get away and a heady atmosphere of freedom enveloped the family. The release from Garreth's supervision was a potent exhilaration and even Neill succumbed to the holiday air that intoxicated them all.

Ellen had much to think about, for so much that was exciting and unexpected had happened. Consequently Breffni's absence did not depress her as much as it normally would have, and Clothilde and Neill were at pains to assure her that it was a mite soon to fret. He had just about reached London by now, and had to be trained before he was sent into battle.

The leaves were falling. Golden, bronze, russet, ochre, a mellow yellow, the country blazed under a huge amber sun and a burnished carpet of gold. The wind was cold. It brightened their eyes and freshened their cheeks.

Avoca House was a square grey stone house sitting calmly in rolling green lawns faced by the Wicklow mountains which loomed in the distance girdled by wisps of grey fog. A small wood lay to the left of the house, and a huge fountain, brought from France in eighteen hundred, played its constant water-music foursquare in the centre of the lawn, facing the house. Stone dolphins spouted water, as did a mermaid, and the central jet leapt several feet into the air. Goldfish swam in the stone basin and moss grew on its sides. The carriages and cars detoured it, for the drive-way divided in two and swept around the fountain in two semi-circles to wind up to the terrace and the main entrance.

The Gormans' Rolls deposited the family, and they were shown to their rooms immediately, their luggage whisked away by the servants. They were familiar with the guest rooms, for they had stayed in Avoca House before, whenever Garreth would allow them.

As Ellen bathed and changed for lunch, she once more felt an overwhelming desire for the luxuries the wealthy took for granted: constant hot water; the ministrations of a well-trained staff; most of all, the living space. The rooms were large and you could walk about in them, breathe in them, expand and have privacy. It was quite unlike the cluttered house in Rathgar with its small rooms that May said were stifling, and limited space. Still, she consoled herself, she was far better off than poor Mary Reilly in her one room.

They lunched on a terrine of duck, a Dover sole, roast beef and a blackberry fool. They had coffee in the drawing-room. Full of light, the large room had French windows which opened onto the terrace. They were closed today against the cold wind that rattled the locks and doors, but no chill penetrated the house, which had the modern heating that Ellen coveted. It seemed to her the height of luxury, and she had to remind herself swiftly of the Reillys' room and count her blessings and ask God under her breath to help her not to compare herself with her sister.

She particularly liked the blue drawing-room. She sat there now, admiring the Aubusson carpet of amazing pattern in all shades of blue; cornflower, azure, forget-me-not, sky, a myriad shining tones that delighted her eye. It lay on a polished parquet floor. The sofas and chairs, Louis Quinze, were covered in embroidered blue silk with gilt legs and scrolled edging around the seat and back. The giant oval mirror over the pink Italian marble mantelpiece was gilt-framed, and the drapes on the windows were midnight-blue velvet. There was a Steinbeck grand piano in one corner and a golden harp near the fireplace. The Irish wolfhounds, Paddy and Patsy, lay comatose before the fire and May poured coffee a servant had brought in on a silver salver. Charles Cavendish passed the cups around with dex-

143

terity and charm, and Lord Gorman sat in his favourite chair hoping he could soon escape to his study for a fine Havana cigar. He would not dream of smoking in the drawing-room and irritating his wife and children.

Lelia and Little Barth sat on either side of their mother. They both had her blond colouring but their looks were, unfortunately, a carbon copy of Big Barth, who was a jolly, good-humoured, placid man with a round full face and no distinguishing features; totally unremarkable. Unfortunately, for Little Barth and especially Lelia, he was plain and plump and his greatest asset, which was no consolation to them, was his kindness. It radiated from him and he was incapable of causing hurt, being considerate in all he did. One had to like him, and Neill, Celestine and Clothilde responded to his friendly hospitality, his concern for their comfort. Ellen in particular loved his company. In her opinion, he was exactly what a man should be: vastly reassuring, never discussing business at home, reliable in a crisis and above all good-humoured and not in the least threatening. The very characteristics that irritated his wife recommended him to his sister-in-law.

'Well, my dear, May tells me Breffni has joined up,' he said to her now.

She nodded and sniffed. 'Yes, Barth, and I'm so worried. You cannot imagine . . .'

'I've told her not to, dearest,' his wife said, sipping her coffee and gently slapping her daughter's hand which kept advancing tentatively to the *petit fours* when she thought her mother was not looking. Lelia had her father's tendency to plumpness.

'Oh I can, my dear, I can,' Lord Gorman addressed his sister-in-law. 'I can imagine just how I would feel if it were Little Barth off to France. But you must not worry. May is right. By the time they have trained him the whole damn thing'll be over. Christmas at the latest, they say.'

Ellen was so relieved she could hardly speak. Hope, which had deserted her on the previous day, flowered again. Everything her brother-in-law said she took as gospel truth. He had an honest man's authority and she believed him completely.

'Do you really think so, Barth? Really? Do you mean there is a chance that he will not see active service?'

'I'd say a very good chance, m'dear. More like a certainty. He's only just joined and, as I say, by the time he's done his

144

basic training the whole party is bound to be over.'

Ellen sighed happily. She wondered how her sister could want any other man when she had this tower of strength to love and guide her. She looked at May in her salmon-pink blouse, the choker of pearls tight about her long white neck, and saw her blue eyes search for Charles over the rim of her coffee cup.

Charles sat between Clothilde and Celestine and they were both laughing at something he was telling them. Ellen sighed. They looked so lovely, her daughters, so very young and untried. She sent up a quick plea to Our Lady to protect them and turned back to Lord Gorman who was saying, 'We'll thrash the Huns, never you fear. Teach them a lesson.'

'But they are simply other women's sons obeying orders,' Neill said, 'I don't expect they have a much clearer idea of why they are fighting than Breffni has.'

'What?' Barth looked at his nephew, slightly perplexed. 'Oh yes. Well,' he rose and bowed to the company. 'Beg pardon, Ellen, you'll excuse me m'dear,' he said, 'if I relieve you of me presence?'

'Go, Barth. Go. Your cigar awaits you.' May gave her husband an affectionate glance.

'I'm going over accounts this afternoon, m'dear. Be in the office if anyone wants me. Otherwise see you at dinner.'

When Barth had closed the door behind him, he let out a sigh of relief. So! Charles Cavendish had fallen for the youngest Connolly gal. He smacked his fist into the open palm of his hand to release some of the excitement and relief he felt. He wanted to cheer. He had been in hell the past months, not knowing which way to turn. He adored his wife, and watching her fall for Cavendish all over again was bitter medicine to swallow. He had known where her heart lay when he had first started to court her, for he had known her all his life.

When he had come down from Oxford, he had seen her, a grown-up May he had not recognized, waltzing at a party in the arms of a young lieutenant, and he had fallen madly, passionately in love with her. She, however, had eyes for no one but her soldier. Dear old O'Meara, rest his soul, had put a stop to that and fate had taken a hand. The Boer War had broken out and the soldier was sent to Africa. May O'Meara had disappeared for seven days after they had been separated; then she had gone to London, where he had followed her. She had fined down: her spontaneous gaiety sharpened; her manner much more grown-up. He had wooed her and won her, with old O'Meara's cognisance; and found in her a jewel of a wife. In bed, he discovered a loving, passionate partner. She ran their home with flair and efficiency. With servants she was particularly gifted, and the staff at Avoca House one and all adored her. She gave him two children, one of whom was the son and heir he craved, and all through the years she had retained her youthful figure and her beauty. He fell more and more in love with her over the years. She had become as necessary to him as breathing.

Then back onto the scene came Captain Charles Cavendish, dashing and reckless as ever, and he had had to stand by and watch his beloved wife literally fall into the man's arms.

Through those months Barth learned all about suffering. His pride was hurt, true, but he did not care about that. He was not a petty man. But he became a prey to jealousy, the virulence of which astonished him. He had not known such torment existed. He spied on his wife, despising himself for doing so and realizing it only made him feel worse, rubbed salt into the wound. He who had always fallen asleep as soon as his head touched the pillow now learned how terrible insomnia could be. Worst of all, he learned to lie and act and pretend and play a game with his wife. The complexity of that game scared him. He, the soul of honour, became of necessity dishonest. For he dared not bring the whole thing out into the open, dared not risk forcing her hand. She might run off to London with her soldier. He was forced to pretend that nothing was happening, that everything was as usual, even though he knew; and he knew she knew he knew.

He also sensed that she was afraid, afraid that Charles did not want her on a permanent basis, that their liaison was, for him, a fling, nothing more than a delightful interlude between battles. Barth thought that she had grounds for her fear, but he did not want anything said that would make it impossible for either one of them to repair their marriage. He did not want either of them to say the unsayable, and then not be able to retract it.

He had often been tempted to tell her what a dilettante Charles was. He had ached to show him up as a womanizing, shallow philanderer. In jealous rages and feverish dreams, he wrote scene after scene in his mind in which Charles Cavendish

146

was revealed as a cad and May, the scales falling from her eyes, turned to her husband in gratitude and love.

But he knew people well enough to know they were seldom grateful to be made aware of a loved-one's worthlessness. So he had tossed and turned in his agony, showing a calm and tranquil face to the world which he knew laughed at him behind his back and called him cuckold.

He had never in his wildest imaginings thought of anything so simple and satisfactory (for him) as that Charles would fall in love with someone else. A young girl at that. May's niece. He knew May would suffer and he did not want that. He was not vindictive. He simply wanted her back, and as she would suffer in any event, it was far better this way than any other. This way would show her Charles' real character but also reveal to her how impossible their liaison had been. She would know what it was like to be made a fool of, and while he did not wish the realization upon her, he felt it the only way to bring her to her senses, and them back together again. It would kill her love for Charles quite dead.

Meantime, she did not know. That much was obvious. She was quite blind to what was happening under her nose. Poor May. He made up his mind that he would encourage Celestine and Charles. But he must not be seen to do so. That would be unwise. Charles would be a good match for Celestine and that, according to May, was the purpose of the child's visit. The Connollys were to stay a week, then return to Dublin leaving Celestine behind at Avoca House, 'to find a suitable husband, dearest,' May had said.

Well, there was a solution to all their problems and Barth sent up a prayer of thanks to whatever saint was looking after him that day.

Dinner that evening was a jolly meal. All the company seemed in high spirits, not least Lord Gorman, who kept a lively conversation going and even brought out the best in Neill and Clothilde.

During the soup, an excellent lobster bisque, Neill asked Charles when he expected to return to the front.

'Quite soon,' was the reply. May and Celestine both put down their spoons abruptly, but he laughed charmingly. 'In army parlance, that means it could take forever. We are getting so bogged down in forms these days, are we not, sir?'

147

Why does he always make me feel so damned middle-aged? Barth wondered. He nodded his head in agreement.

'Indeed, m'boy,' he replied, also wondering wryly why he insisted on treating Charles as if he were his son. 'Triplicate! Everything's in triplicate. Even for us down here in the heart of the country.'

'There are absolutely masses of blackberries at the other side of the woods,' Lelia said. She and Little Barth had been allowed to stay up for dinner because the guests were family.

'Oh, do let's collect some tomorrow,' Celestine cried, her cheeks pink, and Ellen looked at her, surprised, for Celestine usually begged off blackberry picking because, she said, it stained and the thorns covered her soft hands in a million little scratches.

Charles smiled at her, and at Clothilde. 'We'll do it tomorrow morning, first thing. When the dew is still on the grass.'

'Why Charles, how poetic of you,' May said tranquilly. Does she not see? Barth thought, and realized she was still quite blind.

'I'm a very poetic fellow,' Charles replied merrily. 'Underneath this uniform beats the heart of a Shelley or a Byron.'

After dinner they went to the blue drawing-room where Clothilde enchanted the company by playing old folk songs on the harp. Celestine, accompanying herself on the piano, sang in her wistful soprano. She had a modest talent, but to Charles that night her voice sounded purer than Melba's.

'Flow gently, sweet Afton, among thy green vales.' Charles thought his heart would burst within him. The beauty of her sweet, timid smile as he turned the pages of music quite unmanned him. Later, Barth sang a duet with her and his rich baritone blended well with her pure high notes, lending substance and poignancy to their song. It was a lovely evening. Ellen sighed in pure delight at the peace in her heart, the prospect of privacy in her bedroom that night, the comfort of the house and the happy serenity of the atmosphere. The lights were dim in the room and the flickering firelight played on the beloved faces of her children, outlining the curves of Celestine's cheeks, highlighting the sharp angles of Neill's jaw. Clothilde's eyes were half-closed and her lashes cast shadows on her cheeks and made her face mysterious. Barth drowsed in the warmth of the fire, his legs stretched before him, his hands folded on his

148

stomach. Charles spoke quietly to May. Her sister's face had never looked more beautiful, Ellen thought; like an Indian summer, she burned with a very bright glow. Her children at her feet could no longer keep their eyes open when she rose and cried, 'Come children, bed, bed, bed. It's way past your time. Call Miss Bellew. Bid everyone goodnight.'

They said a sleepy adieu and the company broke up in a flurry of goodnights.

Chapter
18

BARTH went to May's room that night. He felt timorous as a newly-wed, hopelessly vulnerable, and, trying to conceal his feelings under a jovial grin, a clown's self-abnegation, he knocked at his wife's bedroom door.

'Not tonight, dear Barth,' she sang out. 'I'm quite worn out after the excitement of the last few days.'

May had been making such excuses quite a lot recently. She sat up in bed, her hair cascading over her shoulders in golden waves. Her face thus framed, seemed small and young, and he stood uncertainly in the doorway wondering what to do. She beckoned him in, and he came towards her looking at her with pleading eyes. She, however, avoided looking at him, and plucked at the lace trim on her pillow with nervous fingers. He longed to put his arms around her and hold her close. They were playing a very dangerous game and he knew that one wrong word, one inappropriate touch, and the whole facade might crumble, leaving destruction behind.

'But come. Sit for a moment and I will tell you all about poor Ellen.'

Her eyes were full of apology when they met his, gently asking him to understand. He smiled at her reassuringly.

'I've promised her I'd take care of Celestine,' she said, taking his hand and playing with his fingers in an absent-minded way. 'The family are staying for a week while the dragon is in London.' She smiled at him and he answered her smile with an understanding nod.

'Neill returns to Dublin for work on Monday, poor boy. He has to take care of the brewery in Garreth's absence. Oh dear, and Ellen tells me he so desperately wants to be a priest. What do you think, Barth?'

'I think Neill would make a very good priest. I'm sure he would *not* make a businessman. His heart is not in commerce.'

'Then we shall have to see what we can do to help him, don't you think? I've told Ellen to speak to you. Or get Neill to.'

Barth nodded. 'You can count on me,' he said.

'Why do you think Garreth goes to London, dearest?' May asked. 'I cannot imagine what he does. It's not business, no matter what he says. Poor Ellen, she is simply not equipped to cope with the monster.'

'Ellen is a sweet and loving woman,' Barth said and May glanced at him, searching his face for irony. She saw nothing there except sincerity.

'She worries too much,' he continued. 'If she cared less about that man's feelings, she would be in a far stronger position.'

'Like me?' May whispered. The query held such dangerous implications that he forbore to pursue the conversation and answered with a question.

'The others are staying, though?'

May nodded. 'Yes, for a week. And I'm keeping Celestine for a month or two.' She shrugged her shoulders, her soft unbound hair rippling with her movements, liquid gold in the lamplight. 'Ellen is worried about Garreth and his attitude to Celestine. She says that Garreth will not allow the girl to marry, but intends to keep her at home forever.' She wrinkled her nose. 'Or at least, I suppose, until he dies. Horrid, don't you think?'

'I cannot believe that,' Barth said and his heart sank, for if it were true, his hopes for Charles and Celestine would be sadly dashed. Another parent whisking away their offspring from the amorous clutches of the soldier, he thought wryly.

But May was speaking incisively. 'In any event I don't intend to pay the smallest attention to his decrees. I intend to find her a husband. She is quite lovely and we should not have any trouble at all.'

What is she going to do when she finds out that her niece and her lover are mad about each other? Barth wondered, and shuddered.

Suddenly, his desire for her and the pain of the situation overcame him and he could bear it no longer. Did May think he was made of stone, that he could sit here while she fiddled with his fingers and he could smell the perfume of her skin? He had to get out of the room.

He rose swiftly and kissed his wife on the forehead. 'Good-night, my love. I must retire. I feel uncommonly sleepy tonight.' Keep up the masquerade at all costs. 'I must rise at dawn tomorrow. Sleep well.'

She knew exactly why he left her so suddenly, and, engulfed in shame and guilt, she buried her face in the pillows as he left the room.

She waited for Charles but he did not come to her. Her body ached for him and she could hardly restrain herself from rushing to his room in abject need. But she did not. She did not for a moment doubt his love for her. They shared a white-hot passion that would be difficult to quench, she knew, or thought she knew. She confused carnal need with love.

'Oh, my darling, beautiful man, come to me, I need you so much,' she whispered, but her arms remained empty, her body unfulfilled.

Chapter

19

CELESTINE usually missed her father when they were apart, but this week she hardly thought of him at all. She felt as if she were in a dream: all her senses heightened; her emotions very near the surface. As the atmosphere in Avoca House was friendly and warm, this was not a problem. Her dear Uncle Barth was continuously thoughtful and kind; her Auntie May was gentle and loving. Little Barth clung to her skirts or sat in her lap, lending her, she knew, the sweet attraction of the 'Madonna'. She would smile up at Charles over the young boy's golden curls, then press her nephew's cheek, always aware of Charles' enamoured glance.

The days were golden. It was an Indian summer. Amber and bronze, the leaves drifted over their feet as they wandered about the estate under the cool sun. They could smell the foliage burning in a hundred fields and woods and could see the wisps of grey smoke rising from a hundred fires. The sun hung daily in the pearly sky, a blinding disc, the heat of the rays deflected by the September breezes. And everywhere, the pearly mist rose and fell like a veil over the brilliant gold of autumn.

And the days passed slowly. Neill left on the Monday morning early. The men at Avoca House were up with the dawn, the women lay a-bed late. Quite shockingly, so it seemed to Ellen, who adored the foreign luxury of sipping an early morning cup of tea in bed and then rising, at her own leisurely pace, to dress with the help of Brindsley and saunter downstairs to find fires blazing in the grates and everything tidied, polished and taken care of in her absence.

They spent their days in a desultory fashion, pottering and

gossiping, and she was not sure she could ever get used to it. She liked a purposeful energetic day and she quite enjoyed being tired at tea-time. Lying about all day made her feel guilty.

Quite a lot of time was taken up with wardrobe. May changed from *negligée* to morning-gown; riding-habit to luncheon dress; tea-gown to *robe-de-chambre* to full dinner-dress. She spent a lot of time, too, ringing bells for servants to supply her needs and issuing occasional instructions to her housekeeper, Mrs Moncrief; all of which Ellen would have preferred to do herself, without bothering the servants. She thought ruefully that she would be a dreadful failure as the lady of the manor. The servants would sit around all day while she rushed about performing menial tasks she should have left to them! The trouble was that she enjoyed the menial tasks at home and loved to join Mamie and Miffy in their chores about the house. Not the excessively difficult ones, like cleaning the grate or tending the fires, but the cooking, the polishing and the general running of the home which seemed to Ellen a useful and absorbing occupation.

May moved from room to room languidly, trailing her sensuous perfume behind her and hardly seeming to expend any effort at all, except when she was in the saddle. She was good-humoured, if edgy, and Ellen did not at all like the tension visible between her and Barth. She wondered if May's lack of energy had anything to do with activity in bed at night; and if her own desire to be worn out by tea-time had anything to do with her own lack of it. She stared at her sister's classic profile and wondered if she 'did that' with both Barth and Charles, and how she managed it; and if she did not, and Barth was boycotted, then, surely, he minded dreadfully? She castigated herself for such thoughts, but they would creep into her mind, though she tried hard to get rid of them. It was all so very puzzling.

Nevertheless, it was divine to be at Avoca House, to suspend worry, to forget about her own problems and just indulge herself.

Breffni impinged on her thoughts constantly, but, obeying May and Barth's instructions she ruthlessly plucked all such worry out of her mind and kept remembering that her son would probably be too late in joining up to see any action.

Clothilde wandered about the estate, a book in her hands.

154

She played with Lelia, and their voices were heard echoing through the house and gardens as they searched for, or laughingly found, each other. She played croquet with Celestine, when Lelia and Little Barth were in the schoolroom with their governess, Miss Bellew, a sharp-faced spinster from Bath, whom the children loved and attended to. In the evening, after dinner, Celestine played the piano and sang, and Clothilde entertained on the harp.

A lot of the time Clothilde preferred to be alone, staring at the horizon, dreaming dreams of something out of reach. And sometimes, as she wandered, the thought of Darragh Quinn thrust itself, unwanted, into her mind, disturbing its smooth waters and creating ripples that spread outward, ever outward, shattering her tranquillity and leaving her cross.

One day May came upon her sitting on the stone balustrade, gazing abstractedly at the mountains, purple, olive and brown in the distance. She was so still that May became worried. She also feared the girl might become chilled, sitting on the stone in her light dress. May fetched a cashmere shawl and brought it to her, laying it over her shoulders.

'What is it, Clo dearest?' May asked gently, and, to her dismay, the girl burst into tears and within minutes had left a large patch of damp on the shoulder of May's pale rose voile tea-gown.

May held her close until the storm was over and Clothilde had calmed down a little.

'I want to be a nun, Auntie May.' Then, as she saw May's lip tremble, she added, 'Oh don't laugh, please. Please, don't. I want to so much and Papa says I cannot and must marry Owen Mulcahy.'

May patted the girl's shoulder and prayed for the right words. 'You know, Clothilde, I decided to be a nun when I was sixteen and . . .'

Clothilde looked at her aunt levelly. 'Unlike you, Aunt, I did not change my mind or grow out of it. I am, have you forgotten, twenty years old.'

May sighed. They had not been the correct words, despite her prayer.

'Well, I don't know what to say, except that Owen Mulcahy is not such a terrible fate after all.' She thought how hypocritical she was being. Owen was exactly like Barth. Oh, he was

155

handsomer, it was true, but his very niceness rendered him boring. And here she was, recommending her own fate to her niece.

'And by the way,' she added, 'he is coming to dinner tonight. I want you to know it was arranged a while ago.'

Clothilde shook her head impatiently. 'That does not matter at all. Owen is not really important, Aunt.' So much for poor Owen, May reflected. 'Owen is a dear and I like him enormously. It's just that I do not want to marry at all,' she said with finality.

'Perhaps you are afraid?' May asked gently and Clothilde was startled.

'Why on earth should I be afraid?' she asked angrily, her face flushed.

May shrugged. 'Oh, I don't know. Many girls are. Then they find out what fun it can be.'

Clothilde thought of her mother and father. 'Fun!' she said derisively. 'Fun!'

'Yes, fun, my dear. Marriage can be quite wonderful,' and, as she said this, she realized she meant every word and specifically about her and Barth.

'Well, I don't want that kind of fun,' Clothilde said firmly. 'There is, Aunt, within me, an ardent desire to give myself to God. A feeling that it is for me the only way to fulfil my life. Do you understand?'

There was a desperate note in her voice. May nodded. 'Yes, my dear. You are so like Neill. He is, after all, your twin. Please don't be annoyed with me for asking, I'm just curious, but are you sure your vocation is not an echo of your brother's? That you have not been influenced by him? He is a powerful person and I believe his vocation is genuine . . .'

She could have bitten her tongue off as the words came out, but Clothilde merely shook her head impatiently.

'Yes. I see. No, Neill has not influenced me.'

'I did not mean that he actually urged you to become a nun, Clothilde. I simply meant his *attitude* might have had a bearing on . . .'

But Clothilde interrupted. She's so feverish, May thought, so tense.

'Well, the problem is that my father will not listen. Will not even hear. And to argue with him or reason with him is useless.'

156

Her voice rose, 'The only way I might get his permission is if I persuade him it is the last thing I want.' She threw despairing hands in the air and May realized that she had never seen her niece in such a state before. She was usually such a calm girl. May had been aware of a fire that smouldered beneath Clothilde's surface. Now she realized just how much passion lay in the heart of the seemingly serene girl. Clothilde turned to her now, eyes flashing

'Oh I cannot bear it, Aunt. He bends us to his will. He is anxious to form an alliance with the Mulcahy clan. As you know, they are wine merchants and eventually the business will be Owen's as the only child. Even I can see how mutually beneficial that would be.'

She was angry and resentful, but she pulled herself together and straightened her back and May could not but admire her.

'I'm sorry, dearest Aunt, to bore you so,' she said.

'You are not boring me, Clothilde, you know you are not. I feel useless though, unable to help you. And I would have liked to so much. Give yourself time. And think on what I said about fear. Your father has had a large influence on his family and I, for one, would not be surprised if his example had made his daughters a little nervous of men. However, I have told your mother I will find a husband for Celestine . . .'

Clothilde acted without thinking. She gave a little laugh and waved her hand towards the trees across the lawn from whose emerald shadows Celestine and Charles had emerged.

'You will not have to look far,' she said before she could stop herself. She felt her aunt's hand tighten on her shoulder and she looked up to see that May's face had suddenly lost its colour, and she looked alarmingly as if she was going to faint.

Clothilde was heartbroken that the words were spoken and that there was no way to retrieve them.

'Oh, Aunt, I thought you knew. I thought everyone could see . . .' she stammered.

Both women looked towards the two figures below them. There was a communion that surrounded them, visible even from this distance. There was tenderness in the way he stooped towards her and love in the way she reached out to him. It hung in the very air that encompassed them.

'Is he then so very unsuitable? Papa will never allow . . .' gauche as a servant caught in an unseemly act, Clothilde's voice

157

trailed on but her aunt did not answer. It was as if Clothilde was alone on the terrace. Pale, frozen-faced, shocked, May stood as if turned to stone.

Celestine and Charles were laughing. He had not dared to touch her. He was terrified that she would run away, that he would lose her. Besides there was no need to rush. He felt none of his usual impatience to get her into bed, to conquer her. He had never wooed anyone before and now he found it breath-takingly exciting. There was a whole arsenal of erotic little moves to be employed. Tiny touches, looks that were expressive, the play of emotions hitherto unexplored until now, went to the head like wine.

He had pursued many women; hunted them; then taken the victor's spoils. But it did not matter too much if they escaped, took flight and ran away from him and his passion. Now it was of the utmost importance that he succeed, and he was sensitive to her every mood and thought. Every time their fingers met and she blushed, his heart stood still. Every time she appeared in the doorway or he saw her sitting in a window or leaning over Little Barth or arm-in-arm with her sister, his heart raced and he thought he would suffocate.

He had not gone to May since the Connollys' arrival. It had not crossed his mind to do so. He was too totally engrossed in his love, in Celestine. It was as if everything before their coming to Avoca House was unreal, another life.

He did not mean to be cruel. It was simply that May had no substance for him now, no reality, as, indeed, no one else had either. People were insubstantial shadows that moved about his beloved and himself. All the other women in his life, as well as his hostess, had become shades, unreal and of no consequence. The only reality for him was Celestine.

They had gathered conkers in the woods that afternoon, prising the heavy casings off the chestnuts.

'They are the colour of your eyes,' he said, and they sat together on a moss-covered log in the cold shadow of the stooping trees.

Her wide eyes were flecked with golden lights and she looked at him so trustingly that he wanted to slay dragons for her. The tangle of her dark chestnut hair haloed her face. He had begged her to cut a tendril, which, after his impassioned pleas, she had snipped off and he kept it now in a pouch under his tunic, for all the world like Ellen and her scapulars.

Reality to him was Celestine's moods. The sunshine of her smile lit up his day. The anxious crease between her brows when she spoke of the war was the most important problem he had to solve. The fear in her eyes worried him, and how he could take away her anxiety and allay her fears became his preoccupation.

He explained that he was a professional soldier and nothing could happen to him.

I'm not one of your Johnnie-come-latelys that don't know one end of a gun from the other,' he said and saw, to his horror, a huge tear, crystal-bright, lying on the soft curve of her cheek and another forming in her eye and castigated himself for a monster and a fool when she told him her little brother was just such a Johnnie-come-lately and had only now gone to England to train. He wiped away the tears and smiled a consoling smile at her, feeling her pain and anxiety.

'The war will be over by Christmas, so you've nothing to worry about. Dashed if I want to miss out, but I may not make it back if this leg don't hurry and become A.1.'

'Don't. Don't say that, please. I couldn't bear it if you . . .'

'If I what?'

She became covered in confusion and he loved her thus. It made him feel incredibly strong and masculine where before he had hated such feminine traits and coyness.

'I hoped . . . I wished you could stay here for some little time more. I'm going to be here for a couple of months and I . . . I . . .' She lowered her head, tearing at her handkerchief. He tilted her face. The sun shone through the leaves, speckling her countenance with golden shadows.

'I love you,' he said.

She drew in a sharp breath and placed her hand over her heart to stop it racing. She said nothing. In her eyes, looking into his, he saw her need of him and her acceptance of him clearly mirrored. She felt what he felt; she loved him as he loved her. His apprehension vanished. He felt an immense gratitude flood his being.

He bent his head and kissed her. She had never been kissed before by a man, he could tell. Her lips were tremulous beneath his and he brushed them gently, fearful of startling her. Her eyes were wide open when he moved his face from hers, and looking

159

at him for a moment, she leaned towards him and pressed her mouth to his. She let herself slip into his embrace, become part of it, her arms winding themselves around his neck. He gently disengaged himself. He had no intention of allowing his passions a free rein. This girl was too precious and had to be treated with great care and respect.

He saw she was trembling. He kissed her forehead in a gesture of ineffable tenderness.

'I will speak to your father,' he said, and for the first time a cloud appeared on the horizon. Her Papa. What would he say? Then instantly she consoled herself. He loved her. When had he ever refused her anything? No, of course it would be all right.

They came out of the wood laughing. He kissed her cheek and her heart gave a joyous leap within her. Looking towards the house, she saw her Aunt May on the terrace. She waved to her and ran up to the house.

Chapter

20

STOCK still May waited for Celestine to cross the lawn. Clothilde watched her curiously, but May revealed nothing of her inner turmoil. It seemed to May as if everything in nature was, for a moment, suspended: Celestine's white figure in flight across the green grass; the shadows of the trees behind her; the diamond cascades shooting from the fountain, veiling Celestine as she ran behind it; Charles' figure striding after her, his shoulders straight; the sun glinting on his shining leather boots; and the tall, thin girl beside her in the shade on the terrace, shading her face with her hand, leaning towards her as if to help.

In a second, she had seen it all; what everyone else must have known and, she thought, Barth must have been aware of since their arrival — the terrible, awful fact that Charles and Celestine were in love. She stifled the cry of agony that almost escaped her lips. She supported her weakening knees by leaning heavily on the pedestal bearing its urn of geraniums. It hid her a little from Clothilde. She could not bear her niece to see the pain writ large, she knew, across her face.

Celestine and Charles. Charles and Celestine. That explained his absence from her bed the last few nights. She had thought it had been out of discretion, that Ellen's presence in the house had inhibited him. But no. It had been because he had fallen in love with her niece. She had not worried overmuch about his apparent lack of attention, but now she realized that it was because his attention was otherwise occupied. What a fool she had been. What an idiot.

The girl ran across the lawn, the fine material of her dress clinging to her slim body, her hat in her hand, her hair escaping its ribboned bondage. May knew she would hold that picture in her head forever. She had her hands full of conkers, May saw, and, as she ran, she dropped some of them. There was an eager radiant smile on her face, and, for a sudden overwhelming moment of blind rage, May wanted to destroy that trusting, innocent face, to damage it beyond repair.

But the moment passed. Her breeding, her training, came to her rescue. No one must ever guess the extent of her pain, or see that she was frightened by the power of the emotion.

Celestine ran up to her aunt, impulsively hugged her; then, surprised at the lack of response, she stood a little back to survey her hostess.

'Auntie May, are you all right?' she asked, looking puzzled.

'I'm perfectly well.' May knew she sounded strange, but it was the best she could do. 'You run along, dearest child, with your sister. I want to speak to Captain Cavendish for a moment.'

Charles had reached the terrace. His face flushed as it suddenly dawned on him the awkward situation he was in.

'Charles is . . . he is . . .' Celestine stammered to a halt; then, embarrassed, she ran to her sister and caught her arm.

'Come on, Clo,' she cried, dragging Clothilde away; and, looking over her shoulder at the others, she said, 'I'll see you all later. At tea?'

It was a question. May nodded and the two white-clad girls disappeared around the corner of the house in the general direction of the orchard.

'They'll pick some apples and swing,' May said casually to Charles. 'I used to do that when I was their age.'

'I remember,' he said; his voice was sad. He looked at her, noticing for the first time the lines at her eyes and throat. She gestured and he followed her to her room. She did not speak as she mounted the wide stairs; and Barth, emerging from the study, quickly returned from whence he had come without being seen. Sometimes he felt like a thief in his own house and he resented it.

She took Charles to her drawing-room, just off her bedroom. The room always welcomed her. But not this time, not today. She had chosen every vase, every painting, each chair and each piece with care and love, and never before had she entered the primrose apartment without a sigh of relief. Now, however, her heart was heavy and her mouth was dry.

She went and sat on the chaise without speaking. She laid her head on the yellow damask and felt her temples throb. Charles stood at the window watching the leaves fall. There was a long heavy silence between them.

At last, May said, 'I think you had better tell me what's going on, Charles.'

'I never meant it to happen, May,' he said sadly. 'It was not planned. It just . . . we fell in love. As soon as I set eyes on her, I . . .'

'I see.'

So, you were not really in love with me. She wanted to ask him, badger him to confess to her. Pick at the wound. What more was there to say? But she could not let it go so easily. Her heart, her life was cut, shredded. No. Yet what more could he say? She rose and went to him where he stood at the window. He had his back to her and she put her arms around him, pressing her body to his. She lifted her hand and touched his ear, then stood on tiptoe and kissed his neck. He turned swiftly and she clung to him as he pivoted. She nearly lost her balance but she clove to him, kissing his face, covering his cheeks and lips with a thousand kisses. Very firmly, he thrust her away.

'No, May. Please. It is over,' he said.

She looked at him sadly. She was too clever to plead, to beg, to humiliate herself, though she longed to. In any event, she did not think it would work. She had done as much as she could without demeaning herself. Better he should remember her with her dignity intact.

'Very well,' she whispered and all her energy left her, and she went and sat down abruptly. 'Now leave me, please.'

There were tears in her voice but he did not hear. Like a child released from class on a summer day, he escaped from the pale yellow room.

May turned her face into the cushion, the hot tears falling down her cheeks. She cried for a while; then reminded herself that at her age she could not afford the devastation that tears would wreak on her beauty. So she stopped, and stared at a shaft of sunlight that fell on the silk carpet, an occasional sob shaking her body. She gazed at the carpet and thought of all the years to be lived without Charles, to be endured alone. No: with Barth. There was always Barth.

163

Then she remembered Ellen's words. Garreth would never allow Celestine to marry. He wanted her kept at home for ever. She blinked. Perhaps there was hope after all. If Garreth refused permission, the girl could not marry, at least not until she was twenty-one. Four years. And men like Charles Cavendish were notoriously fickle in love. It would be a very long time for him to have to wait for his virginal bride, a very long time. What had happened to her could happen to her niece. She could be sent away. May frowned. A tiny crease, like an exclamation mark appeared on her smooth white forehead. She could go, perhaps, to Nellie in Kerry. May would tell Garreth it would be the best thing for a besotted young girl.

All was not lost. She narrowed her eyes in thought. Garreth was not likely to change his mind. He was a very stubborn man. Any idiot could see how he adored Celestine, and if he had said she was not to marry, then he would not allow it. In a tussle of wills, he would win hands down over Charles Cavendish any day. Besides, he held all the cards. Celestine was under age and he was her father. She sighed, a long shuddering sigh; then she threw her drenched handkerchief into the basket for soiled linen and went to her dressing-table. She stared at her silver-backed monogrammed brushes, her tortoise-shell comb, her cut-glass bottles of scent and the bowl of large yellow and white daisies. She raised her eyes fearfully to her mirror. She did not know what to expect.

The face staring back at her was quite perfect. She examined her skin for flaws. There were none. The eyes, clear cornflower-blue, new-washed by the tears, the perfect little pouty mouth, the curves of her brows and the fineness of her nose, all were clearly revealed in the reflection she saw before her. She looked more closely. There were some fine lines around the eyes, to be sure. But the face was as lovely as it had been when she was Celestine's age. She smiled, relieved.

She would get Charles back — given time; given Garreth's wishes. Yes, she smiled again, all was not lost. She would get Charles Cavendish back eventually. She would have to, for without him she would surely die.

Chapter

21

ELLEN was wrong. Avoca House and its staff needed constant vigilance. May disguised her efforts and an onlooker could be forgiven for thinking that she did little to effect the efficiency with which the house was run. Latterly, however, things had been allowed to slip. May's preoccupation with her lover had not blinded her to the fact that tea was sometimes late and that the china sometimes showed faint stains of tannin. May had said nothing. She had been too busy. Now she said nothing because she felt totally drained of life. She had to keep holding onto the hope she had felt when she had looked into her mirror.

It was difficult when she was with Charles and Celestine. They were a source of agonizing pain when she was in their company, as perforce she had to be. She watched Celestine, viewing her as if she had never seen her before. The girl totally lacked artifice and was pretty in a way she, May, had never been: innocent, trusting. May had always been knowing and sexually aware, and for all her beauty she knew she could never compete with the girl's youth and insouciance. She was so sweet, May thought irritably; you could not dislike her. She aimed to please in a straightforward manner; she was without guile. She was totally unaware of the situation. Yet why should she know? How could she guess the true state of affairs for which nothing in her protected life had prepared her?

May sat at tea-time, feeling nothing, her gestures mechanical, her face empty. Charles passed the cups and brought them for refills. He seemed a little subdued. But his exuberance kept breaking through. He was in love, and his head was full of his beloved. He plied her with cakes and biscuits; he hovered over her like a guardian angel. And every so often, she smiled at him and he returned that smile with a look so sweet, so tender that May, catching it, felt her heart pierced by unbearable pain.

'Aunt May, are you all right? You look so pale.' Celestine rushed across the room and sank at her aunt's feet, her face full of concern. 'Dearest Aunt, are you all right? Or, are we being too much for you? Oh, I've been so selfish, thinking only of my happiness, not of you.'

May protested feebly. She thought she was dying. Certainly she was in some kind of hell. She felt she had a fever. She shook her head, wishing this hour was over, aching to escape, unable to move lest something should happen that she could turn to her advantage.

'No, no, Celestine, I am a little faint, that is all. I am tired, but it is not your fault. Oh how could you think so? It's just that . . .' To her horror, she found that she was perilously close to tears. Her lip trembled and a sob rose in her throat.

Barth sprang to her rescue. 'Come, come, by dear. You must go to your room. Rest a little. You have been doing too much of late.'

There was no irony in his voice, she noted. He put his arm around her shoulder and she leaned against him, suddenly dependent on his large strength.

Looking at Ellen, he said, 'She does more than you think, Ellen. Dear wife.' He touched the soft curls over her ear and Ellen reddened, nonplussed that he seemed to have read her mind. But Barth was not trying to devine anyone's thoughts but his wife's.

'I'll go with Mama,' Lelia said, and Barth looked at May enquiringly.

She nodded. 'I would like that, Lelia,' she said, and the three of them left the room.

Behind them, conversation resumed.

'Owen is coming tonight, Clo,' Celestine said. 'Oh please try to be nice to him.'

Clothilde frowned and looked gloomy, and Charles, who had watched May leave with slight irritation, said, 'Why shouldn't she?'

Celestine turned to him a face animated and full of laughter.

'Well, Clo, wants to be a nun and Papa won't let her. He wants her to marry Owen and . . . and . . . it's all a tangle.'

Charles looked at Clothilde as if she had come from another planet, and Clothilde stood up suddenly.

'How dare you, Celestine. Oh, how dare you. Discussing my feelings like that, in front of strangers.' She glared at Charles; stamped her foot. 'How dare you,' she repeated and left the room.

All Ellen's calm left her. The old familiar flutter in her chest made her breathless and she found she could hardly breathe.

Celestine saw her mother's distress. 'Here's a fine how-de-do,' she said, 'just when we were all so happy.' She went to her mother now, as she had gone to her aunt. 'It's all my fault, dearest Mama,' she said ruefully. 'Forgive me.'

Both Charles and Ellen knew that she was far more to blame for the disturbances that had broken out than she knew.

'No, dearest. It is no one's fault.'

'Mrs Connolly, I know this is not the time, but I am anxious. You see, I think Celestine spoke hastily in front of me because she thinks of me . . . or rather, I hope she does . . . what I mean is, I have become family, sort of.' Seeing Mrs Connolly's puzzled face, he continued. 'I want to talk to Mr Connolly about Celestine. Ask for her hand . . .'

Ellen rose, suddenly strong, and looked at Charles Cavendish squarely.

'You are right, Colonel. This is not the time. Now, if you will excuse me?'

'But I may speak to Mr Connolly, may I not? I'm sure he'll understand.'

'I would not count on it at all, Colonel.' Ellen shook her head and her grey curls jiggled. 'Oh no. I would not count on it at all,' she repeated, and swept out of the room.

When she had gone, Charles looked at Celestine, perplexed. 'What on earth does she mean?'

Celestine laughed. She was too happy, too excited to let anything disturb her.

'Dearest, dearest Charles. My father is supposed to be a tyrant.' He looked at her puzzled, but she smiled. 'Sometimes . . . no, mostly, he lays down the law pretty heavily with Mama and the rest of the family. But I have been able to get him to do exactly what I wanted ever since I was a baby.' She laughed again and tossed her head. 'You see? He has never in my whole life refused me anything. Ever,' she added triumphantly. 'Now,

167

kiss me. Kiss me, do. I have only just learned how beautiful it is to kiss a man.'

Charles put his arms around her and gently pressed his mouth to her's. Her lips were soft beneath his, yielding to the sweet pressure. The sensation left him weak and he was glad enough of the interruption when the maid knocked and entered to clear the tea-things. Celestine leapt away from him guiltily.

He was again surprised at his own reaction, for up to now, kissing had been a mere preliminary to bedding a girl. He knew that, for the first time in his life, he wanted to go by the book, obey all the rules, do the socially accepted thing; for he wanted this girl at his side forever. He wanted her to be his friend as well as his lover, his companion in all that was good and bad in life, and the mother of his children. Everything that had happened in the past seemed trivial and unimportant. Now, drawing her arm through his, he led her onto the terrace and told her all that was in his heart.

Chapter

22

THE dinner party that night was plagued by a very unsettled atmosphere. Owen Mulcahy and his parents, unaware of the tensions that rippled through the candle-lit room, thought merely that May was not her usual sparkling self and had probably caught an autumnal chill. She was notorious for drifting about in georgettes and silks, chiffons and laces, even in the midst of winter, and although Avoca House had the new-fangled heating and a fire in every room, still the breezes were treacherous and Mrs Mulcahy felt May had only herself to blame if she had caught a cold.

Barth was his usual genial self; the charming colonel was obviously smitten by the youngest Connolly girl; and Ellen was as nice and good a listener as usual.

Emer and Brendan Mulcahy were a prosperous comfortable pair who adored their only son and heir. Emer was disliked by the male sex in the society they had moved in because she was outspoken, had brains, and did not try to hide the fact. They were a devoted couple; both short and tubby, they were constantly amazed at the good looks of their tall straight son. Owen was not as handsome as the Captain but he was a delightful young man. His features were regular, his face freckled and good-humoured. He genuinely liked people, found excuses for their petty follies, and forgave easily. He was, and always had been, in love with Clothilde. In that alone he was obtuse. It never dawned on him that she simply did not love him. He decided that her desire to become a nun was a passing phase. He was serene in the certainty that eventually Clothilde would marry him and settle down. He loved her severe good

169

looks, her seriousness, the passion that smouldered beneath her cool surface. He thought Celestine's vitality and animation, her ready laughter, tiring, and though he admired her prettiness he did not think she could hold a candle to his darling Clo. He smiled at her now in the candle-glow, thinking how lovely she looked, but she did not meet his eyes.

'The Germans started buying gold a couple of years ago,' Brendan Mulcahy was saying, twirling the stem of his glass between his thumb and forefinger. 'I said then there'd be a war.' He had protruding eyes and one of them worked independently of the other so you were never quite sure where he was looking. 'She called in her debts and built up the strongest army in the world.'

Ellen gasped and Barth coughed and tried to catch the roaming eye.

'Oh, the British Army'll take some beating,' he said, laying a protective hand on Ellen's arm. 'It will be over by Christmas.'

'Brendan doesn't think so, do you, dear?'

Brendan looked with gratitude upon his wife. She could always be relied upon to give him the right cue.

'No, dear, as you say, I do not. It's going to be a long hard struggle from what I hear. And if the Germans do win, it would be no bad thing for us.' He smiled and nodded his head. 'England weakened would be in Ireland's interest.' The Mulcahys held Nationalist views. Both of them were staunch advocates of Home Rule. A lot of the county society consequently found them embarrassing and wished that they would not be so outspoken and would keep their radical views to themselves.

Ellen was by now in a state. Barth could feel her arm tremble beneath his hand.

'Really, Brendan, I do not think that this is a fit subject to discuss at the dinner table,' he said, with some severity for him.

Brendan looked surprised. 'Why ever not?'

God damn him! Barth tried to keep his temper.

'Because there are ladies present,' he said.

Emer laughed. It was a high cackling hoot that May thought, inconsequentially, might drive poor Clothilde mad if she had to live in the Mulcahy mansion in Wexford. Clothilde, however, did not seem to notice it. She was looking anxiously at her mother.

170

We would have all been better if we had never got up this morning, but had stayed in bed and avoided this terrible day, May thought. She nearly broke the stem of her glass as she caught sight of Charles at the other end of the table, touching Celestine's hand and looking at her with an expression of such desire and love that May could hardly contain the hot surge of anger that rose within her.

'What on earth difference does that make?' Emer was saying. 'I should hope we women are modern women and have brains enough to understand what tragic folly you men commit when you go to war. You kill and maim in the name of, what? Freedom? Ideals? Do you think there is a mother in the world who would willingly send her son into battle as their fathers do?' she snorted, and Barth rose from his seat. Ellen had uttered a bleak moan.

'Emer, please. Breffni Connolly has just joined up. He has gone to England. Ellen . . . oh dear . . . are you all right?' He went to the sideboard and poured her some brandy.

Ellen pulled herself together, and sat fully erect.

'I'm all right,' she said with dignity.

Barth returned. 'Here, drink this. It will help.'

'Really, Barth,' Ellen spoke calmly, 'I am perfectly all right.' But everyone could see that she was keeping a very tight rein upon herself and her feelings.

Emer looked across the table in consternation. 'Oh Ellen, I didn't know. I didn't know. Someone should have stopped me.'

Barth forbore to respond.

Emer was a kind woman, and normally her conversation would have been stimulating. But now the harm had been done; the dinner party spoiled. However, despite Ellen's distress and May's despair, the company recovered its spirits over coffee in the drawing-room. Emer, Celestine, Charles and Brendan played bridge, and Owen coaxed Clothilde into the library, where to her consternation he dropped on his knees in front of her.

'Will you marry me, Clo? Please tell me you will. I need you so much.'

Clothilde looked at the anxious face before her. The library was dimly lit, the reflections of the flames from the fire shifting in patterns of light across the ceiling. She felt ill at ease, and where normally she would have told Owen to get up and not be

171

so silly, now she hesitated. She had seen so much pain caused by love that day and she did not want to be the cause of any more grief. Yet she could not tell him what he wanted so much to hear. There was silence in the room. Owen held his breath. He was still on his knees before her.

She repressed a desire to giggle, then said in her usual brisk way, 'Oh, get up, Owen, do. You look a bit silly like that.' She saw the disappointment in his face, like a little boy let down, and she put out her hand and touched his arm. 'Oh, I do not mean to be unkind,' she said contritely. 'But the answer is no. You know that, Owen. It is and always will be no.' She shrugged. 'I cannot help it, Owen, you know that. You've always known that I want to take the veil.'

He knew that what she said was true, but he also knew that her all-powerful father was not at all in favour of the idea. He was well aware that Garreth Connolly liked him, that his suit was acceptable to Clothilde's father not least because of the business the Mulcahys were in. Their wine import and export business was a little further down the Liffey from Connolly's. It would be an ideal alliance; both parties stood to gain a lot. It would allow Garreth to diversify and expand and the same applied to the Mulcahys.

Owen was ambitious. He saw himself eventually as head of the 'whole shebang', as his father phrased it. It was a goal he very much wanted to reach. And it was not so outrageous. Neill and Breffni were neither of them interested in their father's business. They dutifully went to work with Garreth every day, Owen knew, but they were not interested. Whearas he was; immensely interested.

He loved Clothilde with all his heart. He always had. But there was so much more to life than marriage and children. They were a woman's whole world, but a man's existence had many diverse compartments, and business was one of them. It seemed to him a miracle that the woman he loved and his business goal were encompassed in the same family and the head of that family was *au fait* with his ambition, and approved.

Only Clothilde stood in his way. She was being very difficult about the whole thing. It was, in Owen's estimation, a ridiculous ambition to want to become a nun. A priest he could understand, but a nun! He often had to restrain himself at moments like these from being rude about it, and telling

172

Clothilde that it was she who was silly, not he. However, that would not get him anywhere and might put her right off him. He had to keep the avenue open and hope that persistence and her father's will would win the day.

When they were married it would be different. He would be her husband then, and would have a say in how she behaved and thought. A wife's duty was to obey her husband, and he did not doubt Clothilde would make an excellent wife. If she became a nun, God forbid, she would have to take a vow of obedience, along with others of poverty and chastity. He would certainly hope that he could keep his wife in comfort. He believed himself a 'modern' man and he knew he would do his best not to be too demanding in the bedroom, but keep in mind her gentle susceptibilities when seeking his marriage rights. He would, however, be quite adamant about obedience. Any wife of his must bow to his superior judgement and dictates.

He stood up now, a little angry with her but magnanimously prepared to forgive her.

She saw the hurt look on his face and her heart went out to him. 'Oh, Owen, sit down. You look like a child. I don't mean to be rude to you, really I don't. But you see I really do not want to marry. Not you. Not anyone. She thought for a moment of a huge man, a rough man, in a tweed jacket; then, exasperated with herself, she said, 'I don't like men.'

Owen felt renewed hope. This he understood. 'All girls are like that,' he said, 'at first. But you'll change.'

'No, Owen. Your mother is right. We are not the feather-brained creatures you men like to make us out to be.'

'I know you're not, Clothilde. ' He looked shocked. 'You are a very intelligent girl. My mother is clever too, no doubt about that. But you need a man's guiding hand, to protect you, to look after you. Just give me the chance. There is no need for you to be afraid of marriage. You'll find out it is not so bad.'

There it was again. It was precisely what her Aunt May had said. Clothilde sighed. He did not understand. He never would. Explaining was a waste of breath.

And then the thought struck her. Perhaps *she* did not understand. Perhaps Aunt May and Owen were right. Perhaps she was afraid of life. She shuddered. Then she heard Emer calling her son.

'Come, Owen,' she said. 'Your mother is calling you. They must be going home.'

The uneasy evening had come to an end. The Mulcahys piled into their car and Brendan and Emer fell into a discussion about the undercurrents at Avoca House and hazarded guesses, far off the mark, about their causes; while Owen tried to work out how Clothilde could be persuaded to give up her silly female idea of becoming a nun and marry him.

In the corridor outside their rooms, Charles kissed Celestine's cheek and hand and said farewell until the morning. He went to his door and, turning, saw her still looking after him. He hurried back to her and kissed her once more, and then again, because they could not bear to part. Then Celestine and Clothilde sat with their mother until she fell into a fitful sleep.

Then they went to the room they shared and were helped out of their clothes by Brindsley who had finished her duties with Lady Gorman. They brushed their hair, one hundred strokes, and curled up in bed having called goodnight to each other. Both girls were exhausted and fell asleep almost at once, each dreaming a different dream.

Charles climbed into his own bed and taking the handkerchief he had purloined from his beloved in the woods that day he placed it against his lips and breathed in her perfume until he, too, fell asleep.

Barth waited, and when the sounds of the house had died down he opened the connecting door, went through the dressing-rooms and after tapping gently went into May's bedroom. She sat up in bed, her lace and satin negligée framing her pale beauty. For a moment Barth felt cold with fear. It was so fragile, the framework of the whole situation. It could collapse at any moment. It could fall about their ears. But May looked at him standing there, tubby in his pyjamas, balding and paunchy, the expression on his face one of such hopeless pleading that a sob caught in her throat and she opened her arms to him. The dam burst and all the overwhelming emotion bottled up all day, all the tension that had marred the evening, gave way to a flood of tears. He wrapped his arms around her, in gratitude and love, cradling her to him as if she were Lelia, and pressing his lips to her hair, he murmured, 'There, there, my love. There, there. It's all right now.'

174

Chapter

23

NEILL had gone into the brewery that Monday, checked the sacks of malt and silos of grain, and checked the winch that took the sacks to the top of the brewery. He had issued necessary commands, had told the men, 'Run off your wort'; 'Collect the sweet wort'; 'Add aroma hops'; 'Can you clear out the trub?'; and inevitably, 'Make sure the beers are roused'. All the time he was issuing his commands he was aware of the men's anger. They did not show it in gesture or glance. If anything, they worked harder than usual. But it was there all the time, just under the surface. An indefinable simmering.

He knew they were angry about John Joe Reilly. John Joe was popular. He was a good worker. He had a nice wife and a sick child. It galled the men that he had been sacked without just cause. It outraged their sense of justice. And it frightened them.

Neill did what he could to placate them, but they gave him no real chance. He could not blame them. Each time he tried to say something he found himself up against the stone wall of their united front; workers against the boss.

And all the time O'Brien stirred it up. The man, Neill decided, was a toad.

Neill lunched that day on a plate of cold cuts in 'The Golden Harp' with Kerry for company.

'It's a bad thing, Kerry, when I feel ashamed in front of my own workers,' he said.

'Then do something about it, Neill. Oh I know that as long as your father holds the reins you are pretty helpless. But from what I hear he's talkin' all the time of leavin' and lettin' you run

175

the brewery. Wouldn't it be grand now, an' you could change the whole emphasis of the management?'

It was the second time someone had suggested that to him. He knew it would not be easy, but once his father let some of the authority slip from him it would not be too difficult for Neill to make changes. It would have to be slow, but at least it would be sure. Darragh Quinn and he were always discussing the idea of a kind of co-operative between management and workers where the men would receive a bonus if productivity increased. Darragh was terribly against slave labour, as he called it.

'The men are angry over John Joe,' he said to Kerry.

'Well an' I meant to talk to you or Mrs Connolly about that,' Kerry said. She put her freckled hand over his. 'John Joe is sayin' terrible things about yer father, Neill. We're frightened he'll get into trouble. The man is half outa his mind with worry.'

'Oh Kerry, he has every right to be. It's awful what my father has done to him. I don't blame him in the least.'

He saw Kerry shiver. Her eyes gleamed in the gloom of the pub. Sepia light left her face half shadowed. He could see the glow of her auburn hair and the white slant of her high cheek bones.

'I'm afraid, Neill. He's talkin' foolish. Tell yer mother to have a word with Mary.'

Neill sighed. 'Much good that'll do. But I will, Kerry, I will.' Then he said, 'You know, Kerry, I feel responsible for John Joe. I'm not, but I feel it. I wish there was something I could do.'

She looked at him fondly. 'You're a good man, Neill Connolly. Would there were more like you,' she said and returned behind the bar.

Before he left for Rathgar that evening, Neill and O'Brien checked everything. When Garreth Connolly was away, the manager was doubly careful, not wanting to draw the boss's rage down on his head.

When each copper vat was checked for temperature and each member of the night staff and the workers had been warned to keep on the alert, Neill went home to the empty house. It seemed twice as big as usual. The absence of voices, the gap left by his mother's absence, all helped to make the rooms larger and stranger than they had ever seemed before.

Mamie welcomed him, glad of his presence to fuss over and

176

make her feel useful. She was lonely without the family around, and was only too happy to have Master Neill to look after.

He ate alone in the dining-room, listening to the silence broken only by the chiming of the grandfather clock in the hall. The echoes as it tolled the quarters seemed unnaturally loud, and he did not remember ever really noticing that you could hear its musical notes in this room at the back of the house.

After dinner, he drank his coffee in the parlour, listening to the peaceful crackling of the fire and the gentle plop as the ashes cascaded down into the grate and pieces of wood fell with a soughing sound. He felt very tranquil there in his solitude. He sighed and gently murmured to himself the words of his favourite poem which was also his favourite prayer: 'St Patrick's Breastplate'.

'This day God gives me strength of high heaven,
Sun and moon shining, flame in my hearth,
Flashing of lightning, wind in its swiftness,
Deeps of the ocean, firmness of earth.
This day God sends me strength as my steersman,
Night to uphold me, wisdom as guide.
Your eyes are watchful, your ears are listening,
Your lips are speaking, friend at my side.
God's way is my way, God's shield is round me,
God's host defends me, saving from ill.
Angels of Heaven drive from me always
All that would harm me; stand by me still.'

' "God's shield is round me",' he repeated. 'Oh Friend at my side, give me courage. Show me the way to do Your will. Why do I feel this burning to be a priest? Is it Your will or my own? Help me not to try to shape You as I wish You to be, but serve you in the way you know is best for me. Oh Lord, Lord, help me.'

A great peace fell upon his spirit and he dozed off.

When he opened his eyes he thought at first it was the striking of the clock that had roused him. Then he heard the knocking and he thought he was dreaming. But the knocking continued, a loud persistent banging on the front door. It must have been going on for some time, for as he tried to rouse himself he heard Mamie coming down the stairs grumbling to herself and interspersing her grumbles with loud shouts at whoever was knocking at the door.

177

'Hold yer whist, for God's sake,' she yelled, then muttered, 'A body doesn't expect to be disturbed in the middle of the night. It expects to be restin' so it does. Every bone in me body is protestin'. Hold on! Hold on!' she yelled again. 'I'm comin'.'

Neill tried to shake himself awake. He took his watch from his waistcoat pocket and glanced at it. Four o'clock in the morning. It was still dark. He rubbed his eyes. He felt chilled and stiff and the fire was dead.

The knocking had stopped. Mamie had opened the front door. He could feel the blast of freezing air it admitted and he shivered. The unreality persisted and he thought he must be dreaming again when he heard Bill O'Brien's voice. O'Brien's voice in the hall, who had never set foot in this house before? Neill shook his head but the voice obtruded, shrill and panic-stricken. He heard Mamie trying to calm O'Brien and there was a jumble of voices mingling senselessly in the hall. Then, as Mamie seemed to be making no headway in calming the manager, she suddenly assumed the firm commanding tone she had used to the Connollys as children.

'Now you sit there an' hold yer whist, Mr O'Brien. Mr Connolly is, if ye remember, in London. I'll get Master Connolly for you directly. But pull yourself together, man. Shoutin' an' carryin' on'll not hurry things up one smidgeon. What are ye? A bawlin' childer or what? An' you fifty if yer a day. Anyone'ld think there's a fire.'

'But there is . . .' O'Brien spluttered.

Mamie had turned to go upstairs, but now she let out a scream that made O'Brien nearly jump out of his skin as Neill emerged from the parlour.

'Holy Mother o' God. Are ye all tryin' te give me a heart-attack this night? I thought ye were in bed, Master Neill. God, ye fair put the heart across me.'

Neill laid a hand on her arm. 'You go back to bed, Mamie. I'll see to whatever is wrong here.' O'Brien was hopping about the hall, almost incoherent. 'O'Brien, what brings you here?' Neill asked as affably as he could. 'You've never had call to be in this house before. Will you have some coffee?'

Neill saw at once that O'Brien was in a terrible state. He was sweating profusely, whether from heat or fear Neill did not know, but guessed correctly that it was the latter. He kept removing his bowler and mopping his brow, then replacing the hat.

178

'There's no time for coffee, Master Neill. It had nothing to do with me. I want you to know that. I was vigilant, as you said. I, that is we, we just don't understand it.'

'What, man? What are you talking about? For heaven's sake calm yourself and tell me.'

'The brewery, Master Neill. It's on fire. It's been blazing for hours now.'

'Oh good God. Are the men all right? Have there been any casualties?'

O'Brien blinked at him through red-rimmed eyes and Neill thought he had probably left this visit until it was too late in the unrealistic hope that he could somehow contain the fire, and conceal it from Garreth. The man was in total panic.

'Wha'? Wha'?' O'Brien said now, puzzled. The men's welfare did not concern him, only the thought of Garreth's anger on his return to find his brewery gone up in flames.

'Casualties? The men? Are they all right?' Neill resisted the impulse to shake him.

'Oh. Oh yes. I think so. But the brewery is burning. Oh God, Master Neill, Mr Connolly will kill me. He'll have my guts for garters. Oh an' it wasn't my fault. I din' do nuthin'.' The man was in abject terror and Neill felt a chill of revulsion that he tried to shrug away.

'You're not sure, are you?' he said, looking the man straight in the eyes. They slid away from his gaze and Neill shouted, 'Ben. Ben. Come at once.'

Ben-the-Boots, who had been listening at the top of the steps that led to the kitchen, appeared precipitously into the hall.

Neill asked him, 'Is the car ready, Ben?'

The boy flushed. He was pulling on his trousers over his pyjamas and rubbing the sleep from his eyes. 'It's always ready, sir. Always.'

'Then let's go.' And all three left the house in the chill pre-dawn.

It was O'Brien's first time in a motor, but he was not destined to remember much about it, preoccupied as he was with the situation he was in. He had worked for Garreth Connolly since the beginning and he knew his master's methods well. Someone would pay for this, and O'Brien was casting about feverishly for an alternative to himself. Somehow, someone else must be used to deflect the boss's wrath from him. He would have loved to

179

blame Neill but it was no good trying to incriminate him, for he had checked everything in front of witnesses and gone home before the fire had started. O'Brien's thoughts twisted and turned as he tried to think of someone to accuse before Mr Connolly returned from London as he surely would now, in a fury not only because of the fire but also because his visit had been cut short. O'Brien had a shrewd idea what his boss got up to in the big city and he guessed that being interrupted would not put Garreth in the best of moods.

Good God, if he did not find an answer, he could end up without a job. Like John Joe Reilly. Just as swiftly and unjustifiably. He, O'Brien, knew in his heart that John Joe had done very little, if any, harm, yet there he was, one morning an employee of long standing with Connolly & Sons, and a short moment later, out on the street, jobless, penury staring him in the face. He'd end up like John Joe Reilly.

John Joe Reilly. O'Brien's mind suddenly seized on an idea. John Joe Reilly. Of course, of course. The perfect scapegoat. His answer, praise the Lord. And as the man was in trouble already, a little more was neither here nor there. He was asking for trouble. He was asking for prison. He had been saying inflammatory things about Mr Connolly all over the neighbourhood. But softly, softly. Young Master Neill was notoriously softhearted and he was fond of John Joe. Didn't he take him last week, after the sacking, for a jar at 'The Golden Harp'? Softly. Softly. Hold yer whist, as the servant at the Connollys' had told him. He ached to giggle, to hug himself with glee. But he kept his face a blank and his secret to himself.

The car swung down Usher's Quay, then Victoria Quay, and Neill could see to his horror a pink-and-red glow in the sky and a pall of black cloud in the distance. The city was etched dark and featureless against the dawn, like a cameo. The grey waters of the river rolled and curled, silvered under the still present moon. As they drove Neill could see the sky reddening, a fiery dawn. Only it wasn't. It was Connolly's brewery burning.

Neill was saying, 'I cannot understand how you could leave the scene of the fire without first assuring yourself that everyone was safely out.'

'Much whoever started it thought of that,' O'Brien said, preparing the way. He was remembering how Mr Connolly hated John Joe.

Neill looked at him sharply. 'What do you mean? Can't you go any faster, Ben?'

Softly. Softly. Careful, now.

'Nothing, sir. But we were so very careful. I fail to see how else it could have happened. It *must* have been deliberate.'

'Well, I can think of a hundred ways. Father is not one to waste money on safety precautions. The wood was dry as a tinder-box. However, it's no use speculating. You called the Fire Brigade?' He could not keep the sarcasm out of his voice.

'Of course, sir.' Nicely done. The first small hint. Inferring it was deliberate. The first tiny speculation. The ground being laid. O'Brien could not keep the ghost of a smile from his lips.

He was startled on glancing up to meet the steady gaze of Ben-the-Boots in the rear-view mirror.

Chapter

24

THE brewery was ablaze, a white-hot inferno, yellow and red flames, the colour of the autumn leaves licking the shell of the old building that had always been part of Neill's life. The noise was stupendous. He could hear the cackle of the flames consuming everything greedily. It seemed the whole neighbourhood was there, eyes reddened from the cinders, some in their dressing-gowns, all hastily attired. Faces smudged with soot, they ran hither and thither helping, doing what they could to contain the voracious crimson monster. In the dark the flames glowed, and the heat was scorching as hell.

The Fire Brigade had it under control, they said, although to look at it you would not think so. One of the men, coughing and spitting, said they had sacrificed the building to prevent the spread of the flames, a wise decision in Neill's estimation, but one he thought his father would not approve of.

Some of the people were standing in groups, gazing in disbelief at the devastation. The workers, those who lived in Paradise Row and Paradise Street had helped the fire-fighters. Their faces were smudged and blackened and they passed buckets of water, doing what they could. They all had words of sympathy for Neill, words of commiseration. Sparks flew through the air and landed sizzling on the women's skirts and they slapped them out, blowing on their hands as they did so. Some fell harmlessly on the ground. The air was full of the acrid stench of burning, and smoke billowed from the gutted building in giant puffs.

The Quinns were there: Darragh helping the men and Kerry passing around bottles of a rival brand of porter to help quench the fire-fighters' thirst.

The men knew they were looking at the ashes of their lives, for with the burning of the building they could see the end of their employment. No brewery meant no work, no work meant no money. No money meant no food and no rent. In the smoke and flames, they saw penury and homelessness and a terrible fear.

Neill had never felt so helpless. He could see now that what the fireman had said was true. The blaze was diminishing, though it still was a sight to behold. The sheets of flame seemed mainly contained on the left side, away from the houses, where the actual brewery had been, and Neill realized the part that would be saved, if any, was the now quite useless office.

His mind blank, Neill moved slightly around the side of the brewery to where the men fought flames leaping devil's-poker red out into the dawn. He shielded his face with his hands, for the heat was fierce, and looked up. Too late he realized that the side wall was about to collapse on him. In an instinctive move to save himself he tried to run, but instead felt the weight of a man flatten him onto the ground, covering Neill's body with his own. Neill heard the tearing creaking scream as wood and masonry splintered and crashed to the ground. He stayed put a moment or two and then shifted experimentally as the man above him moved. He lifted his head, spitting cinders, for his face had been pressed into the ground, saw a large hand, took it and was pulled to his feet by John Joe Reilly. Neill was surprised to see him there.

'I was in "The Golden Harp" with Darragh,' John Joe said, brushing the dirt from Neill's coat. 'I couldn't refuse to help, now could I? After all, I don't want any other poor eejit in my position, do I? An' if there's no building, there's no jobs.'

'Thank you, John Joe,' Neill said, considerably shaken by his narrow escape. 'You've just saved my life.' Neill was finding it difficult to keep his voice steady. 'Good God, man I could have been badly injured but for you. I'm truly grateful.' He looked at the smouldering beams that had nearly pulverized him and at an evil iron bar that had missed his head by inches.

But John Joe was not listening. He peered through reddened eyes at Neill.

'Ye won't tell yer father, now will ye? That I helped to put it out? It'd kill me if he found out. I'll never give him the satisfaction.'

'An' why not? Why can't Master Neill tell his father?'

183

Neill and John Joe swivelled to face O'Brien. He stood in front of John Joe, his head to one side, a snide expression on his face. 'Eh? Eh?' he said aggressively.

'I don't want Master Neill to give him the satisfaction of knowing I'd helped after he gave me the sack,' John Joe's tone was puzzled.

'Or is it because you had somethin' to do with it startin'?'

John Joe let out a roar and O'Brien darted behind Neill.

'I'll kill ye for that. I'll murder ye,' John Joe shouted, trying to get his hands on the little man, who weaved and dodged behind Neill's back.

'You heard what he said, Master Neill. You heard him,' O'Brien screamed.

'John Joe, pay no attention to him at all,' Neill said. 'Calm down. O'Brien, don't talk such rubbish.'

The police had arrived to question people. The workers wearily answered their queries wiping sooty faces, and Neill tried to calm John Joe. But O'Brien seemed intent on drawing attention to their little group, so inevitably an inspector came over.

'What's all the commotion?' he asked.

'Nothing, officer. Nothing at all,' Neill said in an authoritative manner.

'Oh, I'm not so sure about that, officer,' O'Brien was not be be thwarted.

Neill was very conscious of his twenty-one years against O'Brien's venerable fifty. O'Brien planted himself in front of the inspector.

'I was saying to Master Neill here, he's Mister Connolly's son, officer.' The inspector nodded. 'I was saying that John Joe Reilly there musta set the blaze, an' he intent on revenge.'

John Joe let out another bellow, and though Neill tried to calm the situation, it was no use. The big man seemed as intent on self-destruction as O'Brien was to convict him.

'I'll kill ye for that. I've said it an' I mean it. I'll murder ye.' He pushed the inspector out of the way and grabbed O'Brien by the collar and held him, feet dangling a couple of inches above the ground, shaking him until the teeth rattled in his head. There was no murderous intent in the action but Neill knew that the police now, and a court later, would not see it in the same light as he did. They would simply be told that the big

184

man had attacked the smaller, older man and people would draw their own conclusions.

The inspector had beckoned two policemen to come to his assistance. They had quite a bit of trouble separating John Joe from O'Brien. Prising him out of the big man's grasp, Neill thought, for he was not really hurting O'Brien. They pinned John Joe's arms behind his back. O'Brien was fiddling with his false teeth which had come loose, but he still managed to indict the unfortunate John Joe.

'Sacked he was, last week,' he lisped, trying to reinstate the teeth into their usual secure position. 'Sacked. Swore to avenge himself, he did. I heard him.'

'Well, I did not,' Neill said firmly, 'and I was there.'

O'Brien looked at the inspector. The men about who had heard him shouting were murmuring angrily amongst themselves. Yet they were reluctant to take sides. They, too, could be blacklisted, and John Joe, they saw, was already doomed. No one would take his word against O'Brien's.

'He's a boy, Inspector. Only a boy. I'm the manager here. His father's manager for thirty years I've been. You can ask his father, Mr Connolly, what kind of a man John Joe Reilly is. Just ask him. You'll see.' O'Brien cast a triumphant look at Neill.

'And where is Mr Connolly? Has he been notified?'

Neill had not thought of that. His heart plummeted at the thought of telling his father.

'He's in London with my brother, officer. I'm going to telephone him when I get a chance.'

'I'll do it,' O'Brien said promptly. But Neill was not going to allow that. He could imagine how the affair would be slanted if O'Brien gave the news to Garreth.

'You don't know where he is,' Neill said, realizing as he said it that he didn't know either. However, he was not going to let O'Brien know that. 'I will tell my father, thank you very much.'

John Joe had calmed down and he now looked at Neill, the horror of his situation dawning on him.

'Mr Connolly, I done nuthin', nuthin' at all, except help,' he cried in a disbelieving voice.

Neill could not bear to look into his face as the police snapped handcuffs on him. A Black Maria pulled by two heavy horses had clopped up into the smoke-filled area in front of the brewery.

John Joe looked wide-eyed with fear as the back doors were opened and policemen jumped out. Suddenly realizing the inevitability of what was going to happen, John Joe made a last bid for freedom. But he was no match for the uniformed men. They bundled him into the van despite his protests of innocence and Neill's pleas for clemency. The others in the crowd stood about silently. They were sorry for John Joe, but there was nothing they could do. Darragh and Kerry had joined Neill, and Darragh too tried to reason with the inspector but to no avail.

As they pushed him into the van, John Joe turned an agonized face to Neill and called, 'Tell Mary, Mr Connolly, tell her I did nuthin'. Tell her.'

The door was barred and shut on him. His voice was full of pain and bewilderment and they could hear him as the van drove away. 'Tell Mary, Mr Connolly. Tell her I did nuthin'.'

Neill was shaking with anger. Darragh shot him a warning glance.

'You'll do no good by losing your temper,' he whispered to his friend.

Neill turned and looked at O'Brien beside him. The little man was frightened by the look on Neill's face.

'When my father hands the brewery over to me, O'Brien,' he said slowly, rest assured that the very first thing I will do is sack you.'

He had the dubious satisfaction of seeing all the stuffing knocked out of O'Brien and a look of terror cross his face.

'Now I'll telephone my father,' he said, and strode purposefully away thinking, 'A really good man, a priest, would forgive him. Oh help me, Lord, to see Your image in all men. Even Bill O'Brien.'

Chapter

25

THE next morning, after the dinner party to her vast surprise and consternation, Ellen was called to the telephone. Not having a phone in Rathgar the instrument frightened and unsettled her. She was not at all at home with it. Added to that were her apprehensions about Breffni, the army and the fact that her son and her husband were loose in London. Anything might have happened and in her mind it could only be bad news that warranted a telephone communication. She suffered such a nervous attack at the announcement that the call was for her, that the maid felt it incumbent upon her to inform Lady Gorman that her sister was having some kind of seizure.

To her amazement, the servant found her mistress in bed with her husband. Hiding her confusion, she said that there was a telephone call for Mrs Connolly, but that that lady had taken on so that she, Ellie, was worried for her.

'She's in a terrible state, m'lady. I think she might have a seizure an' I wouldn't know what to do.'

'That's all right, Ellie. I'll go to her.'

The maid left and Barth got out of bed swiftly.

'I'll see to her, my love. She'll calm quicker for me.'

He smiled at May, an intimate smile, recalling last night, but her eyes slewed away from his and she did not meet his glance.

He was right. Ellen responded to his calming influence. She was wrapped in her woollen dressing gown, so different and more practical than his wife's concoctions of satin and lace, and he felt for some reason more comfortable with her than he ever felt with May.

He took her to the little room off the hall, an old cloakroom that had been converted to accommodate the new instrument near to the servants' room so that they could easily hear it.

'I'll take the call if you like, Ellen,' he said, and she gratefully accepted his offer. She had only handled a telephone once and she had hated the experience. She watched Barth apprehensively, fear gnawing at her stomach. Perhaps Breffni had been shot by a German soldier. Although that could not be . . . it was too soon. There were air raids in London: suppose Garreth and Breffni had been bombed in the street? No-one would telephone her to break good news. It had to be a calamity.

Barth was nodding at the phone. He laid his hand on her arm.

'Yes? Yes? Oh, I see.' He covered the mouthpiece. 'It's Neill,' he said.

Neill? Neill? Her heart slowed and she wondered, puzzled what on earth Neill wanted. Barth was nodding at the phone again, then he looked at her once more.

'He says there has been a fire at the brewery. Nothing to be alarmed about. There have been no casualties. However, he wants to phone his father in London, and asks have you any idea the name of the hotel he is staying at?'

Ellen tried to grasp all he was saying. All she could think of was that she wished the telephone had never been invented. Then Neill would have had to deal with the fire and she would not have been frightened and she would not have to worry about Garreth coming home and spoiling her lovely break. She thought, 'But a moment ago I was terrified he might have been in an accident. Dear God, what is the matter with me?'

'It's the Great Western. In Paddington, I think,' she told Barth, who repeated it to Neill.

'Does Neill need me at home?' she asked anxiously. Barth shook his head.

'No. No,' he said. 'Neill was quite clear about that. He said you and the girls must not worry. He said he had everything under control.' He smiled at Ellen. 'Are you all right, my dear?' he asked, anxious to reassure her.

She nodded. 'Yes thank you, Barth.'

'Only I'm late, Ellen. I've got a Hunt Committee meeting and . . .'

'Run along, Barth, do. It's all right . . . I'm all right, truly.'

188

Barth gave her a little hug. 'Don't worry, my dear. Just don't worry,' he said and smiled again, waved and left her.

She dithered a little in the big hall. She took a step forward, then one back. She turned this way, thought, then turned back. Then she shrugged. There was nothing she could do about it, except worry. Well, she would not. She would take Barth's advice. Life, she thought, was too short. All sorts of enlightening and frightening things had happened to her recently and the sky had not fallen. In fact, if she was completely honest, she had to admit that she was quite enjoying all the excitement. Except, of course, for Breffni's joining the army. She really did not like that at all. But then he would never get a chance to fight, Barth said, and she trusted Barth. Should she go home to Rathgar? If Garreth came home early he would expect her to be there. Well, she thought, and why should she? Garreth would not give one fig for her feelings if the roles were reversed.

'I'll please myself this once,' she thought, 'And to pot with the consequences.' She gave a little laugh. Everything that was happening here at Avoca House was certainly very fascinating: May doting on Charles (how could she have the courage?); Charles in love with Celestine (that would certainly be stopped when they returned to Rathgar). Celestine would fight her father tooth and nail for her soldier.

'She might win, too,' Ellen whispered to herself as she climbed the stairs, and smiled at the thought.

And now Garreth's brewery was burnt down. Well certainly he could not blame her for that, although he would try. But if she wasn't at home he couldn't vent his anger on her at all, until the edge had been blunted. He would have to take it out on that little weasel O'Brien.

This was something he would not lay at her door. Her lips tightened into a line. 'And I will not let him,' she murmured firmly. 'No. And when we go home I'll simply let him rant and rave and I'll not pay him a blind bit of notice. I'll not care. Oh it'll be difficult, but I'll do it.' She drew in a deep breath, 'After all,' she said aloud, 'he can't kill me.'

She stood still on the stairs, her chin on the bannister. She thought about the implications. She had never thought that way before. A smile lit her gentle face and she gathered her woollen dressing-gown around her and skipped up the next few stairs.

189

'Sticks and stones may break my bones,' she chanted, 'but names'll never hurt me.' She paused a moment, 'Why didn't anyone explain it to me before?' she said to herself, 'He cannot kill me.' And bunching her dressing-gown up nearly to her knees she jigged up the last stairs, her heart light within her.

Chapter

26

BREFFNI wished wholeheartedly that he was alone. He ached to be in the company of a group of carefree chaps his own age, preferably artists, and not with his rather alarming father.

Garreth had insisted on introducing his son to the pleasures of sex, and Breffni would much rather have found out for himself, even if it was only by trial and error. There was something terribly intimidating about having his father looming over him, egging him on. He was not in tune with Garreth at the best of times, but in the erotic atmosphere of the brothel, he felt awkward in front of and embarrassed by his father.

Garreth took him in high good humour to Flossie's. The rouge patina that hung over the whole place gave it, in Breffni's opinion, a slightly satanic aura. The glow was cast by the crimson plush of the furnishings, the red velvet drapes, the rose lampshades and the fact that Flossie herself sailed about like a scarlet frigate, in flame-coloured satin and rubies, formidable and shimmering as a blazing bonfire.

She chucked Breffni under the chin, squeezed his arm, and remarked lasciviously how tasty a morsel he was and how deliciously young. Breffni felt he was being devoured by a whale. Garreth had been greeted like a long-lost friend by a plump woman called Maggie. She was dressed, or rather *en déshabillé*, in a long transparent black chiffon *robe de chambre*. You could see her white legs and a great deal of her large breasts through the filmy material. Breffni thought all that naked flesh was repulsive, but he dared not show his feelings for fear of being thought gauche.

'My son is a virgin,' Garreth boomed proudly to the

191

assembled company of floosies and whores in various stages of undress. 'He's to be a soldier. He's off to the wars and I don't want anyone to jeer at him,' he said, slapping Breffni on the back. It was as near a gesture of affection as his father could make, and Breffni wondered why it was so important that he shouldn't be jeered. 'No-one'll be able to say Breffni Connolly was a greenhorn. They will never be able to tease you, Breffni my boy.'

He was a little drunk, Breffni realized. He had never seen his father like this before and when Garreth looked at him his son could see real affection in his father's eyes. It disconcerted him and he wondered briefly if perhaps his father did care for him a little after all.

The women flocked about him like birds of prey and gazed on his youth with predatory eyes. Their faces were painted, their cheeks rouged, Breffni thought, like Celestine's dolls. They had the same artificial look, vacant and dull. He desperately wanted the ground to open and swallow him up but there was no chance of that.

From the moment the journey had begun, his father had been in an 'all boys together' mood which Breffni found acutely embarrassing. But then, in this awful place, to his son's relief, Garreth suddenly became more interested in his own pleasure than in showing off to his son. From his eulogy praising himself in the role of father, and Breffni for joining the army he had quickly descended into a mumbled jocular flirtation with the buxom Maggie.

Breffni was not too impressed by his first sexual encounter. He chose the youngest, the freshest of the group of girls available. His father was obviously content with the flashy Maggie, though how he could fancy such a bawdy gross and overpainted individual Breffni could not fathom. He personally liked, insofar as he knew what he liked, maidenly modesty, blushes and a sweet diffidence that made him feel strong and protective. He knew, however, that there was nothing remotely resembling such a girl to be found within these scarlet walls. He was rapidly finding out what he did *not* like.

As it was, his father standing at his side beaming at him as if he were making him a present of Lily Langtry herself, was hurrying him up.

'Choose, lad, choose. We've not got all night,' he laughed

192

coarsely. 'Well, maybe we have at that, but we don't want to spend it down here, now do we, lad? Now, get on with it.' He thrust his clenched fist in an outward jabbing movement that caused the girls to shriek with laughter and his son to feel nausea rise within him. They were all watching him. It was overheated in the dim red room and the faces of the girls seen in the flickering rosy gaslight seemed coarse and lascivious.

His father could hardly conceal his impatience and Breffni knew he had to make up his mind quickly.

'Her,' he said, pointing, and a round of applause went up.

'Lily,' the Red Madam said, winking one kohl-encircled eye and pulling the girl out from the group. She thrust her at a bashful Breffni.

'I've paid for the whole night,' Garreth said, 'I'm not mean. You can have the whole night, m'boy.'

Breffni wanted to die. Most young men, he thought, would envy him. Here he was in a famous London brothel being offered his pick of the girls and all he wanted to do was to rush home to Mama.

His father pushed the two of them towards the flight of stairs that led, he supposed, to the bedrooms. As they ascended, he heard his father say to Rosie, 'Are you sure she's clean?' and Rosie reply. 'Certainly, Mr Connolly. Quite certain. All my girls see the doctor weekly.'

His heart sank, for the effect of the whispered exchange was to dampen any sexual excitement he might have felt. He ploughed up the stairs after Lily and heard his father laugh behind him.

'Like a lamb to the slaughter, isn't he? You'd think he'd show a little more enthusiasm.' There was an irritable edge to his father's voice. 'Well, Maggie, you won't find me lacking,' and he let out a whoop which blended with the prostitutes' raucous laughter.

It was not so bad when they went in to Lily's room. There was a rag-doll on the bed and the chamber was curiously virginal. Lily was often chosen by customers for her little-girl innocence. She looked about fifteen and had, in fact, just passed her sixteenth birthday. The room was childish in its simplicity and it looked to Breffni very like his sisters' rooms at home. He was totally unaware that there could be anything erotic about the sheer childishness of the place and he was simply relieved that there was nothing alarming about where he found himself.

Lily herself was an accomplished whore. Her father had raped her when she was eight years old, a practice he continued, although it ceased to be rape after the first few times. Lily accepted it; it became part of her increasingly squalid existence. She discovered eventually that she could get paid for allowing men to use her as her father had. As soon as she found she could make a good living, she left home and was very happy with her present situation, deeming herself lucky.

Breffni's climax was fast, furious and premature. It left him shaken, amazed and dissatisfied. Fireworks had exploded in his body but his mind had shied away from the experience, and his spirits fell and he immediately felt gloomy and depressed.

He disliked Lily touching him. He felt his privacy had been invaded. He also thought there must be something wrong with him for feeling like this. Other boys boasted of sexual congress. They talked of 'mounting the filly' and 'putting one in' and used all sorts of other suggestive phrases. Breffni believed them. The fact that they could be exaggerating or even lying never entered his head. He did not think for a moment that their boasting might be mere bravado.

When he had rested a little, Lily's hand strayed across his groin to arouse him again.

'This time'll be better,' she said, licking his ear. 'You'll see.'

He stifled the impulse to push her away. 'No, Lily. Leave me alone. I don't want any more.'

'What's the matter? Didn't I treat you well? Don't you fancy me? Oh, don't tell Rosie or she'll beat me.'

'She'll do that?'

'Yes.'

'Well, you needn't worry. I won't say anything.' He looked at the young face on the pillow beside him. 'Does she hurt you, Lily?'

The girl shook her head and said matter-of-factly, 'Not really. She's all noise and wind. Underneath she's soft.' There was contempt in her voice.

'Why do you do it, Lily?' he asked.

Her skin was pale and now that all her paint seemed to have evaporated, her lips and cheeks still had the blush of youth. Her face was thin, like an elf in the Victorian drawings in their fairy-tale book at home.

'Well, what else can I do?' she said practically. 'I got no education. I can't read or write. Nobody cares if I live or die. This is a good life compared to some. It's a hard life for the poor. At least here I don't starve. I reckon I'm well off.'

They lay side by side like corpses, still and silent on the white counterpane. Two children. Breffni shivered.

'This is what it would be like to be dead,' he said. He did not know why he said it. He had his arms crossed over his chest and his fists were clenched.

'Don't say that,' she cried, propping herself upon her elbow. 'Put the eiderdown over you and get warm. You sure you don't want to get 'ot the other way?'

He shook his head. He felt sad and lonely and isolated. He desperately wanted to be at home in Rathgar with Celestine and Clothilde and Neill. He longed for the comforting face of Mamie and most of all he ached to be held in his mother's arms. How silly I am, he thought, ashamed, how stupid. A real man would not feel like this. He bit his lip and she tucked the cover over him, then lay down beside him and putting her thumb in her mouth and her head on his shoulder, she fell asleep.

Breffni lay awake all night, eyes open listening to the girl's even breathing. At dawn there was a banging at the door.

'Come on, you greedy pig. I've been waiting for you. We've got to go.' It was his father's voice.

Breffni dressed. Lily remained in a child's sleep. She did not seem to stir. Her lashes rested on her pale cheeks in black crescents, her lips were parted and her damp thumb lay just out of its soft orifice. He kissed her forehead and tiptoed out.

Chapter
27

THREE days later, when Breffni had gone to Colchester, Garreth got the telegram from Ireland. Unable to get his father on the phone, Neill had sent him the message by the only other way. Garreth had hardly spent any time in the Great Western Hotel, having other more exciting fish to fry. The telegram infuriated him. He had been in wonderful spirits and to receive such news when he was having a jolly good time angered him to the point of fury.

At first he had found Breffni's presence quite a stimulant. Not that he needed one; he had Maggie's assurance on that score. He had brought his son back to Rosie's again on the second night of their stay, assuring him once more that he had paid lavishly so that both of them could remain there all night. If Breffni's response seemed a little cool, it was, Garreth thought, because he was jealous of his father's stamina. He had it from Maggie and she had it in confidence from Lily that the lad had only managed it once in the night.

'My Gawd! You're a bull, Mr Connolly. You wore me out, so you did. Four? Five times? I can't remember. An' your kid only once, Lily said. Body of a young man, you 'ave. Performance of one too, I can tell you. Better, even.'

'Ah! Experience counts,' he roared happily, pleased to be favourably compared to his young son.

Breffni found the repeat experience repulsive. He was embarrassed by his father's lascivious remarks and kept thinking of his mother whom he adored, horrified that his father could be

196

unfaithful to her; and he could not work up the enthusiasm to play games with Lily. He was terribly anxious, too, about his manhood. Did this reluctance mean that there was something wrong with him? He turned cold at the thought and lay stiffly beneath the sheets.

They talked, however. Lying on the bed, he told her about his family and all about joining the army. She could not understand why he wanted to go to war and he had to admit he was not at all sure himself.

'You 'ave a nice 'ome, a mum what loves you, a father 'oo cares for you. Why do you wanna leave it?'

'I dunno.'

'You don't 'ave to over there in Ireland.'

'Oh yes, in a way we do. Ireland is part of the British Empire.'

'Well, I dunno about that.'

'I think it's a fine thing to do,' Breffni said, wondering if he meant it, 'to be a soldier. To fight for your country. No matter what Neill says, England is our's. Our country. We owe it to civilization to see that the killing stops. The war will do that.'

Lily shrugged. 'I don't care about other people,' she said. 'Let them take care of themselves. They never took care of me, so why should I help them? No. But I just don't see why you wanna go.'

There was a loose thread on the counterpane and she plucked and worried at it. Her hands were a child's hands, her nails bitten to the quick. She hugged the rag-doll in her right arm.

'Well, Lily, you're a woman . . . Well, nearly. You don't understand us men,' he said grandly.

She didn't reply, nor did her expression change, but he knew what she was thinking and he blushed.

'Please try to understand Lily, about . . . about . . . it's partly my father. Him being here . . . next door. And Mother. My mother I told you is sweet and gentle. All this is . . . I don't want to upset you, Lily, but it's not what makes me happy.'

Lily sighed philosophically. 'No. I don't 'spect it is. Never mind, lovey. Tell me what does. Make you 'appy, I mean.'

He thought. 'Oh, being quiet. Sitting in the garden and smelling the grass. I prefer the smell of the grass to the most beautifully scented flowers. Having tea with Mother. Twilight

197

when the world is full of changing shadows. Oh, things like that.' He was quiet a moment, then he said, 'Lily, do you think there's something wrong with me? Me not liking sex much?'

'No. Tell you the truth, I don't like it much either,' Lily said.

Breffni thought this was a novel idea. He had imagined because of the sounds of ecstasy she had made that she must love her work.

'Oh. Well . . . well, I expect that's all right. You're a woman, so I s'pose . . .'

'Look, you stop fretting about it. You don't have to like it, now do you? From what I hear, your old man does the work of two. Go to sleep now. Rest.'

Breffni kissed her chastely on the forehead and did just that. The following morning he said farewell. He liked her and he thought that in different circumstances he might have loved her, desired her. He decided he was going to get out of any further visits to Rosie's by leaving for Colchester the next day, and when he told his father Garreth did not object. He had enjoyed showing off in front of Breffni but it was wearing thin and the boy put restraints on him which he found irksome. He longed to be completely free of the shackles of respectability. Now he could let go, take Maggie to the music hall to see Vesta Tilly and, when they went back to Rosie's, have a couple of girls in with them to hot things up and add a bit of variety. Breffni might be shocked.

In anticipation of an exciting night, his senses titillated, he cursed roundly when he found the message Neill had sent him from Ireland:

FIRE IN BREWERY STOP CONSIDERABLE DAMAGE STOP UP TO YOU TO RETURN OR NOT STOP NEILL

In a fury, he stormed up to his room in the hotel, rang for a bell-boy and ordered a brandy. He had also to arrange his return to Dublin earlier than he had booked. His nerves frazzled, exasperated and in a hurry to pack, the full import of the telegram did not hit him until much later. Like a frustrated child, thwarted of a coveted toy, his sweets dashed from his grasp, all he could think of initially was how hard done by he had been. But, on the journey to Kingstown, he suddenly became aware of the words on the yellow piece of paper. 'FIRE'. 'DAMAGE'. They impinged themselves on his consciousness. A feeling of unease invaded him. What had happened? What exactly did Neill mean by 'considerable damage? He strode up and down on the ferry's deck oblivious of the stars carpeting the deep blue sky, of the icy air cutting his skin, of the crashing of the waves against the side of the boat. What state was the brewery in? How bad had the fire been? Cold fear overwhelmed him. He thrust his knuckles into his mouth to stifle his panic. Poverty. Oh God, not poverty again. The fear of it was always there, just under the surface. He remembered the cold; raw hands and ears that stung; inadequate clothes. A shirt, short trousers, his knees bare, a thin patched jacket against the east wind. He remembered hunger gnawing at his belly; never enough to eat. He remembered the helplessness, the hopelessness. He groaned. A man taking a constitutional around the deck heard him and stopped.

'Are you all right, sir?'

He shrank back as Garreth turned blindly, his eyes full of tears and terror, raising his walking-stick and crying out, 'No. No. No.'

It was in this state that Garreth eventually arrived home to discover that his family, except for Neill, were still in Wicklow at Avoca House, behaving for all the world as if nothing had happened.

When he heard this, he relieved his tension and fear by ranting and raving so much that Miffy below in the kitchen broke down and, in an agony of nerves and tears, said she would not, could not, leave its safety. Ben-the-Boots comforted her, sitting her down on a stool and fetching her a hot cup of tea.

Garreth berated Neill as if, Mamie loudly announced, his son was to blame for the fire in the Brewery.

'I cannot leave you, Neill, cannot leave you for five minutes before you allow the business to go up in flames. How dare you? How dare you?'

Neill saw that his father was nearly apoplectic and he decided to leave the house, as nothing he could say would make any difference now.

Garreth paced about, looking for an outlet for his wrath. It came in the form of Mrs Danagher from next door who, he saw when he looked out of the window, was leaning over the wall that separated their gardens. She was clipping the branches of the crab-apple tree that hung over her wall.

He pushed up the window and yelled at her. 'What do ye think you are doing? Leave that tree alone. Don't you cut another twig, woman, do you hear?'

'An' why can't I? Who says so? It's banjaxing my geraniums.'

'Well, Mrs Danagher, didn't I see you picking all the fruit off the ground when it was there? Much you minded it interfering with your geraniums then.' He felt the blood rush to his head.

'It interferes with them gettin' the sun,' Mrs Danagher replied tartly. 'An' yer wife said I could.'

'Leave that tree alone. It's my property. I'm the boss in this house and I'll sue you if you dare to touch it again.'

Mrs Danagher, who loathed Mr Connolly, plonked down the shears on the wall and put her hands on her hips ready to take on all comers.

'Well, fire ahead then. I'd love to see you try, Mr Connolly,' she said triumphantly. 'I'd love to see you empty your pockets, an' all because I cut off a couple of branches hanging into *my* garden, which makes them, Mister high and mighty, *my* property. Have you forgotten that Mr Danagher is a solicitor?' she asked gleefully.

Garreth had indeed forgotten that her husband was in the legal profession. He slammed down the window, defeated, thwarted even in that altercation. He went to bed in a filthy mood with an unsettled and fearful household waiting apprehensively for what he would do next.

He had decided to wait until morning to visit the brewery. He knew full well that his temper was out of control and he did not want an incident like the one with Mrs Danagher to occur at his place of business; better to be calm and in control; better to wait. Tomorrow he would be himself again and he would find out who was at the bottom of all his troubles. For there must be a culprit. He tried to sleep, but sleep evaded him. He tossed and turned angrily, asking Fate why she had decided to pick on him with such virulence. He was frustrated that Ellen was not there so that he could take out his rage on her. She was his wife. She was supposed to be at his side in times of trouble. Instead, she was down with her fancy sister in Wicklow. Enjoying herself, no doubt. Not giving her poor husband a thought. Well, wait until they came home. He would show them. He slaved and slaved to

200

supply them with everything they could want and they could not spare him a thought when he was in trouble. How ungrateful they were. So much for religion. So much for the Holy Catholic church. On this odd thought he fell asleep.

Chapter

28

THE following day Garreth inspected the devastation. The place, blackened and open to the sky, filled him with fear and dismay. But he remembered the insurance. He had been consoling himself with the thought of the insurance since those terror-stricken moments on the boat when he had felt helpless as a child again.

All along the road the workers stood silently, the men holding their caps in their hands as they would have at a funeral. The women covered their heads with shawls. They did not try to speak or gesture to him, they just stood staring at him with pained and pleading eyes. It was not so bad while he was in the car; they lined the roadway like mourners watching a hearse pass. But when he stepped from the car in front of what remained of the brewery he could feel their fear, smell it off their ill-clothed bodies and he wondered if they could smell it from him. He fought it down, the terror.

'What do they want from me? What can I do, for God's sake? Why don't they leave me alone?' he muttered irritably to himself. He knew he was unreasonable, that they wanted to find out what would happen to them. However, he was much more in command of himself today. He was not going to let them see anything on his face.

There was not much to please him on his arrival. The fact that John Joe Reilly had been arrested and taken to Kilmainham Jail was the only piece of information that had given him any relief from his smouldering fury and O'Brien was quick to capitalize on the fact. Garreth commended him for his efficiency in thus having the arsonist detected and arrested so promptly.

They stood in Garreth's office, ironically the only part of the building that had not been destroyed. The walls were scorched and blackened but it had not been too affected by the flames. The devastation had been mainly on the other side of the building, and worse luck, Garreth commented when he inspected the place, it had to be where the work was done.

'Damned nuisance; for we could have functioned without the office and the cloakrooms, but now we can't get any beer brewed or bottled until we get the insurance money and it is all fixed, and that will take some time. Goddammit! I'll be out of pocket, I will.'

Neill was ashamed of his father at that moment, more than he usually was.

'Do you think you could see your way to paying some of the regular workers a retainer?' he suggested. 'After all, they are going to find it difficult to keep afloat.'

His father's face paled. 'Are you mad?' he queried. 'Have you got a screw loose or something?'

'No, Father. I just feel that we are being a little selfish . . .'

'I'll give you selfish,' his father roared, making O'Brien jump. 'Have you any idea how much we have lost? How much it's going to cost me to get into production again?'

'Won't the insurance company pay for that?' Neill asked mildly.

'We'll still have had no saleable produce for the market. No sales, no money. Are you stupid or something, Neill, that you cannot grasp that fact?'

Neill fell silent. Useless to point out to his father that the insurance company would cover the cost of repairs. Useless to point out that his father owned the land all about and that he also owned the house in Rathmines and that they could certainly remain afloat for some considerable time to come. Useless to point out that the workers would starve with the closure of the brewery, would be evicted, would die. Useless. Useless. Useless.

'I've ordered some workmen here to see you, Mr Connolly' O'Brien said, glancing at Neill and smugly smiling. 'Pronto. I did it pronto.' He rubbed his hands together and Neill could see he was basking in Garreth's approval.

'Good man, O'Brien,' his father said.

'Yes sir. The builders will be here first thing Monday.'

'We'll get the skids under them and see they stick at it till we can get some work done.' He shook his head sadly. 'I know how slow repair work is. Irish workmen are slower than tortoises.'

A crafty look came into O'Brien's eyes.

'How if . . .' he began, 'how if I pay them for speed and not until they have finished? You know, make a higher price for the shortest time, and if they go over that time limit, the sum goes down and down accordingly?'

Garreth's face lit up. 'That's a brilliant idea, O'Brien.' He turned to his son. 'That is the kind of help *you* should be giving me, Neill,' he remarked in an aggrieved voice.

Neill did not bother to reply. 'You don't think, you know. You stand here in the ruins of our business, your mind obviously on other things, talking drivel about paying the workmen when they are doing nothing. . .'

'Through no fault of their own,' Neill interrupted.

'Through the fault of *one* of them. My God, what kind of an idiot son have I got? What lofty thoughts are you thinking, I'd like to know?'

Didn't this fool son of his understand how hard, how back-breakingly relentless his father's struggle had been? Didn't this unrealistic boy know anything about poverty? He certainly professed to. Well, he should realize, Garreth thought, that once you've starved as he had you never forget it, never feel secure. And if he could rise, so could they; the grey-faced workers he despised and who were a constant irritation to him. Why didn't they do as he had done? Fools, all of them. Stupid, gormless fools.

His son was looking at him. 'I was worried about John Joe Reilly, if you must know,' he said. When he saw his father's expression he instantly regretted the words. 'I'm certain in my own mind that he did not mean what he said that day. That he did not burn the brewery. That he is innocent.'

'Oh you are, are you? Well, let me tell you I heard what he said.' Garreth jabbed himself in the chest. 'O'Brien heard what he said.' He pointed to his manager. '*You*' —, he waved the finger at Neill — 'are the only one who thinks for some daft sentimental reason that he did not *mean* what he said.'

'The sentimental reason being that he saved my life,' Neill said with asperity. 'He did, you know.'

'He may have had an ulterior motive for doing that. He may . . .'

204

Neill shook his head angrily. 'Oh Father, don't be stupid. It was instinctive. The man is a fine man. His instincts are honourable. And I'm prepared to swear to it.'

'Who's going to believe you? Who?' Garreth banged his fist on the desk. 'No-one,' he said triumphantly. 'No-one.'

'But Father . . .'

'Don't "but Father" me. Why you should choose to take the part of a known agitator, a trouble-maker, and a thug who threatened to kill O'Brien, here, against your own father and his faithful manager I fail completely to understand.' O'Brien was nodding virtuously as Garreth thundered on. 'In any event I don't want to hear another word about it.'

But he was to hear more of it. For an hour Garreth and O'Brien talked, arrangements were made, business details worked out, letters of apology to regulars discussed. Then there was a commotion in the corridor outside the office, and a distraught Mary Reilly burst in on them.

Neill was horrified at her appearance. She had always had a spunky charm, a survivor's optimistic approach to life. Now her eyes were defeated, red with weeping, and her demeanour hopeless, her shoulders bent as she stood before Garreth Connolly.

Garreth was uncertain who she was. He sat behind his desk, motionless and expectant, like an animal ready to spring, looking at the woman who stood bowed before him with simple dignity.

There was a petrified silence in the room, then Mary spoke quietly, piteously.

'For God's sake, Mr Connolly, don't take him from me. He wouldn'a done it, for sure he wouldn'a. If ye told me he was havin' a Union meetin', I'd agree he was guilty. But not the fire. Ah no. Them's his friends workin' there. He couldn'a killed someone. He's not like that. I know him. He's soft in spite of his strength. He couldn'a hurt a fly. Please, Mr Connolly, me heart's broken an' him in jail. All it needs is one word from you.' She fell to her knees, the shawl falling back off her hair as she clasped her hands in supplication. Garreth who had listened to her in stony silence had by now realized who she was. 'I'm beggin' you, Mr Connolly, set him free. Ye sacked him, isn't that enough? Ye took away his livin', isn't that enough? Ah God, have ye no heart at all?'

205

He was staring at her with distaste. He didn't even bother to reply. He turned to O'Brien and said, 'Get that woman out of here.'

O'Brien rushed around and grabbed her by the arm. Neill moved to prevent him, but Mary drew away from him with great dignity.

'Leave me be,' she said gently .'I can manage without your help. I'll go.' She gathered herself together and stood with her head held high and when she spoke her voice was deadly calm. The men sat, meanwhile, as if immobilized by her pose.

'Mr Connolly, what you are doing is evil. And evil attracts evil. It may not seem so now, but one day this will come back to haunt you and you'll curse the day you did this terrible thing.'

Garreth Connolly felt a chill of fear down his back. He screamed again, 'Get that woman out of here.'

But Mary Reilly had already gone.

The next two days Garreth found himself frustrated and thwarted at every turn. Neill, Mamie and Ben-the-Boots turned a deaf ear to his tirades, not reacting to his insults or his rage. They nodded their heads at him absently and deferentially but he knew they were paying him no real attention. Miffy did not show her face and Mamie always had a cast-iron alibi as to her whereabouts when he asked. He was without a scapegoat in the house and without Ellen, he did not seem to be able to get anyone to listen to him. He felt lonely. He telephoned Avoca House to speak to his wife and order her home but the house-keeper told him that Lady Gorman was preparing for a ball that Saturday and Mrs Connolly and her daughters were out, not available to come to the telephone. She told him briskly that she had been asked to tell him if he called that Mrs Connolly and his daughters would be returning to Dublin on Monday morning. He was welcome to join them, the housekeeper said, and rang off. That would have imposed an even greater curb on him, Garreth knew, for he did not dare to give free rein to his moods in Avoca House. He was ill-at-ease with the Gormans, conscious that they were not impressed, either by him or by his achievements, and he was very aware that May Gorman thought him a common brute, for he had heard her call him that and he had never forgiven her for it. It was understood in that 'set' that poor Ellen had married beneath her. The only time he had ever lost his temper there, he had been aware of the ring of coldly critical stares as they had watched him in silence, expressions of distaste on their faces. He had faltered to a stop, ashamed and embarrassed. No, Avoca House was the last place he could find relief from his ill-humour.

Never in his life had Garreth been so impotently furious and frustrated as he was now. He found it impossible to rest, to sleep, to concentrate on his business. The brewery was closed and there were no workers available on whom to vent his spleen. Never had he known such a state of affairs. His mood grew murderous. He could not even rail against his own son, for Neill stayed well out of his way. His father did not know where he was. In fact, Neill had escaped to 'The Golden Harp' and the company of Darragh and Kerry.

The welcome there was warm, the atmosphere within the Quinn family circle was harmonious, and as usual they made him feel relaxed and comfortable.

'Where's the wee fella?' Kerry asked him. 'Has he gone off to England then?'

Neill nodded.

Kerry's eyes flashed. 'Isn't it typical of the bloody Irish?'

'Kerry, don't *use* words like that. You'll shock the man. Remember he's for the priesthood,' her mother admonished her.

Kerry looked at him speculatively. 'An' I'm not too sure about that either,' she said and glanced again at Neill who lowered his eyes. 'How can you want that? Life is a chaotic accident, no more, no less,' Kerry said, heatedly. 'How can you dedicate your life to a God who lets this happen? Who lets poor Mary Reilly down in her hour of need?'

Neill shrugged. '*We* can make order. *We* can make peace. *We* can make life fair and secure for all, or *we* can create chaos. *We* are responsible, not God. We are greedy and acquisitive and selfish. Countries as well as people.'

'Oh, Neill, don't give me a lecture, please. What you say, your vision, is idealistic nonsense. What about plague, famine, death, destruction? What do you tell a man whose home has been demolished by a volcanic eruption or a flood, who has lost his babies an' his wife? Do you tell him to grin an' bear it? That it is God's will?'

'No, because it isn't. Jesus weeps.'

'Then why doesn't He stop it? Or ask His Father to?'

207

'Because he gave us free will. He gave us the choice, Kerry. Without that choice we are but puppets. That was not the grand scheme. We, each of us, have a propensity for good or evil. We must choose.'

'Well, unfortunately, the ones who choose evil, like your Pa, seem to get away with it. They are the rich and prosperous ones.'

Neill thought for a moment then he asked, 'Would you change places with him, Kerry? Do you think he's a happy man? Do you think his life is enviable? I mean what he is, not what he's got?'

Kerry shook her head.

Neill was suddenly tired of justifying his deeply-felt beliefs. He sighed. To him, it was very simple, but fragile as a soap-bubble. The gift of faith was both a blessing and a burden. To explain that Christ was love; that prayer was not magic, was not an abracadabra to get rid of all life's unpleasant happenings, but a request for the strength to bear them with fortitude; that prayer was release into a realm where fate had no relevance, where the vicissitudes of life were accepted; it was all beyond him at this moment. Pain and suffering, he believed, were part of growth; love and laughter and peace only came through it. How could he explain the paradox; without pain there was no joy. Pleasures, yes; content, no.

It was so easy to create scapegoats; parents; the Church; school; life. To apportion the blame. But nothing was achieved thereby. Neill believed that there was no growth in blaming. There could only be progress in forgiveness and acceptance.

Kerry was staring at him. He looked at her, then Darragh. He frowned worriedly.

'I'm thinking of John Joe. Mary's face haunts me, Darragh. My father has fixed all the blame on him for the fire and it is not right. I'm certain he didn't do it.'

'And O'Brien. Don't forget he had a part in it too. Don't forget that little weasel.'

'No indeed, but it's my father who has the power and he's in a foul mood about . . . oh, everything. What can I do?' He banged his glass on the table. 'I feel so impotent,' he said.

Darragh shook his head. He sipped his beer, licking the foam off his top lip.

'Nuthin',' he said. 'Nuthin'.'

208

They sat, legs stretched out before them, in front of the small turf fire glowing in the grate in Mrs Quinn's kitchen. Kerry had started to prepare supper, moving gracefully about the room, listening to them talk. Mostly she was quiet, but she interjected a comment every now and then. Neill loved to watch her calm and measured movements; it rested him, seeing her perform the preparations for the meal; her sure capable hands, her fluid gestures. They had asked him to stay for tea, which was their main meal, and they ate at six o'clock of an evening when the Angelus rang. The meal consisted of bacon and eggs, fried bread, strong tea to drink and home-made fruit cake. Kerry, her freckled arms elbow high in flour, had baked a new batch of soda bread while her mother and father cleared up in the bar preparatory to the evening session. Philomena often called to Kerry from the gloom of the snug, a cheerful call, asking a favour, giving a command: 'Bake some bread, pet, the sour milk is perfection at this very minute'; or, 'Can you dunk these rags, pet? I dunno' what people deposit on the tables in here but I'm tellin' you it's not booze.'

Once their father called, 'Give us a hand wi' the barrels, Darragh,' and his son left Neill brooding in front of the fire for half an hour.

They talked. Darragh surprised Neill by some of his sentiments.

'I sometimes wish I was you, Neill,' he said. 'If I had the brewery or the chance to run it, Gawney, I'd make some changes around here.'

Neill looked at him, smiling. 'What would you do, Darragh?' he asked.

'Well, I'd make it a workers' co-operative,' he said, his eyes shining. 'Think of it, Neill. Every man with a share. Of course there would be a scale. The higher up you went, the harder you worked, the bigger the reward. Think how proud the men would be, how secure. God, man, can you imagine their faces? John Joe Reilly secure for life provided he worked hard? Wouldn't that be a grand thing?'

Neill had never thought in that way before and he was amazed that Darragh had thought of it. He told his friend so.

'It's all I ever think of, Neill,' the red-haired man said bitterly. 'How to help these people. The dice is loaded against them. They haven't a chance. Ah well, talkin' won't help.'

209

It was very peaceful and pleasant, talking, setting the world's problems to rights, or more particularly, Ireland's. Neill decided he couldn't face home so he asked Philomena if he could stay the night.

'I don't want to go home, Mrs Quinn. My father . . .'

'You don't have to explain to us, Neill. Pass the butter, pet.'

Neill took the glass butter dish from Kerry and gave it to Philomena. In her cheerful plump face her eyes were shrewd.

'Ye need a bit of peace,' she said comfortingly. 'You don't have to stand on ceremony here.' She thought a moment and added, 'He can sleep on the mattress an' we'll put it on the floor in your room, Darragh. That suit ye? Or are ye too grand?' Her grin took the sting from her words.

'No. Not guilty,' Neill said.

'There's fresh linen smelling of lavender. I laundered it myself.' Kerry sounded a little on the defensive. 'An' a fluffy blanket.'

Neill hugged her. 'Ah, I know, girl. Don't fret. Yer Ma's only teasing me.'

Darragh turned to Neill. 'Come with me to the meeting,' he said.

Kipper Quinn cast his eyes up to heaven. 'Ah Darragh, yer not goin' to force poor Neill into yer lunatic meetin's, now are ye?'

Philomena leaned forward and patted her son's hand. 'Leave him alone, for God's sake, son,' she said.

'An' that's what we will do if he doesn't come . . . leave him,' Kerry quipped lightly, tossing her radiant hair. 'We're both going, an' you an' Ma will be behind the bar so poor old Neill will be all alone if he doesn't join us.'

'Besides,' Darragh added, 'we won't bite. No one'll force you to join anythin'. But I tell you what, Neill, it'll be educational. That it will. Yer always talkin' about doing good for this poor benighted country. Well, now's yer chance to find out what those of us who are trying *are* doing.'

'Bloody trades union. Gawney, as if it'll get anyone anywhere,' Kipper Quinn sighed. 'Now don't let yerself be bamboozled by them two.'

'It's all right, Mr Quinn,' Neill began but Philomena interrupted.

'Ah Darragh, shut up and don't try to inveigle the poor fella.'

210

'It's all right, really, Mrs Quinn,' Neill reiterated. 'I'd like to go. It would be interesting. I've never been, as you know, and this is a good opportunity to try to understand what Darragh and Kerry are always talking about.'

Kipper rose and scratched his neck and said as usual, 'That was lovely, Mother. Thank you.' Then he looked at Darragh. 'But I still don't think you ought to bring Neill to the meeting. I don't know as I approve of ye two going. They spout a lot of hot air at those things and those two would be better outa it.' Then he grinned at Neill. 'Not that they pay a blind bit o' notice to what I say.' Neill noticed that he seemed to take pride in the fact that his children acted independently of him.

Kipper looked fondly at his offspring and Neill could not help comparing him to Garreth. 'Couldn't ye give it a miss? Just for tonight?' he asked. When had Garreth ever asked such a question?

Darragh shook his head. 'It's a commitment,' he said briefly and Neill looked at Kipper.

'I'd like to go. Really I would. I might learn something.'

'Well, I don't approve of the whole thing. People getting above themselves,' Kipper grumbled. 'There is an order to things. A top a middle and the bottom. Bottom's just as important as the top. Everything's got to have a bottom. Can't be a top without it. Stands to reason. Well, don't go mucking about with the order of things or there'll be chaos. I'm warnin' ye.'

Darragh affectionately rumpled his father's hair and Kipper moved back to the bar.

Philomena smiled at her son. 'Well, go, then, but be careful, son,' she said.

'I will, Ma. Cross my heart.'

She sighed and got to her feet slowly, with effort, as if her body could not bear to move. She started gathering the dishes.

'Give them here, Ma.' Kerry took the dirty plates from her mother and kissed her cheek. 'I've lots of time. You go an' help Da.' She looked after her mother. 'She does too much. She's on her feet from eight in the morning to twelve at night, God help her, an' never a complaint. I tell you I'd have something to say ...' she stopped and glanced at Neill. 'An' sure what would you know about it an' you with servants to do your every command?'

She giggled as Neill leaned over and slapped her bottom

gently. He sipped the last of his tea, his elbows in the debris of the meal on the kitchen table. He let the peace of the place flow over him. It felt so good, so blessed to be here in this warm kitchen in the circle of this loving family. Yet it was not an aesthetically pleasing place. The table was of cheap wood, planks really, and covered with oilcloth gaudily printed with plum-coloured roses. The jam was in a jar and the dishes were of the plainest pattern and not all of the same set; some were chipped. The cutlery was steel. Neill, however, preferred it to the monogrammed Georgian silver of Avoca House or the plain silver cutlery of his own home, where the table was covered in damask and the china was foreign and fine and the lord and master stage-managed the conversation and made sure that no spontaneous joy could erupt. The condiments, here, were in the containers they were bought in, while at home they were trans-ferred into cut-glass pots of beautiful design purchased in Weirs of Grafton Street at exorbitant prices. But in this homely kitchen there was no tension. No cross-currents of anxiety disturbed the peaceful atmosphere. No martinet cast terror into the hearts of those around the table. There was no fear here, only a mutual concern for the welfare of the others, a deep abiding loving exchange. It soothed his troubled spirit and he thought he would put John Joe Reilly out of his mind, just for this evening, and give himself over to the sheer pleasure of being with the Quinns.

Chapter

29

THE meeting that Saturday night was not what Neill had expected at all. He had supposed that he would have to listen to the resentful ravings of jealous men with large chips on their shoulders. He had presumed that even though the complaints were justified, they would be inarticulate and larded with the natural animosity and prejudice of the poor. Instead, he found himself among eloquent speakers who got to the root of the problem, namely, that Irish people did not work for themselves, but were dependent on the British Government who forced them to work for aims, ideals and goals unsuited to the prosperity of Ireland and aimed only at strengthening the British economy. The speakers called for Home Rule. Ireland for the Irish.

'If we are to be poor — I see no reason why we should be, but if we are — let it be our own problem. I tell you though, we won't be. Working for ourselves we'll have new goals, new incentives. Each worker will have a fair wage and a good reason to work hard. It will build up an Irish economy for the good of the Irish people.'

There were a lot of intellectuals, students from Trinity College, as well as working men. There was resentment, too, but everyone seemed set on finding a solution. They went to a little café in a side street after the meeting and drank hot black tea. Darragh and Kerry were flushed and their eyes sparkled with an excitement Neill was beginning to understand. They watched him covertly, trying to gauge his reactions.

Neill's head buzzed with all he had heard. He had never come across ideas expressed so fervently by men who obviously

213

thought proudly of themselves as Irishmen. He thought of how his mother had instilled in them as children the ideal that the English were superior in everything. That imitating their manners, accents and behaviour was the prerequisite to social and business success. He knew his aunt, Lady Gorman, and his uncle-in-law, Barth, Lord Gorman, were held up as the perfect examples of how to be and to conduct oneself, and they were as close to an upper class English couple as you could get. Place them in a London social gathering and not by a syllable or a gesture would they betray their Irish background.

Neill thought now of the cadence of Kerry's speech, of the peasant dignity of Mary Reilly's stance, of Darragh's voice singing 'Dark Rosaleen' of Clothilde plucking the harp, and the purity of the Irish melodies drawn from it. He thought again of his Catholic conception of God, and he saw again the purple Wicklow mountains and the steel-grey rivers and the salmon leaping. He remembered Mamie's stories of Cuchlainn and Finn McCool, the wonderful tales of Emain Mancha; Conor, Emer, Maeve. He recalled the stubborn clinging to a forbidden religion and a banned language over hundreds of years of oppression by a people who raised up their eyes to those beloved mountains and dreamed of freedom. Yes, it was good to belong to those people. It was better he realized at last, to be completely Irish than to be at best a good imitation of an Englishman. Why didn't I see it before? he wondered.

His eyes filled with tears and he leaned forward and met the inquiring gaze of the brother and sister opposite him. They had no trouble with their identity. They knew they were Irish to the core and they were proud of it. He stretched out his arms and covered with his right hand one of Kerry's and with his left one of Darragh's. He held them firmly in a strong grasp.

'I'm with you,' he whispered. 'I'm with you.'

Chapter
30

THE party and dance at Avoca House was a great success. No one realized what an effort it took Lady Gorman to arrange it all and act the part of the perfect hostess.

Barth supported her and his quiet sterling strength gave her the stamina and courage she required to sustain the level of gaiety needed. She did not realize how much she relied on Barth; she simply knew that when the going got rough his arm about her shoulder and his gentle kiss upon her cheek infused her with the energy to continue when all she wanted was to crawl into a corner and die.

Celestine was the belle of the ball which was in her honour. Her hair was looped about her well-shaped head in ringlets held firm with sugar-water, Mamie's special recipe brought in a bottle from Rathgar. Old-gold ribbons and little flowers were laced between the curls that framed her glowing face. Her dress was a credit to Madame McGinty, but what made her stand out from the crowd and made the guests turn to look at her and nod their heads and smile in admiration was the radiance she carried about her, and that was the gift of her lover. That extra patina of excitement, that glow in her cheeks, the dazzling brilliance of her eyes, that came from the knowledge of a woman in love that her love is returned.

They danced together, Charles and Celestine, all evening, and it was obvious to all, including May, that they were oblivious to everyone but each other. Charles danced in a lop-sided way because of his knees, but it did not seem to matter. They danced eight-handed reels, waltzes, polkas and the more modern American steps to the new American music that was beginning to be played in Ireland, much to the disapproval of the older people. Charles and Celestine moved together as if they were isolated from everyone else, alone in perfect harmony with the music and each other, as if in a dream.

Barth saw May's pain. No one else did. He was acutely aware of her suffering and he could not but admire her brave front. She graced the whole affair, remembering to ask after sick relatives, discussing children's problems, the latest gossip, giving what seemed her undivided and sympathetic attention to each and every guest. Only Barth knew the effort it cost her, the strain she was under.

The buffet supper was perfection. The orchestra, in its best form, played full blast and talk and laughter filled the rooms. The service was unobtrusive and the guests enjoyed themselves greatly and reiterated that May Gorman gave the best parties this side of Dublin. Champagne flowed, smoked salmon disappeared down hungry throats, lobster Thermidor was consumed, the marrons glacés and the ginger syllabub were delicious. The band consumed great quantities of porter and the music got livelier as the evening progressed.

Celestine hung on Charles' arm and she never strayed from his side.

'No-one else gets a look-in,' Sive Jeffries grumbled to Clothilde. 'And he the most gorgeous man you could find in three counties.'

She cocked her head to look at Clothilde. 'And aren't you dancing at all, Clothilde? Ah well, your sister was always the vivacious one, your mother said, and you're the serious one.'

Clothilde shrugged and lowered her eyes. She was thinking about the meeting in South King Street and the red-haired man who troubled her so. As she thrust him angrily out of her mind, she recognized Owen Mulcahy's feet. With a sigh and without looking up, she stood and moved into his arms.

'Oh Owen,' she said, 'why do you always turn up when I'm thinking?'

'To stop you,' he replied lightly and waltzed her away.

Ellen, sitting with Barth, gave a contented smile. 'It's good to see them both occupied,' she said, forgetting about May for the moment. 'Celestine and Charles, Clothilde and Owen.'

Barth patted her hand. 'It is that,' he replied. 'Long may it last. Will you dance with me, Ellen?' he asked.

216

'Sure, I'd love to,' she cried, jumping up eagerly, like a friendly puppy he thought fondly. She smiled at him coquettishly and he regretted that he loved May and thought how happy this woman would have made him, and how easily he could have kept her content if only things had been different. Ah well, he smiled back at her, perhaps that would have been too easy.

Ellen loved to dance. It made her feel young again and she could forget how old and plump she had become. She had tiny feet and she twirled on them energetically in his arms and Barth was amused. He could see in her the girl she had once been, and it saddened him to think that all her energy and gaiety had been suppressed and submerged by the boor she had married.

Clothilde waltzed past in Owen's arms, eyes remote, cheeks pale. Barth thought that Celestine, bright as a star on a snowy night, was much more like her mother than the grave and passionate older daughter. He wondered whether Ellen realized the ferment simmering beneath the calm exterior Clothilde showed to the world. Clothilde was more like her aunt, he thought. Not in appearance, but in temperament. Both presented a cool exterior to the world but beneath there was fire.

'Ellen,' he said on impulse and remembering what they had said. 'If it ever gets too much for you in Rathgar, you know you can always come here, don't you? You'll never be abandoned.'

She was immediately on the defensive and he felt her body stiffen in his arms and her steps falter.

'Why on earth would they, Barth?' she asked, flushed, though whether from dancing or his suggestion that anything might be wrong he could not tell. But he was not disconcerted. He simply wanted her to know there was a way out if necessary.

'Oh, I don't know,' he answered mildly. 'Do you mind if we stop? I'm dreadfully out of breath.'

The dance was just over anyhow, and as they came to a halt, Barth gave Ellen an extra twirl and gracefully handed her into a little gilt chair where she sat, fanning herself.

'I'll get you an ice and some champagne,' he said, leaning over her.

She looked up into his gentle eyes. 'You're very gallant,' she said and marvelled again at May's infidelity. 'May is very lucky to have you, Barth,' she added softly.

217

Barth sighed, 'I wish she thought so too,' he said wistfully, looking over the heads of the dancers to where his wife, surrounded by guests, seemed in scintillating form. She was laughing, but her eyes, Barth saw, were following the enchanted couple in the centre of the floor as the music struck up again. Charles and Celestine were moving together, gazing into each other's eyes.

Barth sighed again and looked at Ellen. She caught his eye and the awful realization dawned on her that, perhaps, he knew and she was covered in confusion for his sake. He read her thoughts and wondered again why he could not have chosen this sister. How different life would have been, how much more tranquil. He looked at Ellen's soft round face affectionately, but sadly that was all he felt for her. He loved May passionately, and passionate love was not a tranquil emotion. It was too selfish, too demanding. Perhaps he had asked May for more than she could give. Poor May. A dazzling butterfly skimming through life, needing so much to keep her happy. Ellen needed nothing more than kindness.

He took her hand between his. 'I want to say something to you, Ellen,' he said solemnly, and her heart missed a beat in dread lest he should confront her with something she could not cope with or say something she did not wish to hear. He saw her look and patted her hand reassuringly.

'I simply want to ask you to realize one thing that up to now you may have overlooked. That is your value to Garreth.' She opened her mouth to speak but he hushed her, putting his finger to his lips.

'No, Ellen, hear me out and when I am finished say nothing but think on what I have said.' He leaned over her again and she stopped fanning herself and looked at him, fascinated. 'You have never realized your power, Ellen. Without you, Garreth is lost. He relies on you for all the home comforts, for everything. For prestige as well. He aspired to marry into your family and he won his bride. To lose you would be catastrophic for him. You are essential. I'm saying nothing more. Just do not forget your value and remember it is a weapon. Never be afraid again.' He bowed over her hand and kissed it. 'I'll get the champagne,' he said and left her.

The dancers swirled past her, dresses swishing, perfume wafting to where she sat, music and laughter filling the air

218

around her. Her head was a whirl. The sense of what Barth had said hit her like a sledge-hammer. She had never seen herself in that light before. She could not examine his logic at this moment for she felt suddenly light-hearted. She decided she would think about it later; there must be a snag to what he had said, for it placed her in a completely different position than any she had imagined.

Barth brought the champagne and she drank it thirstily and thought about inveigling Barth to dance with her again, she had enjoyed it so much.

Charles held Celestine lightly in his arms. His knee ached but he did not feel it. He could feel nothing but the softness of her hand in his, the gentle undulating of her waist as they danced. He could see nothing but her face slightly tilted back under the sprinkling lights, and his love for her splashed her countenance with radiance. He could see the tiny pearls of sweat on her upper lip and he ached to kiss them away. He had come from another time, another place, to this moment. A different culture bred him, a much more sophisticated society produced him, and her innocence and purity overwhelmed him. He adored everything about her; all her little uncertainties, her gaucheries, her naturalness, a quality that, before, he had despised in a woman. He had loved hot-house plants, exotic blooms, but no more. Now he had fallen in love more completely than ever before with a garden blossom, an uncultivated creature, ignorant of the ways of the world. With her, the lusty desire to seduce was absent. With her, there was only a warm desire to guard and protect and cherish. He did not analyse his emotions, he simply held Celestine lightly in his arms and felt that time stood still and happiness was, after all, attainable and something you could touch.

Celestine knew that from now on her life, content, peace and stability depended on this man. She trusted him; it did not occur to her not to. She gave him her heart with the confidence of a child.

For them both that night, time was suspended. All the normal rhythms had changed tempo and they floated together on a cloud of unreal enchantment. They asked no sensible questions of each other. They assumed, lover-like, that everyone would join them gladly in a celebration of their love; that no-one could possibly wish them ought but well; that there would be, could be, no opposition to this joy they had found in each other. They waltzed in each other's arms childishly oblivious of a reality they were only too soon to face.

Chapter

31

AT tea in Avoca House the next day the women were alone. The men out riding. 'Blowing the cobwebs away after last night', Barth had said as he and Charles and Owen Mulcahy, who had stayed the night went off for a canter. The women sat about in the blue drawing-room sipping their tea and talking in a desultory way about the ball the night before.

Then Celestine announced that she was returning on Monday with her mother to Dublin. Her face scarlet, she faltered and stammered through a garbled speech that was almost incomprehensible but that everyone seemed to understand.

'It's not you, Auntie May . . . don't think that . . . I know you asked me to stay on and it was so kind of you but . . . it's, well . . . Charles wishes to . . . my father must be told . . . and then we can . . . but you have been so kind, dearest Aunt, and it's not that I don't want to, but, well, we feel . . . or Charles does . . . oh, and of course, I do too, that in order to expiate matters . . . I should, well . . .'

'Oh, sit down, dear child, do,' May said. Her voice was kind though her pulses raced and she wanted to scream. 'We all understand. Of course, you must go.' Then, to her horror, she heard herself add, 'If all goes well for you and your Papa says yes . . .' (And why shouldn't he? she wondered sourly, no matter what Ellen says about him not wishing Celestine to marry anyone. The girl would do well to marry a colonel so handsome and well-to-do.) 'If all goes well, I'll give you the wedding here in Avoca House.'

Oh God, had she run mad? Why was she saying these things?

As if it did not matter, as if her heart was not breaking.

'Oh Auntie May, you are an angel.' Celestine threw herself down at her aunt's feet, almost upsetting her tea. She took May's small white hand between her's and kissed it fervently.

'Oh thank you, thank you, thank you. You see, we want to get married as soon as possible.' Her large brown eyes filled with anxiety. 'Charles may be . . . may be recalled . . . to . . . to active duty.' She could hardly get the words out.

May patted her hand and said quickly, 'Oh my dear, don't think of that now. Charles' injury is not completely mended.'

She closed her eyes and the memory of their naked bodies on her bed, her lips on his scarred and twisted knee, the scent of his flesh, the tickle of his hair and the recollection of his passionate love-making overwhelmed her, and for a moment she thought she might faint. She wondered what the others would think if they could guess what went on behind her expression, which she had arranged smooth as glass. If they but knew her innermost lustful thoughts, how they would despise her. How shocked they would be. Ellen particularly. She glanced at her sister's round good-natured face. She looked anxious and May knew that she was worried about going home to Rathgar. Poor Ellen was happy here in Avoca House. She had a hard time with Garreth Connolly. We all have our problems, she thought, and sighed.

She heard Celestine's voice warble on about her kindness and she was suddenly glad that the girl was going back to Dublin. Even if she took Charles away from Avoca House, anything was better than the torment she was enduring, watching them together.

Chapter

32

LEAVE-taking next day left all of them with mixed feelings. Barth was dreading a return to the *ménage à trois*. Celestine and Charles were devastated at their forthcoming separation. Clothilde and Ellen were filled with apprehension at their return to Rathgar and to Garreth and his inevitable ill-humour. Ellen had put the fact of the fire out of her head, but she knew, now, both it and her husband's wrath would have to be faced. May was nervous, sick with anxiety and dread; for the future, no matter how it turned out, promised nothing but anguish for her.

Barth drew Ellen aside.

'Pardon me, dear Ellen, for perhaps rushing in where angels fear to tread, but do remember what I said to you at the ball.' She had forgotten and was puzzled. Then she remembered his words and the jubilation she had felt at his message to her. She smiled at him, and for a moment her apprehension vanished.

She nodded. 'I'll remember,' she said.

'And if things get awkward, or too difficult for you, well, you know there is always a home here for you.'

Ellen met his sympathetic glance and smiled back at him. His concern made her feel much better. But she knew that at the end of the day she had to sort out her own problems, that she had chosen her situation and that it was up to her to cope with whatever trials and tribulations came her way. So Fr Grogan had told her, and his word was law. Resigned, she patted Barth's arm.

'You are a kind man,' she said, her pale blue eyes misting over. 'And remember, no matter what happens or what has happened, May is a good woman,' she added firmly and turned aside to gather up her children.

Celestine and Charles held hands, their breath mingling in little puffs in the cold September morning. A pearly mist hung over the lawns and the trees gently swayed in the vicious little breeze. A bank of fuchsia glowed cerise, a violent splash of colour against the balustrade, and the autumn leaves gleamed, damp burnt-umber, brilliant scarlet, sienna, gold and brown. The sun was a yellow disc, cool as the moon, pale and misted over, veiled with wisps of cloud.

Charles tucked Celestine's fur closer about her neck. He touched her cheek with his palm. He felt the shock of contact right through his body and he shivered. She watched him with wide dark eyes.

'Oh I do love you so,' he said to her breathlessly, although they had been standing still for ten minutes. 'I love you so much, my darling Celestine, I would die for you.'

'Hush. Don't say that.' She touched his lips with two fingers. 'Oh don't even think it. If you died, I would die too.'

They stared at one another, oblivious of the cold, the damp chill in the air, unconscious of the others bustling about preparing to take their leave.

'I cannot bear to be without you,' he said.

'I know darling, darling Charles, neither can I. Oh do, do hurry to Dublin after me.'

'Tomorrow. I swear. Tomorrow. I'll come in the morning at the crack of dawn.'

She shook her head, laughing. 'No, no. Not too early, my beloved.'

'Then at a reasonable time, but in the morning I'll set my case before your father. He cannot refuse us. Oh, I'm not worthy of you.'

'No, no, no.' She shook her head again, contradicting him lovingly.

'Well I'm not. I've led a shockingly immoderate life. But that was before I met you, my angel. I've been wild; I have not a good reputation . . .'

She giggled, a little grey puff of vapour escaping from her lips. He longed to kiss that rosy mouth but refrained from doing so. It would not be seemly, with her mother and sister about. And May. Every time May came into his head he pushed her

224

firmly out. The thought of her made him uncomfortable. But that was the past. It was over and done.

'Anyone as handsome as you, as wonderful as you are, must have had . . .' She hesitated, then shrugged. She was not sure what he might have had and she did not want to know, but she knew it was unrealistic to expect him not to have loved before. In any event, it was different for men. So her mother had often said. She tightened her grip on his arm.

'But never, never again, except me,' she said fiercely. A shiver of joy shook him at her proprietary manner and, despite her mother and aunt's presence, he leaned over and kissed her cheek.

'I promise, my darling, I promise.'

Ellen saw the kiss and was filled with foreboding at the thought of the inevitable meeting with Garreth and how he was going to react to the news, in fact how he had already reacted to the fire. It would not be long now. She knew he would be in a vile temper; the fire in the brewery and her absence would guarantee that. Celestine was in love with Charles and it was serious, anyone could see that. Poor May. She knew her sister was suffering, she was aware of her unhappiness. She knew that she could not bear it if her daughter was to endure a similar pain. But she also knew her husband, and the chances of him allowing Charles to marry Celestine were nil. What a catastrophe their meeting had been for everyone, except, of course, each other. Ellen sighed wearily and hoped she could summon up enough courage for the scenes ahead. What was it Barth had told her? Not to underestimate her importance to Garreth. She must remember, she really must.

As they journeyed home her dread increased. She tried to caution her daughter and suggested that she should not blurt out the news to Garreth. But Celestine was convinced that her Papa would be happy for her, thrilled at her news; and she was deaf to her mother's warnings. Clothilde worried because she had not become engaged. Her father would ask her about Owen and would be irritated beyond endurance at her tardiness. She, too, prayed for fortitude and courage. Only Celestine, like a glass of champagne, fizzed and bubbled with excitement.

When the Wicklow train reached Amiens Street they hired a cab. The jarvey seemed in no hurry, flicking his whip at the nag in an absentminded way, and they meandered through the traffic at a listless pace.

225

Ellen tried again. Her nerves were reaching breaking-point the nearer they got to home. 'Don't blurt out the news to your father, *please*, Celestine,' she begged again, and, again, Celestine was not disposed to listen to her mother's advice.

'Oh, Mother! Papa will be pleased, I'm sure. He's always happy for my success.'

'He may not see this as success,' Clothilde said dryly.

'Of course he will,' Celestine said tranquilly and she smiled at her mother and sister, certainty in her shining eyes. 'You don't know Papa as I do. Why, never in my whole life has he been cross with me.'

'Oh stop burbling on, Cel. It's not going to be easy, you must realize that,' Clothilde said tartly.

'Fooey. You don't understand. Papa will be happy for me, I know he will.'

'All I ask is that you think of *us* a little,' Ellen interrupted, her voice gentle.

'Oh, Mother, you know I will.'

'No, I don't, Celestine. I don't at all. Just because your father thinks the stars and the moon shine out of your eyes, you sometimes take advantage. It may be all right for you, but it is not all right for me and Clothilde. We sometimes have to pay for you being your father's pet.'

Quick tears had sprung into Celestine's eyes. 'Oh I'm sorry. So sorry. I wouldn't have that for the world. What do you want me to do?' she asked contritely.

'Just don't blurt it all out to your father. Give him time to complain a bit about the fire. He'll want to. Let him tell us and have his little grumble.'

She hoped that was what it would be, a little grumble; not, as she feared a mighty eruption.

Clothilde took up her mother's refrain. 'Try to keep the news to yourself until, say, after supper when he's mellow and relaxed and, perhaps, you have sung him "Kathleen Mavourneen",' she said earnestly.

Ellen nodded in agreement with her eldest daughter and they both looked at Celestine hopefully. She nodded.

'All right, Mother, Clo. I'll do as you ask. I still think Papa will be happy for me. But if you think it is the best way . . .' They nodded in unison. 'Then,' she shrugged, 'all right.'

In the event, the confrontation that Ellen and Clothilde had

226

been dreading was postponed. On arrival they found Nellie's coat on the hall-stand and the third O'Meara sister ensconced in Garreth's chair in the parlour. Garreth was hovering uncharacteristically in alien territory, between the piano and Ellen's chair, which he seemed unable to sit himself in and to which Ellen gravitated now automatically. She studiously avoided her husband's eye as she greeted her sister.

Nellie was a placid, unemotional, tranquil woman who neither loved nor hated to extreme, but was balanced and sweetly reasonable in all things. She was, at this moment, happily unaware of her brother-in-law's ill-concealed irritation at her presence, and would not really have worried about it if she had sensed it anyhow. As far as she was concerned, other people's ill-humour or anger was their own problem and any attempt to draw her into its orbit was doomed to failure. She had had a lot of practice with May's propensity for drama during their girlhood. She hugged Ellen and her nieces and her face lit up at her sister's warm welcome.

Nellie had a fine face, a profile cut in ice, pure and sharp. It was a beautifully boned face; weathered by her outdoor life, her skin was not as well preserved as her sister's, but she was a person people instinctively trusted and liked. She was also a little deaf in one ear.

Ellen was so relieved to see her that she was almost in tears. Garreth would not precipitate a big scene with Nellie here.

So Ellen asked her eagerly and at once, 'You will stay, won't you?'

'Well, you don't think I'm going back to Kerry and I've just arrived?' she asked, laughing. 'Although if it's too much trouble I can go down to the Shelbourne.'

Garreth was busy slipping into his armchair which Nellie had vacated on Ellen's arrival, so his comment, 'You'd probably be far more comfortable there, Nellie,' came under Ellen's loud protest and so got smothered.

'Let you stay in the Shelbourne? My own sister? Never,' Ellen said very firmly.

'The Lord be praised,' she thought. 'This is a reprieve and perhaps Garreth will have mellowed by the morrow.'

'You'll stay here, Nellie. We've got no one in the guest room.' Ellen wanted to make sure that Garreth did not manoeuvre her amicable sister into the hotel.

'Ah well, in that case, Ellen, I'd love it. 'Twill give us time to talk.'

Garreth could see he was losing ground. He rose with dignity, excused himself, and was about to leave the women when his youngest daughter, having removed her coat, hurled herself into the room, throwing her arms around him, hugging and kissing him. He visibly thawed, the black edge to his humour melting away. He greeted Celestine warmly. His 'Oh my dearest child, how good it is to see you' was lost under Celestine's excited gabbling. His embrace and the warmth of his greeting had touched a responding chord in her. He held her for a moment, tightly in his arms. Then, despite her mother's warnings, ignoring her sister's advice, she plunged headlong into an account of the momentous thing that had occured while he was away. She simply could not wait a moment longer; the magnitude of what had happened to her needed instant expression.

'Oh Papa, I am engaged to be married,' she blurted out and Ellen's face went pale. 'Well, Charles has to ask you first, of course, but I told him it would be all right. That you loved me and would give your permission. Oh, and you will love him, Papa, I know you will, for I do. He is so handsome and kind and . . . and . . .'

She had caught sight of her father's face and suddenly her confidence left her. The face was implacable and cold, a stranger's face, not the face of her loving and kind Papa at all. It was a face he had shown her mother and sister and her brothers, but she had never seen it directed towards her. She wished, too late, she had heeded her mother and sister but she had to carry on.

'Oh Papa, Papa, don't be cross with me. Please say you understand. Please, Papa, please. You know how I love you.'

For a second his world had stopped. He could not believe his ears. For a fleeting moment he thought of her going away, not being home when he returned from work, never singing 'Kathleen Mavourneen' to him again. He knew that she had given him the deepest happiness he had ever known in his life. Only with her had he felt relaxed and contented. Only with her was he sure of himself. Only with her did he feel the equal of any man and no longer fearful of his own inadequacies. He did not have to brag and boast to her. She accepted him as he was

228

and loved him for himself. He could not lose her. He dared not lose her. Fear of showing weakness made his voice sound colder than he had intended.

'You say you love me?' he asked icily. 'I do not believe it, Celestine. I did, but I do not believe it any more. I thought you did, but I was mistaken. You say you love me and yet you treat me like this?' His voice now was sorrowful.

'Like what, Papa? Like what? I don't understand.' Celestine was bewildered. She timorously touched the lapels of his jacket, looking at him beseechingly. She could not fathom what was happening. She felt as if her whole life was in turmoil and everything was being turned topsy-turvey. She knew that her father had often been unkind to her mother, her sister and her brothers. Not intentionally, of course, and after all, he was a man, her father, her mother's husband, and so, of course, he had a right to show his displeasure. But up to now, she had never been on the receiving end. She had found her family's fear of Garreth hard to understand. Suddenly, now, she shared their terror of the head of the house.

She had been so sure, so eager to share the happiness that threatened to overflow, to share it with the only other man she had ever loved. But her confidence had been thrown back in her face. Coldly he had questioned her love for him. How could he do that? It was a betrayal.

She tried again. 'Papa, Papa, you know I love you. But I love Charles Cavendish. Not instead of you, but as well as you. Please try to understand. I want to marry him, please.'

'You will never marry him as long as I'm alive.' There was a chill note of finality in his voice that wounded her to the very quick. Then he said slowly, patiently, as if she were an idiot and might not understand, 'I have always told you, my dear, you cannot say I have not. I have always been clear about my plans for you all. Neill, and Breffni when he returns from the war, will take over the brewery. Clothilde will marry Owen Mulcahy and you, you will remain with your mother and me, unmarried, our joy and consolation in old age. You will not see Charles Cavendish any more, do you understand?'

Nellie had been vainly trying to understand and to hear what was going on. Most of it seemed Greek to her, and her faulty hearing prevented her from fully assimilating the conversation between her niece and her brother-in-law. It seemed to her yet another example of Garreth's pontificating, laying down the law to his family, something, she often told her husband, Joe, that she could not have borne. She had been thinking how lucky she was that Joe was not foolish enough to go in for that sort of thing when the name Charles Cavendish impinged on her consciousness.

'Charles Cavendish? Charles Cavendish?' she said loudly. 'Isn't that the young lieutenant May was mad about?'

Garreth Connolly swung around to rebuke her, then realized the full import of what she had said.

'What? What? You mean . . .?'

'Yes. You remember, Ellen?' Nellie asked comfortably. 'Why are you shaking your head like that? Surely you remember? Charles Cavendish, years ago. Papa and Mama took May off to London to put her out of his reach. Oh what a fine to-do it all was.' She burbled on unaware of the effect her words were having. 'And Mama, Grandma O'Meara, told me only the other day that he has come back to Avoca House and that May is misbehaving herself all over again. Mama says that they have been the talk of Wicklow. She's very cross about it. You know what Mama is like, Ellen. Good luck to them, I say, though I'm sorry for poor Barth. He's a very milk-and-water fellow. No dash. No brio. Whereas Charles Cavendish was a devil of a charmer. Still, Barth does not deserve his wife bedding down under his very nose with a soldier, and that soldier a devil like Charles Cavendish.'

Everyone stared at her in horror. She looked from face to face in surprise, then perplexity.

'What have I said? Shouldn't I have told you? Surely Celestine and Clothilde are old enough? Or are they? I sometimes forget. Townsfolk are such a prissy lot, God help us.'

Still there was silence. Still they stared.

'Well, what is it, for heaven's sake? Have I sprouted a wart on my nose? Enlighten me, do.'

Garreth was the first to recover. He had been blindly searching for a reason for his disapproval and suddenly, miraculously, it had been given to him. He had been apoplectic at Nellie's inopportune arrival ten minutes before he expected his wife and family. Now he sent up a silent prayer of thanks for her presence and her tactless soliloquy. All the anger, frustration and impotent fury of the last week left him. Of a sudden, the dark

230

clouds of his pent-up rage rolled away and the sun came out. He smiled at Nellie.

'Charles Cavendish. Of course. I remember him well.' He glanced at Celestine. 'Handsome, my love, he certainly was in a facile, superficial way.' He could not keep the triumphant sarcasm from his voice. 'Your Auntie May's beau.'

'And still is, in a wrong side of the blanket way,' Nellie said. 'Not that I blame May. She always loved Charlie, and Father did rather throw her into Barth's arms. Still, marriage is a sacrament and such hanky-panky should be discouraged. Don't you agree, Ellen? But you've just come from Avoca House, Garreth was telling me. What is all the news? All the latest gossip?'

'Nellie, please, hush up,' Ellen pleaded.

'So the whipper-snapper that trifled with your feelings is your Aunt May's beau. You see, Celestine? How right I was? Your Papa was right. Your Papa loves you and cares for you. You know that well enough. I have your best interests at heart. You can see that now. But you are young and naïve. You have been taken advantage of. I cannot imagine how your mother allowed it to happen.' He glared at Ellen who shrank into herself.

Celestine thought her head would burst. Waves of shock engulfed her. It seemed she did not know the man before her nor the man she had left at Avoca House. She was stunned, not understanding what had happened. She was completely mesmerized by incomprehension. Her father's face seemed to grow and become grotesque as a gargoyle. He was cross with her, angry. Why? She had done nothing wrong. Falling in love was not wrong. How could it be? Papa and Mother must have been in love sometime. Everyone did it, except, of course, nuns and priests. She wanted to whimper like a whipped dog.

And Charles? What of him? Was he really Aunt May's beau? There was a roaring in her ears, a throbbing, beating drum in her head. She looked wildly around the room. Her father was still speaking but she could not hear what he was saying.

'I'm going to be sick.'

She whispered the words to Clothilde who stood beside her. Her sister took her arm and rushed her up the stairs to the bathroom. Ellen followed.

Garreth asked, turning benevolently to Nellie, 'Would you join me in a glass of sherry?'

As Ellen went up the stairs, she heard Nellie say, 'How kind.

Well now, I don't mind if I do. Garreth, did I hear Celestine saying she felt sick? It was the train journey, I'll be bound. Nasty smelly things, trains. Don't really hold with them myself. Or motor vehicles either. Even the velocipede. No. Give me the good old horse any day . . .'

Chapter

33

CLOTHILDE bathed Celestine's face with a cloth wrung out in cold water. The girl was hot and cold by turns and shivered violently. Clothilde and Mamie between them had undressed her and put her to bed after a fit of vomiting that alarmed them and left Celestine weak and exhausted. Now she lay against her pillows, shaken, her face pale and strained. Ellen held her daughter's hand, patting it occasionally. They all knew Garreth would not come up here.

Ellen realized she should go down to her sister but Clothilde said briskly: 'He'll be happy now, Mother. Leave him with Nellie. Stay here awhile and rest yourself. For this is not the last we'll hear of this.'

Ellen sighed. She was miserable to discover that, deep within her, there was a feeling of relief that Celestine was the target of Garreth's wrath for a change. So used to defending the other children, so accustomed to being the object of his anger herself, so tired of being assured by Celestine that Garreth was truly a loving and misunderstood father, it gave her a certain satisfaction to see the man who had caused her so much pain and who was, in her daughter's eyes, a paragon, brought low, revealed in his true colours, and her judgement vindicated. And she was deeply ashamed of her feelings.

Clothilde watched her sister anxiously. Celestine's lips were outlined in white and the usual ripe, red colour had vanished from her mouth and cheeks. All the vitality had gone and she seemed lifeless lying there, a frown furrowing her pale forehead. Mamie fussed about, worried about her darling, and Ellen drooped over her daughter's still form, sighing deeply every few

233

moments. There was silence in the room as Clothilde bathed her sister's brow with gentle movements.

At last, Celestine opened her eyes. She made a feeble attempt at a smile, failed miserably and said to her sister, 'You're so good, Clo. So kind. Mother?'

'Yes, my darling? I'm here.'

'Mother, why didn't you tell me about Charles?' She paused, gulped, and added painfully, 'And Auntie May?'

'I didn't think it mattered.' Ellen shrugged, and realized that she still didn't.

Celestine looked at her mother, surprised.

'That is what I have been thinking. Just now. Why should it matter to me? Oh Mother, I know he loves me.' Life and animation were returning to her cheeks and mouth and eyes. 'Does it matter who he loved before me? He did not know me then. He did not know he was going to meet me and once he met me . . . But then, why didn't he tell me about his involvement with Auntie May? Why?'

'Perhaps he, too, thought it did not matter,' Ellen said.

'Oh Cel, don't get excited. You're all right. Keep calm.' Clothilde held her hand tightly and her sister turned to her.

'No, Clo. Why should it matter? He loves me now. I *know*. I *know*. I know it with every fibre of my being. He loves me.'

Clothilde met her mother's eyes across the bed. They exchanged a look, understanding each other's thoughts well.

Ellen spoke. 'Dearest child, that is not important. About your Auntie May, all that. What is important is your father's attitude. He'll never let you marry Charles.'

'Oh Mother, Mother, I'm sure you're wrong. He needs to get used to the idea.' Celestine's eyes were filling with hope. 'When he meets Charles, when they speak, it will be all right, I know it will.'

Clothilde shook her head and cast here eyes up to heaven.

'Oh dearest sister, you are such an optimist, you always were. But please do not get your hopes up. I know — we, Mother and I — know him better than you . . .'

Celestine blushed, her cheeks flamed red and she said indignantly, 'I don't know what to believe any more. Papa has always been the kindest, sweetest man to me all my life. Just now . . . well, the news was a shock to him. I wish I had listened to you, that's all . . . waited a little. It was a mistake, I'm sure.' But she

234

did not sound very sure herself.

Ellen rose. 'I had better get downstairs and see to things. Mamie will have to make up the bed in the guest-room and put in hot-water bottles for Nellie. Garreth will be angry if dinner is late, although he's quite pleased with himself just now, having upset us all and won the day.'

'Oh Mother, please don't say that,' Celestine pleaded.

But Ellen replied firmly, 'Now, Celestine, no more nonsense from you. I'm sorry, my love, but you are beginning to see your father through our eyes for a change. It is no use getting in a pet about it. Papa will not change his mind about your getting married. He never means to allow you to wed, any more than he means to allow Clothilde to follow her heart and take the veil. What you *do* about it is another matter, but take it from me, if your Papa has his way, you will *not* be married and Clothilde *will* be married to Owen before the year is out. Mark my words.' And, on this ominous sentence, she left the room, and Celestine fell back on the pillows and closed her eyes.

Clothilde sat with her quietly for a while, waiting until her breathing was slow and even. Then she tiptoed out. She went downstairs. Garreth's laugh, echoed by Nellie's, filtered out in muted fashion from the parlour. She crept down the steps to the kitchen and called Miffy. Ellen was there instructing Mamie. Her mother turned to her and asked her what she was doing, creeping about her own house as if she were a thief.

'Oh, Mother, I've told Miffy to go upstairs and sit a while with Celestine. I don't want Cel left alone. I think she's a little in shock. I also think Miffy ought to be out of the line of fire this evening, don't you?'

Her mother nodded and Miffy nodded vigorously beside her. There was nothing Miffy wanted more than to stay upstairs with Celestine, away from her tormentor. She lifted her skirt and fled, fleet of foot, up to Celestine's room.

The evening passed peacefully. Garreth, secure in the knowledge that he had the upper hand, was in great form, joking with Nellie, laughing a lot and being sarcastic about the service and Mamie. Mamie, on her own, was making heavy weather of the dishing up. Neill did not appear and Celestine stayed in her room, Miffy a silent devoted companion. She was worried though about her young mistress who was tossing and turning.

Miffy soothed her as best she could. 'What is it, Miss? Mebbe

235

I can help?' she asked timidly, anxiously.

'What would you know about it, Miffy?' Celestine asked helplessly.

'Well, ye don't have te know about somethin' te help,' Miffy said realistically. So Celestine told the girl all about Charles, omitting the complication of her aunt, which she felt might be too much for the girl's limited intelligence.

'I don't know what to do, Miffy, really I don't,' she said feverishly.

To her surprise Miffy said, 'Well I'd have no doubt at all, Miss Celestine. I'd go wid him. Off an' away. If I loved him.' The servant faltered. 'Now I think I've said enough, Miss, an' you too. Hush up now an' try to rest.'

The longer Celestine lay there in her bed and thought about it, the more she came to realize that perhaps after all her mother was right. So many times she had seen her father angry and sarcastic with her brothers, her sister, and her mother, but she had closed her eyes to their pain. She had never had to traverse that territory herself and, in order to protect herself, she had chosen to be relentlessly blinkered about her relationship with her father. She had assumed that his *tendresse* for her would surmount any difference of opinion. Now she knew that this was not the case. His amiability towards her depended on her total subjection to his wishes. Well, she decided on consideration, so be it. She would have to find the courage to fight him. Somewhere, from the depths of her being, she must draw the strength to contest her father's will. With that realization, part of her died. Part of her trust was buried, and part of her faith, her unclouded innocence, vanished into the mists of her childhood; and what was left of her belief in the familial love of her father was shaken and she questioned, for the first time, his omnipotence.

'Oh Miffy, Miffy, I'm so unhappy,' she cried and Miffy soothed her again.

'There, there, little Missy. Rest. Rest.'

Tired out, released from tension as if she had made some momentous decision, Celestine eventually fell into a troubled sleep.

Chapter

34

FROM her window next morning Celestine saw Charles arrive. She called Clothilde, who came hurrying from her room. She had been in and out of her sister's room all morning, for Celestine was in an agony of excitement and dread that constantly turned to hope. Both girls watched Charles' arrival breathlessly.

He looked splendid in his uniform, every inch the soldier. When the doorbell sounded, Celestine and Clothilde crept to the top of the stairs and sat on the landing. Celestine had a moment of confidence as Charles gave his cap and gloves and coat to Mamie and disappeared into the parlour. Surely her father must be impressed by this distinguished officer.

Her hope was short-lived. They listened to the silence of the house for a moment, staring at the closed parlour door, and then it was broken by Garreth, his voice raised in anger. They could not hear what he said, only his furious shouting. Unable to bear it, Celestine jumped to her feet. Alarmed, Clothilde tried to restrain her, but Celestine pulled away, tearing the sleeve of her blouse with the violence of her movement. Before Clothilde could stop her, she lifted her skirts and ran down the stairs into the parlour. Clothilde's restraining voice echoed after her in vain.

'Oh don't, Cel. For God's sake, don't. Don't interfere. You'll make it worse.'

It was no use. Celestine was gone and she was left holding a button from her sister's sleeve.

Garreth was incensed by the sudden appearance of his daughter. He had felt quite calm waiting for the soldier. Ellen

237

had informed him that the man was coming to see him, and he found himself looking forward to his arrival. He would give him short shrift, he would put him in his place. He had planned to be cold and dismissive and had started that way, but Charles Cavendish's superior air infuriated him and his precarious self-restraint gave way and he began to shout. Once started, it was hard to stop. Charles was not lacking in respect; far from it. However, he seemed to assume his suit would be welcomed, that Garreth would be glad to have him as a son-in-law. It was this last assumption that broke the dam on what little control Garreth possessed, and he turned on Charles in fury.

'By what right do you dare to ask me for my daughter's hand? You, her aunt's lover?' He saw Charles flinch and he thought, aha, my fine superior fellow, you didn't think I knew that, now did you?

'How dare you even think of such a sweet innocent girl at all, let alone ask to marry her?' he continued in a fine rage. 'I forbid you to entertain such a notion. I forbid you to see her again. I forbid you to set foot in this house. I forbid you to have any contact with her, ever. Do you hear me? Ever again. Do you hear?'

'But, sir, I beg of you, . . .'

'You are not fit to do up her bootlaces. You are nothing but a philanderer.'

'Oh, sir, you cannot blame me for anything that happened in the past, before I met Celestine.'

'That is right, Papa,' Celestine cried. She had burst into the room and heard Charles' last sentence and her father's reply. 'You cannot blame him for the past.' She ran to Charles and took his hand in her's. 'I don't, and after all, that is what matters.' The sweet look that passed between them outraged Garreth and he turned his back on them for a moment.

Celestine stood trembling at her lover's side, trying hard to keep back her tears. She was distressed beyond measure at this ugly scene between the two men who meant everything to her.

Her father was amazed to see her. He had been sure Nellie's disclosures the previous evening would disgust his daughter and put her firmly in his camp. It seemed that he was wrong, and the damage was worse than he had feared and this acknowledgement deepened his rage. He struggled for control.

'It is most certainly not what matters.' He turned to her,

238

suddenly quiet. 'I have loved you all your life, Celestine, since you were a baby and I held you in my arms and you clung to my little finger. With your tiny little fist, you held onto my finger.' There were tears in his eyes and Charles felt only disgust at how this man was manipulating the gentle girl beside him.

Celestine had no such insight and she was thrown into terrible confusion at the sight of her father's tears. 'Don't, Papa, please don't,' she sobbed.

'Come here, child,' he said gruffly. She obeyed and he took her face between his hands. Charles stood stiffly as if at attention. He was finding it difficult to restrain himself.

'Look at me,' her father said. 'Have I ever been unfair or unkind to you?' Humbly she shook her head. 'Have I ever been wrong about what's best for you?' Again, she shook her head. 'Well, my dearest child, you must believe me that I'm not wrong now.'

'Oh Papa, Papa, but I love him.'

The tug of her loves drew her both ways. She felt as if she were being torn in two. This man before her had been her god, the be all and the end all of her life up to now. Behind her stood Charles, and she could feel the irresistible pull of her new love. Desire for him, an overwhelming yearning to slip into the circle of his arms, overcame her. Now, here in this room, the old fought with the new.

'Don't do it to me, Father,' she cried out in pain. Her voice entreated him, but he was deaf. She turned to Charles, bewildered. Garreth stepped swiftly between them.

'Leave this house,' he said to Charles. 'I will not ask you again.' He was too clever to allow it to come to fisticuffs and Charles was aware, too, of the danger inherent in such an eventuality. Both men looked upon each other with loathing and Celestine, seeing that look, knew she must choose. There would be no compromise.

Charles drew himself up. 'Sir, I came here to ask for your daughter's hand in marriage. She loves me and I promise you that I will give everything I have to make her happy. I would cheerfully die for her. I am saddened by your attitude . . .'

'You dare to speak to me like that?' Garreth interrupted. 'I think you have lost your reason. I will not ask you again. Leave my house.'

'Then I must go too, Father. I will go with him. You will

break my heart, Father, but I must leave you and the home I love.'

'You will not. I'll have you both arrested.' His voice quivered in fury. 'You will go nowhere unless it be to your room. You forget you are underage, my girl. Besides, no priest in Ireland will marry you without my permission.'

'Your permission. Your permission.' Clothilde stood in the doorway. Alarmed by the loud voices and the piteous sound of her sister's distress, she had opened the door quietly, taken in the scene, and heard enough to make her forget, for a moment, her fear of her father, the respect she knew was his due, and the sin she committed by her audacity in addressing him thus.

'Do we need your permission to breathe? Do we need your permission to exist? Are you indeed God? Or do you think you are, Father?'

Celestine knew the fight was over. For the moment, there was nothing she or Charles could do to melt her father's unreason. There was no need to embroil Clothilde in the trouble.

'Leave this house,' Garreth said once more and Charles bowed and left the room. Celestine was about to follow him, but her father's voice, cold as the North wind, restrained her. 'Stay here. Don't move.'

He listened until he heard the front door shut and the sound of footsteps crunching down the gravel path. He turned to his daughters.

'Go to your room, Celestine. You are not to leave it today. Have your meals there. Mamie or Miffy will serve you. I have nothing more to say to you.' He looked then at Clothilde. 'I will overlook your disgraceful rudeness. It is no wonder that man thinks he can come here and dare to ask for my daughter's hand. He sees you lack respect and therefore treats you as cheap. Your mother will need you, Clothilde, to help in enter-taining Nellie. They are both at Mass at the moment.' Then, as his daughters turned to leave the room, he added, 'I would like to remind you both that I will be here for the next few days. The brewery was burned down. Not that that triviality should interest you. I will be watching your every move. If either of you puts a foot out of place, it will be the worse for you. Remember I am right beside the front door.' He smiled at them. 'You may go now,' he said.

That night Celestine heard the key turn in her bedroom door. The click was loud in the silence of the night and she heard the sound of her father's cough a second later. It seemed to her that he wanted her to hear. He coughed a second time and then there was silence again; the silence of something withdrawn. She could feel his presence moving off though the thick door separated them.

She remained calm. She had made up her mind. In a way, her father had made it easy for her. She had made it up that moment in the parlour when she stood between the men she loved. She would escape this room. She would fly to Charles. A pain tore through her chest when she thought of her Papa, of her love for him. Despite what he had done to her, she still wanted to run to him, apologize to him. For what, she did not know. She simply knew that the habit of obedience and reverence was very strong, and the thought of breaking the custom of a lifetime filled her with guilt. She was determined to quell her reluctance. She was going to take her chances, dare and dare again, and fly to her love. Plans ran around and around in her head and were in turn discarded. She felt sure that Charles would protect her if she escaped. She was certain they could lie low until he could take her to England, to Gretna Green if necessary. It would be shocking, awful, but she was prepared to go to any lengths to win her love. For to her, who had never been out of Ireland, England was a great and protective place. Charles was English, therefore no harm could come to her there. In that invincible country, its soldier-citizen protecting her, she would be safe. Her Papa could not touch her there.

But she had to find a way out of the house. Celestine was aware that Neill, her best hope of escape, was staying away deliberately, and now, in the light of her experience, she did not blame him. But he would not be back for a while and would be in trouble when he did return. She was afraid that Clothilde would be too sensible of the dangers involved to enter wholeheartedly into the idea of escape. Celestine knew that her plan was unformulated and yet she had full confidence that it could work. But she needed a helper. She had discarded both Clothilde and Neill. That left her mother. But Ellen was too frightened of Papa and loved her too much to allow her to attempt it. She thought and sought in her mind for someone who would not mind deceiving Garreth and suddenly she knew:

241

Mamie. And Mamie would get Miffy to help. Yes. The plan would work with Mamie's and Miffy's support. At last, with everything in place in her mind, she slept.

Chapter

35

THE next morning at eight o'clock there was a gentle tap on Celestine's door. It was Mamie. She had brought breakfast on a tray; hot chocolate; fresh-baked brown bread; and a coddled egg. But Celestine was not hungry and could not eat. To Mamie's surprise, she sat up brightly in bed and looked at the servant with pleading eyes.

'Oh Lord, oh Lord, oh Lord,' Mamie glared at Celestine, knowing what was coming next.

'You *must* help me, Mamie,' Celestine said, grabbing the older woman's arm.

'It'd be more than my life's worth, Miss,' Mamie said. Mamie never had to have things explained to her. She always knew what went on in this house. Someone always confided in her, and if they didn't, she guessed.

'But you *must*, you know you must. You're my only hope.' Celestine sounded desperate.

Mamie sighed. She alone of the whole household did not go in fear of Garreth Connolly. She was of peasant stock; her parents had been crofters on the O'Meara land before the girls got married and the big house was sold. Her parents had died long since and Mr O'Meara had given Mamie to Ellen on her marriage to Garreth. Mamie was not frightened of Garreth because she was not frightened of life. She needed little, was satisfied with less than she needed, and was capable of survival. She was also philosophical and well aware of the fact that Lord Gorman would not see her want. Even if he did, she knew she would always get a job, for she was, as Ellen put it, 'a treasure', a superb cook and a hard worker, ready to turn her hand to almost anything. So there was no fear in her, for Garreth did not possess any power over her.

She hated Garreth. Her loathing of the man burned within her like a bright flame. She had watched him, his behaviour to Ellen over the years, his bullying ways, his high-handed tactics with his wife and children, and she had learned to despise him. She knew he was an upstart. She had seen him fumble his table manners, unsure about what was correct, and she had let him see she noticed. She had realized he did not understand a lot of words and allusions used by the family in the worlds of art and music, history and agriculture, and she enjoyed watching him stew in his own juice. She was glad of his discomfiture, for he had not treated her darling Ellen well. She had seen her beloved mistress go in anxiety and fear of him, had watched her shrink more and more within herself.

She protected Ellen as best she could. She took every opportunity to make Garreth's life as difficult as possible, as long as it did not affect her adored Ellen and the rest of the family.

This seemed a ready-made chance, she thought, as she looked at Celestine's upturned face. It was so like her mother's when she was this age, so happy and trusting. This was a chance to thwart him, her adversary. So she sighed and asked Miss Celestine what she wanted done.

'Oh, pack an overnight bag for me, dearest Mamie.' Celestine's face was flushed and Mamie gasped.

'Oh Mother of God. What do ye mean te do?'

'I'm going away with Charles.'

'The soldier? He seems a strong and mature person, but nevertheless, Miss Celestine . . .'

'I love him, Mamie. I love him with all my heart.' She clasped her hands together and looked at the servant with pleading eyes. 'Oh, Mamie, it's no use your making a fuss. I'm going to run away, with your help or without it, or I'll die. I'll go like this if I have to.' She pointed to the chemise she was wearing and Mamie crossed herself.

'Such sauce! Well, an' how are ye goin' to get outa the house?'

Celestine shook her dark mahogany-coloured hair. 'Oh that's easy. The back door. The vegetable garden. Papa forgets it's there. He'll keep his eye on the front door, you can be sure, although I am sure he would never imagine I'd try to escape.

But he's bound to forget the back lane. I'll go that way. Down the stairs and into the kitchen and out into the garden and then, *voilà*, the lane. Miffy can get me a cab.' Celestine was jumping about, well pleased with herself. Her excitement was infectious. 'Mamie, dearest Mamie, you'll help?'

Mamie nodded and was rewarded by a bone-crushing hug.

'Mamie, you must telephone Avoca House. Ask to speak to Charles or Auntie May.' She thought for a moment, feeling a stab of pain as she remembered her godmother's involvement. She shook her head. 'No. No. Better make sure it's Charles. Captain Charles Cavendish. Tell him I'll meet him in the Shelbourne Hotel. Tell him I'll be there at tea-time. Four o'clock. No one will notice me there at that time. It is suitable for young ladies, Mamie, so it's no use you looking so doubtful. Also it will give him time to get there. You'll do it, Mamie, won't you? And be sure to speak to him personally. Please? Pretty please?'

Mamie nodded and Celestine squealed and wrapped her arms again around the old lady, who hushed her. The girl was full of energy now, for with the resilience and passion of youth, she had completely switched her allegiance from her father to the man she loved. Overnight, her father had become a villain and she knew that if she did not condemn him as one she would suffer too much pain. Better cut him out of her affection than be torn apart by a divided loyalty she found unbearable.

Mamie was grumbling in a half-hearted sort of way. 'It's against my better judgement, Miss Celestine, an' I don't know what yer Ma'll say. Girls today! I'm sure it's not right, telephoning a gentleman, making assignations. But if you're set on it, I'll help.' Celestine gave a cry of delight. 'For pity's sake, hush up or you'll have your Mama and sister in on top of us, and then the fat'll be in the fire.'

Celestine fell silent immediately and Mamie continued, 'And another thing, Missy. Try to pretend you are contrite. Be meek and biddable, and after lunch pretend a headache. Say you did not sleep last night and must rest. It is the best thing to do. It'll fool 'em.'

'I'll try, Mamie, I'll try. Although I haven't been good about accepting advice up to now. Oh, thank you. You are the dearest person in the world.' She hugged and kissed Mamie, who

245

snorted and pulled away, but Celestine could see how delighted the servant was.

'Nonsense. We haven't begun. Time to thank me when it's all over and you and Captain Charles are flying to freedom in each other's arms.'

Mamie wanted to believe that Celestine would be happy, that their efforts and the ensuing trouble would be worth it. But she had her doubts. Something in her bones warned her it probably would not be plain sailing.

Mamie told Celestine that to pack her bag would not be too difficult. She said she thought that her best plan was to go downstairs and await the first opportunity to escape and make her telephone call, for upon that depended success.

She managed it much sooner than she expected, for Ellen had run out of senna-pods. Mr Connolly, she told Mamie, had not had a movement that morning and what with her being in Wicklow and all the fuss about the brewery, no one had prepared him his black brew, and as the supply of pods had run out she wanted Mamie to go down to the chemist and get some Syrup of Figs, a laxative that might do the trick. Mamie was happy to oblige and hot-footed it down to Mr Blessed, who also had a telephone, which he was delighted to let Mamie use.

On her return, she told Ellen she would fetch Miss Celestine down for lunch and hurried up to the girl's room where Celestine was waiting in a fever of impatience.

'Did you speak to him? To Charles? To Charles himself?'

'Yes, Miss Celestine. Himself. I asked . . .'

'Oh tell me, Mamie, tell me what he said.'

'I'm trying to. Trying I am, if you'll let me.'

'Well, go on. Please go on.'

Mamie sighed and sat down. 'If you let me get a word in edgewise, Miss Celestine, a word, an' I'll tell you.' She paused and Celestine shut her mouth and looked at Mamie with wide beseeching eyes. 'Well then, I'll tell you. First, I got Lord Gorman. What a lovely gentleman he is, to be sure.' She caught Celestine's eye and hurried on. 'He knew it was me. He got me the captain. Very happy the captain sounded to hear from you. Wanted to know if you were all right. Wanted most particularly to know. Kept asking me if you were all right and I said yes.'

'Oh Mamie, Mamie, tell me . . .'

'Miss, I'm trying. I told him the plan. He promised to get to the Shelbourne early. He said to tell you he would be there without fail. Tell her, he said, I'll be there eagerly waiting for her. That's what he said.'

Celestine was blissfully relieved, but thrown into a state of frenzied activity.

'Let's hurry, hurry, Mamie,' she cried, and Mamie pointed out that she did not have to meet the Captain until four p.m. and it was now only approaching noon.

'I'll run a bath, Miss, calm down. You get bathed and changed and I'll pack your valise. Never you fret. We'll see to your needs. Now off you go, off.' She shooed Celestine into the bathroom for all the world as if she were a mother hen.

Lunch was a tense affair. Ellen and Clothilde jumped to the conclusion that Celestine's nervous excitement derived from her broken romance, and Garreth took her appearance at lunch as a sign of contrition, a misunderstanding she did nothing to contradict. He duly unbent enough to smile at her, indicating his magnanimous desire to forgive and forget. Then he sank back into the uncomfortable state into which the malfunction of his bowels had cast him.

It seemed an interminable meal to Celestine. She was profoundly grateful that her Auntie Nellie kept up a monologue and did not seem to expect her or her mother and sister to take part in a conversation. She knew she would not be capable of it, at all events. Eventually the jam roly-poly and custard had been consumed and the coffee stage was reached and Celestine excused herself and said her head throbbed and that she was going to lie down. No one saw anything amiss in this, and in fact would have been much more surprised if she had elected to stay. They knew she was upset, and her behaviour was in character with such a state of affairs.

Mamie had to wait until the dishes had been washed and dried before she could go upstairs. Her absence from the kitchen would have given rise to suspicion, there was no doubt of that. When eventually they were all done, she hurried back to Celestine's room where she found the girl rushing around, picking things up, laying them down, full of restless excitement. Mamie admonished, entreated, and eventually insisted she settle down and calm herself.

'You'll get nowhere, Miss, if you wind yourself up like the grandfather clock in the hall.'

247

She urged Celestine to take a warm fur wrap, though the girl could see no need for such niceties.

At last, small case packed, fur wrap around the shoulders of her coat, Celestine, hugging Mamie, bidding her a fond if absent-minded goodbye, was at last ready to go.

They crept down the stairs. They could hear the clink of coffee cups from the parlour and Nellie's voice mingling with Ellen's, Clothilde's and Garreth's. A stair creaked and Celestine went pale, for it sounded like thunder in her ears, but the conversation flowed on behind the closed door. She glanced at Mamie who nodded, and they crept past the door and to the stairs to the kitchen, and at last into Mamie's domain, where she could breath a sigh of relief.

Miffy waited, her eyes like saucers, chewing the bottom of her apron.

Celestine ran up to the little maid and hugged her. 'I'm doing it, Miffy. I'm going after my happiness.'

'Good on ye, Miss.' Miffy was in a state of nervous tension mixed with delight for her mistress.

Mamie sent her for a cab. 'Make him wait at the end of the lane. Do ye hear? Never mind what he says. An' if yer worried, pretend yer dumb.' Mamie looked at Celestine and added, 'I don't trust her voice. It comes out strangulated when she's out of control.'

Miffy got the cab. It was easy enough on the Rathgar Road. With a mixture of sign language and squeaks, she managed to make the jarvey understand that she wanted him to park at the bottom of the lane. The jarvey, not the full shilling, was only too happy to wait. Inside the house, in the kitchen, Mamie was alarmed when her bell was rung.

'Mercy, Miss Celestine. They must want more coffee. An' I gave them the big pot an' enough to launch a battleship,' she said. 'Wait there, Miss. Don't *do* anything. I'll go an' see what they want.' To her horror, it appeared that Mr Connolly, in a restless frame of mind, had decided to go down to the brewery after all and, as he said, oversee what was going on. Mamie, thinking all the time of Miffy shivering in the street just down from the front door, where the lane ran out into the main road, helped him into his top-coat and gave him his hat and scarf and umbrella. She opened the door to let him out, and shut it behind him with unmannerly haste.

248

Miffy, standing where she was told, found herself staring in horror as she saw Mr Connolly emerge through the front door. The poor servant nearly had a seizure and was so horror-struck when she saw him that she did exactly the right thing; incapable of movement, she stood frozen to the spot in petrified terror.

The gods were on their side, for Garreth moved stolidly away from the house, never once turning round. Celestine slipped out from the back clutching her valise. She was soon deposited in the cab, aglow with excitement. She was on her way. It kept her warm in the dark interior which smelled of stale cigar smoke. That reminded her of her father and she had to push the thought of him away. The nag took her time, clip-clopping along, and Celestine was in a fever of impatience to reach the hotel. Tucked up in her rug, she peered from the window and saw the sky had darkened and the wind was blowing through the trees. It looked as if a storm was brewing. Autumn had become bleak and the sun had gone. She shivered and drew the rug closer around her. She was not used to being alone.

She glanced towards St Stephen's Green. The grass was browning, bare branches were etched against a silver break in the clouds. A dark day. They reached the Shelbourne at last. She paid the jarvey and went into the hotel.

The staff welcomed her, assuming, because of her case, that she had come for the night. She explained that she was meeting someone, Captain Charles Cavendish. Had he arrived? No, they said, no officer had come into the hotel since lunch. Very well, she would wait. They were happy she should do so and they took her valise and put it in the baggage room.

To the right was the lounge, welcoming, a familiar place often visited with her mother and sister when they went shopping in Grafton Street.

The waitress showed her to a table and served her afternoon tea. In the spacious room with its glittering chandelier and huge mirrors, elegant ladies sipped their tea, exchanged gossip or simply stared at the toings and froings in the hotel. China clinked, silver tinkled against cup and saucer, conversation simmered gently under the music played by three spinster ladies on cello, violin and piano. 'Roses are shining in Picardy' floated through the room, but Charles did not come.

Celestine could not eat. She sipped the tea, fiddled with a cucumber sandwich, her eyes never far from the entrance to the

249

tea-room and the one to the hotel. From where she was, she could see both quite clearly.

She watched, heart throbbing every time someone came into the hotel. Once she half-rose to her feet as a man in a uniform similar to Charles' arrived stamping his feet and, shaking out his great-coat. But it was not Charles. It must be raining for the colonel, she saw it was a colonel, took off his cap and, shaking it vigorously, made the bellboy jump back from the shower of drops that hit him in the face. The colonel apologized and said he was being shipped out later that afternoon and could he have a quick brandy and soda. 'I've got to make a telephone call,' he said. 'I'll take the brandy with me.'

'Yes, sir, right away, sir.' The boy hopped to attention, his face still wet.

Celestine dropped back into her chair disappointed. People came and went constantly but Charles did not come. Her excitement waned. Her heart no longer quickened each time someone entered. She raised her head, still eagerly, but there was a tiny fear now within her.

What had happened? The traffic was bad? He had been delayed? His transport had broken down? But his transport had been the train; trains did not beak down. The station was within walking distance of the hotel. What could have happened?

Had Mamie made a mistake? No. Mamie couldn't, wouldn't. She looked at the gilt clock over the marble mantelpiece; the hands pointed to six thirty. Any moment now the door would swing open and Charles would arrive. She knew he would. Any second now, she would see his face light up as he caught sight of her. Then the explanations, the apologies. She would make him suffer a little for the worry he had caused her. But only a little. She could not bear to be angry with him for too long. Perhaps the train had been held up on the Dublin/Wicklow line. Something wrong with the tracks. There were a thousand reasons why he was not here.

Perhaps he had had an accident. Oh no. Not that. She could not bear the thought. Perhaps he was called back to active service. Only then he would have let her know. It would not be at all difficult to telephone the Shelbourne. No, it must be an accident. But even then he could have made a call, sent a message.

250

But perhaps he was in a coma? Or worse still, dead? Her heart froze at the thought. Now she was filled with dread and her imaginings became wilder. Her father had shot Charles. That was why he had left the house. He had found out and had come to shoot the captain. She visualized his broken bleeding body lying bloodstained in her arms. Ah, God, no.

Her dread turned, with the ticking of the clock, to a dreadful dull feeling of abandonment. For the first time she felt alone in the room, isolated, vulnerable. The waitress fussed over her, sensing her distress. Celestine was humiliated by the girl's attitude. She wanted to stand up and cry out, 'I am not rejected. He will come for me. You will see. He will come.'

But he did not. The trio stopped playing and put their instruments into their cases, the piano-player gathered up the music and they left. The piano-player, who was tall and gaunt, closed the piano lid with a sharp little bang that made Celestine jump.

One by one the lamps went out leaving only one dim light. At eight o'clock she knew she would have to go. Everyone had left the lounge and it was dark and shadowed. Outside in the lobby, the doors of the restaurant had swung open and jewelled women in evening dress with men in formal wear, full of gaiety and laughter, were arriving for dinner.

In the shadows, her little face looked desolate and wiped free of colour. The waitress did not know what to do. She had finished her duty here but she did not like to leave the pale little miss. She had seen Celestine's anxious scrutiny and nervous expectation every time someone came into the hotel. She had seen hope die and anxiety take its place.

At last the girl approached Celestine.

'Miss, Miss.' Celestine was sunk in such a deep gloomy reverie that the waitress had to shake her shoulder to get her attention. 'Miss, I've cleared all the other tables and set them for after-dinner coffee. Are ye intendin' to go or stay? Can I help you?'

The look Celestine gave her was desolate. The waitress was sympathetic and wanted to help.

'Tell me, Miss, can I help ye?' she asked again.

'Someone I expected . . . someone who was to meet me here, hasn't . . . hasn't come. There must have been an accident,' Celestine faltered, speaking through stiff lips as if her mouth was frozen. The waitress had a shrewd idea that the trouble was

251

a boyfriend, though with this class of protected young female it was unusual.

'Why don't you telephone from here? Can you do that?' she asked, trying to be helpful. The girl's face lit up.

'Yes. Yes.' Why hadn't she thought of it before? Why on earth. 'Thank you. Thank you very much,' she cried and jumped up and patted the waitress's hand.

But there was no joy at Avoca House. A servant eventually came to the phone.

'Captain Charles? No, miss. I don't know where he is. Unless it is with Lady Gorman. I know the family are dining out tonight. What? No. No-one went to Dublin today or I'd have known. Lady Gorman always sends the carriage or the motor car and neither have been out. So sorry.'

Celestine went to the desk, where a sympathetic porter took her valise out of the baggage room and called a cab for her. He tucked her into it and gave the jarvey the address in Rathgar. The young lady was distracted and incapable of much communication but the porter, familiar with the ways of drunks (not that he thought for a moment the young lady fell into this category) knew where to look for a record of where she lived. He found it on a label on her valise and duly told the jarvey where to go. He wondered briefly about the pretty girl and what had happened to her. It seemed sad that someone so lovely and young should be so obviously unhappy. Then a motor vehicle pulled up to the curb outside the hotel and he forgot about Celestine in the hustle and bustle of the new guests' arrival.

252

Chapter

36

GARRETH had not realized that Celestine had gone until she returned home in a state of collapse. She was wet to the bone, for she had stood outside the house in Rathgar in the teeming rain refusing to enter, until the jarvey, driven to distraction by her obvious distress and disorientation, literally dragged her up the pathway and deposited her in the front hall.

The door had been opened by Mamie who tried to guide her young mistress up the stairs without anyone seeing her, only to be halted by Garreth, who had come out of the parlour to see what all the commotion was about.

'The young lady was in a state of distress, sir,' the jarvey stammered, somewhat put out by Garreth's glare. He had expected thanks and a handsome tip but it was not to be. Instead of thanks, he received a mighty dressing-down as if, he said afterwards, he had been responsible for the state the girl was in.

'Where did you pick her up?' the girl's father asked him.

'Why, outside the Shelbourne, sir. It's my pitch, so it is, sir.'

'Well, where was she? On the street?'

'No, sir. In the hotel, sir. The porter said she was waitin' for someone who never turned up.'

The jarvey was pleased enough to escape without his tip, for the nasty look that crossed the gentleman's face when he told him this. It was fierce awful, he told his missus. Like he was pleased the sweet young lady was in such a state.

Ellen and Nellie were bewildered when they arrived to see what all the noise was about. Neither of them had realized that Celestine was not at home, and Clothilde was in the same position.

'So, my fine young lady, he has jilted you.' Garreth turned on Celestine in righteous anger. 'I warned you. I warned you what he was like. I was right, wasn't I? You see what comes of disobeying me?'

'For God's sake, leave her alone. Don't you see the state she's in?' Clothilde ran to help Mamie, who held the near senseless girl in her arms.

'And so well she might be. Defying her father. Retribution, I call it. Serves her right. Now perhaps she'll see I have her best interests at heart.'

What happened next astonished everyone. Ellen pushed him aside. For a moment, he could not believe it and neither could she. Ellen had actually shoved him away from the foot of the stairs as she went to her daughter. She had done it without thinking.

'Stop it at once, Garreth,' she said. He could not believe his ears. 'Just be quiet. You've said quite enough.' As if he were one of the children. Appalled, he looked at her open-mouthed. She moved firmly up the stairs. Nothing happened. 'The sky,' she thought, 'has not fallen in.'

'Clothilde, help me with Celestine. Mamie, run on up and put a hot-water bottle in her bed. We must get these wet clothes off at once. The child is half dead.'

'I'll get Miffy to prepare a hot drink,' Nellie called from the hallway to the kitchen, and she disappeared below stairs.

Between them, they got Celestine to her room. All was bustle and fuss. It reminded Garreth of those times when Ellen was giving birth, when the house was full of activities with which he had no active connection. He felt superfluous.

He had received a nasty shock. Ellen's brisk treatment of him came as a complete surprise. She had never spoken to him in that tone before. Then there was the fact that Celestine was capable of defying him. Even after his most stringent instructions, she had had the courage to pay him no heed. It was unsettling. That one or other of the members of his household was involved seemed likely, but he knew in advance that there was no use trying to find out who. No one would tell him. He sensed to his horror a tiny crack in the edifice of his authority, a weakening of his absolute power, and he was chilled by its appearance.

But, he consoled himself quickly, he had been right. He had

254

warned his child about Captain Charles Cavendish and he had been proved right. Full of righteous self-justification, he turned his back on all the activity and swaggered into the parlour to finish his after-dinner coffee in peace.

Chapter
37

CHARLES had just put down the phone after Mamie's call when it rang again. He nearly did not answer it, but, being beside it, it seemed churlish not to. He was at once furious that he had done so for it was a call instructing him to report at once for active duty. At once. No delay. The voice on the other end of the line informed him that things were hotting up out there and there was a boat waiting for him at Kingstown. He was to join a battalion of men who were being shipped to France that day. His marching orders had come through. It was news that would normally have filled him with excitement but today it threw him into despair. To add insult to injury, if he had not answered the phone himself, he could have received the message late and taken a tender to the boat, giving him enough time to reach Celestine at the Shelbourne. He heard that Colonel Masterson was staying there, but whether he had left or not Charles did not know. In any event, the colonel could not help him in his dilemma. There was no wangling a few extra hours, not now that they had spoken to him in Avoca House, and Kingstown stood between Wicklow and Dublin. So he bowed to the inevitable. He was a first-class soldier and his duty to the army came before all else. Even, in this case, Celestine.

But he loved her so, and desperately wanted to see her before he left for France. There was no time to go to the Shelbourne and he knew she had no phone at home. He doubted that even if the Connollys had a phone, she would get the message. So there was only one thing to do. He went to May.

She was in the blue drawing-room sipping coffee pre-lunch and playing with her lapdog, Flea. She stretched out her hand to him and held his briefly when he gave it to her. She patted the sofa beside her.

'Sit here, Charles, where I can see you. My, how handsome you look. Love suits you.'

He looked into her china-blue eyes for sarcasm but they were as expressionless as glass.

'May, darling, will you do me a favour?'

She looked lovely, he thought, her silver-gold hair dressed simply in a fold at the nape of her neck, a frill of lace framing her chin and the pink lobes of her ears.

'Of course anything, my darling. You know that. Just ask.'

'I've been called back on active service.'

She drew in a sharp breath and her hand went involuntarily to her heart. 'Oh no.'

'Yes. But it's Celestine I'm worried about.' He was looking out of the window at the grey day, imagining his love, so he did not see her blue eyes narrow.

'I am supposed to meet her at the Shelbourne Hotel at tea-time. You see, dearest May, I went to see her father. He did not approve of me at all; I don't know why.' He rose and paced the room restlessly. May kept silent. There was hope here; hope of getting him back. If she could keep his confidence in her. Listen, she told herself, listen sympathetically.

'I'm not a bad match. But he was appalling to me. Refused to entertain the idea of marriage at all. Said he would never allow it.'

May could imagine the scene. No, she was quite sure Garreth would not give an inch. And so much the better for her. This man would intimidate Garreth, his cool sophistication would put Garreth at a disadvantage and he would hate him for that.

'I'm sure he'll change his mind,' she said lightly. 'After all, darling, it must have been a shock to him. Give him time.' Her voice was soothing. 'I'm sure he'll come round.'

'Do you really think so? Oh, May, you fill me with hope.' A frown creased his brow. 'But about today. She is going to meet me for tea in the Shelbourne. I intend to send her to my Aunt Agatha Stokes in London. Celestine will be safe with her. But you see I cannot get word to her . . . Celestine, I mean.' May could feel her heart leap. 'That is where you come in.'

May frowned. 'How do you know she is meeting you?' she asked.

'Today, Mamie, her servant, telephoned here. She said Celestine wanted to meet me in the Shelbourne Hotel, for me to be there at four o'clock. It is so important and I cannot go. She has been so brave. I *must* be sure to get a message to her there, so that she will not have a moment's anxiety. That is where I must depend on you, May.' He turned to her impulsively and she felt her limbs go weak with desire for him.

'Of course, my dear,' she said blandly, keeping her expression smooth.

'I could telephone the Shelbourne,' he said, looking distracted, 'but what message could I leave that would not alarm her? If I have her paged, I might embarrass her. She might mind, if there is a reason for her to be incognito. Heavens, I don't know. Then what?' He glanced at May who had her head bent. 'To tell her I have been sent overseas? The shock. It would upset her and she has been through so much already, I'll be bound, with that father of hers. My heart breaks for her. I would have to tell her in a message, for I'll be gone by then; she would have to read all this in a message. "Captain Charles Cavendish says you are to go to his Aunt Agatha Stokes in Hampstead", someone she has never heard of. No. It would never do. So I beg you, plead with you, to go to the Shelbourne for me and tell her all. Will you, dearest May? For all that we have been to each other?' He knelt before her, looking intently at her. She smiled and touched his cheek. She looked at the curve of his mouth and ached for him.

'We'll always be good friends, May? Oh I'm so very grateful to you. I cannot bear to think of her being upset, you know.'

Again she smiled, 'I would do anything to help you,' she said.

He breathed a sigh of relief. 'Ah, thank you, I knew I could rely on you. Put her on the first boat to England. Tell Barth to use his influence if there is any difficulty and tell Barth that Colonel Masterson is staying at the Shelbourne and he can ask him to pull strings. The old fellow would do anything for me, really he would.'

You assume that of everyone, my darling, May thought, as she went on smiling.

'See that she has money and the address which I'll leave you, with a letter. You'll do it beautifully, my dear, I know you will.'

She nodded again. 'Of course,' she said and, if her smile had become by now a little false, he did not notice.

258

'You'll be sure, won't you? You'll be there in time? Tell her I love her. I'll see her soon. I'll count the minutes. I'll write to Aunt Agatha. May, you do promise, don't you?'

Once more she nodded. But she had crossed her fingers in a childish gesture. If only she could stop his dreadful concern for her niece. Well, she *would* go to the Shelbourne tomorrow. She felt the butterfly flutters of guilt in her stomach. But there was never any real doubt in her mind of what she would do. Or rather, she amended, what she would not do.

They lunched together, *à deux*. Barth had left soon after Mamie's call to go to a horse auction in Meath and was away from home. Charles talked to her of Celestine. But not too much. He seemed to feel he had settled all that. He was confident that May would meet his love in the Shelbourne, take her under her wing, get her on the first available boat-train and at the other end Celestine would go by train to London and thence to Hampstead. It would all be looked after. Simple. He trusted her.

She smiled her dazzling smile at him and he covered her hand on the table with his.

'I knew I could depend on you,' he said. 'What a wonder you are, May.'

She wrestled with her demons, and for a moment she nearly relented. But his smile at her, his glance in her eyes, the gentle frisson of his breath on her cheeks and the touch of his hands over her's took her breath away, left her desperate for his love.

He would forget Celestine. The girl was an *ingénue*, an innocent, and Charles was nothing if not worldly. She thought he must surely grow bored with her niece. It was inevitable. And she, May, would be there waiting. Soldiers coming home from war needed understanding women, not giddy girls, to help them forget the horrors they had been through. She never doubted his attraction to her. She was serenely certain of his passion if she could get rid of Celestine, whom she was sure was a passing fancy. Celestine's innocent, insouciant quality that held him in thrall was the very characteristic that would bore him after a time.

She was determined on a course of action foreign to her nature, which was kindly. An implacable resolve to hold onto the only man she had ever loved swamped her decency and her honour. This man was her man. He belonged to her. Her parents had separated them. He had drifted from woman to woman until he had met her again and their passion had deepened and for her become a necessity. He had had a fling with her young impressionable niece. It was a match Celestine's father disapproved of, and, she reasoned, she would be wanting in her duty if she encouraged the young couple to elope. It would be an irresponsible and foolish act on her part, and Garreth would be furious with her. Besides, she was convinced that her sister Ellen was not in on the plot. How could she, May, do that to her sister? Garreth would give his wife hell if he found out that May had been involved in his beloved daughter's escape.

Of course, Celestine would suffer. The young always suffer. And recover. She had suffered when Charles had left her that first time and her father had taken her to London. But the young are resilient. She had married Barth and been happy. She shut her mind firmly on the memory of any pain she had suffered afterwards. She refused to dwell on that. She did not want to be reminded of its intensity and that she was thrusting a similar pain on her niece. She refused to think of Celestine.

She had never really forgotten Charles and she would not lose him again. She could not bear to. She wanted him back. He was the only man who excited her. His hold on her was total, but he did not know this. She had held him lightly, for she had not wanted to frighten him away. Her obsession with him rendered her pitiless in her pursuit of him. Celestine could wait. She had time. May's time was running out. Celestine would break her heart a little but she would recover. Bereft of Charles, May knew she herself would wither. In the heat of battle, the bloodbath of France, he would forget the immediacy of his infatuation for Celestine (she insisted of thinking of it as that: an infatuation). She knew that he had not made love to Celestine. They had not shared those moments of ecstasy when two bodies joined in love reach an overwhelming fulfilment. What did Celestine know of the beauty of his naked body, and how could she, May, live without it?

May knew too what he was like, fresh from combat, battle-weary and feverish for release. Their love-making was an ardent coupling, wild and abandoned. He awakened her, roused her, satisfied her as no other could.

She knew her niece and believed that that innocent little creature was incapable of reaching such heights of passion.

260

She would write to Charles. He had left her a forwarding address and asked her to give it to Celestine. She would not give it to her niece. She would write to Charles and tell him that Garreth was not going to allow Celestine to go anywhere, that he had discovered her attempt to escape and that the girl herself had decided to obey him. He must know how dutiful she was, and what else could a good Catholic girl do? To leave would break her parents' heart and she was too caring a child to do such a heinous thing to the mother and father she loved so much. Charles must have known how dearly she cared for her darling Papa.

May was clear on what she would do; but it did not make her happy. A black melancholy descended upon her, weighing down her spirit and overwhelming her soul. Her eyes had remained dry as she watched Charles leave. The motor car had slid down the gravel drive, the rain dancing on the shiny black roof. It disappeared out of sight and still she did not move.

When Charles had gone, she sat by the window in the blue drawing-room and looked at the rain. Her hands lay idle in her lap and there were no tears in her eyes. The clock ticked on monotonously and she did not move but remained transfixed, staring out at the fountain.

The drawing-room was darkening when Weems came in.

'Oh, m'lady, you're in the dark. Let me turn on the lights. There. My, you look pale. Let me bring you some nice tea.'

As he left the room May called, 'What time is it, Weems?'

Weems stopped and looked curiously at his mistress. There was a clock on the mantelpiece that Lady Gorman could see just by turning her head a fraction. But May could not bear to turn her head.

'It's six o'clock, m'lady.'

Six o'clock. Celestine had waited a long time by now. She would have to give up soon and go home. Or perhaps she had done so already. May gazed steadily out of the window. The grounds of Avoca House were shrouded in a pearly mist that blurred the edges of the trees. The sycamore was aflame, its leaves descending in slow motion, but May now could not even see the fountain right in front of her. Her eyes had misted over. An awful regret pierced her heart. For a moment she felt so soul-sick that she nearly jumped to her feet, but her body remained fixed and still. A sob tore her chest and she laid her head on the cool window-pane.

261

'Oh my God, oh my God, help me', she cried, and sobbing pressed her forehead harder against the glass.

No, it would not do, she told herself when the storm had passed. Her course was charted. She loved him so desperately, her first love, her last love, she could not let him go. She felt tired, so tired sitting there.

Weems brought in the tea. May dabbed her eyes with her handkerchief, and sipped the hot liquid and still sat at the window, looking at the rain.

Charles would be well on his way. Most probably he has put both of us out of his mind, she thought wryly, men are like that. Celestine would have gone home by now. Her mother and Clothilde would look after her and surround her with love. Garreth would cry triumphantly 'I told you so', but he, too, would be happy to have his adored child at home safely with him.

'I'm doing the right thing,' May thought. 'She should be with her loved ones. She is too young to helter-skelter off to London on a wild goose-chase to Charles' Aunt Agatha.'

She put down her tea cup. It was dark outside now. 'I'm doing it for all the wrong reasons,' she added to herself. 'Reasons unworthy of me. Yet, God help me, I cannot stop myself.' She heard the ticking of the clock, loud in the silence of the room.

A moment later the door opened and Barth came in. 'My dear. All alone? Where are the children?'

She glanced up at him. She was pale as death. 'They are over at Usher. A party,' she said, her voice lifeless. 'They ought to be back soon.'

'And Charles?' He did not betray by the quiver of an eyelid how he felt.

'He's left. Unexpectedly. For the front.'

She lowered her gaze from his. So that's why she's so pale and distraught, he thought, and he felt a surge of relief at the departure from his house of the man who had caused him so much pain. There was silence in the room except for the patter of the rain on the window.

May sighed. 'It's been a very long afternoon,' she said wearily.

He smiled reassuringly at her. 'Well, it's over now,' he said, 'It's over.'

262

PART TWO

Chapter

38

FRANCE

I am in hell. Not the hell the priests frightened me with at school, but worse. Much, much worse. They did not have the imagination to invent anything so horrible as this. I think sometimes that I have gone to another planet, like in the stories I used to read by Jules Verne. I used to think them daft and impossible, but not any more. This strange and alien place contains neither the days of the week nor the seasons of the year as clocks and guides. It is diametrically opposite to the world I used to live in. Nothing I have learned at school or at home has prepared me in any way for the battlefields of France.

The aims here are simple in the extreme: advance an inch; a yard; a quarter of a mile. This is the purpose and focus of my existence. The fabric of life here is composed of blood and naked bone, death and terror, fear and the screams of men engulfed in the scarlet shimmer of explosion and gun-shot. Grenades and bullets are the currency. Warm beds, tasty meals, the benign presence of females have no place here. Prayers are no longer the family rosary or Mass in an incense-filled church, the soothing rhythms of Gregorian plain chant in St Hilda's. Prayers, now, are implorings, screamed in agony, or, more often, the names of God and Jesus are a curse spat out in anger and horror. Obscenity is prayer too, I find, and I am getting used to it. No, nothing in my life has prepared me for this war. I think I was sent here too soon. I had hardly registered than I found myself here. I look strong. The men think I'm tough. Little do they know I'm barely held together.

I know it is winter. It is raining and it is cold and we went forward a few yards today, then back, then forward again. We maimed. We slaughtered. We killed to advance a useless mile to nowhere, in a country that is not ours and whose language I do not understand. We are fighting an enemy who is a foreigner here too. It makes no sense to me. I hope someone is wiser than I am.

'What are we accomplishing?' I asked Bert, my friend.

'Damned if I know, Irish,' he replied. 'Just do as you're told and don't think.'

It is madness. It is a hostile world and it seems to me that the days are scarlet, the colour of blood.

Dearest Mother,

I am well. Thank you for your letters. I love to hear from you. It xxxxcensored xxdxxxxxicensoredxx xxxxdxxlx xxex censored xxxxj getting on fine. Give my love to Celestine and Clo and Neill and Father.

Your loving son,

Breffni.

Chapter

39

MARY sat in the silent room. A very nice woman, who said she was a friend of Mrs Connolly, had come that morning. She was wearing a long black velour coat with a neat little astrakhan collar and an astrakhan toque on her greying hair. She looked very smart and had a kindly face. She wore gloves. Mary had never owned such things. She thought them the height of luxury. In the winter when it was bitterly cold and her fingers were numb she boiled a pot of hot water then she let the anger go off it. When it was tolerable and she could bear the heat, she put her hands in the water to thaw them out. The heat made her fingers tingle. Life came back to them. It was painful but pleasant.

The lady had come for Delia. Mary had stood by mutely while two men wrapped Delia in blankets and took her down to the ambulance. Delia was frightened, Mary could see, even though she had explained to her daughter what was going to happen, and that these people would care for her and make her well. Nevertheless, she was frightened, Mary could see it in her eyes.

The child had missed her father, even though John Joe had only been gone a short time. She loved his big reassuring presence, and when she realized he was gone, she had got the idea into her head that one by one some outside force that she did not understand was splitting up the family.

But she was being brave. Though terrified, she was trying not to upset her mother. Mary could see it; and it broke her heart.

It was very kind of them, Mrs Connolly and this lady, for otherwise Delia would surely die. Why then did she feel so angry with her benefactors? Why did she want to hit the lady, punch her arms and tell her to leave Delia, that she, Mary, was quite capable of caring for her, that she did not understand? Yes, she was very good, very Christian, but she had not lost her husband and her child.

She crossed herself at her thoughts and castigated herself for thinking such unworthy and evil things, but it did not take the feelings away. The woman was lucky. Did she know how lucky she was, with a comfortable house and husband and children, safe and secure to go home to? Her husband would be corpulent from good living and two helpings of everything. The meals, Mary had been told, in well-to-do houses were three courses, and they had wine with it. The lady's house would have many rooms, all full of furniture, and the house would be warm in winter, cool in summer.

She looked around the small room her family occupied. She had done her best, but it was pitifully little. Delia had gone into the care of strangers. Her husband was in jail. She had no one to look after now.

Neill had said he would go bail for John Joe, but he had been refused bail at the hearing on the grounds that John Joe was a menace to the public. This, on the evidence of Garreth Connolly and Bill O'Brien. So John Joe had been committed to jail pending trial and Mary Reilly had not slept since the night of the fire with the worry of it.

She watched the ambulance until it disappeared down Paradise Row and around past the Connolly Brewery. The building still seemed to be smouldering, yet she knew it could not be. Too much time had passed. Perhaps it was because the ashes were still there. No one had cleaned up and they blew around, casting a pall and blackening the walls of the already dirty houses. She hated that place. She hated Mr Connolly with an implacable hatred.

She looked at her windows. The fire had made them dirty. She had always kept the room clean as a new pin. She galvanized herself now into action. She boiled a pail of water and set to wiping down the cracked window, vigorously polishing it.

When it was done she sank exhausted on their one and only chair. It was her's now, now that John Joe had gone. All her energy ebbed away.

She was alone. Alone as she had never been before.

Completely alone. They had taken all she loved from her.

John Joe. She sighed and the sound that came from her was ragged and uneven. John Joe. All her life, he had been there loving her. They had played together as children. He had protected and guarded her even then, his large strength ensuring her safe journey through life. He had been her friend. In his arms, she had found a physical completion, ecstatic and fulfilling. Oh yes, he had been her lover. He had also been the father she had never really had, for her own was a helpless drunk. John Joe had been the best of men. And he was gone. Gone because of lying men. Gone because no-one knew him like she did. No-one believed that he was incapable of such an action. Christ in heaven, all you had to do was look into the kindness of his eyes to see that he was incapable of such an act. Now he was shut away. Away from the sunlight. Away from her.

She looked up and saw his coat on the hook on the back of the door. She stood and slowly took it down. The material had once been good but it was a Connolly cast-off. It had been worn for a long time before it reached, through Mrs Connolly's kindness, the Reilly household. John Joe had been wearing it these five years or more. It smelled of him, and it was that familiar dear smell that broke her. She crumpled to her knees onto the floor holding the coat to her face and wept as if her heart would break.

'Oh John Joe, me darlin'. Yiz'll be so cold in the prison without this. So cold, me darlin'. An' Delia, ye'll miss me so, my lamb, ye'll miss me. An' then ye'll forget me. Ah God. Have ye no mercy? What'll I do? What'll I do? What'll I do?'

No one answered. The silence was profound.

Chapter

40

FRANCE

The colour has turned to grey. From scarlet to grey. I cannot believe that there is so much grey in the world; grey mud; grey sky; grey landscape; grass beaten grey by army boots; and grey rain. Rain, rain, rain. Heavy saturating rain that stultifies, blinds and depresses. Dave crying out in pain and jerking beside me; the captain shouting 'Don't let him go into shock'. With a bullet tearing him apart, Chalkey screaming, a loud raucous sound, like a bird, a macaw, an inhuman sound like none I have ever heard before, I am surrounded by a bloody cacophony.

I keep telling myself, over and over again like a mantra, 'We're fighting for freedom. We're fighting for freedom. We're fighting for freedom.' *They* told me I was fighting for a free society. But society seems very far away and freedom seems an unobtainable thing. Who in this world is free?

One by one, the boys I have trained with have died. Or disappeared. I don't know why I am still alive. Bert was one of the first to die. His head was blown clean off. I shit and wet myself at the same time. Then I vomited. His body, headless, twitched and jerked for a full minute before it was still and he died. The next morning I saw in the cracked little mirror that my hair had gone grey overnight.

I remember so many isolated incidents, but I can never recall the sequence of events. I remember the band playing 'Soldiers of the King' when I was embarking. I felt so proud and excited. I remember arriving in France. I remember making jokes about 'Mamsel from Ar/men/teers' as the boys deliberately mispronounced it. I remember sliding the magazine into the chamber, and the gun being loaded and cocked as I advanced and killed, advanced and killed. All the other things, the deaths of my friends, the blood, the rain, the mud, I sometimes think about and sometimes forget. I realize I am in a place, an alien place somewhere, and sometimes I wonder why. What am I being punished for? What did I or any other human being do that was so appalling that we were sent to this hell-hole? Then I remember about society and freedom. I have thought a great deal and I have come to the conclusion, eventually, that I am not Breffni. Not really. I am 'Irish'. The others called me that, or they did when they were alive. The ones who took their places call me 'Irish' too, as a name, and they look on me as a veteran. In their newcomer eyes I am a combat-tried and true old-timer. That's the mortality rate here. Bert had christened me 'Irish'. 'Good on yourself, Irish,' he had cried in admiration when I took him to Rosie's with me. A pre-combat treat. He was so surprised and admiring that I knew such a place. And that the girls there knew me. Then I remember his twitching headless torso, the body that had lain hotly with Sally in the bordello in Paddington. Bert had called me 'Irish', so I am 'Irish'. I have left Breffni at home in Ireland where silver rain fell, gentle rain, a benediction on my face. It is quite different from the drowning, soul-destroying deluge that drenches me here. Breffni will keep that soft sweet world safe for me.

I cannot bear to think of the gentle face of my mother any more. To think of her makes her part of this slaughter so I blot out memories of her and of my sisters and the dark, intense and kindly face of my brother. The only face that comes to me in the blankness of these days is the face of my father. That comfortless face seems to sit easily in my mind in its present state. The mind of 'Irish'.

'Look at me, Father,' I cry silently as I learn to kill. 'Be proud of me. See how brave I am.'

The pitifully brief crash-course in soldiering I have been through in Colchester has hardly prepared me for this alien world. I dream sometimes of Kerry and Darragh, but when I crawl along in the mud on all fours, I do not think of anyone. I am not Breffni then. I am 'Irish'.

Some of the lads laugh. I know they are scared shitless, but they tell coarse jokes to cover their faces. Some, though, do not seem to care. They do what they are told, unimaginitive, blindly obedient.

'Do you know why we are fighting?' It is not a popular question. No one wants to face it. But then, I am not a popular soldier. I am a silent machine. They think I am hard as nails. But I ask questions. 'You're like granite;' they say. 'But shut up, for Christ's sake.' They do not want me to use my brains here, to ask, to question. They do not want cleverness or imagination. Just force. Besides, I am like an automaton. They are even a little afraid of me now. I know I seem quite mad to them sometimes.

They do not know that I am isolated in shock which I wrap around myself like a cloak. When the captain asked me not to let Dave go into shock he did not realize that I had gone instead and I have never recovered, that the chattering of my nerves is concealed beneath this cool exterior. I function normally, in so far as one could be normal here. I obediently do what I am told, I move, I walk, crawl, eat and kill. The staccato sounds of shooting, the dull boom of gunfire and hand-grenades echo in my brain. The screams of my fellow men sing in my ears. Explosions have ceased to make me jump. From a greenhorn I have become a professional. The tightness in my muscles has slackened into numbness. I feel unconscious most of the time and I long to be Breffni again.

Dearest Mother,

All is well here. We are ~~john xxxo~~ censored ~~xxlathru~~ censored ~~xx~~ winning and the morale of the lads is very good.

I long to see the daffodils. Do you still have tea on the lawn? I'll ~~skajdmkd~~ censored ~~xmxkxjjd~~ love to Clo and Celestine. Give big brother a hug for me. Give Father my love. Tell him I'll help him when I get home.

Your loving son,

Breffni.

Chapter

41

BILL O'Brien stood at the open front door of the brewery. He was waiting for his lord and master and he was very frightened. This time there would be no scapegoat to shift the blame to, to deflect it away from him. This time everything would fall squarely on his shoulders, even though it was not his fault.

Garreth Connolly had been pestering him for the letter. He had expected it ages ago. But it had not arrived. That was, until this morning. Bill wondered why it could not have gone to his boss's home. Why did it have to have come here? And above all, why was it he who had opened it? He wished for the thousandth time that he could put the clock back. He was sweating, and his face had broken out in a rash of unbecoming blotches. He stood leaning against the doorpost, casting about in his mind for excuses, for some reason that would get him off the hook, but he could not. Yet, as he reiterated to himself, it could not be construed as his fault. Nevertheless, he knew that Garreth Connolly would blame him. That was as sure as he was standing there, and it was grossly unfair.

His son caught his eye. Not so much his son as what his son was doing.

He had often thought that Dorsel was a half-wit. His tolerance was stretched to its fullest extent by his son. His wife was a mousey nondescript person who blended with the furniture and was anonymous to the point of non-existence until Dorsel came to grief at the expense of his father's tongue. Overcome with maternal love, she would spring to his defence, a lioness defending her cub.

But no matter how his wife felt about their offspring, it did

273

not change the fact that Dorsel was somewhat strange. He had an empty face which could look very knowing or very stupid depending on how one saw him. Bill O'Brien informed everyone that his son was a highly intelligent boy, so his lack of expression was put down to intelligent pre-occupation by those who believed Bill O'Brien, and Garreth Connolly was such a one. Not that Garreth trusted him with much. He acted as an errand boy in the brewery, but he was on quite a high salary for anyone in Connolly's. He was general dogsbody and agreed loudly with Mr Connolly whenever his boss uttered a word, which was a sure way into that gentleman's good graces.

Dorsel smoked cigarettes. He rolled his own, using his own brand of Golden Virginia tobacco. He carried boxes of matches in his pocket. What Bill O'Brien saw now was a sight that alarmed him to the point of panic. Dorsel was leaning against the wall facing the smudged and empty space where the part of the brewery that had burned down used to stand. He saw with horror what his son, in an aimless, lackadaisical way was doing.

At that moment, the Connolly car driven by Ben-the-Boots drove up to the entrance where O'Brien stood transfixed. Garreth Connolly blundered out of the car and over to Bill, followed by Neill. Neill's attention was caught by the manager's appalled stare and he followed his gaze to where Dorsel was lighting matches and flicking the flaming sticks into the water in the stone horse-trough that stood a couple of feet away from him. The matches gave a loud hiss as they hit the water, then died.

Only he was missing the horse-trough at least twice as often as he hit it. Then the lighted matches fell into the debris of what was left of the building, where the firemen said the fire had started. That side of the wall was where the logs of wood and the turf used for the furnace were usually stored and the straw for the horse food. The men would replenish the pile of logs and hay daily as the mound was used up, and at night it was covered with oil-skin to protect it from the rain. Today it was not raining. The sky was clear and cold and sunny. The matches flared and died, flared and died, as Garreth stepped from the car while Ben-the-Boots held the door for him.

Garreth slapped Bill O'Brien on the back and drew him into the office. They disappeared. Neill remained outside, watching Dorsel, fascinated, as he played his game with the casual familiarity of someone to whom this was an oft-repeated almost mindless occupation.

Ben-the-Boots had come up behind Neill as he stood and was watching too. Neill glanced at the chauffeur.

'Have you ever seen Dorsel O'Brien do that before?' he asked.

Ben nodded. 'I thought you'd never cotton, sir, deedn' I didn't. Sure he's at it all the time.'

'For God's sake, why didn't you say so? Why didn't you tell me?'

'Well'n I was goin' to, but you've hardly been home since. It wasn't my place to go out huntin' you, now was it? I was waitin' and waitin' an' then I began to think I had a nasty evil mind, seein' as for no cause I can't abide that apology of a human' bein' sir. But now I see you have the same thought I had sir . . . well, I'm that glad.'

Inside the office, Garreth Connolly had sat down abruptly, his face a shocked mask. He looked incredulously at his manager who sat perched on a chair before him. He was running on the spot while stuck to the chair, his little feet tapping out his near hysteria. He was unconsciously wringing his hands and his eyes slewed around in terror as the door burst open and Neill entered, holding Dorsel by the ear.

Garreth looked at Neill, his face changing from disbelief to anger.

'What the hell are you doing here, boy?'

Neill tweaked Dorsel's ear and the boy gave an outraged yelp.

'Lemme go. Lemme go.'

'Not until you tell my father what you were busy doing just now and what you were seen doing the night of the fire.'

'I didn't know . . . how was I supposed. . . . I don't believe it was me. Da said it was John Joe Reilly. Nothin' to do wi' me.'

Garreth banged his fist on the desk.

'Be quiet,' he cried, and when there was silence except for Dorsel's squeals, he looked coldly at Neill, 'What is all this about? I am in no mood to listen to any nonsense at this moment. Our lives, our whole lives, are at stake and you come barging in here bothering me with trivialities . . .'

'Sit down, Father, and listen.' Neill's voice was firm. 'This "nonsense" as you call it, this "triviality" is a man's life. A

275

woman's life. A family's happiness. You have a moral obligation to listen.'

Garreth rounded in fury on his son. 'How dare you speak to me like that? You have become far too obstreperous of late. You say you want to be a priest, yet you stand here and criticize your father. I will not have it, do you hear?'

The O'Briens looked from father to son as if watching a tennis match.

'Then, Father, you leave me no option but to call in the police.' Neill turned to go. Bill O'Brien let out a wild snort of panic, a high whining sound, like a baby pig in pain, and Dorsel sank to his knees, his arms around Neill's legs, impeding his exit and causing him very nearly to fall.

'Oh don't do that. Don't do that,' Dorsel squealed. 'I'll do anything you say. Anything. Beat me, punish me, but please don't tell the polis, don't.'

Neill looked down at the boy with distaste. A ring of saliva circled his mouth and he blubbered mindlessly, holding Neill in a panic-stricken tackle.

'What are you talking about?' It was Garreth, looking puzzled, who spoke. He was at a loss to understand what was going on, so preoccupied was he by the shock he had just sustained.

'Let me go,' Neill cried and the boy instantly released him. He remained on the floor uttering little moans of fear.

Neill turned to his father. 'That apology for a human being was, just now, playing a game with matches. Outside. Right beside the wall where the wood and hay is kept and where the fire started. He lights them and throws them into the horse-trough. Only, half the matches don't make it. They drop into the burnt-out ruins of your brewery, Father. And I am told that Dorsel O'Brien admitted in front of witnesses . . .'

Bill O'Brien let out a whistle of pain. 'Oh no. You little fool.'

'Oh yes,' Neill continued. 'He admitted in front of witnesses that he was playing his little game with the matches the night of the fire.'

Garreth Connolly stared at his son. 'So?' he asked coldly.

'Haven't you forgotten, Father, that there is a man in prison, wrongly accused of arson?'

Garreth waved his hand as if brushing away a fly. 'Oh, we'll sort that out in a day or two. I have other, more important, matters on my mind.'

276

Neill looked at his father in disbelief. 'There is nothing, I repeat, nothing, more important at this moment than John Joe Reilly.'

Again his father shook his head as if to brush away Neill's words.

'Father, if you do not come at once with me to the proper authorities, I shall, I promise you, telephone for the police and ask them to come here. Then you will have some very awkward questions to answer. You might even be giving John Joe Reilly grounds for legal complaint.' He did not believe this for a moment. It would be stretching the imagination for a native Irishman even to bring such a case against the rich or powerful much less to win it. Certainly, a working-class man or a peasant would have little redress for wrongful treatment. But his father could not be sure of that. Neill looked at his father and noticed, for the first time, how grey his face was, how shocked. Garreth met his gaze, an expression of appeal in his eyes. Neill was startled.

However, his father took a deep breath and said, 'Neill, what you don't know . . . Neill, you don't know what has happened.' His voice was angry, but there was anguish and hysteria just beneath the blustering tones. 'O'Brien, here, just informed me that we are not insured.'

Neill stood silently, staring at him. 'What?' Neill could not believe his ears. 'But there must be some mistake. We are insured with Lloyd's of London. A safe policy that covers fire. Surely, Father, there *must* be some mistake?'

Garreth spread his hands. 'No, Neill, there is no mistake,' he said. Then, in a sudden burst of anger, he rounded on O'Brien, just as that gentleman feared he might. 'This link-headed bastard, this fool, did not answer the letter and send the cheque to renew the policy when it was due.' His voice rose in pitch. 'He let the policy lapse. He bloody let the policy lapse,' he shouted.

O'Brien cried in as nearly panicked a voice, 'But no, sir, no sir, no sir.'

Garreth turned on him as if he would strike the little man. 'But yes, sir, yes sir, yes sir,' he screamed back.

This time it was Neill and Dorsel whose heads turned, metronome-like, from Garreth to Bill as their voices reached a shrill crescendo.

O'Brien cried now righteously, 'I'm not allowed to write cheques or make payments. I told you before, Mr Connolly, that it was due. I reminded you before your trip to London, reminded you for the fourth time. But you must have forgot. You must,' he finished feebly. He knew he was lost, even though what he said was true, and he quailed before Garreth's furious gaze.

'I did not forget. How dare you suggest I did.' It was your bounden duty, your job, to tell me it was due, to point it out to me. What the devil do you think I employ a manager *for*? Hey? Ah no. You were too busy with your "yes sir" and "no sir" to bring it to my *immediate* attention. Well, from now on you are *not* my manager. You are sacked. Fired. Without a reference. Out, out, out. The both of you. Out of my office for ever.'

O'Brien saw he meant it. He had worked for Garreth Connolly long enough to know that once he had sacked a man he never relented. He prided himself on the fact. He could never bring himself to forgive or admit he was wrong. O'Brien looked at Garreth, his world crumbling around him. All his grandiose plans evaporated and he knew now how John Joe Reilly had felt and why Mary Reilly had cried. He stood as tall as his five foot six inches could muster.

'You're a cruel, selfish man, Mr Connolly, that you are,' he said swiftly, astonishing Garreth by his nerve. 'Sure, I reminded you that day. It is not my place to run after you an' you would have shouted at me if I did that, an' if I had made a habit of it you would have sacked me anyhow. An' if you had trusted me I'd have sent the money. I'd have posted the cheque. It was not my fault an' no impartial person would blame me for what happened.'

Garreth sat staring morosely at his desk. He knew that what the little man said was true, but he could not now go back on his word.

Bill O'Brien took his bowler from the stand in the corner. 'Well it seems I'd have lost the job anyhow, for there's no brewery now. Connolly's Brewery is dust an' ashes an' it serves you right. Come, Dorsel. We're going.'

'Oh no you're not,' Neill said. 'I must say I do not agree with my father in this matter. I do not think you are guilty of this, and you should not be blamed for it. However, there is the other matter. This fellow has some explaining to do to the

278

police. It is no use gainsaying me, I will have my way. Come, Father. You must come too. I want you to withdraw charges, get a lawyer, whatever you have to do, to get John Joe Reilly out of jail and explain there has been a miscarriage of justice.'

'Not now, Neill. This is a tragedy. You don't seem to realize we are facing disaster.' His father's face was a sickly grey but Neill did not see.

'*Now*, Father,' he said firmly. 'Now, or I'll bring the police here.' Garreth's eyes dropped before his son's. He looked at the floor and thereby gave in.

As they left the office, Garreth Connolly, Bill O'Brien and his son were filled with loneliness, panic and fear. Their lives had been bound up in this building and each other. It had been the centre of their existence. Too late they realized, all three, what they were losing. It was not just the brewery. It was the game they had played, the game of boss and manager, of strong and weak, of tyrant and victim. They had enjoyed it, each feeling they were well cast in their parts. The hours they had spent together gave their lives purpose and importance. And now it was all over. There was no future in the place they had worked in all their adult lives. The mainstay of their existence had crumbled to dust. The familiar was gone. Arid vistas of unemployment stared Bill O'Brien and his son in the face. Their security had flown, disappeared, leaving them like landed fish, out of their element. And Garreth was without a centre, in a void.

But Neill's heart was lighter than it had ever been and his steps were buoyant as he walked away from the brewery he had always hated; walked towards the freeing of John Joe Reilly.

Chapter

42

IT was the most painful time Celestine had ever known. She felt she had been smashed in little pieces, that every inch of her had been wounded, that every particle of her suffered. Her muscles ached, her bones hurt, every sinew and fibre of her being seemed in agony. But most of all her heart was bruised. It mourned. Her spirits sank in depression and she felt she could not bear to live. Life had lost its savour. The world was coloured grey.

She had been happy, content at home with her mother and her sister, looking forward each day to her brothers' return from work, then tea, and then, the best moment, her father's home-coming. He had brought with him an enveloping love and his strong arms about her each evening gave her complete security. It had never occurred to her that there were strings attached. It had never occurred to her that her father's love for her depended on her obedience to his will. It had never occurred to her that his will for her could be such a crippling thing, a demand that she remain single forever, stay at home with her parents until they died. Then what? Be an old woman, dried-up, lonely and alone? Never to bear children? Never to have her own family? Never to know love?

What had happened to Charles? She could not believe he had deserted her, let her down. She was sure she would have known if he had been toying with her affections. Yet she had been wrong about her father. Couldn't she also have been wrong about Charles?

Her confidence in her judgement had been severely shaken. Her trust, the implicit trust in life that she took for granted, had been shattered. Bruised, hurt, whimpering and beaten, she stayed in her room, licking her wounds and suffering, incapable of moving forward, her life at a standstill.

Mamie and Miffy looked after her. They brought her meals, snacks to tempt her; they brought her fresh linen; they brought her sympathy and support.

'How is she?' Ben-the-Boots asked Miffy one morning.

'Like a dead thing,' Miffy said. She looked at him and sniffed. 'It makes me sad. She's all floppy.'

Mamie nodded. 'She's like a rag-doll. No life in her. God, 'n' she used to be so full of life.'

Ellen put her head around the kitchen door. 'Have you coped with the steak and kidney, Mamie?' she called.

'I've tucked it up nicely under the pastry, Mrs Connolly.'

Ellen's head vanished and Mamie, wiping her hands on her apron, said, 'I'll set the table, Miff. Don't want you crossin' Mr Connolly's path in these troubled times, God help us,' and she left the kitchen.

Ben-the-Boots looked up from polishing the silver. He was not used in his capacity as chauffeur these days, not since the fire had Mr Connolly taken him out regularly. As he hated to be idle, he turned his hand to anything that needed doing about the house. He put down the yellow cloth he had been using and went over to the waif-like figure at the range.

'When are you goin' to stop bein' scared of the big man, Miff?' he asked her gently.

She shook her head. 'I'll always be afraid of him,' she said.

'Why?' he asked.

'I couldn't bear to be sent back. He can send me back to that place. He's always sayin' he will an' it would be the end of me; to go back there.' She looked around at him, her eyes wide with fright at the idea of 'The Institution'.

Ben-the-Boots shook his head. 'Ye needn't go,' he said simply.

She looked at him perplexed and he laughed.

'Ye don't have te. They won't want ye back anyhows. Yer too old.'

Miffy stared at him, unable to believe her ears.

'Don't yer see, Miff? You're long growed. If the big man sent ye back, they'd soon send ye packin'. Send ye off te get a job. They've no interest in adults. They're only for children. An you

. . . you could get a job anywhere. Yer a great worker.'

Miffy still doubted the truth of what she was hearing. The nightmare of all her years was suddenly, quite casually, being removed. She was being told it did not exist any more.

''s that true, Ben?' she asked breathlessly.

He nodded.' Mrs Danagher next door asked me one day . . . I was polishin' the car an' she said, she asked me, would ye leave the Connolly's, go to work for her? Said she needs some-one an' you'd be perfect, if Mamie had trained ye. Said she'd pay ye, too.'

'No . . . I don't believe it.' Miffy looked at him, incredulous. 'No. Not really?' she said, shaking her head each time she said no. 'No, never.' The idea was preposterous. She had been so trapped by her fear of Mr Connolly and his threats, and now Ben-the-Boots was showing her the road to freedom and she could not quite take it in.

He was nodding his head just as vehemently as she was shaking her's. 'Yes. Yes, Miffy.'

'I wouldn't want to leave here,' she said, then added doubt-fully, 'It's all I've ever known. Except for the other place. The Institution.' She looked at him and smiled suddenly. 'I can say it now without being afraid,' she said and put back her head, 'Institution'. She called. 'Institution. Institution.' She laughed and he joined in the happy sound. Then she paused and added, 'I wouldn't want to leave Miss Celestine or Mrs Connolly. Oh, an' I wouldn't want to leave Mamie.' She dropped her chin on her bony little chest. 'Or you,' she whispered.

Ben-the-Boots cleared his throat and his face became suffused with colour: brick-red.

'Well, now, I know a way ye could stay here an' still not be afraid;' he said seriously.

'Do ye?' She looked at him genuinely puzzled, enquiry in her eyes.

He nodded again. 'Yea,' he said. He gulped and took a deep breath. 'Marry me. Why don't ye?'

Miffy sat down abruptly on the stool by the range. She looked like a landed fish, her mouth opening and closing word-lessly, her eyes near popping out of her head. She remained speechless. Ben-the-Boots waited.

At last he said, pretending impatience. 'Oh, well, if ye don't wanna.' Then he added sadly, 'I know I'm not good enough for ye . . .'

282

She leapt to her feet, stung by his words. 'Not good enough? Not good enough? Ah Ben, ye must be jokin'.'

'No I'm not. An' ye can stop thinkin' of yerself as dirt beneath the Connollys' feet right now, Miffy Mulligan. Yer worth more than the whole of them put together. Ye have more love and understandin' in yer little finger than . . . than . . . Yer special to me. Yer special to Mamie an' them upstairs, too, if ye think about it. Well?'

She was trying to grasp all these new and very attractive ideas.

He squatted before the range, taking her by the shoulders. 'Well?' he asked.

'Well what?' she said, bemused.

'Will ye marry me, Miffy? You an' I would do well. We have nobody but each other. No family but each other. I'd look out for ye. I'd be proud to. Give us some purpose. You an' me. An' maybe start our own family.'

She was staring at him with shining eyes. 'Our own family. Our very own.' She could not believe the possibility.

'A baby. Of my own.' It was too fantastic, too wonderful.

'Well, will ye?' Ben-the-Boots' impatience this time was real.

She nodded. 'Yes,' she said breathlessly. 'Yes. Oh yes.'

As he shyly kissed her cheek, Mamie came rushing back into the kitchen.'

'All hell's broken loose upstairs. Listen, Ben, get up there, will ye, an listen. I don't want to miss anythin'. There's the mother an' father of a row blowin' up.'

'What's happened?' Ben asked and Mamie looked at him with irritation.

'If I knew, would I ask? I said get up there an' listen, will ye?'

'What'll I say I'm doin' if anyone sees me?'

'Oh, think, man, think,' Miffy cried. 'Say ye've come to see if Mr Connolly wants to go . . . anywhere, because you were goin' to wash the car.' Mamie and Ben both looked astonished at Miffy's flushed little face as she said this. Mamie was rendered speechless by the unexpected eloquence of her kitchen-maid and the confidence in her voice.

'Exactly. Never heard ye talk like that before, Miffy, deed'n I didn't,' Mamie said when she had recovered. Then she shooed Ben-the-Boots out of the kitchen. 'Off ye go an' keep yer ears open. There's talk Mr Connolly is ruined, an' as that fact wouldn't

283

keep me from sleep I want to be ready in case I have to protect the mistress.'

Ben clattered off, making a great racket and Mamie cast her eyes to heaven. 'God'n' he needn't *announce* he's eavesdropping fer cryin' out loud,' she said, exasperated.

She turned to Miffy who still sat on the stool looking bemused.

'Miffy, what *is* the matter wi' ye? I've never seen ye so . . . relaxed . . . calm, sittin' there like Lady Gorman herself, doin' nuthin'.'

'Ben-the-Boots an' me has come to an understandin',' Miffy said with simple dignity.

Mamie forgot her preoccupation with the family for a moment.

'Ah God, I'm glad, Miffy,' she said, rushing over to the girl and enveloping her in her huge smothering embrace. It was an embrace that Miffy loved and enjoyed. Mamie's was the only embrace she had ever known. Large tears filled her eyes and slid down her cheeks.

'I'm so happy, Mamie, I just can't believe it.'

'Well, now, I'm happy too. Ye deserve it; a bit o' happiness in yer life. Ben's a good boy. An old head on young shoulders. Still, that's no harm. He'll look after ye; never fear.'

She listened, herself again and alert to the doings of the household.

'There's excitin' things happenin' above, Miffy. I don't want to miss it.' She took down the large Georgian silver tray. 'Put the best china cups on it, Miffy. I'll wet the tea. Oh I never thought I'd live to see the day the master would be home for tea,' she said. 'An' now it looks like we'll never be rid of him again.'

Chapter

43

GARRETH sat in his chair, his head in his hands. He is enjoying this in some perverse way, Ellen thought coolly. She had been feeling her way tentatively along the road to independence, amazed at how easy it became as she went along, how quickly she progressed and how she gained in self-confidence. Since she had come back from Avoca House after the fire she had taken tiny steps forward in not allowing Garreth to get away with bullying her. She kept remembering Barth's words. She wondered why no-one had told her before, then realized that she had never given anyone the opportunity. She had been too busy defending Garreth. Well, no more. Enough was enough. The children were grown up now. There were adult battles to fight. The namby-pamby days were over, she told herself fiercely.

The house had been in hiatus since yesterday. Neill had come home late with his father and then he had left, saying he had things to do, but telling her about John Joe Reilly and that it was Dorsel O'Brien who had set the brewery on fire. All charges against John Joe were dropped and he was out of prison and for that Ellen was profoundly grateful. She had been terribly worried about Mary Reilly. Now that that situation was satisfactorily concluded she felt she could relax. But there was Garreth's dilemma.

'We're ruined. Ruined,' he moaned. 'Penury stares us in the face. Everything gone.'

She felt sudden contempt for him, sitting there full of self-pity. The Garreth she had known, the bully, the successful businessman, was infinitely preferable to this snivelling creature.

'We still have the site and Paradise Row and Square and the Street,' Ellen said ticking them off on her fingers. Garreth looked up at her. She was calm, totally unfussed and unlike her usual self. She had no right to remain unconcerned, Garreth thought, she should be in a state, worried about their future.

'*I* still have the site. *I* still have the streets, foul places that they are.'

'Oh it's "I still have the site", but it's "*we* are facing penury",' Ellen said and her husband's jaw dropped open at the tone of her voice. He could not believe his ears.

'You are facing ruin, woman, and all you can do is make snide remarks. Really, Ellen, your stupidity over the years has astonished me. You don't seem to be able to grasp the seriousness of the situation you are in.'

'How quickly we travel from "we" to "I" to "you". *I'm* not in a serious situation, Garreth. *You* are,' she replied calmly. The sky had not fallen in.

He looked at her astounded. Once more the unworried tone, the tranquil expression. Ellen, to his fury, sat crocheting serenely, unaffected by his prophecies of doom. It was as if she had changed character and turned into a stranger. He was incredulous enough to be stung into a question that immediately put him at a disadvantage.

'What do you mean?' he asked in astonishment.

'Oh, if . . . and I say if advisedly, for I am sure, Garreth, that things are not quite as bad as you paint them. You have always had a tendency to dramatize.' Garreth gave an apoplectic squeak. He was too surprised to round on her for impertinence. 'If', she continued, 'we are, as you say, ruined, then I can always find a home with either of my sisters. Nellie was saying that she felt it was time I went to Kerry for a protracted stay and Barth was only telling me a while ago how welcome I would always be at Avoca House. It seems I am popular. So I'm not really worried at all. You see, Garreth, you have never allowed me to share your business life with you. The problem, I'm afraid, is yours.'

'Nellie said? When she was here? What made her? And Barth? Why should he say? What are you talking about?' Garreth spluttered, unable to find his bearings in this sort of conversation. Was it not enough that his brewery had gone up in flames, that the insurance on it had lapsed? Here in the

286

bosom of his family, where he had a right to expect support and sympathy, he was being treated in a cavalier fashion, as if he was a casual acquaintance instead of the master of the house. He sat silent, his eyes popping at this utterly uncharacteristic display of indifference.

Mamie entered the room bearing a laden tea-tray. She put it on the occasional table near Ellen, saying, 'Will I pour, Mam, or will you?'

'Mrs Connolly will pour, Mamie, thank you.' Garreth looked at her ferociously. 'Now get out of here at once, if you please.'

'Don't speak to Mamie like that, dear.' Ellen's voice was calmly authoritative. There was no plea, no fear in it. Once more Garreth was rendered speechless, was disconcerted by her change of character.

'I think you have taken leave of your senses, Ellen' he said at last, when Mamie had left the room, a smirk on her face that she did not try to conceal.

'No, my dear,' she answered calmly. 'No. I had, you see, a little chat with my brother-in-law . . .'

'Barth.' Garreth spat the name out, interrupting her.

She nodded. 'Yes. Barth. He asked me why I was always so afraid, so nervous, so unsure. I knew that it was because of you, dear. You've always made me feel as if I were a half-wit, an idiot, a nuisance in this house that was my home. It was a home you often told me that you gave me out of the goodness of your heart.'

She smiled into the fire, then turned and took the cosy off the tea-pot and started to pour.

'Well, it was good of me,' Garreth said defensively.

'No.' Ellen shook her head. 'It was the least you could do.' She handed him his tea. He fought the impulse to knock the cup out of her hand, to get some positive response from this calm stranger opposite him.

'Well, Barth explained to me that I must not be like that any more. He explained it to me, as if I was a child, which indeed my behaviour has resembled up to now even though I am a middle-aged mother of four. He said I could always to go Avoca House. That I need never be homeless despite your threats. I decided to take his advice. In the last weeks, since the fire, since you behaved so unreasonably to John Joe Reilly and have been so beastly to Celestine, well, I simply made up my mind never to be afraid of you any more. Would you like more tea, dear?'

Without a word, full of impotent fury, Garreth Connolly stood up and left the room. His wife did not follow him into the hall as she usually did. He put on his hat and coat without help, and with no idea of what he was going to do, he left the house.

'The world has gone off its head,' he said, baffled, as he strode up the Rathgar Road. 'Off its head entirely.'

Chapter

44

HALFWAY down the Rathgar Road Garreth hailed a cab. He had suddenly got the bright idea of going to his club. He liked to pop in there each evening after work. Or he had done in those far-off normal days.

The Gentleman's Club was in Leeson Street. He liked to stroll into the silent womb-like reading room and self-importantly choose 'his' chair, a chair earned through position, power and money. And time. Not least of all time. True, his chair was an unimportant chair, a chair to the back and side of the room, a chair in a dark corner away from the wide bay windows where the Fitzgeralds, the Jeffries, and the O'Brien-Twohigs sat. True, it was not in the centre of the room beneath the warm light from the chandelier where the Vestries, the O'Sheas and the Gormans had seats. But that was relative. The men who sat in the centre chairs and the ones near the windows were extremely important, indeed, leaders of industry, politicians, members of old monied families, men he never thought he would keep company with. In his wildest dreams as a poor boy, he had never ever aimed this high.

He had clawed his way up to the position he was now in. He had worked singlemindedly to make the brewery and his properties into a thriving concern and that it had been until the fire destroyed it. He had married the daughter of one of the old families and earned himself a small place in this gentlemen's club. He was quite happy to remain a satellite here, to stay on the fringes.

He never entered its portals without an upsurge of pride and self-congratulation. He would walk with measured tread, looking neither to right nor left, for there were few he could call acquaintances here. He would sit in his chair and pull the service cord. When the waiter arrived, slowly, for all the waiters here were old (and most tended to be alcoholic), he would order a Jameson and soda. Then he would sit and sip his drink slowly and savour the good important feeling, the feeling of achievement, of being a part, however small, of this world of old leather and old names, of prosperity and understated wealth. He enjoyed every moment, relishing each drop of his whiskey. Then he would leave. With the exception of Brendan Mulcahy he spoke to no-one and no-one spoke to him.

Brendan had no desire to become too friendly within these walls. But he wanted the alliance between his son Owen and Garreth's daughter, Clothilde, and he did not overlook the fact that Connolly was a brother-in-law of Lord Gorman, and to such an opportunist as Mr Mulcahy, one never knew where something like that might lead. In any event, the merger would be attractive to both men, a fact he was fond of pointing out to Garreth.

Today when Garreth arrived he made his usual entrance and with dignified steps he walked over to his chair, pulled the service cord and ordered his usual drink. At least here everything remained the same. Chaos might reign at home, the brewery might be destroyed, but his club provided its usual sanctuary.

He stretched out his legs, sipped his drink and speculated on his woes, listing in his head a roll-call of people whom he had reason to resent. The list was headed by O'Brien, his manager, and Ellen, his wife. He was making up fantasies of what he would do to them when his reverie was interrupted by a voice in his ear asking to speak to him. Surprised at being spoken to so unexpectedly, he cursed inwardly at yet another deviation from the normal. Then he saw the intruder on his privacy was Brendan Mulcahy.

'Good evening, Mulcahy,' he said, starting to rise. But Mulcahy pressed him back into his chair and signalled to the ancient and desiccated servant who pushed over an easy chair at a snail's pace and with grunts of effort as loud as he dared.

'Wanted a word, Connolly.' Brendan Mulcahy cleared his throat and sat in the chair which the waiter had arranged facing Garreth. He signalled to the waiter, saying 'Same again.'

Garreth did not protest, even though he never took a second drink. One drink in the club was his habit. However, today seemed a day for breaking rules and Garreth sighed and sipped at his second John Jameson wondering how his world, so tidy and ordered, so trim and predictable, had turned into a shambles where he seemed unable to control events or people any more.

Brendan Mulcahy cleared his throat. 'Aw . . . Connolly, old fellow. Heard of the fire. Bad luck. Very bad luck indeed. I do sympathize.'

Brendan spoke with a plum in his mouth, thereby earning the respect of his associates who aped the upper-class English accent. They thought it a sign of culture and breeding.

Garreth nodded. 'It was that,' he said dolefully.

Brendan stirred in his chair, his body uneasy, eyeing the large man opposite with a wary eye.

'Rumour has it that the brewery was not insured?'

It was Garreth's turn to move uneasily. He did not like the turn the conversation had taken. He never discussed business with outsiders and felt Mulcahy's question to be an intrusion into his private concerns. However, the question left no room for tactful evasion.

The little man opposite, dapper and alert as he waited for a reply, and the effect of the second John Jameson, caused him to be more candid than perhaps he would have been had the situation been different.

'Rumour this time is correct. It's all the fault of that God-damned manager of mine. He forgot to send the renewal payment when it was due. He let it lapse.' A distinct note of self-pity crept into the last sentence.

'Did he now?' Brendan Mulcahy knew nonsense when he heard it. Connolly was not the kind of man to entrust payments to his manager. 'You could prosecute him? Perhaps get compensation that way?'

Garreth glanced swiftly at Mulcahy, trying to decide if the little man was making fun of him. Mulcahy sat back, very relaxed now, looking at him slyly, his fingertips touching across his belly. He had a gold watch-chain which was plaited through the fingers of his right hand and you could see the outline of his watch in the pocket of his waist-coat.

Garreth did not like his tone. He snorted. 'O'Brien wouldn't be worth prosecuting,' he said. 'He's not worth much.'

Brendan Mulcahy smiled at him beningly. 'You surprise me. I would have thought after working for you all those years he would be worth a tidy sum. After all, one must pay one's manager a decent wage.' Garreth, unused to this kind of cut and thrust, was confused. Mulcahy continued. 'I am glad to know the truth. Can't trust rumour, y'know. Well, what I had in mind, no offence meant, was to put in an offer for the land and the streets you own thereabouts. Onwards and upwards, y'know. Let us say . . .' He named a figure well below the market price that made Garreth splutter and nearly choke. 'Think it over, old fellow. Think it over.'

When Garreth had caught his breath he slammed the glass down on the small table beside him, causing some of the other occupants of the room to lower their papers or glare in mute protest. Garreth glared back at them, and Brendan, who had paused, cleared his throat, lowered his eyes and continued.

'I'm afraid Clothilde must put all thoughts of marriage to Owen out of her head.' He leaned forward and said confidentially, 'Owen's wife will be expected to bring to a union with my son a decent dowry . . .'

But he was talking to himself. Garreth had risen, and now walked, head held high, out of the room, and out of the club, without another word.

292

Chapter

45

CLOTHILDE was haunted. All during her stay at Avoca House the face of Darragh Quinn had interposed itself between Clothilde and everything she did. Always when she least expected it he was there. The face repelled her. She shied away from its craggy roughness, its strong earthy peasant quality and most of all from the unveiled candour of its eyes. People she knew shielded their thoughts, censored their communication and conveyed what was on their minds with a subtle consideration for the recipient. Except her father whom she hated. And Darragh Quinn.

She was too honest not to query the violence of her emotions. Why hate a man she had only met once, whom she would never meet again? He had behaved impeccably for one of his sort. He had only been helpful that night in South King Street. It seemed so many moons ago, such a long time for her to remember. It was simply his eyes, the familiarity with which he had looked at her, his bold expression. He had hidden nothing; his admiration was there for all to see. She shivered and blushed when she thought of him and she thought of him a lot. Too much. Not deliberately, but wherever she looked, Darragh's face often seemed to be there. Like the Cheshire Cat in 'Alice in Wonderland', part of him had lingered on, and try as she might, she could not shake him off.

He interfered with her prayers, too. Her clear straight line to God, her uncluttered channel of communication, became suddenly snarled; and she struggled to get through but to no avail.

She knelt beside her bed night after night trying to make

293

contact, but God seemed to have deserted her.

She did not know what to do. There seemed no way out of the trap she found herself in. She tossed and turned through the nights, trying vainly to sleep, but did not succeed very well.

She thought matters might improve when she returned to Rathgar and the familiarity of her own room, but they got worse. And as time passed they grew worse yet. Time made the face more vivid instead of less so. She felt guilty, a scarlet woman, evil in some undefined way, yet she had done nothing wrong. It was as if she were possessed, and she did not know how to exorcise the demon. The demon was Darragh Quinn.

He was with her when she danced, sang, played the harp, was her companion when she went riding, walking, shopping. He sat with her in the motor car or the carriage, shared the compartment with her on the train. He sat with her at meals, interfered with her reading and did not allow her to concentrate on what she was saying. Worst of all he was with her in her bedroom, and he came between her and her prayers. Sometimes he refused to allow her to sleep. He came to her when she was unconscious. He slipped into her head when her limbs were languid and she was defenceless.

She would get him out of her mind for an hour or two. Relieved, she would start something, to read perhaps, but there he was again in the pages of the book. She would sip her tea but he was once more her silent companion.

She went to confession. The priest said that she was becoming human, that she should put the idea of taking the veil out of her mind and concentrate on doing a line with an eligible young Catholic boy. Did the young fella fit the bill? Mortified, she hurried out, not waiting for her penance.

She decided to confide in Neill. Her twin would understand. He was her friend as well as her brother and she trusted him. She had been glad to help Celestine. She could look after her sister and no one noticed her preoccupation. She had always been the quiet one. She sat with Celestine and held her hand while she tried to catch Neill on his few visits to the house. She soothed Celestine and comforted her, but noticed little of what else was happening in the house. She was vaguely aware that her father was at home most of the time and seemed subdued. She also heard her mother countermand her father's orders and thought how odd that was. She heard Miffy singing on the stairs

294

and was surprised at the servant's happiness, for Miffy had never been known to sing. And she waited for Neill.

Garreth was there all the time. Mamie ordered him from one room to the other while they were cleaned. She did it with relish, and Garreth meekly obeyed. He had no choice. He was a fish out of water, a man in a woman's domain at the wrong time. He had nowhere to go and he did not know the rules of the game in his own home, so unfamiliar now in the daytime. He could lay down no laws here, for when he did, it ended in discomfort and chaos in the established routine. The first time it happened he had told Mamie to go away and leave him alone in the parlour after breakfast, for he wanted to drink some coffee and read the newspaper at leisure. She had said, 'Yes, sir,' and with a shrug left him. Uneasily, he shut himself up, not noticing that there was no fire in the grate. He enjoyed the papers for a while, then realized he was freezing. He pulled the bell for Mamie but Miffy came. He looked in irritation at the little servant who stared back at him unblinking. She did not appear to be afraid of him any more, and he found to his consternation that she was making him uneasy. Her stare was cool and seemed to dare him to be unreasonable and shout. She was getting like Mamie, he thought. Cheeky. Lacking in respect.

'Light the fire, Miffy,' he said. 'I'm cold in here.'

'Yes, sir,' she said and bobbed a curtsey. 'It's usually laid after breakfast, sir. Ye'll have te move.' He looked puzzled and she added, 'The grate has to be cleared out, sir. Ben-the-Boots does it after he drops you at work.' A flicker of a smile came into Miffy's eyes. 'He's waitin' in the kitchen until yer finished here for a chance to get it done.'

She left the room as if she had scored a victory and he had no option but to retire to the bedroom, hoping to find some peace but there he found Mamie shaking out sheets, the room an unfamiliar place draped in white. When he had backed out and hurried to the dining-room, Ellen, sitting at the table, looked coolly at him and like a stern headmistress said, 'Not now, Garreth, I'm doing the laundry lists,' and bent her head in dismissal. He felt like an intruder in his own home, and though he blustered and commanded and yelled, no one seemed to take any notice of him or, if they did, it threw everything out of kilter.

Something had snapped and he did not know what it was.

295

He knew it had something to do with the fire and him losing the brewery but it was not that alone. Ellen had changed since her last visit to Avoca House. Celestine had changed. Clothilde had changed. Even Miffy and Ben-the-Boots had changed. He found it unnerving.

He was full of impotent fury when he saw Clothilde coming down the stairs one cold morning. It was the time of the day he hated most in the house: morning. Ben-the-Boots was cleaning the grate and setting the fire in the parlour. Miffy was clearing away the breakfast in the dining-room. Celestine was as usual still in her room. He missed her sorely yet every attempt he had made at reconciliation she had rebuffed. When she came downstairs, which was not often, she seemed like a ghost of her former self, infinitely remote. Ellen and Mamie were in the bedroom doing God knows what and Garreth, with no place to go, hovered uneasily between the parlour and the hall, waiting for Ben-the-Boots to finish.

Clothilde was dressed for the street when she came down the stairs. Mamie came out of the bedroom and Clothilde called up to her, 'I must find Neill. Do you know where he is?'

Mamie shook her head. 'The lace doilies need mending, Mam. I'll take them up to the Blind School with the wicker chairs from the kitchen for fixing.'

'Very well, Mamie. That sounds fine. I've got to go to Switzers for some more pillow-slips.' Ellen's disembodied voice came from the bedroom.

Clothilde had paused on the stairs. She said in a pleading voice, 'Mamie, *please* tell me. I've got to see him.'

'He's with those common public-house people. He spends all his time there instead of helping me to find a solution to our problems.' Garreth had called up the stairs from the hall. He felt like a thief standing there. Clothilde said, 'Thank you, Father.'

Ellen came out of the bedroom and stood at the top of the stairs, a lace traycloth in her hands.

'Here, Mamie. This needs mending too. No, Garreth. They are not common people. They were very nice to us, very helpful that evening at the opera.'

'Out of here at once,' Garreth roared at Ben-the-Boots, who dropped the poker he had been using, and leaving a pile of ashes on a newspaper spread out in front of the half-cleaned fireplace, calmly left the parlour and disappeared down the stairs to the kitchen, leaving Garreth purple and helpless.

'I'm off to Mass, Mother,' Clothilde called and ran down the rest of the stairs but Garreth stopped her.

'I suppose you know you've lost Owen?'

'Well?' said his daughter shrugging. 'An' so what?'

'Don't you dare to speak to me like that, young lady. Your mother brought you up to speak properly.'

But Clothilde had slipped past him and left the house and when she was halfway down the gravel path she turned and waved to him, much to his annoyance.

'Church again,' he muttered. 'Damned church. But I thought she said something about Neill . . .'

It was only when she had disappeared down the road that Garreth noticed that it was raining heavily. He stood for a moment watching the grey sheets spatter the pavement, a feeling of fear sweeping over him as the rain was sweeping over the trees, causing them both to bend beneath the weight. He thought, 'She didn't have an umbrella,' but he said nothing and anyhow it was too late. Then he closed the door behind her.

Chapter

46

WHEN she left the house Clothilde did not turn towards the church, instead she made her way to the city. It was a bitter cold day. Black clouds scudded overhead in the wind and every so often released a torrent of rain which beat upon the pavements in a deluge. The trees waved bare branches black against a steel-grey sky. The streets beneath her booted feet were shiny with puddles. But Clothilde did not notice the weather. She was filled with a feverish excitement. She wanted to talk to Neill. And Neill, she knew even before her father had told her, would be at 'The Golden Harp' with the Quinns.

She would lay the ghost. At last she would free herself of the man who had haunted her for months now. If she wanted to see Neill she would have to go to the Quinns, and that necessitated seeing Darragh. Well, she would face up to the situation. She was now certain that when she actually saw him he would cease to be a threat. He would shrink and his importance would vanish. He was, after all, a working man who helped his father in a pub. The mere sight of him would probably be enough to release her from bondage. She wondered why she had not done this before.

She hurried down the street, her hair caught in the wind for she had forgotten her hat. She saw a hackney and hailed it, directing the driver simply to take her to Connolly's Brewery on the Liffey. He seemed to know where she meant and he clicked at his nag and they clopped along at a leisurely pace.

Clothilde had never been near her father's place of business so when the cabby turned down the Quays and the streets became meaner she found herself in another world. She was

298

horrified and forgot to be nervous in her amazement at the squalor all about her.

At last the cabby stopped and came around to ask her exactly where she wanted to go.

'It's not very . . . er . . . suitable here, Miss, for the likes of you, an' the Connolly Brewery burnt down to the ground months ago,' he said. 'There'll be no one there,' he said, spitting tobacco out of the side of his mouth and wiping the back of his hand across his nose.

'I know that,' she said, eyeing him with cool appraisal. 'If you knew and you thought I did not, why didn't you tell me before?' He became shifty and uneasy under her stare but she continued, 'I'm looking for a public house.' The jarvey shrugged; now he had heard everything. But the lady went on smoothly, 'Owned by a family called Quinn. Do you know it?'

The driver looked relieved. 'Sure. O' course I do. "The Golden Harp". We'll be there in a mo'.' He climbed back up and clicked to his nag again, and fair enough they had stopped in minutes in front of a neat little pub.

It was in sharp contrast to the streets around it. The tall, four-storey Georgian houses of the neighbourhood were in a ruinous state. They looked like those in a war-torn city to Clothilde. In the Irish Press she had seen photographs of such places in Europe and this street looked a lot like the newspaper pictures. Roofs tilted lopsidedly. Chimneys had collapsed. The front doors were mostly missing, the windows broken and patched with wood or straw or left gaping. People moved like wraiths in and out in the rain. She could see their shadows on blinds where lights burned on this dark day. She shivered and paid the man.

'Will ye be all right, Miss? D'ye want me to wait?' he asked and Clothilde could see an unexpected flicker of concern in his rheumy eyes.

She shook her head. 'My brother will be here,' she said. 'Thank you.'

She opened the door of the public house and was greeted by a blast of warmth and a great guffaw of laughter. Then there was silence. She looked around, trying to accustom her eyes to the gloom of the interior.

There was a group of men in front of the counter, pints of beer in their hands. The man behind the bar she identified at once as Darragh's father. Every line of his face was familiar, though older and less clear-cut. The men were in open-necked, collarless shirts and patched jackets. They wore boots and had the rough weather-beaten faces of working men. They were all looking at her, curiosity writ large on their faces.

Opposite the bar a huge fire burned cheerfully in a grate. She made for the fire, slightly nervous of actually approaching the men at the bar. To her astonishment a thought came unbidden into her mind. 'I'll be all right. Darragh is here.' Not Neill is here, but Darragh. She shook her head and went and stood before the fire, warming her hands which were frozen.

A voice in her ear made her jump.

'Can I help you, Miss?' Same voice. It made her blush and stammer as she replied, 'I'm looking for my brother, Neill Connolly.'

Kipper Quinn's face broke into a grin. 'Aw Gawney Mac, why didn't ye say so? Aw, come inside, *astore*, an' not sit here with strangers. Kipper. Kipper Quinn at yer service.' He grabbed her hand, pumping it firmly up and down. 'You must be Clothilde? Celestine's the one that's sick.' Without waiting for a reply he steered her into a big warm kitchen. A large woman and the girl Kerry whom she had met outside the Opera, were elbow deep in flour, raisins, and sweet-smelling spices, with bowls and wooden spoons. In front of another fire, feet up, peaceful and looking as if this was his home, sat her brother Neill.

And Darragh. She felt her knees go weak at the sight of him and when he saw her his face lit up and he looked delighted.

She had turned him over the weeks into an enemy, an adversary. Now all such animosity left her and she was flooded with relief, as if he was dear and familiar and they had been separated for a long time.

'Clothilde. Is anything wrong at home? It's not Breffni?' Neill had jumped to his feet and everyone in the kitchen looked at her anxiously.

'No. Oh no.'

Darragh touched her shoulder. 'You're saturated,' he said. 'Take off your jacket. Didn't you wear a top-coat? Mam, this is Neill's sister. She's as wet as a drowned rat.'

'Didn't I gather that?' Philomena said with wounded pride. 'Come to the fire, lovey, sit yourself down an' I'll pour you a hot cup o' tay. Just let me wipe my hands. We're makin' the puddin' for Christmas.'

Darragh took her coat and shook it. Kerry smiled at her and when Neill took a chair from the table to sit her in, Kerry draped a shawl over her shoulders and settled her in front of the fire. Clothilde was so overwhelmed by their instinctive kindness that she burst into tears.

Neill cried, 'Oh what is it, Clo? It must be Breffni? You never cry. Please tell me.'

'It's not. I swear it's not.'

'Leave her be. Let her rest. Give her the tay, Mam.' Darragh's voice was quiet and infinitely kind. She turned to him instinctively, as a child turns to authority. She looked at him fearfully but there was no hostility in those kindly hazel eyes. There was only sympathy there, a desire to help. In her imagination she had caricatured his face and made it cruel. Now all she could see was a gentle expression of concern.

'I'm so confused,' she said.

'What is it, Clo? Is something wrong at home?'

'Let her have her tea first,' Philomena said. 'Let her set awhile in peace.'

Clothilde sipped the tea gratefully. She looked shyly about. The women went back to the pudding. There were two white porcelain pudding bowls on the table; mounds of chopped candied peel, raisins, amber sultanas and nuts lay on plates; and there was a bottle of brandy and one of port. Philomena and Kerry were stirring the ingredients in a large copper basin. Their faces were flushed with effort, pink-cheeked and moist in the heat of the kitchen. They reminded Clothilde of Celestine's face at jam-making, before all the turmoil and she thought sadly of that time, their unworried innocence then, gone now forever.

The men sat on either side of her, Neill and Darragh, silent, peaceful, looking into the fire reflectively. They are not afraid of silence here, she thought. Darragh sucked a pipe. His profile was strong, almost severe. He must have felt her gaze for he looked around and caught her eyes. She glanced down shyly.

'Do you feel better?' he asked softly. She nodded.

'Why did you come here?' Neill asked.

'I don't know,' she said. 'But I'm glad I did. I feel more peaceful.' She could hear the rain outside. The noise was soothing; a steady patter making her feel warm and protected and

301

safe. Mrs Quinn smiled at her when she looked around, and taking the brown teapot off the hob, manoeuvred her large body around the table and topped up her cup. She smiled again at Clothilde but did not seem to feel the need to say anything.

There was such accord here in this kitchen that Clothilde was afraid to move lest she break the mood, shatter the tranquillity. No wonder Neill loved to be here. No-one hurried her or asked her to explain anything. there was no sense of urgency here, no feeling of rush.

At last she said, 'What is that street we are on, across the road? Near the brewery?'

Darragh glanced at Neill. 'Paradise Street. And Paradise Square. Paradise Row. It's an ironical name for them, don't you think?'

She looked at Neill, eyes wide and anxious. 'Father's streets? His tenements?'

Neill nodded.

'I did not know such places existed. It's like hell,' she said.

'Well, it is. Hell for the occupants, that is,' Darragh answered dispassionately. But his eyes were bright with anger.

'Oh don't go soundin' off, Darragh. Can't you see the poor girl's in a state? I'm sure it's no concern of her's,' Philomena said in a placatory tone.

'It's everyone's concern,' Kerry said calmly but without accusation. 'When people are forced to live like that it is all our responsibilities.'

Clothilde put her cup down and stood, 'I agree. It is our responsibility,' she said. 'But you must believe me that I didn't know. To this day I did not know. Oh, I knew father owned Paradise Street and Square and Row and that Neill was always arguing with him about how awful those places were but it had no reality for me. As God is my judge, I did not know that they were like that, as bad as that.' She shook her head. 'I'll never forgive my father for this. Never. How dare he? How could he? I don't understand.'

Darragh stood up. 'Come with me,' he said.

Philomena placed herself between them. 'Now no! No, Darragh. The young woman is exhausted, shocked and still wet. Can't you see? Leave her be.' She turned to Clothilde. 'He's terrible,' she added ruefully. 'He's impossible. Forgive him.'

Clothilde was looking into the clear eyes of the man opposite.

302

'No,' she said. 'I'll go with him. I'd like to go.'

'All right then.' Philomena glanced at one and then the other as they looked at each other across her. She blessed herself, and lifted her hands, palms upwards in the air. 'Take the umbrella. She's a lady, Darragh, an' not used to the wet like you are. An' bring her back here so's she can have a bite o' food an' Kerry'll give her a fresh skirt while her things dry before the fire.'

Clothilde put on her jacket. Neill stood up to accompany them but Darragh shook his head without saying anything and Neill sank back in his comfortable chair and relaxed.

Outside the rain had eased somewhat. In the slate-grey day the houses wore a desolate aspect; ghost-houses. They walked down the street and turned into the square. Clothilde felt as if she had wandered by accident into a nightmare. Women scuttled past, shawls over their heads, their faces gaunt. Children ran barefoot in the water and their legs were like sticks. They looked cold and pinched. Men stood about in groups in the gaping doorways sharing a cigarette. They seemed to be waiting. There was an atmosphere of sad resignation about the place that Clothilde had never come across before.

Standing in the dark and dingy street that danced with grotesque shadows Clothilde looked up at Darragh.

'I'll never forgive Father,' she said again, her face serious. 'Never. He does not know what it is like down here. He does not know.'

Darragh took her hand gently. She jumped and pulled away, then she blushed.

'Oh I didn't mean . . . I wasn't being rude, I . . .'

Darragh smiled at her reassuringly. 'I understand. It is all right. I feel I know you, through Neill. We're good friends.'

She nodded. 'I know,' she whispered. 'I can see that.'

She stretched out her hand tentatively and touched his sleeve. 'We have been very . . . protected. My father does not encourage us to have anything to do with outsiders, so I . . .' She hesitated and looked up to see Darragh's face above her's. She suddenly felt very safe here with him, very secure.

'I know,' he said. 'You do not have to explain to me.'

'But how I feel . . . about my father. You see, sometimes I hate him so much. It fills me with poison. It is . . . not right.' She groped for words and glancing up again saw he was nodding vigorously.

'There is something I have to show you,' he said quietly.

'But . . .'

He covered her ungloved hand with his. 'Hush. Trust me. Just trust me. I would never harm you, you know that.'

And she did. She stood quite still on the gloomy pavement and gazed deep into his eyes and knew exactly what he was saying to her. How could she ever have thought ill of him? It had been fear, she knew that now. She felt as if a benign hand had softly wiped away all the violent feelings she had felt a moment before, indeed had been a prey to most of her life. In the stillness of the moment he patted her hand and smiled at her. It was a smile of such sweetness that her eyes filled with tears and she withdrew her gaze from his.

'Come,' he said.

He led her down Paradise Square. Off the square was a small lane. The houses here were even meaner than in the streets they had left, for here were no remains of former glory. The Georgians had not bothered with the architecture of the stables and in these shacks, pitted with holes, dark entrances leading to cave-like dwellings, people, Clothilde saw, lived and breathed in the foulest of conditions.

She could not bear to look. Out of the corner of her eye she saw a ragged child, half-clothed, barefoot and wide-eyed, staring vacantly at her from a doorway. She caught a glimpse of a gaunt-faced mother, hollow-cheeked, a midget-sized babe with a monstrous head in her arms, who watched her with that same expressionless look.

'Why?' she whispered and Darragh said, 'Hush' again and led her on. She did not want to go any further. She felt sick and angry and ashamed at what she saw. It was a reproach to their whole family that their father could be responsible for this. How could she eat again, sleep in her fine bed, dance at balls and parties, drink champagne and nibble canapés with Auntie May with the faces of these people to haunt her? How could she live comfortably when not far away people existed in this misery? She shook her head wearily. Why was Darragh making her look at this? Did he intend to shame her? Make her feel guilty? But she knew that was not so. There was something else. Her ankle twisted beneath her in the filth and muck of the lane and still he drew her on. A man, unshaven and coarse-faced, reeled out of the dark yawning entrance of one of the hovels, uttered an

304

obscenity and staggered on towards the lights of the street. She shrank away from him, shivering.

Darragh came to a halt in front of a closed door, the only closed door in the lane. It was a two-storied little tigeen and the slates were missing from the roof and the wood of the door was pock-marked. There were no curtains on the windows and the glass was mostly broken and cracked. Someone had put cardboard instead of a pane in the downstairs' frame.

Darragh knocked on the door. Quite soon it was opened by an old gaffer, a toothless, creased, grizzled, ugly old fellow in a dirty collarless shirt and stuff pants that looked as if he'd slept in them. His eyes were almost hidden in the creases and folds of his wizened face but when Clothilde caught sight of them they were like an eagle's, piercing and intelligent, unblinking and fierce.

At first she understood little of what was said: the ould fellow spoke in such thick Dublinese that she did not know what he was talking about. But bit by bit her ear became attuned to the cadences and idiosyncrasies of his speech.

It appeared his name was Sean Henny and he had lived here, he said, for sixty years: most of his life. His Mam had brought him from Mayo when her husband had been drowned in the wild Atlantic Ocean. His curragh had overturned and him not able to swim and he a fisherman. The old man laughed mirthlessly, wheezing like a broken clock. 'Them fishermen don't learn te swim on account if ye know how, it takes ye longer to drown.'

He spoke, eloquently and reflectively, leaning against the doorframe. 'No, this place did him fine, 'twas suitable for his needs an' there was nothing he wanted more than to die in peace inside'n the bed. He had his baccy an' his bread-and-jam an' a pot o' tae was allus on the hob. 'Twas all right wi' him.'

There was a pause as the old man squinted up at the patch of grey sky and Clothilde wondered what on earth was the point of all this.

'Who else lived with you in this house, Sean?'

'Foe Gawd's sake, Darragh, ye know that. I told yiz before an' we talked about it over an' again.'

'I know, Sean. I want you to tell this lady.'

Clothilde caught the bright piercing glance again and the old codger cleared his throat and spat into the filthy lane.

305

'Well, it was Mr Connolly that owns the brewery above. Him. He lived here. That is, until he left.' Clothilde's knees almost gave way beneath her. She felt Darragh's firm steadying grip on her arm. 'His mam an' his da lived above on the top floor,' Sean continued gesturing above with his head which he jerked backwards and upwards. 'His mam was a clingin' sorta woman. No starch. The chizzler, Garreth, was a solitary little fella. Kept to hisself. People didn't take te him. God, his da, though, he was a terrible man. A giant he was. Drunk mornin', noon, and night. Bashed his head agin' the lintel every time he came in or outa dat door. Beast he was. Beat up de missus somethin' shockin'. Beat up the nipper. Garreth. Chizzler was skeered of him. Oh, a terrible man.' He paused, reflectively. 'Died in de lane here,' he said dramatically. He pointed to the middle of the small muddy road. Darragh and Clothilde glanced over their shoulders to where the old man pointed. The rain bounced in the puddles of muddy water. It was a terrible place to die.

'Drunk he was. Came back from de 'Paradise' pub. Got violent when he got drunk. Well, somethin' had te happen. Stands te reason. Well, he came home this night pissed outa his mind. Beat up young Garreth and then the missus. Screamin' an' crying she was, wringin' her hands when she staggered after him inta the street.' Sean sniffed and spat. 'Everyone was hangin' outa their windows, watchin' the spectacle, includin' young Garreth. Hangin' outa the top winder up there, cryin' his eyes out, whimperin' an snivellin' he was. His mam tried to hold his da back. "Don't go," she kept sobbin', "Don't go," though I could never understand why she wanted te hold him back. Wouldn't ye think she'd want te be shot of him, wouldn't ye? But no, hung onta him, she did, wouldn't let go. Well he roared like a maddened bull, pulled his arms outa his jacket. He was staggerin' around, drunk as a lord. 'Twas rainin' that night too, just like tonight, fit te baptise ye an' slippery underfoot. Well, in the heel o' the hunt he suddenly wheeled around, like a top, an' fell.' He paused and pointed to a bollard just across the lane opposite the house. 'There. Went down like a felled ox. Hit his head on that bollard dere. We could hear de crack. Everyone heard de crack. De little fella musta heard de crack.' He looked up. 'Killed him, it did. Stone dead.' He shook his head. 'Terrible shame on the family. Shamed they were. Ever after until Garreth left an' went te better himself, the kids called after him "Yer da died drunk in the street. Yer da died drunk in the street. Yer da died drunk in the street." Yelled after him over an' over. Teased him unmercifully. Oh they gave him hell. Me mam used to say she heard him every night cryin' hisself to sleep. How he managed to rise above hisself is one o' the great miracles of the world, so it is. An' he did. Went scrivin and' crawlin' an' workin' hisself morn and night. Determination it was. Gawd'n' it was a mighty thing te see. Fanatic, I said. I often wonder what he got up te an' he clawin' to the top o' the heap.'

The old man gave a caper. He was like some old scarecrow clothed in rags suddenly come to life.

'But he done it.' The man clapped his hands together in relish. 'An' got his own back on the wans that mocked him. Gawney Mac, he made it. Just shows. Well, I'm off in now, Darragh. Bid ye the time o' day. I'll be in tomorrow mornin' an' God willin' as usual fer my jar, directly after Mass, so I will.

He slammed the door in their faces, leaving them standing in the rain.

307

Chapter

47

THE women of Rathgar were worried about Celestine Connolly. No-one knew the family intimately, no-one was on visiting terms with the Connollys, but the word went out that the sweet youngest girl was ill in bed. The newsagent spread the news when Clothilde came in for the *Wicklow People*, a special order, and she came in alone instead of with her sister. Clothilde, they thought, was a serious girl, an' sure why wouldn't she be and her the eldest. But the bright and happy Celestine, why, it cheered you up just to look at her, and her all sweetness and good-humour. The priests heard that she was not well, confined to bed, and a Mass was said. The shop-keepers inquired about her progress from Ellen, Mamie and Miffy, but no one asked exactly what the matter was. They would not be so intrusive. It was not polite. They simply enquired about her and seemed sorry to hear that she did not get better.

Then Miffy, all sniffles, told the chemist Roderick Callaghan, an old maid of a man if ever there was one, and a gossip, all about the unhappy love affair with the handsome soldier and didn't Roddy Callaghan spread the story which was avidly seized upon by the neighbourhood, picked over, discussed, and Celestine overnight became a local tragic heroine. There was not a woman in the district that did not shed a surreptitious tear for the young girl dying of love, they said. They compared her to Juliet and Heloise, to Cathy and Deirdrea of the Sorrows.

They blamed Garreth Connolly. They had no evidence that it was his fault and Miffy had not mentioned his name, but they did not like him, (nasty bully of a man who was uncivil and ill-humoured). So they blamed him. Ellen (a walking 'saint' if ever there was one) they adored. The doctor's wife, Mrs Meagher, was fond of saying that Mrs Connolly had more crosses to bear than Jesus Himself if the truth were known.

They prayed for the poor wee girleen. They quizzed Miffy and Mamie but the news remained the same: Celestine Connolly's condition did not improve.

Dr Meagher shook his head over the lassitude that seemed to envelop her. Her loss of appetite, her lethargy, worried him but he could think of no cure without the girl's full cooperation. He begged her to buck up and take an interest in life, in her sister and family, in clothes and fun and everything around her, but she seemed incapable of it. She tried feebly, stitching her sampler of 'Home Sweet Home', writing in her diary or pressing flowers, but she nearly always let the work fall from her hands while large tears slipped down her cheeks.

'I have lost them both,' she thought. 'I have lost my dearest Papa and the man I love. How can it be? Oh how can it be?' and she slipped further into her depression.

Ellen worried about her constantly, trying to think of new things to divert her. Her husband's problems seemed trivial beside her daughter's sickness of spirit. Neill combed the book-shops of Dublin and spent a fortune in Easons buying her illus-trated books and papers and exciting new novels to take her mind off things. But the books lay unread between her fingers or face down, open on the counterpane.

Garreth went in to see her nightly and delivered a mono-logue which mostly went unheard. It was just as well, for it was a heavy mixture of reproach and invective, rebuke larded with self-pity, with all the smugness of one who has been proved right. She simply turned her face to the wall when he arrived and switched her mind off so all of it passed over her head. Her inertia increased as the days passed and Dr Meagher despaired of her.

Chapter

48

THE next three weeks after her visit to 'The Golden Harp' Clothilde spent in a daze. She tried in vain to assimilate her feelings but found she could not. She was a mass of stormy emotions, tempest-tossed, unable to get her bearings and not at all sure that she wanted to find her way. She refused to come to grips with all that had happened to her, refused to look calmly and dispassionately at the change she had undergone. She was not capable of being detached. All she knew, all she could think of, was Darragh. Like a somnambulant she moved through the days and nights in a trance. She felt no urgency. She did not want to see him again just yet. That time would come, but not yet. She wanted to hold on to her feelings, hold on to the over-whelming fact of Darragh.

There was no doubt in her mind that they belonged together and that he knew it too. He would be waiting for her, that much she was sure of. It was a wondrous feeling. It overwhelmed her and made her indifferent to her sister's decline, her mother's anxiety over Celestine and Breffni, and her father's mounting and constant state of rage. What had once worried or terrified her now left her curiously detached. She realized one evening after dinner as her father ranted and raved at her that she did not care much what he said, what he did. He had lost his power over her, she was no longer afraid of him. She smiled when she realized this and Garreth Connolly felt the blood rush to his head when he realized that she was not listening and he saw that smile.

'Just you wait, my fine young lady. I'll lock you in your room if you do not behave in a manner appropriate for a female dependent in this house.'

She turned and looked at him calmly. 'No you won't, Father,' she said and stood up. 'If you'll excuse me, Mother? I'm going out.'

Speechless, he watched as she left the room. He sat gazing after her. He did not understand what was happening. His whole world was crumbling about his ears. First the brewery: his loss of prestige; his loss of the position that had given him his identity. Next John Joe's victory over him: he had had to go down to the jail and to the Superintendent of Police and sign forms and papers and all the time Mary Reilly was crying her joy all over Neill. That was how he saw it. Mary bobbing and hopping about in her excitement, blithely exultant. Grateful to him too, which irritated him intensely. As if he was negotiating her wretched husband's release. He saw the whole episode as a triumph for 'Workers' over 'Boss'. He shook his head whenever he thought of it. It would be a terrible future when the workers had the power of protest that Neill felt they should. He hoped Neill would live to regret his attitudes. Garreth saw the whole affair as a personal insult, a slight on his credibility and authority. He hated to admit it, but he missed O'Brien. He missed the little man's toadying, his flattery. His fawning obsequiousness had become a drug to Garreth and like an addict he suffered withdrawal symptoms with its loss.

And now there was all this insubordination in the very centre of his life, the seat of his power, the place where until now he had been dictator and god.

Neill was rarely home these days and he did not bother to tell them any more when he would be absent. He dodged in and out, and although Garreth left strict instructions that he was to report to his father as soon as he entered the house in Rathgar, he never accounted for himself. Mamie and his wife were evasive about his comings and goings, and so far Neill had not seen fit to have any contact at all with his father since John Joe's release from jail.

Garreth missed Celestine's companionship desperately. He ached for her gentle touch, her coaxing ways, her uncritical love and her gaiety. But he could not think of a way out of the situation. A stranger to tact or diplomacy, subtlety of any sort was beyond his ken. He had no idea how to go about repairing the breach and bringing about the reconciliation he so desired.

Each evening when he went to her room he went with a view

311

to forgiving her and allowing her to become his darling again, the light of his eyes. But the scene was never played as he envisioned it should be. She had not apologized. She had not been dutifully repentant. She had given him no opportunity of saying, 'It's all right, my pet.'

And Ellen. Her mouth had developed a stubborn expression strangely reminiscent of Mamie, and latterly Miffy. She had taken to leaving the house without telling him where she was going. Also, there was something in her manner, a detached independence that was most unladylike and out of character. What angered him most of all was that Ellen did nothing that he could rightly accuse her of.

And now Clothilde. She had been disobeying him as the others had but this was too much. Open mutiny. The way she had looked at him. Icily, with scorn. How dare she? He was her father. She had no right to behave towards him in that manner. He felt very tired; bone tired and for a moment he remembered the little boy he had been — alone in the garret room in the foul street, learning how to read, teaching himself the basics, slowly with infinite patience, for school was too painful a learning place.

He pulled the napkin from under his chin and threw it on the table. Ellen stood.

'Sit down,' he ordered. She paid no attention.

'Sit down,' he repeated.

'I'm going to Devotions, dear,' she said as if she had not heard him and tranquilly moved towards the door.

A feeling of hopelessness overwhelmed him. There seemed nothing to say or do. Overcome with inertia he sat on, speechless, after Ellen had left the room. His bones felt weary. He thought of his life, of the horror of his youth, of the mother who had died prematurely of exhaustion and lack of correct nourishment. He thought of the unfairness of it all. He had started with nothing. God, he thought, had given him nothing, no help at all. He had fought for everything he had. He had let no opportunity slip past him. He lived on nothing. He ate little in those days, but dreamed of the day when he could be lavish. He curbed his appetites, storing within himself the promise of excess when he had reached his goal as reach it he knew he must. And he did. But by then the carefree days of youth had passed him by, never to return. Buying the land little by little.

312

Building the brewery. He did not know why he had bought the mean streets from whence he came. A kind of flying in the face of God, of shaking his fist at heaven, he supposed. Besides, he knew the territory, was familiar with it. He felt at home there. He could stride the streets, fat, well-fed, prosperous, his shoes leather, polished by Ben-the-Boots, his servant, the watch and chain he wore in his waistcoat solid gold, his cane ebony and ivory, silver-tipped. And he wore a hat, not a cap, and puffed on a cigar for all the world to see.

And he despised the working men who had not succeeded in rising above the dirt, poverty and ignorance of their birth-place. He loathed the fact that they crawled and grovelled to him to get work and the fact that they were well content to do the meanest of jobs. Yet he needed them, not only to keep his business going but to feed his ego and confirm to him that they were not as he. He had swaggered amongst them, looking down on their lack of ambition as if they had a contagious disease.

He had married Ellen, far above his station, and at first he had been terrified of her, waiting to be 'found out' and expecting her to pour contempt on him for his ignorance, his crass mistakes. She was too much of a lady to do so and as time passed he began to despise her. He saw her fear of him as weakness and she began to irritate him. Incapable of returning her generous love he lost it. He did not see her worth; did not value her gentle nature.

By now he had everything he wanted: a comfortable house, servants, a wife and children over whom he had total authority. His business thrived and his trips to London, his erotic gambols with Maggie in Paddington had completed his life to his total satisfaction.

Then it had all collapsed. He had been afraid over the past weeks to examine his finances. He knew he could not continue indefinitely without income from the brewery. What would happen now filled him with a terror he felt unable to grapple with. He had never felt like this before, helpless and afraid. When he was young he had never had anything to lose. Now he stood in danger of sinking into the mire from which he had come. And he knew he had not the energy within him to rise a second time. He would become part of that throng of losers he so loathed.

His only course of action to save himself would be to sell the land. Sell Paradise Row, Paradise Square, Paradise Street and the brewery, or rather, the site the brewery had stood on. But he could not bring himself to do that. In the weeks that had followed the fire he had tried to accept the fact that he would probably have to dispose of his holdings, but it went against the grain. It irked him. He was used to holding his possessions close and he doubted if he could ever let them go. The area represented to him his achievement. Standing at the entrance to his brewery he could see where he had come from and where he was going. The past and the future. Failure and success; failure that he had turned into success. It was his identity. Without it he became insubstantial and a nobody. Like now. Sitting here, stupefied, in his own dining-room whilst his family ignored him and went their merry way. And Ellen disobeyed him.

An unfamiliar feeling enveloped him and he could not identify it for he had never felt like this before. To his horror tears came into his eyes. Any sign of emotion other than righteous anger or indignation was a sign of weakness to him.

He stood up hurriedly and left the room. He went upstairs. He would go to London, to Paddington, to Maggie. It had been what he had always done when he was disturbed, and although this time it was different, surely it would work? He felt a surge of relief. He would feel like a man again. Maggie would make him feel in charge again, restore his vanished pride, and he would once more be the man he used to be. He would go to bed early. It was still only morning. But he was very tired; excruciatingly tired. He had never felt so tired in his life before. He would rest. He would get O'Brien to get him tickets on the Mail Boat. O'Brien? No. He had given him the sack. He would have to ask Ellen.

He got undressed very slowly. Each movement seemed painful to him and took him ages to accomplish. The thought came that Ellen might refuse to get his ticket. Well, it did not matter now. He must sleep. Yes. That was all he needed. Sleep.

He climbed into bed and with a sigh fell into darkness.

Chapter

49

THE library was Barth's favourite room in Avoca House and he was often to be found there in the late afternoon before tea, checking accounts, reading the *Times* or *Punch* or just cogitating. The library was warm and pleasant. The walls were lined with leather-bound books which were rarely disturbed as Barth and May were not great readers. Today he was expecting Neill to call and while he sat waiting for him he looked out at the rain which fell softly on a nearly barren world. Soon it would be Christmas. It would be a long time before the snowdrops heralded Spring. Daffodils. He thought of the fields behind Avoca House and how they looked in Spring when the daffodils and narcissi marched down to the river, their golden trumpets nodding in the soft breezes. He looked out over the lawn and imagined the sea of purple and violet, yellow and pearly white of the crocuses that each year clustered at the base of the huge grey-sinewed lime trees. The orchards would be drifts of blossom, the canopy of the trees falling to carpet green earth.

Not for a long time yet. Not for months. He sighed.

He had sent for his nephew, asking him to come to Avoca House in the early afternoon and stay to dine and remain overnight. The boy had telephoned his acceptance and now Barth waited patiently for his arrival. He had sent Buckley, the chauffeur, to meet the three o'clock train and at exactly three-thirty Barth saw the Rolls make its stately journey up the drive, around the fountain and the last lap to draw up in front of the house. The dogs barked and a moment later his tall nephew was ushered into the library by Weems.

Barth held Neill's hand in a firm clasp, then indicated the

315

chair on the other side of the fire. Weems hovered in the doorway awaiting instructions.

'Your Aunt May is having tea in the blue drawing-room, so you may have some tea if you wish. Sit down, m'boy, sit down. But I think you and I might prefer a whiskey and soda? Eh?'

Neill smiled at his uncle and nodded his head. He loved his uncle and he was always touched by Barth's innate goodness.

'That would be most welcome, Uncle.'

Barth nodded over at Weems. 'You may go, Weems. Neill will pour.'

Weems shook his head. 'Yes, my lord,' he said, then tut-tutted and left the library reluctantly. Barth burst out laughing while Neill went to the whiskey decanter on a table across the room and poured a generous measure into two cut-glass tumblers.

'Weems would treat us all as invalids if we allowed him. He cannot bear us to do anything for ourselves,' Barth said.

'I'm not entirely sure he's still alive, Uncle,' Neill said.

Barth crossed his right leg over his left, pulling up his trouser as he did so, chuckling as Neill handed him the tumbler and squirted soda into the glass.

'Not sure you're not right, m'boy. He moves about Avoca House like a zombie. He's long past being much use but I've known him since I was a lad. He came to Avoca House with me when I got married. I'm much too fond of him to retire him.'

Neill nodded. 'Of course you couldn't do that, Uncle. Avoca House just wouldn't be the same without Weems.'

'Have a pleasant journey, m'boy?' Barth asked. Neill nodded.

The two men settled back comfortably and sipped their drinks for a moment. The fire flickered merrily in the grate and they looked into its heart as they drank. Neill broke the silence.

'What did you want to see me about, Uncle?'

Barth examined his nephew. He liked Neill's tall spare good looks. He had a directness and honesty that Barth admired.

'Neill, what exactly has been happening in your family?' he asked thoughtfully. 'May and I have been concerned. Is it as bad as we hear? Rumour has it your father is ruined. Tell me what happened.'

'Well, that's easily answered, sir. The brewery went on fire. The fire was caused by my father's manager's son. He was careless. It was an accident. But my father's insurance of the brewery had lapsed. My father blames his manager, but knowing Papa I'm fairly certain the blame was his alone. My father was not one to allow his manager access to funds for the payment of bills,' he said dryly.

Barth nodded. 'Mmm. No. I cannot see Garreth trusting his manager that far. Indeed, I don't allow our manager here to make the larger payments. Not that I don't trust him, it's just that in the event of a mistake I know where the blame lies. With me.'

'Precisely,' Neill said.

'How has it affected your family, Neill? You must know we are concerned about your mother.'

'I understand. I hardly know yet. There has scarcely been time for us to realize our position. Certainly Father is not destitute. He owns the land the brewery was built on, a prime sight. And those hideous blots on the face of the earth: Paradise Row and Square and Street. He is landlord of that terrible slum. But he has lost all the rest. I don't think he realizes the extent of his loss just yet.' Neill shrugged. 'I really don't know his plans.'

'Well, Neill, I thought that might be the case and I have considered what I should do. I am prepared to buy the land from Garreth. I don't *want* it. I don't particularly like the idea of becoming responsible for "the hideous blot" as you call it.' He looked at his nephew. 'Is it really as bad as that?'

Neill nodded. 'It's worse, sir. You can have no conception.'

'Well, you may tell your father that I'll give him a good price for it.'

'He will refuse, Uncle. You know my father.'

Barth smiled. 'Yes, you are right. He'll refuse it. At first. Then he'll have a look at his bank balance. Then you must give him an opening, tactfully, to reconsider my offer. A few remarks about gossip, people finding out too much about his situation, and perhaps a suggestion that if he sells to me he can make the excuse that he became disenchanted with the works after the fire but wanted to keep it in the family; some such reasoning might persuade him to change his mind about my buying the land. What do you think?'

'I think you may be right, sir. But why should you do this for us?'

Barth sighed. 'Your mother, Neill. She is a very special

317

person and May and I love her dearly. She'll never be hurt as long as we are here to look after her. I don't want her to worry. Besides, you are family. I could never see my family needy. For anything. Do you understand?'

Neill nodded. 'Yes, sir. Thank you very much, sir.'

Barth held up his hand. 'There are conditions, Neill.'

Neill looked at his uncle enquiringly. 'What do you mean, Uncle?' he asked.

'Well, if I buy the land, etc., I'll give your father the market price, which is considerable. It will be in your mother's name, though. I insist on that. Now that transaction depends on certain conditions.' He smiled at Neill's questioning face. 'Firstly, I have no use for a brewery or those terrible houses in the Paradise group. So I'll make Clothilde a wedding present of it. If she needs it.' He saw Neill's look of enquiry. 'Owen Mulcahy. Mulcahy was telling me he withdrew his agreement to Clothilde's union with his son. Silly old bastard. I thought it a pretty poor show.'

'Yes, sir.' Neill kept his thoughts to himself. It was not his affair to speak for his sister.

Barth continued, 'I don't want the damn responsibility of the place and if it would settle things for Clothilde, then it's a good investment. She can, of course, give me shares in it. Put me on the board of directors, eh? Eh? So Clothilde may have the brewery, for what it's worth, and the lands thereabout. Understood?'

Neill smiled at his uncle. 'Yes, sir. You are most kind,' he said.

'Nonsense. I'll recoup quite a lot of my investment, I shouldn't wonder.'

Neill nodded and Barth clasped his hands together, aligned his two forefingers and put the tips against his lips. How to broach the subject nearest his heart? he wondered, then decided to speak simply.

'Secondly, I'll buy it on condition that your father withdraws his objection to Celestine marrying Charles Cavendish.' Neill looked embarrassed but Barth continued smoothly, 'And his objection to you becoming a priest. Are you serious about that? And are you quite sure that's what you want, Neill?'

He looked across the fire at his nephew. Neill looked back, untroubled by his uncle's scrutiny.

318

'Oh yes, Uncle. For a while I wondered if perhaps God's will for me was that I take over the brewery as my father wished and be of service that way.' He smiled ruefully. 'But I reckon God answered that question very clearly.'

Barth laughed. 'Well then, my boy, you must do what you feel is right for your future, without interference from your father.'

'It will cost money, Uncle.'

'I am aware of that, Neill. You need have no worries on that score.'

'How can I thank you, sir? But I do. Very much.' A frown creased his forehead.

'What is it, Neill?'

'It's about Celestine, sir. She was let down by Charles Cavendish. She was to meet him. He was to take her away. He never turned up. She is . . . well, she has been terribly upset. Tell the truth, sir, she has been ill ever since.'

Barth had been contemplating the leaping flames. A log fell and he pushed it with the toe of his boot. He wondered how much Neill knew. Or guessed. He was a bright lad. He did not miss much.

He looked up, 'Yes I know. I just found out,' he said.

Damn, he thought, as he caught Neill's swift sideways glance. He must not give everything away. He had watched, observed his wife, listened to her sister, put two and two together and come up with the obvious answer. May had lied and cheated. It was not a nice discovery; that she was prepared to go that far, act in so foul a way for Charles Cavendish. It was completely out of character. He consoled himself with that thought. He forgave her. He smiled wryly. What was the quality May had that made him love her so? What power did she wield that held him in thrall? No matter what she did he would love her. He was ashamed of that. However, he knew she was not bad. He could not have loved a bad woman. Rather she was a spoiled one. She had always had everything she desired. Really, it was the fault of those who had given in to her over the years. Her parents in particular had doted on her. They had been quite old when she was born and they had refused her nothing. Except Charles. Perhaps that had made him more desirable in her eyes. They had not allowed her Charles.

He had been no better than her parents, Barth reflected; he

had given her whatever she craved. His vast wealth enabled him to realize her every whim. May was cultivated and unostentatious, she would never make a vulgar display. Nevertheless he had showered her with paintings and *objets d'art*, jewels and furs, houses and horses. Everything she wanted. Except Charles. He would not allow her Charles.

He had watched her over the past months sink into the trap she had set for herself. She had betrayed a confidence, she had gone against her own nature and behaved in an appalling manner to her niece. Driven by an obsession before which she was helpless, she had done something despicable and she was suffering for it. Each day he saw her pain; in the taut lines around her mouth, in the haunted depths of her blue eyes. Barth believed that a lot of people brought about their own destruction. He was desperately worried, for it seemed to him that that was what May was doing. She was in the middle of totally wrecking her life. She was pulling her world down around her ears without a thought for the future. And she could not stop, could not untangle herself from the web she had spun. And that was what he was trying to do for her now. He was going to fight his corner with every weapon he had.

He nodded, satisfied, and Neill saw the pain in the curve of his mouth.

'There was a message for Celestine from Captain Charles,' he said lightly. 'It went astray. That afternoon, when he was supposed to meet Celestine, he was on his way to France. He does not know that Celestine is not with his aunt in Hampstead. Or if his aunt has told him she is not there; he thinks Celestine is on her way. Perhaps you will tell your sister and give her this with my apologies.'

The letter had been crumpled up. It had subsequently been smoothed out and refolded. It had no envelope. Someone must have thrown the envelope away, read the letter, crushed it and discarded it. Someone else must have rescued it and smoothed it out.

Neill looked at it. He saw the writing. 'My dearest darling girl, Oh my Celestine, I miss you, my love.' He read no further. He looked at Barth and met his uncle's calm blue gaze. Ah poor man, he knows of his wife's infidelity, Neill thought, and looked away.

'Of course I will, sir. I will deliver it and my sister to Hampstead.'

320

Barth nodded, satisfied.

'And, Uncle? Thank you.'

Barth stood up. He put down his glass and eased his shoulders backwards.

'Thank *you*, Neill. I believe we understand each other.'

Neill rose too but Barth pressed him back into the chair.

'No. Sit awhile. Then you can bathe and change for dinner when you are ready. It's the usual time. I'll leave you alone now.'

He left his nephew staring into the leaping licking flames, a relaxed smile on his face.

Chapter
50

CLOTHILDE looked at Darragh. He was alone in the little kitchen behind 'The Golden Harp'. She would not much have cared who else was there. She would not have noticed others present. Her whole mind was full of Darragh.

'I knew you would come,' he said, seeing her there. 'At least, I hoped . . .'

She nodded. 'No. You knew I would. But I had to . . . think. I had to sort out my feelings. It was as if I had gone into a storm-centre and I was being whirled about like a leaf in the wind.'

He smiled. 'I know,' he said. 'It took courage.' She looked at him enquiringly. 'We come from different worlds,' he said.

She shook her head. 'That is of no account. No. I simply had to sort out a whole series of wrong ideas. Wrong emphases. It is not God I want to serve. It is you.'

He looked angry for a moment. 'Not serve. Not that.'

She smiled up at him and put out her hand and touched his cheek.

'Oh yes,' she breathed. 'Serve. Each other. It is love.' She turned from him and sat at the kitchen table. There were pots of jam and marmalade, salt and pepper canisters and a news-paper. 'I want to explain,' she said. 'You may not understand.'

She looked so vulnerable, he thought, her face naked of guile. Her eyes told him everything he needed to know but he did not tell her that. Let her explain, he thought, for her own sake.

'I thought it was God, but it was love looking for a home. There was no-one in my world . . . big enough. No-one of the largeness I needed. Then I found you and my love rested there.

322

But it felt at first like sacrilege. It was not. God had been trying to show me that. I've been so wayward and confused. So emotional and serious. And Father didn't help. I sometimes did things just to get back at him. Childish. I know what to do with all these feelings now that I have found you.'

She smiled a little timorously. He took her hands, slowly drawing her to her feet.

'I'll rest in you,' she said. 'You're love for me. We'll work together for the people here. Together. We'll manage it somehow. You'll know what to do.'

He was stunned by her understanding. She had put into plain words the exact crystallization of all he most wanted in life, all he ached to achieve and be. So simply. So clearly. Love her and work for his poor and wretched neighbours.

'How did you know I loved you?'

She looked at him calmly. 'Don't play games, Darragh,' she said. 'We both knew instantly. I knew that you knew and vice versa. These past months I needed, not to find that out, but to sort out what I wanted to *do* about it.'

'Your father?'

'You have taken away my fear of him forever. The hatred too. I feel sorry for him. I had to work that out as well. He has no more power over me. When I think how frightened I used to be . . . Now I realize he cannot force me to do anything I don't want to do. Mother will understand, I think. It's hard to forgive what he has done to her and to Celestine. Perhaps it was better not to be his favourite.'

'That kind of love can be a terrible burden,' Darragh remarked and she nodded, smiling at him.

'I remember being so jealous of her, of his love for her, of her privileged position in the family. I was often sharp with her. But I don't feel like that any more. I'm so sorry for her.'

She put her hands on his lapels and slowly, tenderly, he put his arms around her.

'I must not touch you or I'll forget you are a lady,' he said softly.

'I don't care.' She kissed his lips at each corner, then kissed his mouth standing on tiptoe to reach him.

'Ah, don't darlin'.' He held her gently from him. 'I want you so much I could ravish you here and now.' He smiled a little and he spoke lightly but his lips trembled and his hands shook.

323

'Why don't you? For I love you with all my heart and soul and body too,' she said breathlessly.

'No, my darling. No. We will wait. We will take pride in waiting. No-one, least of all ourselves, need ever accuse us of indiscretion or impatience. My sweet girl, we will do it the right way. You will never feel guilty because of me.'

'But I won't feel guilty . . .'

'You don't know that. You cannot be sure. I will treat you with honour, my darling.' He kissed her then, a deep satisfying kiss, and shaken they looked at each other.

'I cannot see your father giving his consent,' Darragh said at last with a sigh. 'I cannot imagine your mother standing up to him. Not if what Neill says . . .'

'I say what?'

They had not heard him come in. He stood behind them looking at them, understanding dawning in his eyes.

'Oh Jesus,' he said and sat down at the table and put his hands over his face.

'Don't be like that, Neill. Be happy for us.'

He looked up. 'Ah my dears. How wonderful it would be. Two of the people I love best. But Father will never allow it. He'll kill you first, Clothilde.'

'He won't know. We'll run away. I'm old enough. I'm not going to let him ruin my life as he has ruined Celestine's.'

'He may not.' Neill glanced at his sister. 'Sit down,' he said.

Kerry arrived in the doorway. 'Will ye look at all of yiz an' not a drop of tea poured out. Darragh you should be ashamed. Neglecting your guests!' She bustled about putting cups and saucers before them, her bright eyes darting from face to face, trying to assess what was happening. She saw Darragh cover Clothilde's hand with his hand and she had only to look at their faces to see how the land lay there. 'Well, well, well, here's a fine to-do,' she said to herself and set about brewing the tea.

'Besides, Father has changed, Neill.' Clothilde was saying. 'He seems much weaker now. As if he has lost his bearings.'

'Father will never lose his bearings.'

'Oh, Neill! You haven't been home in ages. You haven't seen him. Where exactly *have* you been? I thought you were here.'

Neill looked up. 'Oh. Sorry. Well I've been to Avoca House. Uncle Barth sent for me. He's going to pay for my studies to be a priest.'

324

Clothilde jumped up and went around the table and hugged her brother. 'Oh Neill I'm so pleased for you. So very pleased. Oh it's what you've always wanted. I'm afraid I've let you down. Me and Darragh . . .'

'I *told* you, Clo, that it was not the same for you as it was for me. I'm glad about you and Darragh. I could not be better pleased. I'm just terrified for you both if Father finds out.'

'I'm not afraid of him any more, Neill. Darragh showed me the house and introduced me to Sean.'

Neill glanced at his friend. Kerry banged the teapot down and they all jumped.

'I wish someone would tell me what's going on,' she said in an aggrieved voice. 'I'm a human being, amn't I? And I'm simply dying of curiosity.'

'Ah sorry, Kerry,' Darragh said. 'Look, pour us some tea, there's a lassie, and we'll tell you all.'

They sat around the kitchen table and sipped black tea, sweet and strong, and Darragh told Kerry how he would marry Clothilde and they would work together. Neill told them of his Uncle Barth's generous offer and also mentioned how he had found out that Charles had not deserted Celestine.

'The messages went astray,' he said by way of explanation. 'They got mixed up. He was sent back to the front. He could not come to Cel. He left a message that never reached her.'

Clothilde thought of her aunt's tragic face, the passion in her eyes when she looked at the handsome soldier, and she made a shrewd and accurate guess at what had really happened. Contempt and anger overwhelmed her at the thought of the damage her aunt had done. Then she looked at Darragh and knew that if someone threatened to take him away from her she was perfectly capable of acting in the same way. Perhaps. She decided she could not afford to be judgemental. She shivered but said nothing.

'We must tell Celestine,' Neill said. 'The child is like a bird with a broken wing.'

'What you told me about Uncle Barth and his offering me the brewery, Neill: it's very interesting.'

'I think he meant it if it was an obstacle to your marriage to Owen Mulcahy. As a dowry.'

Darragh frowned. 'Who is this fellow?' he asked and Clothilde giggled.

'Ah, a nobody. A non-existent person, my love. But it's of interest to me. Of great interest, Neill.'

'Whatever you say, dear,' Neill replied. 'Though I can't see
. . .'

'Don't trouble your brain about it now, Neill. Let's just sit here, all of us, and be thankful for each other.' Clothilde smiled at the assembled company and realized how dear all the people there were to her. Warmth filled her being. A great peace came over her and she squeezed Darragh's hand.

'In my own mind,' she said, 'I'm quite certain that everything is going to be all right.'

Chapter

51

THAT night, as Clothilde lay sleepless in bed, she sent up a profound and almost superstitious prayer of thanks. Suddenly everything seemed to be changing for the better; not just in her own life but in the lives of those she loved. She had a lover's desire to see the whole world happy and it looked a little as if her wish might be granted.

When she had let herself in quietly by the back door she had surprised Ben-the-Boots with his arm around Miffy. They did not spring apart but had turned to her, shy smiles on their faces. She had nodded to them, understanding now Miffy's songs on the stairs, and went upstairs as quietly as she could.

She tiptoed into her sister's room. Celestine lay propped up in bed. Her face seemed smaller and thinner and the sparkling vitality that had lit up her eyes and added lustre to them had gone. She looked anxiously at her sister, 'Clo? Clo? I'm glad to see you. Papa has not been in to see me today. I do hate to upset him and I constantly do. I'm wicked, I know. He was right, you see, and I was wrong. He keeps telling me so and I know it to be true, yet I feel so unrepentant. My head aches all the time, Clo. Oh am I evil as Father says and damned to hell for disobeying him? I cannot sleep, dearest Clo, for worrying.'

'Hush, hush, sweet sister.' Clothilde soothed her, gently smoothing the damp tangle of hair off her forehead. Celestine had been mildly feverish all day. 'I have something to tell you, Celestine, and you must promise me that you will keep calm.'

Celestine sat up in bed. The lamp cast shadows beneath her eyes and her cheeks looked hollow. The pillow was wet where her head had been.

'What? What? Oh Clo, it is not bad news? Breffni is not . . .'

Clothilde hastened to reassure her. 'No, no. Nothing to do with Breffni. Listen, my sweet. Neill has been to see Uncle Barth. He told Neill that that day that Charles was to meet you in the Shelbourne he was called back to active service.' Celestine was watching Clothilde with wide startled eyes. 'He sent a message explaining that to you and asking you to go to his Aunt Agatha, I think, or it could have been Agnes . . .'

'It's Agatha. Agatha,' Celestine cried. 'Oh go on, Clo. Go on . . .'

'Well, you were to go to Aunt Agatha in London and wait for him there.' Clothilde cleared her throat and lowered her eyes. She could not look into her sister's. 'It must have gone astray. Uncle Barth said it was mislaid,' she added.

There was silence in the room. Clothilde could hear Mamie's voice calling Miffy to help her take in the washing from the yard.

'Shoulda' been done hours ago. I don't know what ye can have bin up to.' Her admonishing tones floated up through the window which was open a crack to prevent the room becoming stuffy.

Clothilde looked at Celestine. Her sister was struggling with her emotions, expressions of joy, anger, fear and hope passing across her face as she tried to take in the news Clothilde had given her.

'It's pitch out here, Mamie, an' I can't see a thing.' Miffy's plaintive voice drifted up, followed by Ben-the-Boots' firm tones,

'I'll do it for ye. Quit worrying, the both of ye. I'll do it.'

Clothilde looked over to the window and she almost did not hear Celestine's remark, 'It was Auntie May.'

Clothilde, startled, looked back at her sister.

'What? Why do you say that?'

Celestine's eyes had begun to sparkle and she clasped her hands around her knees. 'Oh it's obvious, Clothilde. Oh why did I never think of it before? Why? It never occurred to me that she could do such a terrible thing.' There was nothing censorious in Celestine's voice, she just seemed surprised at her own stupidity and immeasurabley relieved. 'Oh it's all obvious now. Charles must have asked her to let me know and she just couldn't do it. Poor woman. She loves him so.'

'Don't you hate her? I would.'

328

Celestine shook her head. 'No. No, that's not important now. What is important is that I must go to his aunt. Where is the address? Oh where?'

'Neill has it. He'll be home soon. He told me all this and he has all the information.' She smiled at her sister. 'And the right name,' she added, 'of his aunt.'

She leaned forward and touched Celestine's cheek. 'You look better already, Cel,' she said softly.

'Of course I do. There was never but one thing wrong with me and you've cured that.' Celestine pulled her sister into her arms and hugged her. She took her sister's hand in hers and kissed it, pressing it to her cheek.

'Oh Clo, I was right all the time. I knew I was. I kept trying to understand Papa, trying to believe that Charles had deserted me and I just could not. It was like being torn apart.' Her voice broke suddenly and she burst into tears.

'Oh dear darling Cel. It's all right now. It's all right.' Clothilde looked at her sister's tears splashing down her cheeks.

'I'm so happy. I'm so happy,' she sobbed.

'You'll sleep tonight. Sleep well. We'll smuggle you over the water somehow, dearest. Uncle Barth will help, Neill says.' Celestine nodded and Clothilde settled her sister down, taking away the two damp lace-trimmed pillows and plumping up the bolster underneath. She lifted her sister's hair away from her neck and tenderly covered her shoulders with the sheets and blankets. She waited beside her bed until all she could hear was Celestine's even breathing punctuated with jagged intakes of breath, the last residue of her tears. Then she turned down the light and tiptoed from the room.

Chapter

52

THAT night Ellen had found Garreth in bed when she came home. She had not seen him all day, but had decided not to worry about it. It was a startling thing, however, to find him in bed before her. He barely acknowledged her appearance in the room. He said something about going to London next day and so saying turned over on his side and went to sleep. She tiptoed around the room, undressing as quietly as she could, hoping not to disturb him.

She felt bemused by her own behaviour. Since her conversation with Barth, Garreth's moods, his anger and the threat of his displeasure, had ceased to hold sway over her. She, little by little, had become, not indifferent, for she could never be that, but less anxious, less worried, less interested, even, in her husband's state of mind. She felt as if a sheet of glass had been erected between them and he could no longer touch her. She ceased to quiver at his every mood-change or cringe before his bad temper. She moved about as if in a dream, wondering why she had not known this long ago. Why had not someone told her? All the agony she could have avoided! All the pain she need not have felt. There should be books to tell people about fear: that it is self-generating; that it is all in one's own mind; that it is all one's own doing; that it is stupid to let it spoil your life. She realized that it was partly her own fault that she had been unhappy. Her fear had made Garreth a tyrant. She remembered what May had said and knew her sister would never have tolerated such behaviour from a husband. She would have set the tone of their marriage from the beginning. She had had the weapon in her own hands and she had not

330

realized it. Garreth had started their marriage in awe of her. But she had not capitalized on her assets, had not known how to use her power. So he walked all over her and she cringed and let him see her fear, and the more she did the crueller he became.

Then all the confusing things had happened to her: her conversation with Barth; the fire; the unusual fact of Garreth's presence here at home with her at all hours of the day and night; and the news that the brewery had not been insured and her feelings on receipt of that news. She had felt contempt for Garreth over the whole business of John Joe Reilly and she was irritated by his presence in the house. Once she had disobeyed him, it became easier and easier on subsequent occasions to do so.

She pulled her nightgown over her greying hair and climbed into bed, careful not to lift the bedclothes from her husband. Usually when he felt her move in the bed he gave a groan. She knew he was letting her know she had disturbed him. Tonight there was no sound.

She lay for a while composing herself for the night. She was glad he was going to London. That is, if he really meant it. There was a lot she had to do, a lot she had to find out.

What, for instance was Clothilde up to, blooming and blossoming like a rose in the sun? She would sort out Celestine's problem for once and for all, even if she had to find Charles Cavendish herself and ask him bluntly what he was up to. She wanted to get over to Mary Reilly and tell her that Delia had made a spectacular recovery and could come home. That lovely news she was impatient to deliver. Oh she had so much energy. Life, she thought, was good. If it wasn't for Breffni.

She sighed. His letters troubled her. They were censored, but it was not only that fact that upset her. She could not understand the stilted sentences that told her nothing. Those terrible short missives she got from the front: 'I am well.' 'How are you?' Incomprehensible, she thought, and unlike Breffni, whose writing had always been descriptive if nothing else.

She snuggled lower in bed. Well, it would all be over soon, the terrible war. Everyone said so. She would not worry about it. After all, she got his letters regularly so she mustn't complain. It was tempting fate.

She fell into a deep sleep.

331

Chapter

53

THE next morning Ellen was up and about early. She tiptoed about the bedroom for she did not want to disturb Garreth who murmured restlessly in his sleep.

She felt sorry for him this morning. She had a hundred things to do today, shopping, changing her books at the lending library, supplies to be checked with Mamie, groceries to be ordered, a million and one little jobs. She loved her role of housewife, just as she thought Garreth had loved his role of boss. He had lost his place in life, poor man. He had nowhere to go this morning. He rattled around her domain, a lost soul.

Well, she would not disturb him now. Let him sleep awhile. It would also keep him out from under her feet.

Early as she was, Clothilde was at the breakfast table before her. The fragrance of fresh coffee, bacon and newly baked bread filled the room and she kissed the top of her daughter's head.

'Good morning, Clothilde,' she said and went and sat at her place at the table.

'Good morning, Mother.' Something in her daughter's tone made Ellen pause and look at her.

'Are you all right, dear?' she asked, noticing Clothilde's vividly flushed cheeks and sparkling eyes. 'More like Celestine used to be,' she thought and she had begun to worry about Celestine when her second daughter burst into the room looking . . . radiant. Ellen decided that was the only word for her.

'Mother, Mother . . .' she ran to Ellen, smothered her in kisses and sat down and poured herself a cup of coffee from the silver pot on the table.

'Well my dear, I must say you seem . . .' Ellen began, but Clothilde, drawing back a corner of the white linen napkin that covered the hot-cakes, interrupted,

'Mother, you have no idea how . . .'

At that moment Neill arrived, though whether from his bed or from outside Ellen could not be sure. He spent so much time now with the Quinns.

'Well, girls?' he said, rubbing his hands. 'Have you told Mother?'

'Told me what?' Ellen looked around at her family. 'Told me what?'

'Can we have more coffee, Mamie, please? My sisters have drunk it all.'

'Neill, don't be beastly,' Celestine and Clothilde said together and Mamie hooted in the doorway.

'Told me what?' Ellen asked plaintively.

'About *everything*,' Neill cried.

'I'll kill one of you if you don't explain.' Ellen was beginning to sound exasperated.

'Mother, Charles didn't jilt me. Papa was wrong. He was called back to the front. He had to go. That day . . . that day . . . well, you see . . . he sent a message,' she stammered. 'It never . . . never . . . arrived at the Shelbourne . . . and . . . well, he thought I was being taken care of,' she finished lamely.

'Oh I see.' Ellen's voice was subdued. 'I see.'

Sadly she did. Oh May, May, she thought. You were always headstrong and foolish. This was such a stupid thing to do. You were bound to be found out. Oh you foolish woman. I'd be so angry, only that it has turned out so well for Celestine.

'He wants me to go to London to his Aunt Agatha. I cannot wait, Mother. I want to go right away . . . this minute.' She jumped up and ran to her mother as if her joy was too much to contain.

Throwing her arms about Ellen she cried, 'I'm so happy, so happy. I'm going to marry Charles,' she sang out and Clothilde, Neill and Ellen laughed with her, happy in her happiness.

He heard their laughter in the hall. He felt suddenly terribly alone. He had never laughed like that, never been included in such a joyous sound. He heard the words Celestine was singing out and he was filled once again with a powerful fury, a rage he had not been able to muster since he had lost the brewery. It made him feel master again.

333

'Have you taken leave of your senses?'

They had not seen him come in. He loomed in the doorway dressed in his best business suit, the one that Mr Goldblat had just made for him. He filled the dark space there, making it darker.

'Papa . . .' Celestine's voice trembled. 'I didn't see you.'

'Of course you didn't, child. Have you not listened to anything I've said to you? Have you not heard?'

He looked at her benevolently, his face full of kindness, and she thought for a moment it was the beloved papa of her childhood back again. But the import of his words slowly penetrated her consciousness.

'You are going nowhere,' he spoke softly. 'I forbid it. And if you disobey me I'll follow you to the ends of the earth and I'll find you. Do you hear? I'll find you and I'll bring you back. Now go to your room.'

'Oh Garreth, don't speak to her like that,' Ellen said firmly. 'She's been ill.'

'And well she may. It behoves no-one to disobey their father. Sit down, Ellen, and shut up.' His commanding tones forced her to obey. 'I am going to the brewery,' he continued. 'We shall see what we can do to salvage what we can. Oh, no, don't write off Garreth Connolly yet.' His voice swelled with confidence and he surveyed them all, one at a time, then left the room. They heard him pause at the front door, then the sound of it slamming as he left the house.

They were still, looking at each other in dismay. Gone was the gaiety, the buoyancy that had held them up in a high and happy mood. They stared now at the ruin of their dreams, the death of all their hopes.

They sat for a long time like that, trying to think of something, anything that would help them.

At first they did not notice the commotion, so sunk were they all in gloom. At first they were deaf to the noise outside; the shouts, the banging on the door. They heard Mamie calling from the kitchen, then Ellen was the first in the room to raise her head and look outward.

'There's something happening . . .' she said uncertainly.

Neill was next. 'Banging,' he murmured. 'Like the night of the fire.'

'What is it, Mother?' Celestine asked in a frightened whisper.

Clothilde purposefully walked out of the room. 'Let's see what calamity has befallen us now,' she said, but as she got into the hall, followed by the others, she was met by Miffy in a state, though whether of consternation or excitement they could not tell.

'It's the Master, Mum,' she cried. 'Lyin' in the street, he is. On his back, like a landed fish. For all the world to see. Like a drunk he is. Out cold.'

'Oh my God, Clothilde, your father . . .' Ellen plucked at the front door with trembling fingers.

'Here, let me help you, Mother,' Neill said. Between them they got the door open and opening it, drew back at the sight that met their eyes.

The front gate was open and half the neighbourhood stood about whispering to each other, staring at the great Garreth Connolly on his back on the pavement.

'For God's sake, have you no pity?' Ellen cried. 'Will no-one help?'

'We've sent for the ambulance, Mrs Connolly,' Mrs Danagher said in an aggrieved voice.

'An' we don't like to move him in case he's broken something,' Mr Blessed said.

'Ah, good morning, Celestine,' Mr Callaghan cried. 'Nice to see you up and about again.'

'Oh thank you, Mr Callaghan,' Celestine said.

Mamie was beside Garreth. When Ellen got to his side she realized he was immobile, but his eyes . . . his eyes, they stared in horror at her, beseeching her.

'Move away, please,' she said. 'Move away, give him a little space please.'

She looked into those eyes again. She had never seen such an expression of fear on anyone's face. It made the fear she had felt before seem mundane, a small emotion next to this stark horror. He was like a terrified child imploring to be saved from nameless nightmares.

'It's all right, dear,' she said, patting his hand as she used to pat Breffni's. 'Don't worry, I'm here. The ambulance is coming. Never fear, it will be all right.'

335

Chapter

54

THE household was in chaos for the next few days. Celestine, who had overestimated her strength that first morning, took time to recover properly and get her 'sea-legs' back, as Mamie put it, otherwise she would have gone rushing off to London immediately. The latter was run off her feet. She complained and grumbled constantly, but a curious holiday atmosphere pervaded the house, and its inhabitants sang when they forgot to remember that the lord and master was mortally sick. Clothilde was living in a state of suspended reality which seemed more real to her than life ever had been before. She was aware of every limb and nerve, every fibre of her being, each beat of her heart. 'So this is what being alive is all about,' she thought and hugged herself ecstatically.

Normal routine vanished. The authoritarian in eclipse, the house relaxed. Ellen went her own way, busy with Garreth. This left the girls and Neill to themselves. In the new freedom Clothilde's love affair blossomed, unimpeded by rules and regulations. She and Darragh met and planned and grew used to each other.

He showed her a Dublin she had never seen before. They went for walks up the tow-path of the weed-choked Royal Canal to Harcourt Terrace. They lingered on misty days at the docks and watched the ships at anchor and listened to the sea-gulls cry. He took her to Howth Head where he watched her cheeks redden in the whip-lash wind as she looked at the grey seas crash thunderously against the rocks. The spray reached them even at a distance, so that she could taste the salt on her lips and feel the dampness of it curl her heavy hair.

'We may not have to run away,' she told him one day on their return to 'The Golden Harp'. He had removed her coat and wondered as he caught the smell of the sea breezes from her hair and looked at the dark curls around the smooth nape of her neck, how much longer he could hold his passion in check. She leaned on him so. She bent to him, her body languid with desire, and he knew his self-control could not withstand such longing, indefinitely.

He poured tar-coloured tea into cups, the Quinns' best, from the pot which had been brewing on the hob.

'What do you mean?' he asked.

'Well, Mother says that Papa may stay in this state, this paralysed state, for a long time. If not forever. Mother won't stop us marrying; and the only impediment was Father.'

'Oh, my darling, we could do it out in the open. March up the aisle for all the world to see. Ye, my queen, on my arm. We can post the banns. I can get you a golden ring for your finger and we can tell the world an' the hell with it.' Darragh laughed, loud and strong and Clothilde joined him.

Kerry came into the kitchen. 'I'm always findin' you two here laughin' your heads off,' she remarked wryly. 'Well, it's better than cryin', I suppose. So what's it on this occasion?'

'Clothilde and I are goin' to get married,' he said.

'So tell me somethin' I didn't already know,' Kerry said with a smile, then impulsively she went around the table and hugged her future sister-in-law. 'Aw, I could'na wanted a nicer sister,' she said, and kissed Clothilde's cheek and hugged her again.

'Nor I.' Clothilde was moved by the Quinns' wholehearted acceptance of her. They poured their love out unconditionally and she received their generosity with a full heart.

'Mebbe you'll be able to stop his foolishness,' Philomena said. 'Stop him goin' te these meetin's. One of these days he'll be caught an' they'll clap him in gaol.'

Clothilde's hand flew to her mouth. 'Oh, no,' she cried, her eyes dilating with fear. 'No, no. Of course you must not go to the meetings if there is danger there.'

'Oh bless us, lamb, don't take on so. We don't get so alarmed in this family.' Philomena patted her hand.'

'Well, he must not take the risk. I won't allow it.'

Darragh and Kerry laughed. Clothilde glanced around the table at their kindly faces looking at her with concern. She

337

realized how dear they had grown to her, how much she loved them. Kipper's great red face expressed his reverence, for he thought of her as an exquisite remote being from a more rarified world come amongst them. They must protect her and honour her, as Darragh had said.

'Ye treat her like the bloody Virgin Mary,' Kerry had shocked her father by saying.

'Wash yer mouth out wi' soap,' he had told her crossly.

But it was true.

Philomena, too, put her on a pedestal and flattered her by asking her advice about creams and lotions to help keep her skin smooth and perfumes to make her body smell sweet. Clothilde came to understand that there was a great and passionate love for each other housed in the unprepossessing bodies of Kipper and Philomena. The latter was as anxious as Cleopatra to seduce and allure.

Kerry treated her with a casual accepting camaraderie that was good for Clothilde. Her teasing and irreverent joshing light-ened Clothilde's gravity and encouraged her to take herself less seriously.

And Darragh. His strong face and palpably male body filled her with desire and love and admiration. He gave her a confidence in herself that she had never felt before. He made her feel whole and womanly and gloriously right within herself. She knew the tension had vanished from her mouth, that her lips now were full and ripe as the soft purple loganberries at the bottom of the garden. She knew the critical, analytical glint had lifted from her eyes and they sparkled now with an uncritical eagerness for life and love. She saw the change reflected back to her in her mirror. She touched her breasts and they felt fuller. She saw her cheeks glow and her hair crackle and spark with vitality when she brushed it and she knew that Darragh had done all this for her. He had single-handedly brought her to life.

Her heart was too full of gratitude to speak as she looked around the table. All she could do was smile at them and touch their hands. But they knew. They smiled back at her, seeing her love for them, her gratitude to them, and they touched her hands in return.

Kerry at last jumped up.

'Aw!' she cried, breaking the tension. 'Come on. Let's have another cup o' tea.'

338

Chapter

55

GARRETH was put in the Bon Secours Nursing Home. He lay passive, unable to move, only his eyes mobile. The nuns were brisk and kindly. Ellen went to see him every morning and afternoon. Then, as his condition did not improve, she came once a day, either afternoon or evening.

She hated going. She dreaded the visits. Garreth had always done the talking; led the conversation. She could think of nothing to say to him. He lay there, a huge immobile mound in the bed and she sat dutifully beside him, beginning sentences she could not finish: 'Celestine is better these days because . . .; 'Clothilde has fallen in . . .'; 'We got a brief letter from Breffni. He doesn't seem to like the . . .'; 'Neill is very happy since he's . . .'

It was no use. A huge gulf yawned between them and there was no bridging it. Too many years of his pontificating while she meekly listened, his bullying and her submissiveness, had entrenched them in their roles so that now it was impossible for her to change. She eventually stopped trying to chatter. She did not give him the news. She sat there, mute, staring at his huge inert bulk on the bed in the spartan-clean hospital room. She would gaze at the ceiling light, at the white walls and counterpane, at the paraphernalia of medicine, and sigh. She wondered vaguely what he was thinking about, if he thought at all. She wished she could care. She was horrified at her indifference and prayed each morning at ten o'clock Mass that God would forgive her for her unnatural lack of concern. She felt dreadfully guilty as if it was all somehow her fault. It seemed to her that if she had cared more, been more dutiful, that Garreth might not have had his stroke.

He was paralysed. He could move the fingers of one hand and his eyes were alive, but he was otherwise immobilized. When she had tried to hold the hand he could move he had flicked her fingers away. This had hurt her more than she could believe. His eyes were angry. She did not care to look into them. He seemed trapped in his head with his anger. Alone. She was glad when she could escape and go home.

For a few moments when she had knelt beside him on the pavement and he had looked at her, his eyes pleading and full of fear, she had felt closer to him than ever before. He had held her hand then, but now he could not accept her help. He had rejected her desire to care for him, soothe him, mother him, comfort him. He had closed the door on her and isolated himself, his fear turned to anger. He had left her outside in the cold with no nourishment and she found quite soon she did not care.

Within a week Celestine was ready and packed to go to London. Barth, fortuitously, said he had some business to attend to in England and he would deem it a privilege to escort her himself to Charles' Aunt Agatha who had been appraised of the situation and who had communicated her bewilderment at the delay.

'For Charles said quite definitely that she would be here months ago. He has been sending letters and I did not know what to do with them. I've been quite out of my mind with worry, not quite knowing what to do. What with bombs and Charles away and his "lovely young lady", that's what he calls her, his lovely young lady not arriving I've been quite addled. However, all's well that ends well, and I'm glad to hear that she is being escorted. We live in terrible times! It would not do at all for a lovely young lady to wander from Dublin to London all by herself. I look forward very much to meeting her and her dear Uncle. Yours, etc.'

Lord Gorman called for Celestine one sunny cold morning in December. Well groomed, smelling of cologne, expensively clad, he always gave Ellen a feeling of confidence. 'No thank you, Ellen,' he said, holding her hand and smiling at her, 'I won't have anything, thank you. We must cut along. How are you, my dear? And how is Garreth?'

'The same Barth. The same.' A sob caught her throat. It was unexpected. He looked at her keenly.

'I hope you are not blaming yourself for any of this? That would be the height of folly, and very unnecessary, my dear.'

Tears flowed down Ellen's cheeks. 'Oh I was, Barth, I was. I felt so guilty. I cannot seem to care too much, you see.'

'Well. That is to be expected. Garreth has never been the, er, most lovable of men. What he did not give you, you could not be expected to give back. Guilt is quite unjustified. Oh forgive me, Ellen. I do not mean to be brutal. It is perfectly understandable that you should feel guilty and helpless. However you must stop all that right now. It will do Garreth no good at all. You must promise me not to let this get you down.'

Ellen, responding to his reassurances, was comforted. She smiled through her tears. 'You are so kind, Barth.'

'Why don't you send for Nellie? She is such a sane and cheerful person to have about at a time like this. Now that Celestine is going away.'

Ellen nodded, drying her tears. 'What a good idea, Barth.'

'What did Dr Meagher say?' he asked.

'Nothing. You know doctors. He says things like, he is improving, that I must be patient. Platitudes.'

'Well, my dear Ellen, all I can reiterate is that you do not blame yourself. I will not hear of it. It is no crime to enjoy yourself a little. You will not help Garreth one whit by being miserable or guilty or whatever. Remember the good Lord's instructions, "Which one of you by worrying can add one . . ." whatever . . . you must obey Him, my dear.'

He turned and looked up at the stairs to where Celestine had appeared all in pale grey.

'Who is this vision, this princess? Can it be my little niece? Bless me, I'm honoured to be escorting such a ravishing creature, to be sure.'

Celestine gave a delighted chuckle and tripped down the stairs and flew into Barth's arms.

'Oh dearest, dearest Uncle. How wonderful you are. How wonderful life is. Oh it's good to see you, it surely is.' She seemed so full of excitement, she might bubble over.

'Well now. This is going to be a pleasant journey. Ben, put the valise on the back of the motor. Mamie, don't cry. She is off on the wings of love.'

'Oh I'm that happy for her, m'lord. That happy.' Mamie sniffed, dabbing her eyes. Miffy had followed her into the hall where she shyly waited. Celestine went to the little maid.

'I want you to take care of yourself, Miffy and tell Ben that if you're not married to him and happy by the time I return with my darling Charles, well, he'll have to answer to me.'

Miffy squealed and threw her apron over her head, covering it completely, and Ellen blinked, wondering if she had heard alright. Then she realized that of course she had heard correctly and that accounted for Miffy's state of euphoria the last few weeks, only she, Ellen, had been too preoccupied to notice.

Then at last in the crowded hall, Ellen wrapped her arms round her daughter, holding her in a fierce embrace. She felt that now familiar pain of separation as she said farewell to yet another child.

'Be happy, my love. Life is meant to be happy,' she whispered and kissed her daughter's cheeks.

It was Clothilde's turn to say goodbye and she found she could not speak but that it did not matter. Celestine knew all that was in her heart and the sisters held each other close and let each other go without words.

They all stood on the steps and waved as Barth tucked a rug about Celestine's legs. Neil rushed up the street in time to kiss his sister and waved too as Lord Gorman's chauffeur revved up the car and they drove away.

For a little while the party stood on the steps, their hands still held up in salute. Neill walked up the garden path backwards watching the car disappear up the Rathgar Road until it was out of sight. Then arms were languidly lowered and slowly they turned, Ellen and Mamie, Miffy and Neill, Clothilde and Ben, and went into the house.

Chapter
56

THE next day Clothilde called the family together. She thought how diminished in number they were: Garreth in the nursing home; Breffni in the war; Celestine journeying to her love in London. Now there were just Neill, herself and her mother.

'What's it all about, Clothilde?' her mother asked briskly. Clothilde looked at her sharply. Ellen seemed different, more spritely.

'Sit down, Mother, Neill.'

'Well, Clo? No need to be formal.' Neill looked around the room. They were in the parlour and it was cold. The fire was never lit there until evening.

But he asked, 'Why can't we have a fire here, Mother? Why not? Just because Father . . .' Neill broke off and looked guiltily at his mother. 'I suppose that's not very kind. But I thought we might at least be comfortable . . .'

His mother stood up. 'And why not?' she said cheerfully and rang the bell.

Mamie came in a moment later.

'Mamie, we want the fire lit. Here. Now. Mr Connolly is not here to order it, so I shall. Can you get Ben-the-Boots to build it?'

If Mamie was surprised she gave no indication. 'Well now and why not?' she cried, echoing Ellen. 'Twill do ye good to be warm and cheerful. It's not only himself that needs to be warm.' She went to the door, then hesitated and turned to face the three seated Connollys. 'Would ye like a pot o' tea? An' a biscuit? An' why not? It's near eleven of the morning. A cup o' tea would warm ye even more.'

The Connollys showed for a second that the wind had been taken out of their sails. Then Neill rubbed his hands together in glee.

'Tea would be a grand idea. Just grand. Wouldn't it, Mother?' He saw a smile of sheer pleasure light up his mother's face.

'Just grand,' she said.

They watched Ben-the-Boots as he laid the fire and lit it. Mamie pushed the heavy velvet curtains back and shafts of sunlight, alive with drifting dust motes, splashed the carpet gold. They were all three silent, thinking how unusual the situation was, having tea in the morning in front of a fire in the parlour.

Ellen stared at the shaft of sun. 'Your father would have said it was fading the carpet. I don't really care if it does,' she said, and giggled.

When Mamie had finished pouring the tea and had left the room, Ellen looked with bright enquiry at Clothilde.

'Well, my dear?' she prompted gently.

'Well, Mother, Neill. What I wanted to say, well, suggest rather . . . Oh dear, this is more difficult than I thought.'

'Mother knows about you and Darragh, Clo. She asked me were you in love. You have been looking radiant of late. I told her about Darragh. I did not think you'd mind.'

Clothilde smiled. 'No, of course I don't mind, Neill. I knew Mother wouldn't mind. I guessed she knew.' She looked at Ellen. 'You didn't seem concerned.'

Ellen shook her head. 'No I'm not,' she said. 'I cannot explain it, children. Your Uncle Barth told me not to worry and I took his advice.'

'Ah. Uncle Barth,' Neill said.

His mother continued, 'Do you know, I do not allow anything to upset me too much these days? It is such a relief not to feel you have to worry. To think that you are somehow remiss if you don't is such a bore. It indicates that you are not a person that cares and that is simply not true. Worry never helped any situation so I've given it up. All I want for you all, and heaven knows you are old enough, is for you to be happy. I trust you. Your instincts are fine. So I think you will all find it in your own way now that . . .' her voice petered out, faltering to a stop.

'Now that Father is not around to spoil things for us,' Clothilde said.

344

Two spots of red appeared on Ellen's cheeks. 'No, Clothilde. Do not speak like that. I will not allow you to malign your father now that he is sick. It is disloyal and ill-mannered.' Clothilde hung her head. 'It is all right, Clothilde. But he *was* right about you. You did not have a vocation.'

'Yes, but Owen Mulcahy . . .' Clothilde said contemptuously.

'Owen will make some girl a wonderful husband, Clothilde. But I will not hear one word against your father. Is that clear?' Neill and Clothilde both nodded and Ellen continued, 'But that does not mean we cannot be happy. Or that I need worry.' She patted her skirt and took up her crochet. 'Now. Go on, Clothilde.'

'Well, Mother, is it all right about Darragh? You don't mind?

'Heavens, Clothilde, *I'm* not marrying him. As it happened I thought he was a fine young man the night we met him. He was certainly more successful at getting us to the theatre than anyone else would have been. That kind of masterful man I do admire.' She sighed. 'But do go on, Clothilde. I doubt if you have called us here to ask me that. I'd say your mind was quite made up no matter what I thought.' She gave her daughter an amused glance.

'Well, Mother, I was thinking about the brewery and the Paradise streets and, well, Darragh and me . . .'

Neill leapt to his feet. 'Of course! But of course. Gosh, you're a genius, Clo. I should have thought . . .' He gave a joyful little leap. 'Brilliant,' he cried. 'Brilliant!'

'Do you really think so, Neill? I must say I thought it a jolly good idea.'

'What are you both talking about? You're not making any sense at all,' Ellen cried, exasperated.

'Well, Mother, what I think Clothilde is trying to suggest is that Darragh run the brewery — as her husband of course.'

Clothilde nodded, eyes sparkling with excitement.

'But I don't understand. There *is* no brewery. I don't know how . . .' Ellen looked at Neill.

'We are in a very tricky position, Mother. So are the men of the Paradise streets.'

'I have felt responsible for them, Mother, since I've been down there,' Clothilde said, her forehead creased.

Ellen nodded. 'I've always felt responsible. That's why I have always tried to help. But I don't see what . . .'

345

'Oh it would be wonderful, Clo,' Neill said.

'Will someone *please* explain all this to me?' Ellen asked.

'All right, Mother. It's this. Neill is going to be a priest. Celestine will be married to Charles. I doubt if Breffni when he comes home will want to run the brewery, but in any event I don't think we can afford to wait to find out. Not with Father's hospital and doctors' bills. If Breffni eventually does, why, he can join us.' She paused. 'You see, Mother, Uncle Barth has said he'll buy the brewery and the Paradise streets. For me. I don't know why.'

Ellen's eyes met Neill's. She realized that he knew why. So did she. It was Barth's way of trying to make up for some of the damage May had done. 'I'd like to be generous', he had said once to Ellen, 'I can afford it.'

Clothilde went on.' He would buy it for me as a dowry, if I wanted to marry Owen Mulcahy. He thought I did, and he knew that Owen's father had withdrawn his consent to our union because of Father's downfall.'

'Did he, indeed? Well I never.' Ellen was furious. 'Well, I always thought those Mulcahys were upstarts. Do you remember how tactless she was at the party? Do you? No breeding.'

'Well, Mother, that does not really matter, because I'm marrying Darragh. And Uncle Barth is not a mean man. He is so generous and he'll not withdraw his offer, I'm sure, and he'll be the major shareholder. We'll pay him back. I haven't said a word yet to Darragh . . .'

'But he will be delighted. It's an answer to all our prayers,' Neill interrupted.

'You see, Mother, he loves those people, he really cares for them. All he wants to do is help. See, he could get the men to rebuild the brewery and then they could work there, then they could share in the . . . what? profits . . . it's . . . oh Neill?' she turned to him for help.

'Co-operative. Darragh talks about it all the time. Workers having a share in the success of the business.'

Ellen looked at them aghast. 'But that's unheard of. Your father would never allow it.'

'Then we will starve, Mother,' Clothilde said coldly. 'Father is, alas, in no position to forbid us. Look, Mother, what alternative have we? We have very little money. Eventually it will run out. Rebuilding with the men who will be anxious to help us

346

to make as much profit as possible we'll be bound to do well. We cannot be bounden to Uncle Barth for everything. I would like us to be independent of him eventually. I would like to pay him back every penny. That is not to say I'm not very grateful to him. But you understand, Mother, do you not? How lovely it would be to be self-sufficient? Darragh and I will marry. It will still be in the family. He knows about running a pub . . .' She was struck by a thought. 'Why, we could amalgamate the two . . .'

Neill looked at his sister with admiration. 'Gosh, Clo, you're wonderful. I think you must be Darragh's partner!'

'Of course,' Clothilde said with delight.

'Oh no. Not in business. A lady, Clothilde, does not go into business. And certainly not into a brewery.' Ellen was shocked.

'Well, I will, Mother. I've never been so excited.'

Neill held up his hand. 'I think it's a brilliant idea,' he said. 'The men of Paradise Row and Square and Street will be employed. We can pay back our debt to them bit by bit. We can start them on a minimal wage and tell them that when the business starts to show a profit their remuneration will go up accordingly.'

'Will they believe you?' Ellen asked.

'They'll believe Darragh. It's perfect. Then I can go and get on with my studies with a clear conscience. Oh Clo, you're a wonder.' He hugged his sister.

'So you agree? she asked. He nodded. 'Mother?'

'On one condition.'

'What's that?'

'That John Joe Reilly gets to be something important.'

'I promise,' Clothilde said.

'It sounds,' Ellen smiled, 'just grand.'

Chapter

57

CELESTINE took to Aunt Agatha instantaneously. A tubby, fluttery, over-anxious maiden lady of sixty-five, dressed in the style of an earlier age, her hair was arranged in hundreds of grey sausage ringlets that trembled at her every move. Her dithering uncertainty gave Celestine a maternal feeling towards Charles' aunt and from being the baby of the family she graduated to the novel position of motherly authority. Aunt Agatha threw herself in an abandoned fashion on everyone's goodwill. Friends felt they were helping her out of a hopeless muddle; servants adored her, she gave them the feeling that they were invaluable and she could not do without them. Which was true.

She clasped Celestine to her ample bosom, crying, 'At last. At last.' She refused to allow the girl to stray from her side and flirted outrageously with Barth.

'And you were escorted by your uncle.' She flashed him an adoring glance. 'Lucky, lucky girl. What a comfort he must have been. No lady should travel without a gentleman. Cases, luggage, boats and trains. Gentlemen understand these things. Ladies do not. I simply would not know which *direction* to take.'

Her parlour was overcrowded and two champagne-coloured Pekinese scurried around the legs of innumerable occasional tables covered by fringed cloths and topped with an amazing assortment of bric-a-brac.

A faded maid, approximately the same age as her mistress, served tea, and an assortment of stale fairy cakes that Barth Gorman, thinking of his digestion, firmly refused.

There was a painted Chinese screen in front of the fireplace and a gas fire in front of that.

'I love it,' Aunt Agatha confided in Barth. 'Saves Bagshot here all that cleaning and coal and nasty smoke. This fireplace

348

never worked properly. Brrrrr.' She shuddered. 'Dear Lord Gorman, do have a cake. I'm sure you need it. What a comfortable figure you cut, to be sure. The sort that gives a poor female confidence.'

Barth laughed heartily and Celestine, near Aunt Agatha, smiled happily. She liked this lady more and more.

Lord Gorman took his leave, reassured that Celestine was content and in good hands, for despite her fluttery personality Barth sensed that together with a warm heart Aunt Agatha ran her life along precisely the lines she wished and that appearances can be deceptive.

He went to his club in Jermyn Street for his two-day stay, but kept in touch with the house in Hampstead.

Aunt Agatha took Celestine the very next day on a shopping spree to Bond Street and afterwards to tea at the Ritz. Within a week the pair were on the most intimate of terms, Celestine having confided every detail of her life-story and love affair with Charles to this most sympathetic of listeners.

Aunt Agatha was voraciously curious. Because she lived alone and had never married she had a child-like interest in the doings of others. She was intrigued by Celestine's family, particularly her father, whom she admired even more than Lord Gorman. She would shiver as Celestine talked of Garreth and his tyranny.

'A firm man, oh, a firm gentleman,' she would whisper in a thrilled voice. 'Like Mr Rochester. Oh, I admire Mr Rochester above all other heroes in fiction. Don't you?'

The escape from her problem and her separation from her family made Celestine see her father in a much more mellow light. She preferred to remember the happier days of her life when she was her father's pet, before heart-break was familiar to her. Her memory drew a merciful blank over the sharpness of her recent pain.

Barth had given Celestine a fistful of letters. 'You must be generous, Celestine, if you can, and forgive her,' he said quietly. Celestine knew what he meant. She had nodded. It was the only time that Barth had mentioned, even obliquely, the situation Celestine was in and the reasons for her being in it.

Celestine read the letters avidly. She was in tears when Aunt Agatha knocked on her door after she had spent an afternoon at her own request reading Charles' letters.

'Oh Aunt, dearest Aunt, I'm so happy.' She turned a tear-stained face to the old lady who promptly burst into sympathetic tears herself. 'He loves me so.'

'How could he help himself, dear child?' Aunt Agatha dabbed her eyes and blew her nose violently into a lace-edged handkerchief.

For Charles' letters were outpourings of love both passionate and tender. Celestine spared a moment of sympathy for her rival. Poor sad Auntie May. It must have sent a knife through her heart to read what Charles had written. Three of the letters had been opened. The remaining twenty-four were still sealed and he had sent many more to Hampstead where his Aunt Agatha had kept them for Celestine. Celestine had felt moments of white-hot rage when she had realized that her aunt had had the temerity actually to read three of Charles' letters to her. However, her anger soon left her and a great sadness for her aunt's pain took its place.

Celestine had grown up. She knew about pain. She had felt adult emotions and she could imagine how her aunt had suffered. She neither approved nor disapproved May's initial involvement with Charles. But having accepted that when she had met Charles this involvement was a fact, she could have nothing but sympathy for the loser. She dimly realized how agonizing it must be for an older woman to lose her lover to a younger one, and that her niece.

However, she did not dwell on these things but put them firmly from her, concentrating on the future. She was, after all, the winner and she did not want any bitter feelings to mar her tranquillity. Realizing how anxious Charles must have been, she wrote him a long and tender letter, glossing over the damage May Gorman had perpetrated and reiterating over and over again her love for him and her anxiety for his safety.

It was with alarm followed by relief that she learned that he had been wounded again and was coming home.

So at last, in the spring, when the crocuses carpeted the grass under the chestnut trees in Hampstead, when the daffodils bloomed beside the green hedgerows at the edge of the heath and the sky was madonna-blue washed with platinum, Charles was coming home to his love. She did not know when he would arrive, she just waited patiently and sometimes impatiently, her heart full, his Aunt Agatha beside her.

350

Chapter

58

FRANCE

The land spreads out before me, dun-coloured. There is a reddish glow over the earth and I don't know whether it is an optical illusion or reality. The trench zig-zags across the face of the land and it is home. An unreliable security, protem. Not Rathgar, Mother, oh no, but it is home. Where I spend my time. It is better than open country. Safer. Out there the horror reigns and men become dismembered.

Where is God now, Neill? God belongs to the softer sex. God dwells with women in far-off cosy homes, beside Christmas tables groaning with food, in the faces of children singing carols, in the smiles of my sisters' innocent faces, Celestine and Clothilde. God has no place here.

But I must not blame God. Neill was right. Men made this hell for themselves and we dwell in it. Some uneasily, I have to say some at ease, comfortable in its demands of violence and callousness. Those men need the stimulus of war to satisfy some lack within them, some appetite that needs to be appeased, like a voracious ancient God who demands human sacrifice.

My eyes hurt me. I obey commands but within me my spirit whimpers. Like a beaten pup I silently whine, a muted sound of protest that no-one hears. I move as if in a dream across the slaughter-painted land, over alien soil, move at the behest of others in a direction that always follows gun-fire. Why? Who in his right mind runs after death? What kind of lunatics relentlessly and at their own peril seek out others of their species to destroy?

Hooray! Today we travelled two miles north. We moved slowly and half of us were killed or maimed. But we got there. Clap medals on our chests, sing songs at home.

'Goodbye, Dolly, I must leave you,
Though it breaks my heart to go . . .'

You kiss the girls and make them cry. Mother's tears. The softness of her breasts beneath my cheek when I was hurt and needed comfort. Her all-embracing arms. Will I ever see her again? Will I ever be able to look upon that gentle face knowing what I have done, having witnessed what I have seen?

Lily was in a brothel in London. With my father. Dear old lad. How pitiful he now seems. I have had leave since I came to France. A short break. Rest and recuperation. There was another Lily. Where? I cannot remember. It was a red place too and she was a broken doll with painted lips and thin arms. She spoke French and I could not understand her. But the language sounded soft and sexy. I cried afterwards. It was the only emotion I have shown since I left home. Funny. But the sexual release had triggered my emotions, I suppose, and I could not stop crying. She cradled me in her thin arms. Then I suddenly stopped. I felt like a stone. Cold and still. I dare not think of my friends now dead and gone. Bert, Dave, Chalkey and all the others. The faces of their successors seem like theirs, sometimes so alike that I think they have come back. I feel sorry for them, for the enemy, for the Hun, for mankind. I weep inwardly because men can use each other so. I cry in my heart because of the innocence I have lost and the sure knowledge that I will never again belong in that pre-war world, never again be care-free. I will always now be on the outside looking in. I know secrets that are unbearable yet I must bear them. I have night-mare memories that I can never get rid of.

I cannot sleep, Mother.

It was with relief that I felt, one murky day in the mêlée of dirt and gun-fire, something tear into my back. The sensation I had longed for enveloped me: a merciful blackout.

Dear Mother,

I have been wounded. It's nothing much. They'll be sending me home soon. I'll see you then.
Love to Father, Neill, Clothilde and Celestine.

Your fond son,
Breffni

352

Chapter

59

'I ALWAYS seem to be digging bullets out of you, Captain. You are a lucky devil, you know. They never seem to be on target. At least, not lethal target.'

Charles laughed and grimaced in pain. 'Ouch! Hey, go easy. That's better. No. I know I'm a lucky bastard.'

Dr Darbley snipped away at the dressing and glanced at his patient. A worried frown was creasing Charles' brow.

'You still worried about the mail?'

Charles nodded. 'No word from the girl I'm going to marry. No word. It's been months now. I can't understand it. No word from Aunt Agatha either.'

'Well, don't worry, Captain. The mail here is pretty dodgy. You know that. Ah! That's much better. By the by, I hear you're in line for a medal. Well deserved.'

Charles made a deprecating gesture and winced again as Dr Darbley swabbed out the wound.

'Ah, that's lovely,' he said with exactly the same expression, Charles thought, as Aunt Agatha wore when she looked at her helping of treacle tart before she took the first mouthful. 'Lovely. Yes. You're a reckless blighter, though, charging up that hill alone. Foolhardy. Bloody silly, really.'

'I captured it, didn't I?' Charles retorted and yelled, 'Ouch!' Then he lapsed into silence.

It had been a rough few months, but all in all he had not done too badly. They were sending him home. He was no use to them any more. His wounds had left him too battered for active service, so, he thought, like an old shoe they threw him out. He was just as glad. He would see Celestine. His heart lifted. But

353

hard on that lovely thought the nagging worry came. Why had he not heard from her? Why? He had written care of May. Surely nothing was wrong? He had sent letters to Hampstead. Dear God, he prayed all was well.

Dr Darbley was waffling on when something he said caught Charles' attention. '. . . all as nonchalant as you, old son. It's chaps like poor Connolly bear the brunt. Can't take it, poor blighters. Daft to send them in the first place. But I suppose the army can't afford to be choosy these days. Selectivity out the door.' The doctor paused and was amazed to find himself clutched by the usually unexcitable officer.

'Connolly? Did you say Connolly?'

'Yes. But why? Breffni Connolly. The lad's a mess. Never showed it. Fellows and his C.O. thought he was made of ice. After his mate was killed he showed no emotion. That should have told them something. But you know these army wallahs. Dim about the mind. Poor fellow must have been in shock for months.'

'Breffni . . . then it is! God, Doctor, I've got to see him. He is my fiancee's brother.'

'Oh nonsense. There must be a hundred Connollys in the army. Thousands. What makes you think . . .?'

'Not Breffnis. Breffni is an unusual name. No, I'm sure it's the same. What's happened to him? A mess? What do you mean?'

'His back. Piece of shrapnel. He'll never walk again.' The doctor frowned. 'But all that was all right — or as right as it could be. Took it like a man, he did. First class. Then suddenly,' he snapped his fingers, 'just like that, his head went. Pow. Just like that.'

'What do you mean?'

'Shell shock. Belated. Shell shock. When I see him and soldiers like him I know the price is too high.' Dr Darbley had let a bitter note creep into his normally light and casual tones.

'The price could not be too high. You talk of domination or freedom, Doctor. There is no price too high to pay for that,' Charles said hotly. Then he asked anxiously, 'He's bad? Very bad?'

The doctor nodded. 'As bad as can be. The best thing would be for him to go home. They will send him, of course. Whether he'll ever be . . . normal again, either mentally or physically, is not something I'd like to bet on.'

'Is there any chance I could take him with me?'

The doctor looked at Charles' anxious face. 'You are serious, aren't you? I don't know. He'll have to go by ambulance. For the initial journey. It will be complicated.'

'Oh come on, Doctor. Dispense with the red tape for once,' Charles coaxed. 'For a war-hero?'

The doctor shrugged. 'Oh, if it were only up to me . . . but . . .'

'You can swing it if you really try. For me. Please.'

The doctor sighed. 'I'll do what I can. Always assuming it's the right man.'

'Oh it's the right man, I can promise you that. Will you promise?'

'I'll try,' the doctor said.

Chapter
60

THE thing that drew the two women closest together, that bound Aunt Agatha and Celestine as nothing else could, was their mutual love for Charles. As both women were generous, their love not of a possessive kind, they had an overwhelming interest in anything, however trivial, that pertained to, affected, or was connected in any way with, their beloved Charles.

They spent happy hours extolling his virtues to each other, praising his good looks, admiring his equable temperament. They never lacked conversation, were never stuck for words in each other's company. They were of a similar mind about their paragon. So they were wonderfully content in each other's company, found each other sympathetic, and each thought the other a wise and warmly wonderful companion.

Celestine did not, after all, see Charles turn down the little lane in Hampstead and walk across to No. 3. She had pictured it all so clearly in her mind. How she would see him from her window on the second floor, his tall figure, weary from battle and his wound, limping slowly and painfully down the lane. She would run downstairs to open the front door and fall into his arms for all the world to see.

In the event that was not the way it happened at all. The first she knew of it was Bagshot, Aunt Agatha's maid, calling her at breakfast time one morning. She had slept late for they had been to the Savoy Opera, to see the D'Oyley Carte Company in 'The Pirates of Penzance' the previous night and had had supper afterwards at the Café Royal with old Lord Penrose, an elderly earl who had been courting Aunt Agatha for fifty-one years, ever since she was eighteen.

Bagshot calling awakened Celestine and without paying any attention to what the maid said she ran to her bathroom, splashed some cold water on her face, cleaned her teeth, then leaving her hair tousled and uncombed, and clad only in her rose velvet dressing-gown, she raced down the stairs.

Halfway down she saw him. He stood at the bottom, not at all weary, his eyes sparkling, his lips curved in a tender smile. She paused for a moment, heart beating, then she flew into his open arms. It felt like flying, for her feet hardly touched the stairs. He enfolded her, wrapped his arms around her. He buried his face in the soft waves of her dark hair, filling his nostrils with her scent. They were both crying and laughing and murmuring endearments.

'I'll never let you out of my sight again,' he cried fiercely.

'I thought I'd lost you, oh Charles, I thought you'd deserted me.' She clung to him greedily, kissing his mouth, his nose, his cheeks.

'Don't let's talk about that, my peach, my love, my life.' He swung her off her feet.

'Darling, darling Charles, I love you, I-love-you, Oh I-love-you.' She punctuated each declaration of love with a kiss.

'I want to eat you all up. Oh Celestine, the sweetness of you,' he said and he buried his face once more in her hair.

A discrete cough interrupted them. 'The mistress says, will you go up to her room soon Captain Charles and see her. She longs to greet you.'

'Of course I will . . . Go to her. Tell her I'm coming to her at once.' Charles nodded to the maid, then turned back to Celestine. His face was suddenly serious.

'But first Celestine, my beloved . . .' He hesitated.

She searched his face, anxiety creasing her brow.

'Something is wrong. I can feel it,' she said. 'Oh my darling, you're not going to leave? Go back to the front? You can stay? Oh what could it be?' She tried to fathom why his face had darkened, why his eyes were sombre at this happiest of times.

'It's not us, beloved. Nothing shall come between us. They will not send me away so soon again, my darling.'

Relief flooded her and she leaned her head on his breast, clinging close to him. He stroked her hair, then touched her chin with his fingers.

'No, it's not us,' he said quietly. 'It's your brother. It's

357

Breffni.' She looked at him, surprised. 'Breffni . . . ? How? What ?. . .'

'Your brother, Celestine, is very . . . very . . .'

Her eyes widened. 'He's not dead? Tell me he's not dead?'

Charles shook his head. 'No, darling. He's sick. Then, as she was about to speak, he said, 'Hush. Listen. He's suffering from what they call shell shock. His mind is a little unhinged. Some men can't take it, the war. It can be pretty frightful, you know. Some of the boys they have to send over there are not the stuff soldiers are made of. It's all right for us professional blokes. We're trained for it. Anyhow, I don't want you to be alarmed. But he's going to need all our love and care and attention.'

She was staring at him, compassion flooding her face.

'Where is he?' she asked. 'Let's go to him as soon as you've seen Aunt Agatha.'

'No. No, my love. I wouldn't leave him. I've brought him home to you. He's in there.' He jerked his head towards the parlour. As she turned to hurry into the room he restrained her. 'Compose yourself. Take a deep breath. We need to be very calm and reassuring around him. He's very broken.' Charles' eyes were warning her and giving her courage at the same time. 'You go in and I'll go up to my aunt. We'll have some tea in the parlour, Bagshot.'

'But breakfast is served in the dining-room and . . .'

'Well, we'll have tea in the parlour just the same, please.' Charles reiterated firmly. 'Perhaps we'll have breakfast, later Bagshot. We'll see.'

He steered Celestine towards the parlour door, watched her as she opened it and entered, then bounded up the stairs, two at a time, to see his beloved aunt.

Chapter

61

AT first Celestine could not see anyone in the parlour. It was dark, as the curtains were still half-drawn. Then she made out a shape sitting dejected in front of the empty grate.

'Breffni?' Her voice was soft and hesitant. She did not want to startle him. There was something so defeated in the droop of his shoulders, the curve of his back. His chin had been sunk on his chest and he raised his head wearily and looked at her.

She drew in her breath sharply. Yes, it was Breffni's face, but no, it was not. The eyes were tormented. They were the eyes of a man who had been in hell, she thought. The face was bearded, gaunt and bony, the skin scarred. Breffni's face had been full and his eyes clear, an idealist's eyes, a poet's eyes. Now they were dark and sunken. The light had gone out. He looked like an old man, his body stooped and bent, his face shrunken.

And yet, too, he looked like a child. He had the helpless look an infant has and the bewildered expression of a lost, hurt little boy.

At first he did not seem to know her. His eyes searched the room. 'Charles? Charles?' he whispered and she could see he was panicking, thinking he was alone in the half-light.

'Oh, Breffni, it's all right,' she cried, her soft heart touched by his tragic look. She hurried over to him and tentatively put her hand out. He shrank back from her as if she might strike him.

'Charles?' he cried again, looking about desperately.

'Charles is upstairs with Aunt Agatha.' She forced back her tears. 'Oh Breffni, Breffni, what have they done to you?' He looked at her again, staring blankly at her. 'Breffni, it's me,

Celestine. Don't you know me?' Her voice was piteous. 'Please, it's Celestine, your sister.' For a moment he looked frightened, then bewildered.

'Celestine? Celestine?' he cried, a frown of concentration furrowing his forehead, 'Celestine?' Then a light dawned slowly. 'Yes, my sister,' he said, and looked at her puzzled, then added with a sigh, 'Ireland.'

'Yes, dearest, Ireland.'

His countenance lit up. He smiled at her and as she moved to him, he broke down, his face crumpled and dissolved into a quivering mass, like a baby, and tears flowed down the sunken cheeks as sobs tore through the wasted body.

'I want Mother,' he wept and she took him in her arms, cradling him and hushing and soothing him. He wept for a long time, but Celestine felt the tension leave his body and he relaxed and leaned against her helplessly.

Charles and Aunt Agatha found them like that: Celestine holding her brother, who shook and sobbed in her arms. Bagshot followed them into the room with a tray upon which stood a pot of tea under a cosy, three cups and saucers, milk and sugar.

Breffni looked up and smiled at Charles, tears streaking his face.

'It's Celestine. My sister,' he said.

Charles patted his hand. 'Yes, old fellow. And I'm going to marry her. So we'll all be together.'

Celestine felt her heart swell at her lover's kindness. He was obviously very close to her brother and he had assumed a kind of fatherly authority over Breffni. It was obvious the boy adored him.

'Mother? I'd love to see Mother.' It was said wistfully, with longing, as if he had not seen his mother for a hundred years, as if in her lay rest.

Charles nodded. 'Yes. We'll go to Ireland with you, old boy. We'll take you there when the doctors give their permission.' He looked at Celestine. 'He's under doctor's orders still. I had to promise to take him to the Middlesex for a check-up as soon as possible after we arrived. We'll go later today.' He turned back to Breffni, bending down to him.' Breffni, this is my Aunt Agatha. Aunt, this is Breffni, Celestine's brother.'

Breffni was trying to rise but he could not. Charles told her later that he often forgot he could not walk.

Aunt Agatha said, 'You stay still, young man. Your sister's spoken of you and there's a speaking likeness. Anyone she loves, well, so must I. So there.' She nodded to the boy briskly, finding it hard to return his bewildered gaze.

Charles said gently. 'Breffni, you are with friends here. But we'll take you home soon, never you fear. We'll take you home.'

Breffni smiled trustingly at Charles, then that expression of fear the Celestine had seen before crossed his face again.

'Not Father, though. I couldn't face Father.' He shivered.

Celestine squeezed his hand. 'Father's very ill, Breffni. He's had a stroke. He cannot move. He'll not harm you.'

Breffni shook his head. 'Father? Not move? He was a giant, Charles. How could anyone, anything stop him? Are you sure, Celestine?'

She nodded. 'He's quite helpless. Mother's in charge now. Neill too. And Clo. We're all independent now.'

Breffni looked puzzled, then began to laugh. The sound was harsh.

'Can't move! Father can't move! How priceless. How fitting. Oh God, what jokes you play. You bastard.' He stopped suddenly and looked at his sister. 'Why?' he asked seriously. 'Can you tell me why? Do you think God has a sense of humour after all?'

'I don't know, Breffni,' she said seriously. 'I simply don't know. I'm not Neill or Clothilde. I have never been serious and questioning like them. I'm not too clever. I only know that we try to survive. We do what we can. We just struggle along when things are bad and wait for them to get better. They always do eventually.'

But Breffni was shaking his head. 'No-one can give me an answer,' he said, 'No-one. I've asked and asked, but no-one seems to know.'

'What, old boy?' Charles asked.

'Neill said God gave us a choice. He doesn't make wars but we do. What I want to know is why there is so much, Neill? Why do so many people choose to be bad?'

Charles shook his head. 'They don't, Breffni. There are only the few. The powerful, the ones who desire to be powerful. Dictators, invaders — unscrupulous men.'

'So the evil are more powerful?'

'We have to fight them, Breffni.'

Breffni shook his head. 'No, that's wrong,' he said. 'That's not the right way. That only breaks the good men and makes them bad.' He sighed wearily. 'I'm tired,' he said. 'So very tired.'

Aunt Agatha rang for Bagshot.

'Of course it's not the right way,' she said briskly. Her tone broke the mood in the room and as if to change the atmosphere she turned up the lights, and they all blinked. 'The only civilized way is to educate people. Do away with ignorance forever.' Her grey curls shook as she spoke. 'Now let us get you to bed, young man. You need to rest.'

Breffni slept for a long time. Charles said that it was a good sign. 'We've had such trouble, you know,' he told Celestine and Aunt Agatha as they all three drank their after-lunch coffee in the parlour, huddling close to the gas fire for warmth. 'First, to get him home. There was such a lot of red tape. God, bureaucracy drives me mad. The whole thing was a nightmare.'

Aunt Agatha nodded. 'It's difficult these days. We live in such awkward times. But you managed, Charles, and that's the main thing.'

Charles nodded. 'Yes. Eventually. And I got to know Breffni. He should never have been sent to the front. He had hardly any training.' He looked at Celestine. 'Some God-awful mix up at headquarters, they say. I'm not sure that that's true. They're being mown down so fast in France that they are sending as many raw recruits as they decently can, as fast as they can.'

He saw Celestine's pained face. 'Oh my dear, I'm sorry. I don't want to distress you. But I'm afraid it's true.'

'Oh Charles, I can't bear it.' She looked at him fearfully. 'Will you have to go back?'

He looked at her sideways and smiled. 'I have a long leave, dearest, so let's live for the day and face that when it comes.' He smiled at her. 'Do you want to hear my plan?' he asked.

She nodded. She noted sadly that he had not answered her question, and she realized with a sinking heart that partings from the man she loved would probably make up a big portion of her life from now on. She said nothing. Used to obeying Garreth, she wore the habit of acquiescence easily.

'Well, I have it all planned. I hope you agree. I propose to marry you, my darling, as soon as I possibly can.'

Celestine had risen and crossed the room to him. He took her hands in his and pressed them firmly.

'But . . . but . . . what about . . . what about . . .?' Aunt Agatha spluttered.

'What, dearest Aunt? Don't worry, I'll do it all by the book. I need to be instructed, don't I, dearest? You see, Breffni told me all about it. It's just that . . .' He frowned. 'I may be recalled . . .' A cry escaped Celestine but she bit her lip quickly and he hastened to reassure her. 'It won't be for a while, I'm still quite weak yet, sweet girl, so don't worry. But I would like to marry you as quickly as possible.'

She nodded, looking at him anxiously. 'It's just that . . . it's just that . . .' she stammered.

'What, my dearest?' he asked.

'I'm a Catholic and . . .'

He looked at Celestine, tilting her chin so that he could see into her eyes. 'My precious one, I want us to be married. I am prepared to do anything that's necessary to have you Mrs Charles Cavendish, and then I'll know that you will have that status and will be under its protection if anything happens to me.' As she drew in her breath he laid his finger on her lips. 'It won't, my darling. Aunt will tell you what a lucky devil I am. But if it did, you would be taken care of materially. You would be independent. We will get married in a Catholic church in Ireland as soon as we can. I can take instructions here, I believe.' He looked at her enquiringly. 'Breffni said I have to promise to let you bring our children up in your faith, isn't that correct?'

'Oh, Charles.' She hated the contingencies upon which the Church based its permission for a Catholic to marry a Protestant. 'I would not ask it except for Mother. She'll be so worried and distressed otherwise.'

'I'm not at all upset, dearest. Whatever it takes. I have never been much on church, and if it makes you happy . . . All I want is that legal document as soon as possible.'

Celestine smiled at him. She did not care about church and rules. At the moment all she knew was that Charles wanted her, wanted to look after her, wanted to cherish her, and that was what she wanted too. With a complete faith in him that had never really been shaken, she put her trust and her future in his hands and said yes.

363

'Charles, what's all this about Ireland?' Aunt Agatha asked. 'I suppose that if I want to see you married I'll have to go across the sea to that barbaric outpost of the British Empire.'

Charles laughed. 'Of course you'll come, Celestine will need a chaperone.'

'I think you're very wise, my boy,' Aunt Agatha said.

'And then when you are away, perhaps Celestine would like to stay with me here in Hampstead?'

'I think she would like to be with her family,' he replied.

But Celestine shook her head. 'No, I'd rather be with you, dearest. But failing that I think I'd like to be here. Aunt Agatha is the only person in the world who won't be bored out of her mind if I go on and on about you.'

'How dreadful,' he remarked, smiling.

'No, seriously, I want to wait in Hampstead and listen to you,' she put her hand on the old woman's arm, 'tell me all about Charles' childhood, what he was like as a little boy. And I don't think I want to stay at home. They'll treat me as a baby. Of course I'll visit Mother and Clothilde often. Did I tell you she's married? Oh it's all so exciting.'

'We'll have to take Breffni back,' Charles said seriously. 'We'll let your mother know we're coming to get married. And to bring home her son.'

Chapter
62

THEY brought Breffni home to Ellen. They let her know when they were coming so that she could prepare herself to meet her son.

Word had spread of the homecoming. When the car drew up before the Connollys' front gate a crowd had gathered: Mrs Danagher, her arms crossed over her bosom; Mrs Blessed leaning against the lamp-post and reminding Mr Blessed that the last time they had stood like this, Mr Garreth Connolly had lain on his back on the pavement. 'Felled,' she said. 'Felled.' Mr Roderick Callaghan was there, his eyes blinking rapidly behind his spectacles, and Mrs Fahy and Mr Findlay from the news-agent on the corner. Neighbours stood on the steps and waited and watched.

Ellen stood at the front door. Her body was stiff from the effort of restraint, but she dared not walk down the path for fear her legs would give way under her. She stood, a frozen smile on her lips, the periphery of her vision blurred. She tried to see more clearly and shook her head but it was no use. There was a film over her eyes and she saw everything through a veil of unshed tears. She had been at the door, holding onto its side, for a long time, waiting, waiting for the return. She stared down the road, her eyes searching for the arrival of the car, her sight dim, her throat tight, making it painful to swallow.

Her heart stopped, then jumped into life again. There it was, the car, turning the corner, approaching.

She took a deep breath, seeing nothing except for the car. She could feel her legs trembling. She watched it, oblivious of Clothilde behind her, of the people in the street. She saw it draw to a stop outside the house and Charles get out. Then Charles removed the wheelchair and then lifted something from the motor car. She wondered what it was he carried so tenderly and thought for a moment it was Celestine. But it was not Celestine that the captain carried, for she was behind him. Ellen took a few hesitant steps forward.

It was her son, her darling, her baby. Held like a child, the bottom half of his trouser legs dangling over Charles' arms, his hands clasping the captain's neck. His face was a blur as her tears splashed, at last, down her face and they wet the face of her son, bathing his cheeks and eyes as she kissed him, murmuring the endearments mothers have always used. 'My baby, my lamb, you're home, sweetness, you're here, Mother's here, near the fire, here, here, my darling, my pet, my own.'

He did not notice that they had put him in his father's chair. Mother and son clung to each other as if they would never let go. She kept touching and kissing his face as if to reassure herself that he was really there and would not disappear. And Breffni held onto Ellen, held onto his mother for dear life, clinging to her arms, his hands holding one of hers, kissing her fingers, brushing his lips on her rings. The smell of her, the texture of her soft creased skin, the blue eyes anxious, puffed and pink from her tears, all brought his whole childhood crowding into his mind, driving away the nightmare memories of violence. With one tender look that familiar face had erased the torment. Reverting to the trust of extreme youth, he wordlessly laid his agony at her feet, expecting a miracle, and because he expected it, it happened. For a while anyway there was a surcease of strain, a cessation of the terror. Their tears healed, their embraces restored, their reunion mended.

Celestine took Charles from the room, beckoning Clothilde to follow them. In the hall Mamie waited to greet them. She hugged 'her girl', as she called Celestine, and wished her joy. 'Oh, darlin', darlin' girl, we've missed yer sunny smile.'

Miffy whispered to Celestine that she was married. 'I'm missus now,' she said proudly. 'We kept my name, Miss Celestine. Mulligan. Ben, ye see, dun't know his. So I'm Missus Mulligan, not miss.'

'Puffed up, she is. Puffed,' Mamie cried. 'I'm tellin' ye, Miss Celestine, we thought she'd burst. She's like a struttin' cock, so she is, an' . . . an' . . .' The old servant's eyes were full of tears

366

and she wiped her face with her sleeve and sniffed and gulped.

'It's so good to see ye, Miss Celestine. It's so good to have ye home.'

'Oh Mamie, Mamie, dearest Mamie.' Celestine gave a little sniff herself, then hugged the servant and gave her a shake. 'Now you bustle off, Mamie, and Miffy too, and prepare some lunch for us. We're very hungry and I can't wait to taste some of your cooking again.' Mamie gave a delighted squeal and hurried Miffy down the stairs to the kitchen.

Celestine and Charles had decided that he would stay in the Shelbourne for the time being. Aunt Agatha, coming for the wedding, would stay there too. They hated to be parted even for a moment, but, as Charles pointed out, it would not be for long.

'With your father ill and now Breffni home, your mother will have her hands full and probably no room for me,' he said.

'I can't bear to have you out of my sight for a moment,' she said. 'If you knew how I feel when I look up, no matter what I'm doing, and see you there; the joy I get from your presence. Oh my darling, darling man.'

'I'll haunt Rathgar,' he said, laughing.

Ben-the-Boots took him and his suitcase to the hotel after lunch while Celestine went upstairs to see her father. He was installed on the fourth floor in the guest room. Ellen had got a nurse, a formidable woman, to look after him.

'She's been a tower of strength, Celestine,' Ellen told her as they went upstairs. 'Mrs Pugh, she's called, a most willing woman. She can help me with Breffni. She has Neill's room now he's away in the seminary.'

Celestine noticed that her mother was puffing, out of breath from the climb up the stairs.

'Oh Mother, I made you climb the stairs too quickly. Oh dearest, I'm sorry.'

'It's all right, my love.' She stopped outside the guest-room door, put her hand on Celestine's arm and waited until she got her breath. Then she looked at her daughter. 'Thank you for bringing Breffni home to me,' she whispered and Celestine embraced her mother tenderly.

'It was Charles that found him in France,' she said. 'He organized everything. Oh Mother, he's so good. I love him so.'

'But Celestine, you will get married in the Church, won't you?'

367

Celestine squeezed her arm. 'Of course, Mother, of course. Charles has the letter from Rev. Johnston in Spanish Place. He's got his baptism certificate for Father Grogan too. Everything is in order.'

She did not tell her mother how she had badgered Father Johnston and how that cleric regretted what he called Charles' unholy hurry to get into the Church, or, more likely, into bed with Celestine. However, he had to admit that Charles knew his catechism and answered all the questions correctly. He was a soldier, after all, and he was returning to the front.

'We live in dangerous times,' he said, 'and I suppose that means desperate measures.'

'We'll arrange the wedding as soon as possible,' Ellen said. 'Clothilde is married, you know.'

'Yes, Mother, I do. She wrote and told me. I'll talk to her when I go downstairs. Breffni has taken our minds off everything else.'

'I intend to turn the parlour into a bed-sitting-room for Breffni. Charles won't be here all the time to carry him.'

Charles had taken Breffni to his old room after lunch and the boy was now sleeping peacefully, exhausted after his long journey and the emotional reunion with his mother.

'Oh I was wrong about that man,' Ellen said. 'Watching him with Breffni . . .'

'He's devoted to him, Mother.'

Ellen looked at her daughter. 'Charles could have gone either way,' she said. 'Seeing Celestine's puzzled look, she explained, 'I mean, he could have racketed along going from one woman to another, leading a hedonistic life with not a thought for anything except his own pleasure. But he met you, my dear, and he changed all that. You have brought out the finest in him.'

At that moment an enormous square person in the uniform of a nurse opened the guest-room door. It could not, Celestine decided, be anyone but Mrs Pugh. She reminded Celestine of the Catholic sergeant-major who had stood as Charles' godfather at his baptism, and like the sergeant-major her uncommonly plain face was kindly.

'What's all the talk? Could ye lower yer voices?' she asked. 'It upsets him. Either come in or go out, could ye?'

'Oh Mrs Pugh, it's my daughter Celestine.'

The woman bent her head and pumped Celestine's proffered hand until she thought her arm would fall off.

'Ah, yer name brings a smile to his lips,' she said, winking broadly at Celestine.

Ellen snorted. 'What rubbish. He can't move, Celestine. He can't move an inch. Only a flicker in the eye or the tiny quiver of the hand, and I think even that is involuntary.

'He gives a smile when *her* name is mentioned. I know. I can see,' Mrs Pugh said firmly and Ellen glared at her.

Ellen liked to be in command. Garreth was, after all, her husband, but Mrs Pugh had taken over. She had not known Garreth Connolly in any other than a paralysed state, and she tended, much to Ellen's annoyance, to treat him as if he were a sweet and helpless child in her care. Which, Ellen realized in her more rational moments, he was, to the nurse. Unable to bully or make his wishes known or even speak, he was, to her, a dependent little boy. Ellen wondered if he could hear Mrs Pugh's loud voice and hectoring admonitions. He would hate it, she thought, if he could. But she did not really think that possible. Dr Meagher said he couldn't and the specialist Mr Banks said that they did not know, that they could not be sure.

'I'd like to see him alone, if I may?' Celestine asked Mrs Pugh, who looked a little disappointed. She liked to be in attendance at all times.

'I was hopin' to see him smile,' she said to Celestine, much to Ellen's exasperation. 'For,' she said later to Mamie, 'he was never a smiling man.'

The nurse stepped out into the hall to let Celestine into the sick man's room. She saw him lying there, unmoving, a macabre figure. She shivered in the doorway, looking at the inert body of her father. He had been her god once, now he lay helpless and mute. She moved to his side.

'Oh Papa, Papa,' she whispered and sank to her knees, her warm heart melting in sympathy. She forgot the recent months of pain, the harsh words spoken, the unfair treatment she had suffered at her father's hands. She remembered only the long years during which he had loved and pampered her. Impulsive and soft-hearted, she was full of sorrow at his collapse and saddened that the big strong man she had worshipped had been brought so low.

What did he think and feel, lying there? she wondered. Did

369

he hear Mrs Pugh and Ellen talk about him? Did he hear the noises from downstairs? Or was he to all intents and purposes, dead? She laid her hand on his brow and looked into his eyes. They seemed blank to her. But she could not be sure.

'Dearest Papa. It's me. It's Celestine. Oh I'm so sorry you're like this.' She paused a moment. 'I know you were worried about me. About Charles. But it's all right, dearest Papa. It really is. We're going to be married.'

She thought she saw his eyes move. It gave her a horrible fright. Did his hand tighten? It was certainly clutching the sheet now. She could not be sure, but she thought that hand had been slack when she had first come in.

'Oh Papa, can you hear me?' No move. Nothing.

'I know you would have relented, Papa, I know you would. About Charles. We love each other so. He is so good to me. You need not worry.' She paused again, then continued, 'Oh dearest Papa, you were wrong, you see. Charles and I are so happy. So happy. And he brought Breffni home from the front. Breffni's home now. He can't come to see you because . . .' She faltered for a moment, then said, 'He cannot walk, Papa. We brought him home to Mother. She's so terribly happy to have him here. We cannot stay long, Charles and I. We have to go back to London. We will live there, you see.' There it was again, a tensing of the fingers of one hand. Or did she imagine it? She probably did. She was not sure. She leaned her forehead against the bed. 'Oh Papa, Papa, I wish I could help you.'

She heard the door open and turning her head saw her sister come in.

Clothilde stood a little way from the bed as if reluctant to come too near her father. Her face had a serenity it had never had before. 'I rarely come here,' she whispered. 'I should, I suppose. I just can't . . . bear to . . .'

'I understand. Do you think he can hear us? Mother doesn't think so. Mrs Pugh says he smiles when he hears my name but I don't think so.' She frowned. 'I thought . . . I thought . . . his hand . . . I don't think.'

'Well, and does it matter?' Clothilde said coolly. 'He never listened to us anyway. He's hardly likely to begin now.'

She paused and Celestine said, 'He was always good to me.'

Clothilde looked at her incredulously. 'You are amazing, Cel, you really are. You're quite determined to keep Papa as the

370

hero, even though he tried to ruin your life and nearly killed you while doing it.'

'No, Clothilde, I haven't forgotten. But bitterness is no use to me. What good will it do me to remember that awful time? It will keep it alive and I want to erase the memory.'

Clothilde sighed. 'You were always better than me,' she said, 'And I was the one who wanted to become a nun.'

Celestine laughed. 'That's not true. I wasn't better than you. We just had different temperaments, that's all. We were such babies then, Clo. Do you remember that jam-making? I could only think about my ball-gown and Madame McGinty, and you thought you wanted to become a nun.'

'Oh Celestine, Celestine,' Clothilde laughed. 'I'd have made a terrible nun.'

Celestine giggled. 'It would have been the wrong thing entirely. Papa was right about that, at least.'

They both looked at him. He did not seem to be real. He seemed more like a wax effigy, an inanimate copy of his former self.

'Oh look, Clo. I think I saw it again. His eye flickered.' They examined him intently and Clothilde shook her head.

'No. No, you're imagining it, Celestine,' she said. She looked down at her sister. 'I'm expecting a baby, Cel. Isn't it wonderful?'

'Oh Clothilde, I'm so happy for you.' Celestine leaned forward and put her arms around her sister's waist. Clothilde gently stroked her sister's hair.

'I'm looking forward to the wedding, Cel. I'm sorry you weren't at mine,' she said.

'I couldn't get away. I was quite determined, you see, to marry Charles as soon as he came home and I wanted to be there when he did. I wanted to be with him when he received instruction. He thinks it was all his idea, though.' She giggled. 'I desperately wanted to be with you,' she added, 'but this was more important.'

'And we thought you were the weak one, Celestine. Oh how strange. You and Mother, we thought, would do anything to avoid struggle or strife. Oh how wrong we were.'

Celestine smiled. 'We bend, Mother and I. We bend and we don't break. We try to see the best in people. So there's no residue of poison to cope with. Perhaps that's why we both tried to champion Papa.' She shrugged, looking at her father's help-less body lying under the bed covers. 'It doesn't matter now.'

'I'll miss you, Cel,' Clothilde said. 'I feel I don't know you at all and I'd like to rectify that.'

Her sister laughed. 'Oh no, you won't miss me that much. You'll be too busy with the baby and Darragh. And the brewery. By the way, how is it progressing? Besides, you'll have Breffni and Mother here. And we will be coming to Ireland too, so we'll be able to spend some time together, dear. Won't it be wonderful? You and me and our babies.' She turned to Clothilde. 'Oh Clo, don't you feel grown up?' she asked.

'I do now. I really do now. We were such children then.'

The sisters laughed together.

'It's all worked out so wonderfully well for us.' Clothilde kissed her sister's cheek. 'Darragh and you? You're happy too?'

'Darragh and I are so . . .' Clothilde rolled her eyes, 'settled. So comfortable together. So content. We are aged . . . um . . . about forty. Ah no! No, Cel. You'll get the idea I don't love him as much as I do. I adore him. I'm mad about the man. He's a wonder. You asked about the brewery. He's determined to make a success out of it. And he will. The men are behind him. He's strong. I need someone strong. I'm very,' she creased her forehead, 'wilful. I need a masterful man and Darragh is that.' She put her hands over her mouth and gasped. 'Oh Cel, is it really me saying this? No, but he's wonderful. He's formed a co-operative. Everyone in Paradise Row, Paradise Street and Paradise Square, every able-bodied man in the area, has a share in it. It hasn't all been easy. I'm not saying that. It hasn't all been plain sailing, but by heck it's been a challenge.' Her eyes glowed. 'And John Joe Reilly . . . all charges against him were dropped, did you know?' Celestine shook her head. She wasn't sure who John Joe Reilly was. 'Darragh's made him foreman. He's full of energy and purpose, one of the best workers there. He's so proud. He's great at the job, too. He knows the men, speaks their language. Mother says John Joe is a man again. She's been to see Mary who says all she ever wanted was to have John Joe with her. Mother says the room they live in is painted now, and it's bright and warm and Delia is home, and it's all thanks to my husband. Oh yes. I'm very, very happy.'

Then she gasped. 'Oh my God, you're right, Cel. Papa's hand moved. Oh God, look at his eyes. He's staring at me. His

372

eyes are . . . hatred . . . Oh Celestine . . . Oh God.' She crossed herself and hurried from the room.

'Papa? Are you all right?' Celstine asked as Mrs Pugh came into the room.

'It's no use talkin' to him,' she said briskly. 'He's probably tired. Two visitors in one day.'

'Goodbye, Papa, for the moment. I'll come to see you tomorrow,' Celestine said.

'It's no use, I told you,' Mrs Pugh insisted. 'Then she winked at Celestine. 'I tell yer Ma he smiles. Keeps her happy. But there: look. His eyes are closed. See?'

'They weren't. They were open just now.'

'An' did he smile?' Was the woman being sarcastic? Celestine couldn't tell.

'No. No. He didn't smile,' she said. 'He looked as if he . . .' Celestine shuddered.

Mrs Pugh sighed. 'It's always the same. People imagine. You stare at a painting. If you stare long enough, it moves. It comes alive. I often tell my patient's family that the patient smiles. Cheers them up no end. You're a fanciful one now, aren't ye? Sure, the man's like a slab o'meat. Now off ye go an' leave the poor man in peace. Ups-a-daisy, its time now for your movement.'

Celestine went. There had been no peace in her father's eyes before he closed them. But perhaps Mrs Pugh was right and it was all her imagination. Mrs Pugh was the nurse. She would know.

Chapter

63

DAYS just flew past. Life was pleasant. The women around the vicinity of the Rathgar Road did two things: they took Breffni in his wheelchair to their hearts; and they all pitched in to make the church look beautiful for Celestine Connolly's wedding. They were delighted at the turn of events. They had been on hand to wave her off to London in her rich uncle's car and they were thrilled when they learned from Miffy that the young pair were back together again, all misunderstandings over. 'Ahahha-hhahh,' they murmured in heartfelt sympathy and remembered the past, when they were young and romantic, and sighed for the loss of it. Miffy confided that the young pair were coming to Dublin to get married in St Hilda's.

'Isn't he a Prod, then?' Roddy Callaghan asked Mamie when she was in buying some lanolin for Mrs Connolly's hands and some Golden Ointment for her own eye. She had a nasty stye and Roddy Callaghan swore by Golden Ointment for sties.

'He's been takin' instruction in the Spanish Church over in London. The Catholic one,' Mamie told the chemist. 'Though it beats me why he has to go to a Spanish church to be a Catholic.' She shrugged. 'Sure, you never know the ways of the people in a big city,' she said, 'but at any rate at the end of it he's a Catholic an' if it's good enough for Fr Grogan it's good enough for me.'

The women of Rathgar, especially those involved in the Women's Sodality on a Wednesday and who helped the little nun to keep the church not only spick and span but gleaming with wax, ablaze with brass and silver and bedecked with flowers winter and summer, were determined to give Celestine a bower-like setting to be wed in.

They told Ellen not to worry about flowers. They asked her to allow them to decorate the church as a tribute to the triumph of true love and because they liked Celestine.

Since Garreth had become ill Ellen had relaxed and invited her Sodality neighbours in for afternoon tea. They had accepted her invitations with delight and asked her to their homes in return. They exchanged recipes and household hints, talked of the latest novels approved by the Church, although some of them risked reading books on the banned list, and discussed the various difficulties of running a house and servants in Rathgar. They were most satisfactory afternoons, and Ellen looked forward to them hugely. When they had left she would sit amid the debris and ponder on what had been said, sending a prayer of thanks that the sound of the key in the lock would not disturb her tranquillity. She hoped, briefly, that their chatter had not disturbed Garreth upstairs.

The wedding preparations went ahead. Celestine was in seventh heaven, Charles constantly at her side. Madame McGinty was making the wedding-dress, an exquisite affair of Limerick lace and wax orange-blossoms, slipper satin and veiling so gossamer it fitted through her mother's wedding ring.

Charles' sweet nature delighted everyone and he was so good to Breffni, who clung to him and to Ellen with the dependency of a child. He needed his mother more now than when he had been an infant.

The question of May came up. No one had seen her since that week they had spent in Avoca House so long ago. Celestine was determined that Barth give her away. Barth delightedly agreed. An invitation was sent out. A reply was received in Rathgar graciously accepting on behalf of Lord and Lady Gorman and their children.

'Are you sure you don't mind, Celestine?' Charles asked her. 'I'd understand completely if you refused to set eyes on her again.'

'Me too,' Clothilde remarked.

They were unpacking wedding presents in the parlour. Breffni was watching them from the big winged leather chair that was once his father's. There was tissue paper everywhere.

'Look at this. It's beautiful. Truly beautiful.' 'It' was a

375

Georgian silver tea service: teapot, tray, jug and sugar basin and tongs. It was exquisitely wrought.

'Who sent that?' Charles asked, examining it. 'It's quite perfect.'

'Speak of the devil.' Clothilde laughed, looking at a tiny engraved card. 'It's from the Gormans.'

'Well, I hope Auntie May does come,' Celestine said. 'I feel sorry for her. If she stays away she'll lose face and it will be awful for her.'

'A terrible admission.' Clothilde remarked. 'Everyone will know why.'

'But Uncle Barth assures me she'll come,' Celestine said.

'She must do as she sees fit,' Ellen said. 'She's my sister and I think she will come, if only to show everyone.'

'She must be suffering so,' Celestine said. 'Poor Aunt. Well, it's a beautiful present at any rate and I'm sure we're very grateful for it, aren't we, darling?'

Charles nodded and the conversation turned to other things.

Chapter

64

'I WON'T go, Barth. I can't.'

It was the morning of the wedding. Barth had come into his wife's dressing-room. She sat in her long champagne-coloured georgette dress. The material flowed about her slim body, fluid as water. Her nails were polished to a pink shine, but her beautiful face was pale. She was fiddling with her hat.

'I won't go, Barth,' she reiterated. He saw she was shaking all over. They both knew what she was talking about. All the pain she had caused him, caused Celestine and her family, passed through his mind. He reminded himself that she had suffered as well, perhaps more than any of them could comprehend, and her's was the least popular role; she knew they all hated her. He went over and stood behind her.

'You must, May,' he said quietly. She glanced up, her great sapphire eyes looking at him full of defiance.

'I'm sorry, but I insist,' he continued. 'You've never been a coward before.' She flinched and turned away. 'It's not just the bride and groom, it's the whole Connolly family and our own children. Lelia and Little Barth are so looking forward to it.'

'You go, Barth. You can take the children. They'll not miss me.'

He turned away from her. They had never discussed it but now, he thought, they would have to.

'Oh May, I give up. How selfish you have become. I haven't wanted to speak of it but you force me. You played a foul trick on Celestine.' He saw her wince.

'She is the injured party, not you. Yet she had the generosity to forgive you and invite you to her wedding. I'm sure she did it

377

for the sake of the family, but that is neither here nor there. It was large-spirited of her.' As he said this, he realized that Celestine could afford to be magnanimous. She was the winner. He sighed.

'I hope you'll find it in your heart to forget your . . . er . . . differences and put the family first, just for today. I never thought I would have to ask you that. I doubt if I can forgive you if you let us down today.' He turned and quietly left the room. She sighed and sat staring vacantly at herself in the mirror.

Yes, she was a coward, she knew that, but she had been striving to keep her sanity and she was frightened that if she went to the wedding and saw Charles she would slip back into the pool of black misery that she had clawed her way out of slowly, so slowly. She felt her hold on reality was very fragile. No one knew of the storms that had shaken her to the very core, the despair that had gripped her soul. She realized dimly that it was not just Charles, her passion for him and her loss of him. It was more than that. It was her youth, her life, her beauty.

She had become aware of her mortality, of the body's decay. As long as she had kept Charles it had seemed to her that she had triumphed over age's encroachment. But she had lost him, and now, in her despair, she felt Time's greedy hands squeezing her youth and beauty away.

For the first time in weeks she looked at her reflection with critical eyes. The face was certainly lovely but it was the face of a mature woman, no longer a girl. There were lines and puffs, a blurring here, a pull there, the masks of time irrevocably etched. It was the face of a woman who knew life, who was experienced, who had borne children. She shuddered. She was on a road that she could not retrace. Each step she took brought her further away from beauty and smooth skin, from elasticity of body and lightness of step, and nearer and nearer to old age and death.

She thought of all the pain she had caused. She had not wanted to. She had been driven. Poor Celestine. How she had suffered. She loved Celestine; she did not want her hurt. Yet May knew that she would have fought for Charles, no matter what wanton pain she caused by her actions, for she could not think of him without her heart stopping. When she remembered his love-making, when, solitary in her bed, she relived his embraces, she could not breathe with the fierceness of her longing for him. Her arms ached to hold him. She needed him as an alcoholic needs drink.

She remembered Barth's words. The situation was dangerous. He was nearing the end of his tether. She shuddered at the abyss she was facing. She suddenly felt overwhelmingly vulnerable, and as she looked at her face her eyes brimmed with tears that spilled onto her cheeks.

'Damn,' she cried. 'Damn. Damn. Damn.'

Chapter

65

CHARLES was going with Neill to the church from the Shelbourne. They were bringing Aunt Agatha with them. The old
lady was a vision in cerise crêpe and feathers.

Neill realized that Charles was nervous. He kept fiddling with
his buttons.

'I'm not really good enough for her, Neill,' he said suddenly
as they drank coffee and ate some hot rolls to tide them through
until the reception. Neill spluttered over his cup, but seeing
Charles' serious face forbore to laugh.

'I've caused her much pain already,' Charles continued. 'I've
behaved badly and I'm so ashamed.'

'Then you haven't made a proper Confession,' Neill said,
smiling, and Charles shook his head vigorously.

'Oh yes I did. "A firm intention of *not* repeating my sins",'
he cried in triumph. 'There, you see? I remembered.'

'Well then, your past is all behind you.' Neill retorted. 'In the
sacrament of Confession all our sins are forgiven, provided we
have a sincere resolve not to repeat them.' He grinned at
Charles. 'And I can see you have that. You have repented,' he
said chuckling.

On the way to the church in the car there was a strange tense
silence from the groom, until he suddenly clutched Neill's arm.
'My limp!' he cried.

'What about your limp?' Neill asked mildly.

'It's awful for a young girl to have a husband who limps,'
Charles said wildly. 'I'm like a cripple. I'm so wounded. My legs
are like a Swiss cheese. Oh God, what will she do when she sees
them? Faint?'

Neill could contain his mirth no longer. He guffawed and Aunt Agatha who was in the front with the chauffeur turned around and said witheringly, 'Celestine is not feeble-minded, Charles. If she had wanted a perfect young specimen, I have no doubt she would have got herself one. She wants you, though I must admit I can't see for the life of me why, when you are behaving like an idiot.'

They went into the church together. The interior was full of the scent and beauty and colour of a million blooms. The back of the church was packed with smiling neighbours, with the eager expectant faces of well-wishers, who touched Charles' sleeve for luck as he made his way up the aisle. Neill and Charles sat at the front just inside the altar-rails. The groom heard a stir behind him and started to turn around but Neill restrained him.

'You mustn't look. Not until you hear the wedding march,' he whispered. But Neill himself turned around and saw that his Aunt May had arrived. She moved like a ghost to the left side, genuflected and sat in the seat the usher had guided her to. There was an empty seat for Barth beside her. Neill saw that she was very pale. When she knelt down she looked neither to the right nor left; she did not even glance at himself or the groom, but bowed her head, her slim white neck curving like a swan. She stayed like that for a long time.

Aunt Agatha sat on the other side, Charles' only relative except for a few obscure cousins who had been invited and had decided to make the trip though they neither knew or cared very much about Charles nor had ever been on intimate terms with him. However, the food was plentiful in Ireland and it had been a long time since they had had a really good meal so it seemed a good idea to accept and make the journey. Aunt Agatha, who had been told the shocking details of May's life and her intimate connection with her nephew, could not take her fascinated gaze off the beautiful Lady Gorman. But May never raised her head whilst Charles sat unmoving with back ramrod straight, waiting for his bride.

Mamie and Breffni arrived. Mamie was pushing Breffni's wheelchair and the boy was smiling. He waved at Neill who had turned around at their entrance. But Charles did not turn. Then Clothilde and Darragh came and sat beside them. Clothilde looked quite lovely and there was confidence and authority in her movements and serenity in her look. There were hugs and kisses all round, as if, Mamie remarked, they had not seen each other for weeks instead of yesterday. Miffy entered with Ben-the-Boots. She bustled and glowed and she had two red spots on her cheeks from her excitement and her importance in the scheme of things. From a shivering scivvy afraid of being sent back to the 'Institution', she had graduated into a lady's maid, married to the chauffeur, content and protected. She could hardly contain her happiness.

Ellen arrived with Nellie and Joe. She sailed up the aisle like a pouter pigeon land-bound, all in dove-grey, her walk and bearing full of dash and brio. Quietly, behind Aunt Agatha, almost apologizing for their presence, John Joe Reilly and his family settled themselves. Mary had bought herself a new dress for the occasion and John Joe had a new jacket. Their presence drew waves of greeting from all the others and Mary blushed with pride and her eyes filled with tears and she sent up a prayer of thanksgiving and gratitude.

There was only Barth, Celestine and her attendants, Lelia and Little Barth, to come now and the only member of the family missing was Garreth.

Celestine had crept up to the guest-room early that morning. She could see her father lying on the bed, a huge mound, immobile, quiet as death. She waved to Mrs Pugh to leave and the smiling nurse had left the room. Celestine wished she would stop smiling. So much good humour could get on your nerves.

She sat by her father for a long time. It was quiet in the room. Outside she could hear the birds sing. In the distance car doors slammed, horses' hooves clopped on the cobblestones and there was the rattle of milk-churns in the yard.

She took his hand. It was clammy. She held it between her own as if the warmth of her grasp would rouse him into movement and life. But it lay still in her clasp. She sighed. A feeling of desolation flowed over her and for a moment she was afraid. It seemed to her that all her illusions had tumbled down and she stood shivering at the foot of her life, looking up at the road she would have to climb. It was a long road and it would be punctuated by terrible partings, worry, and pain. There would be happiness there too, and love. Joy and wonderful moments. She knew now that there were no such things as fairy tales, as 'happy ever after', that the only way to survive was to fight for what you believed in, take the knocks with the happiness, learn by the pain you suffered.

'I love you, Papa,' she whispered to him. 'I love you and I forgive you. I'm so happy. So you must forgive me.' She did not know if he heard. She kissed his pale cold forehead and left the room.

Clothilde had dressed her. Mamie had been too sick with excitement. Her hands trembled and she could not fasten up the tiny buttons. Miffy had proved deft at dressing Celestine's unruly curls and she had studded them with little wax orange-blossom blooms until her dark hair was starred with flowers.

Ellen had wept as Celestine lowered her veil. Then they heard Barth's car-horn hoot outside and Clothilde had pressed her sister's hand, smiling into her radiant face. Ellen and her daughter had left Celestine alone for a moment, and hurried down to greet Barth and leave for the church.

Celestine looked around her room. It was another wrenching, a tearing away from the known, the familiar. She would never again be Daddy's little girl, innocently unaware of pain, happy in the bosom of her family, unthinking, unworried. Then her heart flooded with delight. She had not known such joy existed, for, in those untroubled days of childhood, if she had been unaware of pain she had not known that such happiness existed either. She was going to marry Charles. It was worth all she had suffered in the past.

'Well, then, hurry along. Don't want to be late.' Barth's voice floated up to her. 'Left May at the church, Lelia and Little Barth await you in the car. So hurry down, little bride . . .' He faltered to a stop as Celestine rounded the curve of the stairs and quick tears stung the back of his eyes. There was something so very vulnerable and trusting about his young niece as she paused at the top of the stairs. She was so touchingly beautiful as she looked down into his face. They stared at each other, love in their eyes, and he swallowed, gulping the lump in his throat for fear he would weep at her lovely innocent hope. Then she tripped down the stairs and into his arms.

'I'm proud to have you on my arm, my dearest girl,' he whispered. 'You are the most beautiful bride I have ever seen. Except for May.' He could have bitten his tongue out, but she pressed his arm and her returning smile was grateful and happy.

383

'Thank you, Uncle Barth. Thank you.'

He held her arm through his, and her hand in his, right through the drive. He handed her carefully out of the car when they arrived at the church and led her to the door. The organ started the Wedding March, the assembled guests stood and Charles saw his bride. The sun slanted through the high stained-glass windows, dappling her in prisms of colour. Ethereal in white, her dress billowing about her, she seemed to float on Barth's arm up to Charles and he felt his heart stop for a second. He knew at last that all his worries were nonsense.

The ceremony proceeded. Fr Grogan was officiating. He had known Celestine all his life and she felt surrounded by friends that loved her and when she looked into Charles' eyes the expression she saw there filled her with a kind of wonder. Barth handed her over to Charles. He left the altar and went to sit beside his wife. Her head was still bowed over her clasped hands.

'Are you all right?' he asked her softly. The sympathy in his voice touched her and she lifted her eyes reluctantly. Barth's tender concern made her blink and for a moment she was afraid that she would cry. Then she looked away and she saw him. Charles. He was smiling at his bride and there was something reverential in his look.

But nothing happened. Her pulse rate did not increase, nor did her heart miss a beat. Her knees did not go weak and her mouth did not go dry. That awful stomach lurch was absent and she could look at him, calmly, coolly. She stared at the man who had almost ruined her life and there was nothing: not a tremor, not an ache, nothing. Bewildered, she glanced at the kindly face of her husband. She sighed. Tentatively she touched Barth's arm and sighed again. And smiled. The music swelled and the young newly-weds turned and came down the aisle. They too smiled.

Chapter

66

ELLEN was very content. Her life had slipped into pleasurable grooves. She was a busy woman these days. When Celestine had married Charles, she had had some nasty moments, worrying about loneliness. Clothilde and Darragh lived in Phoenix Street. Neill was in Maynooth and Celestine had told her that she would wait for Charles with Aunt Agatha in Hampstead. It left her alone in the house with Breffni, Garreth and Mrs Pugh. She was afraid she would miss her daughters dreadfully. Their companionship had always been dear to her. But the worry, as Barth had told her, was wasted. She had been invited to sit on several more committees. As well as her charity work, she was now involved with the Royal Dublin Horticultural Society, the Rathmines and Rathgar Musical Society, and, of course, numerous church activities.

She made many new friends. They asked her to their houses and she asked them to hers. She entertained. She took Barth's advice and gave up worry. She had grown plumper but she did not mind. Like a sailing-ship breasting the sea she forged ahead with energy and confidence.

She relished her isolation in the large double bed. She had purchased a new mattress in Arnott's in Henry Street and each night as she slid into the middle, pulled the sweet-smelling sheets about her ears and wiggled her legs until she found the most comfortable position, she sent up a prayer of gratitude that Garreth was not there and she had been released from bondage.

She laughed a lot these days. And cried. The spring of her emotions was near the surface, the tap easily turned on. She spent time with Garreth. She did her duty. The spare-room had

385

been fixed up and it was almost a copy of the one in the nursing home. Mrs Pugh had all she needed in order to provide first-class care for Garreth Connolly. Or what was left of him.

He had no power now, she thought. No-one quailed at the sound of his voice. No-one trembled at his glance. And, most of all, no-one's equilibrium depended on his mood.

How did he feel as he lay there, unable to move? Ellen wondered. She sat beside him every day; an hour in the morning and an hour after lunch. She did not like to meet his eyes. She had caught him staring at her once or twice as she rose or sat. There was a point in her progress from seated to standing or vice-versa, when their eyes reached the same level. It seemed to her that he hated her; the expression was one of such loathing. Mrs Pugh said she imagined it and she wanted to believe her. It made her want to cry, but she never let him see that. She made sure she avoided his eyes after that. He looked as if he were in hell. Not like Breffni, whose eyes were tormented. He had been the victim of something threatening his sanity and the pain in his face aroused only a desire to console and help. No, Garreth looked as she imagined a devil, a power in Hades, would look whose will was frustrated, and whose anger could find no outlet.

She could not imagine the condition his mind must be in. She could not have endured such immobilization, the inability to tell the children she loved them, to hold Breffni in her arms and reassure him. She felt infinitely sorry for her husband. But she was practical. There was nothing she could do more than she was already doing.

Except love him. She could not pretend to love him. She sat beside him, her heart indifferent to him, and she thought he knew it. He had blown his chance, she thought, and it was too late now. Love needed to be tended. Both people had to work at it. He had had his chance but he had muffed it. She thought how different the invalids were. People flocked to Breffni. He gave out to them a hope for their affection, a plea for their love and understanding, and that was what he got in return. Garreth had never asked anyone for love and affection and he got none. She often wondered why he had never spoken to her of his mother or father. She wondered briefly and for the millionth time what sort of a home he came from. But she knew better these days than to spend too much time pondering unanswerables.

Ellen had developed in other ways. One day at Yvette's in Dawson Street she allowed herself to be persuaded to try on a cloche of pale mauve felt with an artificial bunch of lilac over one ear. It was frivolous and enchanting, and, Ellen thought, too audacious for a staid married woman. It was much more suited to her sister May, but Yvette herself insisted she try it and put the hat on her head, tucking in her hair and arranging a tiny veil over her eyes and nose. To her amazed delight Ellen found that not only did the hat suit her but she herself *felt* quite different. She felt dashing. Holding her head high, she sailed out of the shop, hat on head, as if she were the Queen of England.

Feeling inspired, the next day she prevailed on Clothilde to accompany her to Cleary's, where she purchased yards of lilac moirée with a view to getting Madame McGinty to run up a spring suit in the new shorter slimmer line.

They had tea, as usual when they went shopping, in the Shelbourne.

'You look wonderful these days, Clothilde,' Ellen began, pouring the tea from the silver teapot. The sun shone outside and the new young leaves trembled on the trees, shivering in the gentle breeze. Clothilde could see the bronze statue of the slave-girl outside the window of the hotel and a red-nosed little gurrier selling papers.

'I feel wonderful, Mother,' Clothilde replied, smiling. 'I can return the compliment, indeed I can. But I'll be glad when we get a larger home of our own. The little house in Phoenix Street is only temporary, as you know. Darragh is aiming to convert one of the Paradise Street houses back to its former glory. We hope it will be ready by the time we start a family. She blushed. 'The men are working like demons for us. It's amazing what a little good-will will do.' She hesitated, then said, 'Mother, we haven't talked much since I married Darragh, at least, not alone. We've all been so busy . . . Celestine's wedding and so on. I wanted to ask . . . well, I hope you don't mind . . . that you're not upset about Darragh.'

'Why should I be?' Ellen asked, surprised.

'Well, he's . . . he's not what you wanted for me.'

'He's not want your father wanted,' Ellen corrected her. 'No. He's not. But things have become topsy-turvy, Clothilde. I cannot explain it. It's the war, I think. Poor Breffni. Boys like that, suffering most horribly. Women having to look after them most intimately. Understanding things they were protected from before. The world has changed completely and I think sometimes its for the best. Certainly the new . . . freedom . . . suits me much better. I love the truth so. It clarifies everything. You understand people's motives, good or bad, and *see* why they do things. Secrets are like cancers. They eat the soul. No. I must honestly admit I would never have chosen Darragh Quinn for you myself. But knowing him, seeing his love for you, I have to admit that you were wiser than I.' She nodded her head and smiled at her daughter, 'He is a good man, Clothilde. An honourable man. A man of clear vision. You have chosen well.' She paused then added, 'I've heard Breffni say things. You see, I've changed too. I've grown up. He . . . he talks sometimes of a prostitute called Lily. She gave him some comfort. Well, I found I was not shocked by this. Oh I know I'm *supposed* to be horrified. Most of the women on the Rathgar Road would be.'

Clothilde raised her eyebrows. 'How do you know that, Mother?' she asked.

'Ah, you're right. I presume. But it's seeing my son in the state he is in. Smashed, like a broken toy. His body, that I bore, a ruined thing . . .' Tears had welled into her eyes. Clothilde covered her mother's hand with hers and Ellen hurriedly blinked them back. 'Sorry . . . I did not mean . . . Men are such fools. Since when has violence cured anything?' She shrugged. 'Well, I'm not at all shocked about Lily. I can only feel gratitude to her.' She looked at her daughter. 'You knew about all these things that I'm just finding out about, didn't you? They say "the children of this generation are wiser than the children of light". I never knew what that meant. How did you know, Clothilde?'

'I don't know, Mother. You just grow up realizing some things simply cannot be right.'

Ellen nodded. 'I wish someone had explained life to me before and not just given me a set of attitudes to strike when certain things happened. Do you understand?'

Clothilde sighed. 'I do, Mother, perfectly. But we all have to find out in our own time.'

'Well, you have certainly learned, so young, what has taken me half a lifetime.'

'I have learned from Darragh, Mother. And Neill. So many things. Not to condemn others. We, none of us have the right to sit in judgement. To keep an open mind. To try to see the other's point of view. That both sides can be right and both sides can be wrong. Another thing I've learned is that we've been made to feel ashamed of being Irish. But we should be proud. We are quite different from the British, temperamentally, artistically and spiritually. It does not mean that we are wrong because of that difference. Or that they are. It simply means we are different. We can be proud of our heritage; they of theirs. But they are not identical.'

Ellen smiled at her daughter's earnest face. 'I know,' she said. 'I understand. So much of our behaviour is in-bred in us. Knowledge gives us the ability to see things clearly. To get away from prejudice and blinkered vision. Oh my darling, I was in a tunnel for so long. It's nice to be out.'

Clothilde laughed. 'You look wonderful, Mother. You have emerged, like a butterfly.'

The waitress, the same who had served Celestine her tea on that ill-fated afternoon so long ago, replenished the hot water and removed the empty plate that had held the sandwiches. People drifted in and out and the sunlight streamed through the windows, catching the gleam of the silver on the tables and the jewels that glittered in the women's ears. Conversation was muted. A laugh tinkled above the gentle murmur and the quartet played. 'I Dreamt that I Dwelt In Marble Halls' very enthusiastically. Ellen sipped her tea and looked about with bright eyes. It was fun to be able to have tea with her daughter and not worry about the time.

Clothilde laid a hand on her mother's arm. 'I wanted to tell you, mother. I hope you'll be pleased. I'm expecting a baby.'

'Oh darling.' Ellen shook her head. 'How wonderful. I'm going to be a grandmother.' How lovely that is, she thought, how delightful. She kissed her daughter. 'Watch out,' she said. 'I intend to spoil my grandchild dreadfully. I never had a chance with you . . .' she added wistfully.

'Oh Mother darling. I think you did a marvellous job. We haven't turned out too badly, have we? Let's go, dearest, Darragh will be waiting.'

'I'm so pleased about my purchases, Clothilde. I'll give this to Madame McGinty tomorrow and see what she recommends as the latest fashion.'

389

Chapter
67

THE next day Ellen was in the garden. Ben-the-Boots had brought Breffni out and he sat in his wheelchair under the tree. He had the book Charles had given her for him, open on his lap. Before Charles had returned to London, he had given her the book.

He had found her in the study one evening after dinner,

'How is he?' he had asked. She knew he meant Breffni.

'He's . . . making progress, Charles. It's very slow. Sometimes he's very angry.'

'Does he talk about it? That helps.'

Ellen shook her head. 'He says he can't remember anything. It's all a jumble in his mind.'

Charles nodded. He handed her a small brown paper parcel.

'This is his,' he said. 'They gave it to me in France. It was salvaged. His name is on the flyleaf.' He cleared his throat. 'It's in the form of a diary, I suppose, although there are no dates. They might not have given it back if there were.'

'What is it?' Ellen asked, confused.

'Writing. I only read enough to see that it was . . . important to keep. For Breffni. It might be healing for him, I mean.'

'Writing?' Ellen said. 'Breffni always wanted to write. Poetry.'

'Well,' Charles said, 'maybe this will help. But give it to him at your discretion.'

Breffni had been reading it the last few days and it had made him cry, but he had seemed so much better afterwards.

His face was peaceful now. The sun slanted through the branches of the tree, speckling him with light. He looked at her and waved. She waved back.

She had had a letter from Celestine in Hampstead. Charles had gone back to France. Celestine was sure the war would be over soon. She too was expecting a baby. She sounded very happy. Ellen would be a grandmother twice over and the mother of a priest. What woman could ask for more? The family had never been closer, she thought. Even May, it seemed, had begun to mend. Barth had popped in after lunch to tell her that his dividends in the brewery had realized a huge profit. The co-operative was doing exceptionally well and he and May were hoping that she and Breffni could spend a week in Avoca House, next week or the week after? She had agreed to the following week and noted to herself that all must be well between them. She was glad. Barth deserved to be happy.

Ellen sighed. Life went on. Not smoothly, never smoothly. You just had to relax as much as you could as you went over the bumps. She snipped off the deadheads, casting them into the trug at her feet.

'Yes that's what happens.' When you cease to contribute to the world you live in, you have to be lobbed off. You die. Or atrophy: it had nothing to do with age or work. It had to do with helpfulness. There were moments when people got chances. Garreth had been given a few and he had blown them. If he had sat down that morning and talked kindly to his children about their hopes and plans, he might not have collapsed in the street.

May was at least trying. Would she ever let go of youth grace-fully? Ellen prayed she might. It would bring such happiness to her family if she did. It was nice to know one's place in the scheme of things. All her children now seemed in the situation most conducive to their happiness. She remembered what Clothilde had said the previous day and she smiled. Her children were nice people, she thought. The house was united. She laid her secateurs on the table. Breffni looked up and smiled at her.

She saw Miffy appear from the kitchen. She called to her at the bottom of the garden. 'Miffy, tell Mamie we'll have tea now. We'll have it out here, under the tree.' She nodded to herself and smiled.

391